"T'Vrel, what is it?"

"The helm is slow to respond," the Vulcan replied. "I am having difficulty arresting our speed."

On the screen, Gralafi's surface was now highlighted by a reddish-purple sky occupying the image's upper third. The ground continued to rush past, and terrain features now were clearly visible, growing larger and more ominous with each passing second. A single thought echoed in Ronald Arens's mind.

We're not going to make it.

"Helm control is failing," T'Vrel reported, and this time even her stoic demeanor seemed to be cracking around the edges. "Captain, I cannot prevent a crash landing."

Without hesitation, Arens once more hit the intercom switch with his fist. "All hands, this is the captain! Crash protocols! Brace for impact!" Then, looking to Hebert, he said, "Launch the buoy."

As the first officer moved to comply with the order, Arens could do nothing except watch as the last sliver of sky disappeared from the top of the viewscreen, leaving only the barren, uninviting surface of the planetoid to draw ever closer.

STAR TREK®

THAT WHICH DIVIDES

Dayton Ward

STORY BY
Dayton Ward & Kevin Dilmore

Based upon *Star Trek*
created by Gene Roddenberry

POCKET BOOKS
New York ▪ London ▪ Toronto ▪ Sydney ▪ New Delhi

Pocket Books
A Division of Simon & Schuster, Inc.
1230 Avenue of the Americas
New York, NY 10020

This book is a work of fiction. Names, characters, places, and incidents either are products of the author's imagination or are used fictitiously. Any resemblance to actual events or locales or persons, living or dead, is entirely coincidental.

First Pocket Books paperback edition March 2012

POCKET and colophon are registered trademarks of Simon & Schuster, Inc.

For information about special discounts for bulk purchases, please contact Simon & Schuster Special Sales at 1-866-506-1949 or business@simonandschuster.com.

The Simon & Schuster Speakers Bureau can bring authors to your live event. For more information or to book an event, contact the Simon & Schuster Speakers Bureau at 1-866-248-3049 or visit our website at www.simonspeakers.com.

Manufactured in the United States of America

10 9 8 7 6 5 4 3 2

ISBN 978-1-4516-5068-6
ISBN 978-1-4516-5069-3 (ebook)

For Michi, Addison, and Erin,
who give me the time and space needed to do this,
and who make sure I'm well-fed and loved along the way.

Historian's Note

The events in this story take place in late 2269 (ACE), during the fourth year of James Kirk's five-year mission as captain of the *U.S.S. Enterprise* NCC-1701.

ONE

As a former science officer and now the captain of a science vessel, Ronald Arens had encountered his share of interesting stellar phenomena. There had been the odd black hole or quasar, stars in the midst of going nova, and the occasional nebula here and there. He even had spent two weeks studying a rogue pulsar. Nothing Arens had seen with his own eyes or read about in reports submitted by those observing even stranger examples of spatial oddities compared to the image now displayed on the main viewscreen of the *U.S.S. Huang Zhong*'s bridge.

"Okay," Arens said, rising from his command chair and moving closer to the screen, "I think this qualifies as an impressive welcome to the Kondaii system, especially considering how we nearly blew out our engines trying to get here." Built for speed, the *Huang Zhong*, an *Archer*-class scout ship configured to hold an enhanced suite of sensor arrays and other science-related information-gathering equipment, had proceeded here at maximum speed after its abrupt reassignment from patrol duty. Despite his comment, the dependable little craft had handled with ease the exertion of traveling at high warp for nearly a week. As for why they had been dispatched, the captain had been told that the ship originally assigned to be here, the *U.S.S. Lexington*, had been deployed elsewhere on a task of greater priority. Though his ship's science equipment would do in a pinch, Arens knew it could not substitute for a *Constitution*-class vessel. To that end, the *Enterprise* was being redirected to the Kondaii system to take on the brunt of the survey and research tasks. Until then, it was the *Huang Zhong*'s show.

Fine by me, Arens mused as he contemplated the anomaly on the viewscreen. To him, it appeared to be something of a cross between a plasma storm and a matter-antimatter explosion. It was an amorphous mass of energy, shifting and undulating in space, all while staying confined within what Arens already had been told was more or less a spherical area less than five hundred kilometers in diameter. Within that region was chaos, in the form of a kaleidoscopic maelstrom of light and color that seemed to fold back on itself, only to surge forth anew moments later. At the center of the field was a dark area, roughly circular in shape, which seemed to beckon to him. It took Arens an extra minute to realize that he had become all but mesmerized by the imagery.

"Captain?" a voice said from behind him, and Arens blinked as he turned to see Lieutenant Samuel Boma, a slightly-built man of African descent wearing a blue uniform tunic and regarding him with an expression that indicated the younger man had been waiting for his commanding officer with both patience and amusement.

Clearing his throat, Arens smiled. "I was daydreaming again, wasn't I?"

The *Huang Zhong*'s science officer's features remained fixed as he shook his head in melodramatic fashion. "I'm not qualified to speculate on that topic, sir. *At all.*"

"Damned right, you're not." Arens's smile grew wider.

Their easy banter, something the captain had missed, was a product of his and Boma's service together years earlier. Arens at the time was the science officer on the *Constellation*, while Boma had been a fresh-faced junior-grade lieutenant fresh out of Starfleet Academy's advanced astrophysics school. The friendship begun during that joint tour of duty continued even after both men went their separate ways to different assignments. Boma had joined the *Huang Zhong*'s crew less than six months earlier, transferring from a ground posting at Starbase 12 following a less than stellar performance while serving aboard the *Enterprise*. After Boma had run into trouble stemming from insubordination charges that resulted in a permanent notation in his service record, he had requested a transfer to any ship or station. When Arens found out that his friend was available, he had petitioned Starfleet Command to have Boma join his crew. Starfleet granted the request, allowing Arens to make sure that Boma was afforded a chance to redeem himself.

Gesturing toward the viewscreen, Arens said, "All right, let's get down to business. What can you tell me about this thing?"

Boma replied, "Not much; at least, not yet. As the initial reports indicated, it's about eight hundred thousand kilometers from the system's fourth planet. According to my calculations, it maintains a consistent elliptical orbit with a duration of seventeen point six days." He paused, pointing to the screen and indicating the dark area at the center of the energy field. "Most of the time, it's impassable, but the rift we're seeing appears at intervals that compute out to be approximately two point seven Earth years, give or take as much as two months. The rift stays open for a period of about thirty-eight days, again plus or minus a day or three, though it doesn't just close; it shrinks over a period of several days before fading altogether. From the reports we've received, once the rift's closed, that's it until the next time it opens. No way in or out." He gestured toward the screen. "The locals have a name for it that translates more or less as 'the Pass.' Seems appropriate enough for me."

"Damnedest thing I've ever heard of," Arens said, reaching up to rub the back of his bald head. Since being given the assignment to observe this phenomenon, he had familiarized himself with whatever information he could find on the Kondaii system, or System 965, as it had been catalogued after initial surveys by unmanned Starfleet reconnaissance probes more than a decade earlier. From the reports he had read, such as those provided by Federation first-contact teams that had visited the Kondaii system more than a year earlier as well as the most recent accounts submitted by continuing contact specialists and diplomatic envoys, the people who called the fourth planet, Dolysia, their home had always been aware of the phenomenon. Like their sun or the pair of moons orbiting their planet or even the other seven worlds occupying the Kondaii system, the mysterious anomaly had always been a part of the Dolysian people's history.

"What about its interior?" Arens asked. "Anything on the moon or planetoid or whatever it is hiding in there?"

The science officer shook his head. "Not much, really. The locals call it 'Gralafi,' which in their language translates to something like 'playful child,' no doubt owing to the way it plays hide-and-seek from within the anomaly. It has a Class-M environment like the Dolysians' own planet, so I suppose that's a huge plus." He shrugged. "By all accounts, it may be a dwarf planet, but there's no way to know if it originally was part of this system and became trapped within that region, or if it's from somewhere else. We won't know anything until we get a closer look at it, run some scans, and see if it shares any properties with the planets here."

"Regardless of where it came from," Arens said, "or where it might belong, the Dolysians have certainly made the best of it." The revelation that a spatial body had been discovered inside the rift residing within a form of pocket or other compartmentalized region of space had come as a surprise to him. Even more astonishing was learning that the Dolysians had explored and even settled upon it, having found a means of working with the rift's sporadic if mostly predictable accessibility. A largely self-sufficient mining colony, constructed on the planetoid decades earlier, now played a vital role in meeting the energy production needs of several of Dolysia's nation-states. "This mineral they extract, erinadium? It's present on the home planet's two moons, right?"

Boma replied, "Yes, sir, and it's also on the planet itself, though in all three cases it's not found in nearly the same abundance. The Dolysians had made the transition to using the material to meet their energy needs decades before the first probes into the anomaly found the planetoid and discovered its rich erinadium deposits. Once they knew that, there was a focused effort to get a permanent facility up and running. According to their projections, there's enough erinadium on the planetoid to keep the lights on for a couple of centuries."

"Wow," Arens said, impressed at the effort the Dolysians

had expended and the rewards they seemed to be enjoying for their work. "Well, that'd certainly justify the risk you'd think would be inherent in a project of this magnitude. On a different note, it suggests the planetoid might be native to this system, after all. It'll be interesting to see if we can offer them some new insight."

Boma replied, "That's going to be easier said than done, though, as our sensor scans are being scattered as they come into contact with the rift's . . . the *anomaly's* outer boundary."

Noting the other man's change of word choice, Arens cocked his head as he regarded his friend. "You don't think it's an interspatial rift?" The idea that this might be a doorway of sorts—to another part of the universe or to another universe or reality entirely—made the captain's mind race to consider the possibilities. "It wouldn't be the first time something like that's been encountered, after all." Shrugging, he added, "Though it'd be a first for me."

"Rifts such as those," Boma replied, "at least the ones we know about, have usually been found to have some common characteristics. Energy distortion fields, chroniton or verteron particle emissions, time dilation effects, and so on. I'm not picking up anything like that from this thing."

Arens frowned, crossing his arms before reaching up to stroke his thin, close-cropped beard. "Absence of such characteristics doesn't automatically rule out this being some kind of interspatial rift or conduit."

"Which is why I'm going to stick with my story of not having the first clue what it is, sir," Boma said. "If it *is* a conduit, then what's on the other side? Where's the other end, where does it go, and what—or who—might be there?"

"Those are all interesting questions which we have also

asked, Captain, though we have been unable to answer them."

Arens and Boma turned in response to the new voice to see the *Huang Zhong*'s first officer, Commander April Hebert, standing near the bridge's doorway. With her was the guest to whom the ship was playing host, a Dolysian female who earlier had introduced herself as Rzaelir Zihl du Molidin. Though she was humanoid in appearance, at least in a general sense, there still were several exterior differences in her physiology when compared to humans. Her skin was a pale yellow with a hint of green; a Vulcan-like pigmentation, Arens thought. The pupils of her eyes were almost devoid of color, with only the slightest shade of red encircling tiny irises. Rather than cartilage forming a nose, there was only a slight indentation beneath her eyes with a trio of small holes which Arens took to be nostrils. The upper portion of her rounded skull flared outward at a point just above small openings on each side, which seemed to serve as her ears. What little hair she possessed was confined to a single narrow strip that began just above the groove between her eyes and continued up and over her head to the nape of her long, thin neck. From there, the hair hung down below her shoulders, braided and intertwined with a strand of black material. The result resembled a ponytail, which hung down across the front of the Dolysian's right shoulder so that Arens could see a decorative silver band encircling its end. Her clothing consisted of a single-piece, floor-length gown tailored to her trim, almost petite physique. The garment had been fashioned from a shiny material that reminded Arens of silk, colored a light tan with threads of white and silver woven into the fabric.

Smiling, Arens said, "Advisor Zihl, welcome to the

bridge." When he had all but choked during his first attempt at mimicking her pronunciation, the Dolysian had taken apparent pity on him by explaining that in her society—one of however many that called her planet home—names acted as a means of honoring respected family members. When a member died, others in the family might be inspired to add a portion of that person's name to their own, a process that continued throughout the lives of those offering such tributes. In the case of Rzaelir Zihl du Molidin, Zihl was her given name, and her title of "advisor" was given to her while operating in her role as one of numerous liaisons between the Federation and the various Dolysian governments.

"Thank you, Captain," she replied, bowing her head for a brief moment. "It is an honor to be here."

Arens repeated Zihl's gesture. "I hope you enjoyed the tour, such as it was."

"The fastest five minutes you'll ever spend," Hebert replied, reaching up to brush a lock of her dark hair away from her eyes. As though attempting to decipher the meaning of the first officer's words, Zihl's expression changed to what Arens thought might be a look of confusion.

"What she means is that because our ship is so small, such tours often don't take that much time," he said, before offering another smile. Starfleet linguistic experts had done a phenomenal job creating a database from which universal translation protocols assisted in communicating with the Dolysian people, using more than one hundred of their known languages. Despite such an achievement, bridging the gap with respect to odd turns of phrase unfamiliar to one party or the other would always present a challenge.

Boma added, "On the other hand, it's easy to keep clean."

Archer-class scouts were designed for speed, their missions entailing getting in and out of places in a hurry and often working in stealth. Their size made them ideal for clandestine surveillance duties, such as monitoring activities along borders separating Federation territory from that of rival powers such as the Klingon and Romulan empires. The *Huang Zhong*, like her sister vessels of this type, possessed few frills or creature comforts for its fourteen-person crew to enjoy. Commander Hebert, like the ship's other female crew members, wore the female officer's version of uniform tunic and trousers rather than the skirt variant. Given the vessel's lack of turbolifts, the uniform choice made for traversing the ship's ladders and crawl spaces in a more dignified manner.

Even billet space aboard the *Huang Zhong* was at a premium, with only the captain and first officer entitled to a private cabin. As for the rest of the ship's complement, though each of them was formally assigned to one of the four remaining crew compartments, each room only possessed one berth, necessitating the practice of "hot-bunking," or sharing the beds by virtue of working and sleeping during different duty shifts. Given the often fluctuating nature of life aboard ship, any open bunk was fair game to anyone when their off-duty shift came around. The situation was tolerable, because most of the *Huang Zhong*'s missions were of limited duration and were interspersed with rotations at the ship's home station, Starbase 23. That the crew was one of the most tight-knit groups with which Arens had ever served also went a long way toward defusing any problems that might arise from being stuffed into such a compact vessel for lengthy periods of time.

Remember that, Arens warned himself, *when Hebert sticks you with the bar tab our first night back in port.*

Seemingly satisfied with his explanation, Zihl nodded. "As I said, the commander is an excellent guide. Your technology is wondrous, particularly your engines which allow you to travel faster than light." She paused, glancing toward the viewscreen. "Such feats are only fodder for stories to my people. Our attempts at interstellar travel must seem so quaint to you, but I hope that one day we too will be able to move among the stars as you do."

"You will," Hebert replied, "one day."

Zihl said, "We have been told by your diplomatic envoys that it is atypical for your Federation even to interact with a weaker species such as mine until after we have reached that technological milestone."

"Not weaker," Boma countered, his tone light and respectful, "just less advanced. Our laws prohibit us from revealing ourselves to such a culture, or to interfere with it, except in very special circumstances."

When Zihl's expression once again conveyed her lack of understanding, Arens added, "We believe that every society has the right to develop on its own, without influence from outside parties such as ourselves."

"That seems like a noble sentiment," Zihl replied, "though I suspect such a philosophy would be problematic from time to time, such as with my people. I am grateful you chose to make an exception on our behalf."

Though the budding relationship between Dolysia and the Federation was continuing to grow and prosper since formal first-contact protocols had been initiated fourteen months earlier, the initial meeting between the two almost did not come to pass. Only fortunate happenstance had seen to it that the *U.S.S. Resolute*, a Starfleet border patrol ship on assignment several sectors away from the Kondaii system in Federation space, crossed paths with a Dolysian cargo freighter adrift in space.

"It was a pretty bold experiment," Boma said, "converting that old freighter into a sleeper ship."

Zihl nodded. "I imagine you find such notions rather simplistic, given your ability to travel faster than light itself."

"Not at all," Hebert replied. "Hibernation ships are a normal first step when developing interstellar travel. Our planet did the same thing, hundreds of years ago."

"Ours was an experiment," Zihl said, "testing whether long-term cryogenics would be a feasible means of traveling to the other planets in our system. I am not familiar with the specifics of the mission, but I do not believe interstellar flight was a goal, at least not so early in the process."

Arens recalled what he had been told of the Dolysians' initial forays into long-duration spaceflight. A trio of scientists had volunteered to be placed in hibernation for a period of several years while the vessel transited the Kondaii system. During the flight, an error in the ship's onboard computer system caused an unplanned ignition of the vessel's engines, sending the freighter on a trajectory that eventually sent it out of the system and into interstellar space. Engineers on Dolysia remained in contact with the ship for a time while frantic plans were considered in order to attempt a retrieval. Though contact with the vessel was sporadic, a minor update to the computer's software allowed the computer to extend the crew's planned hibernation cycle. As the ship continued to travel farther away, a more extensive update to alter its course and redirect it back toward Dolysia failed, taking with it any hope—realistic or otherwise—of rescue.

Several years later, the *Resolute*'s sensors had picked up the ship, registering its low, battery-generated power readings and what was determined to be a distress signal. Upon intercepting the stricken vessel for closer investigation and then detecting life signs aboard, the *Resolute*'s captain made the decision to render assistance, resulting in the first Federation-Dolysian meeting. After the captain made her report to Starfleet Command, a decision was made to send a Federation first-contact team with the *Resolute* when it towed the freighter back to the Kondaii system.

"Captain," a female voice called out from behind him, and Arens turned to where his helm officer, Lieutenant T'Vrel, sat at her station. "Sensors are registering a vessel emerging from the rift."

"One of the ore freighters?" Arens asked, redirecting his attention back to the main viewscreen.

The Vulcan did not reply at first, leaning forward in her seat to peer into the scanner that had extended upward from her console. Then, she said, "Affirmative, sir."

"I've been waiting to see this," Boma said, moving back to his own station. "I want to monitor the energy readings from the rift as a ship passes through."

"So," Arens said, unable to resist the opening his science officer had provided him, "we're calling it a rift again?"

"Quiet, sir," Boma replied. "People are working here, and you're distracting them."

Hebert smiled. "I assume that was said with all due respect?"

"If it makes you feel better." As he bent over his console

and looked into his station's scanner viewport, Boma's face was bathed in the soft blue glow emanating from the instruments.

Arens turned back to Zihl. "Advisor, how many of these cargo runs do your freighters make while the rift is open?" He glanced over his shoulder at Boma as he asked the question, but the younger man either had not heard him or was choosing not to react to the gentle needling.

"Each season is different," the Dolysian replied, "and we always endeavor to establish and maintain a safety deadline, after which no ships are permitted to transit the Pass. For as long as my people have known about the energy field and Gralafi, we have been able to predict within a margin of error when the Pass will open and close." She paused, then added, "Of course, there have been a few miscalculations, as well, but those were long ago, and infrequent."

Hebert asked, "You've had ships in transit when the rift's closed?"

The advisor nodded, bowing her head. "A few times, yes. On those occasions, the ship making the journey was destroyed."

"And nothing can penetrate the field after that?" Boma asked.

"That is correct, Lieutenant," Zihl replied. "When my people first perfected space travel, we sent automated probes to the energy field, followed by larger ships piloted remotely from ground stations on my planet. In every case, the vehicles were lost. So far as our technology can determine, the field is impenetrable except for when the Pass is open."

Arens could not help imagining the *Huang Zhong* in such a situation. Not liking where his musings were taking him, he returned his gaze to the viewscreen, watching as the freighter emerged from the energy field and into normal space. Having been born into a family of low-warp, long-distance cargo haulers with a history going back to the earliest days of the Federation more than a century earlier, it was easy for him to see that the vessel had been constructed with function and practicality taking a priority over aesthetics. The ship was comprised of a forward section, which likely held the navigational and other control areas as well as crew berthing, and an aft segment from which protruded a quartet of engine bells that provided the ship's propulsion and expended waste products from whatever it used as a propellant. The two sections were linked by a long support pylon that Arens figured must contain crawl spaces and other work areas, and beneath which were connected six modular containers of differing colors. Even from this distance, Arens could see that the ship and its components were well-worn, with missing paint or no paint at all, replaced hull plates, and other signs of age and constant use.

"By the time the Pass closes again," Zihl said, "enough erinadium will have been obtained to supply the energy needs of my entire planet for one of your years. Combined with the other mining facilities we have operating on our planet's two moons as well as other sources of production on Dolysia itself, we are able to meet our energy requirements with ease."

Arens nodded. "It's an impressive operation, that's for sure. I don't know that I've ever seen anything like it; not on this scale, and certainly not with the added wrinkle of only being able to get the ore to your planet every three years." Then, he shrugged. "On the other hand, I suppose you've had plenty of time to iron out all the wrinkles."

Seeing the renewed look of confusion on Zihl's face, he was about to explain the idiom when Boma called out from his science station.

"Captain," he said, lifting his face away from his scanner's viewfinder. "You should have a look at this. Based on what we've been told about how stable the conduit is and how it doesn't seem to react to ships passing through it, I didn't expect to pick up any sensor fluctuations, but that's exactly what I'm seeing here."

Frowning, Arens asked, "You caught something as the freighter was coming through?"

Boma nodded. "The rift does react to the passage of ship traffic, but not in any way that's immediately noticeable. Look." He tapped a series of controls on his console, and one of the overhead screens began to display what Arens recognized as a computer-generated graphic of the energy field. "I don't know how to describe it except to say that it was sort of a rippling effect. I was able to pick it up on this side of the rift, but then our sensor beams scattered again. From what I can tell, the effect started from the other side and worked its way in this direction, tracking with the freighter's course. It's only a minor deviation from the readings I've collected to this point, but it was still enough to catch our attention."

"Advisor," Hebert said, her brow furrowed in confusion. "Has this sort of thing ever happened before?"

"Not that I know of, Commander," Zihl replied. "Though our monitoring devices possess nothing approaching the ability of your equipment, no probe we have ever dispatched to study the Pass has ever discovered anything which might hint at its being unstable."

"This probably sounds like a stupid question," Hebert

said, "but could any disruption or whatever you want to call it be caused by our sensors?"

Boma replied, "I don't think so, Commander. We've been conducting full sensor sweeps since we got here. This is the first indication of anything out of the ordinary." He shrugged. "To be honest? I don't think it's an instability. It's almost as if the field was . . . I don't know . . . sweeping over the freighter as it passed."

"Like some sort of scan?" Arens asked. "But that would mean . . ."

"It'd mean the field isn't a natural phenomenon," Boma finished. "If that's the case, then it's not like anything on record. Captain, we need to check this out."

Arens nodded. "Agreed." What might such a revelation mean, particularly for the Dolysians? As interesting as chasing down this mystery sounded to him, the captain knew he needed to proceed with care. Prudence was a fine watchword, at least for the moment, but that did not mean sitting idle. "Would it help if we got you a little closer?" Arens asked.

"It certainly wouldn't hurt," the science officer said. "We were planning to take a look at the other side, anyway."

Turning to Zihl, Arens said, "Advisor, would you be able to obtain the necessary permissions to allow my ship to enter the Pass?"

Zihl replied, "Certainly."

Arens nodded, his anticipation at the thought of getting to see firsthand whatever might lay beyond the rift tempered with concern over what Boma's sensor readings might be trying to tell them. Could he and his ship be responsible—without malice but through simple ignorance—for introducing some new, random element into whatever mix had conspired to create and sustain the enigmatic energy field before them? Had they endangered the planet it shielded, along with the resources that world possessed and upon which the Dolysian people had come to depend?

Despite his conflicting and troubling thoughts, Arens could not help the mounting excitement he felt as he regarded the main viewscreen and the image of the anomaly. "Okay, then. Let's go have ourselves a look."

TWO

James Kirk stared across the table, schooling his features to match the implacable expression on the face of his first officer. Spock, as always, offered no overt clues, but Kirk also could discern no subtle hints or unconscious facial tics or eye movements; nothing that offered the slightest insight into what the Vulcan might be thinking. The best Kirk could do was match his friend's unreadable expression, and see how the next moments played out.

"What do you want to do, sir?" asked Montgomery Scott from where he sat to Kirk's left, eyeing him with unrestrained amusement. On the table before him was a partially depleted deck of playing cards, on top of which the *Enterprise*'s chief engineer had placed a blue poker chip.

Staring at Spock over the five cards he and the first officer each held in their hands, Kirk did not move his eyes as he replied, "Don't rush me."

"I think he's bluffing," Scott said, offering a mischievous grin.

Sitting across the table from the engineer and holding cards of his own, Leonard McCoy snapped, "You had your chance, and you folded. Now give the man time to think, why don't you?" Then, he reached toward Kirk and tapped the table next to his friend's elbow. "I don't mean to rush you, Captain, but would you mind hurrying the hell up?"

"What happened to giving me time to think?" Kirk asked, unable to resist a small smile even though he did not direct his gaze to McCoy.

The ship's chief medical officer cleared his throat, then reached for the glass of brandy sitting on the table near his right arm. "That was until you decided to make a career out of this. I've performed operations that didn't take this long." He punctuated his statement by raising his glass in mock salute before sipping the brandy. After the current hand's opening round of betting and drawing of cards from Scott, who had volunteered to be the dealer for the evening's session, Spock had with no hesitation bet a few of the blue chips stacked before him on the table—the equivalent of twenty Federation credits—and McCoy had matched the wager. Though the chips had no real monetary value, in keeping with standing policy aboard ship prohibiting actual gambling, Kirk still remembered the physician's blunt opinions regarding the matter on the first occasion the officers had assembled for poker: "You can't play poker without poker chips. That's against the law, and if it's not then it damned well ought to be."

"I thought you said patience was a virtue, Bones?" Kirk said, reaching for his own stack of chips and selecting a few without taking his eyes from Spock.

McCoy snorted. "I never said that."

Across the table, Scott countered, "I'd stake my life on having heard you say that very thing, Doctor."

"Keep it up, and a hearing test will be only the first stage of a very prolonged, uncomfortable physical for the both of you." The comment was loud enough to elicit laughter not only from Kirk and Scott, but also from other crew members seated at nearby tables or standing near the recreation room's bank of food synthesizers. For the first time, Kirk realized that their friendly game had acquired a bevy of curious onlookers.

McCoy's conduct might have him in trouble with the captain of just about any other ship in Starfleet, and though Kirk himself had on occasion been required to rein in the doctor, the truth was that he enjoyed his friend's often cantankerous nature—a good deal of which was exaggerated for one reason or another, depending on the situation. The doctor's utter fearlessness when it came to questioning authority had come in handy more than once; indeed, one of McCoy's greatest virtues was that he was unmoved by whatever professional fallout might come his way should his behavior be viewed with less tolerance by an admiral, government official, or anyone else. Anyone who knew Leonard McCoy knew the man's primary motivation was providing quality care to his patients, along with the opportunities Starfleet afforded to increase his knowledge and understanding of medicine and how it was practiced by the various cultures he might encounter in his travels. Beyond that, McCoy had little use for just about everything else pertaining to the service, its rules, or most of the people who occupied its upper command echelons, and Kirk derived great enjoyment from the thought that his friend was only humoring him by consenting to wear a uniform at all.

Whatever you do, Bones, promise me you won't ever change.

Deciding against responding to his friend's good-natured jabs, Kirk instead kept his attention on the game and the enigmatic opponent sitting across from him. "Mister Spock, you seem entirely too comfortable for my taste, so let's see what we can do about that." With his free hand he counted chips from his stack and with a gentle toss deposited them on top of the small yet growing pile at the center of the table. "I see your twenty credits, and raise you another forty."

Spock's face betrayed not one hint of reaction, as though his features had been carved from granite. "A bold wager, Captain." Without looking at the table or the cards in his left hand, the first officer retrieved a quartet of blue chips from his stack and put them on the pile. "I see your forty." With a quick movement he took four more chips from his collection. "And I raise an additional forty." Shifting his gaze to McCoy, he added, "To you, Doctor."

"My mother raised no fools," McCoy said, placing his cards facedown on the table. "Fold."

Kirk, keeping his own expression neutral, once again searched for some kind of tell on Spock's face, but the Vulcan betrayed nothing. "Doctor McCoy taught you well, Mister Spock, but I think he may have left out a few things." Reaching for his chips, he grabbed enough to match the first officer's raise, then reached for five more. "Fifty."

Without the slightest pause, Spock matched the bet. "I call, sir."

Extending his arm, Kirk laid his cards face up on the table. Three kings—diamonds, clubs, and hearts—were complemented by two nines—spades and clubs. "Full house; kings full of nines."

"A most excellent hand, Captain. I congratulate you on your near victory." He spread his own cards on the table, revealing an ace of spades along with four tens. Scott's immediate reaction was to release a hearty laugh, which was accompanied by McCoy's bright, wide smile. From the nearby tables, Kirk heard a quiet chorus of amused reactions and even some soft applause.

"Ladies and gentlemen," McCoy said, "I present to you my finest creation: a Vulcan card shark."

Unable to resist chuckling himself, Kirk shook his head. "I could've sworn you were bluffing."

Reaching to the center of the table to retrieve the pile of chips he had won, Spock replied, "May I remind you, Captain, that Vulcans do not bluff?"

Kirk chuckled again. "Of course not, Mister Spock. Please accept my apologies."

"You should try it some time," Scott said. "Heaven knows you've got the perfect face for it."

"Quite unnecessary, Mister Scott," Spock said, pausing as he began the process of distributing his chips into stacks. "As the captain so astutely pointed out, Doctor McCoy's guidance was most adequate to the task at hand."

Offering what Kirk took to be a mock scowl, McCoy shook his head and released an audible sigh. "Thanks. I think."

"You were the one who offered to teach him how to play," Kirk said.

McCoy nodded while sipping from his brandy. "Sure, but I never thought he'd actually take me up on it." Turning his attention to Spock, the doctor added, "For my next trick, Spock, I think I'm going to help you master the fine art of winning at Texas Hold'em."

"I am somewhat familiar with this poker variant," Spock replied. Now finished ordering his chips, he sat with his hands folded before him, the tips of his forefingers touching. "I look forward to honing my skills during actual game play."

"And I suppose I should save up my chips," Kirk said, leaning back in his chair. As Scott retrieved the cards and began shuffling the deck in preparation for the next hand, the captain let his gaze wander about the recreation room to where other officers had returned their attention to their own activities. Poker and other card games were under way at adjacent tables, and Kirk spied Lieutenant Arex Na Eth sitting in one corner, engaging another crewman in a game of tri-dimensional chess, using the third of his three upper extremities—the one extending from the center of his torso—to move his pieces. A few members of the crew were relaxing in lounge chairs, reading from data slates or actual books. Other personnel were engaged in conversation in small groups, but Kirk also caught sight of a couple sitting on a couch in one corner of the room, speaking in softer tones and seemingly oblivious to everyone and everything around them.

Glancing over at McCoy, he saw that the doctor was conducting his own observations of the crew around him, monitoring whatever obvious or hidden clues might point to something working against an individual's physical or psychological well being. Having noted the couple in the corner, he shared a knowing look with Kirk, gratified that they along with everyone else in the room seemed to be in good spirits. For his part, the captain was pleased to see his crew taking the time to enjoy themselves and each other, stealing a few precious moments away from the demands of their duties. Far from home, tasked with a primary mission of deep space exploration augmented with diplomatic and humanitarian missions as well as whatever errands might be conjured by some bored admiral, life aboard a starship could be a challenge. Kirk knew that if anyone deserved a bit of downtime whenever the opportunity presented itself, it was the men and women under his command.

"Is this the boy's club, or can anyone sit in?"

Kirk turned at the sound of the new voice to see Ambassador Dana Sortino standing behind Spock, making no effort to hide a playful grin. She was slim though not petite, possessing a build that reminded Kirk of a swimmer's physique. Her features were framed by dark red hair cut in a short style that left the nape of her neck exposed. Though her skin was smooth and free of wrinkles, light gray highlights scattered through her hair offered the only clue as to her actual age, which Kirk knew to be early fifties according to the dossier he had been provided. Unlike the tailored business attire she had worn when she had first come aboard ship and during his previous meetings with her, the ambassador now wore cream-colored pants and a brilliant blue silk blouse that matched the color of her eyes. Her entire demeanor seemed to have changed along with her clothes, and she seemed more relaxed, as befitted the rec room's casual air.

"Good evening, Ambassador," Kirk said as he and his officers rose from their seats. "What can I do for you? Is there something you need?"

Sortino shook her head. "Not at all, Captain, unless you can direct me to some of whatever that is Doctor McCoy's drinking."

"Allow me, Ambassador," the doctor replied, reaching for the bottle of brandy he had brought to the game and turning to look for a glass.

Indicating the table with a wave of her hand, Sortino asked, "So, what's a lady have to do to get into a decent card game around here?"

Kirk gestured to the chair Scott had acquired from an

adjacent table and was moving into position between them. "By all means." Nodding in his first officer's direction, he added, "I'll warn you that Mister Spock seems to be something of a poker prodigy, thanks to the efforts of Doctor McCoy. If his luck holds out, it could be a long night for the rest of us."

"I like a challenge," Sortino said, smiling as she accepted a glass of brandy from McCoy. "I've spent my share of off-duty hours honing my own poker skills, though it's been a while since I've had the chance to play. Maybe I can knock some of the rust off."

"The brandy should help with that," McCoy replied. "I'd go easy with it."

Scott added, "And when you're finished with that and need to cleanse your palate, just let me know, Ambassador. I've got a bottle of scotch in my quarters I've been saving for a special occasion."

"Just one?" Kirk asked, offering a knowing grin.

Sortino nodded. "It's a deal, Commander."

"Please," the engineer replied, "call me Scotty."

"Only if you call me Dana."

Settling back into his chair, McCoy reached for his own drink. "I have to say, Dana, that you're not like most of the other ambassadors we run into from time to time."

The comment elicited a laugh from Sortino, who nodded. "Yes, I've read some of the reports from my colleagues about their various adventures aboard the *Enterprise*." She looked at Kirk, her left eyebrow rising in almost Vulcan-like fashion. "They warned me about you, Captain, and you'll be happy to know that there's a dartboard in the break room at the Diplomatic Corps HQ in San Francisco with your picture on it."

Kirk raised his drink in salute. "It's nice to be loved."

As he sipped his brandy, the captain reflected on the diplomats he had encountered in recent years. He viewed many if not most of them as myopic, vexing bureaucrats who seemed to find their way to the *Enterprise* with alarming regularity, armed with an incessant need to prove something. On the other hand, Dana Sortino seemed comfortable and confident in her role and the authority she carried, but without any apparent need to demonstrate that clout to anyone and everyone in close proximity to her. One of the marked distinctions between her and other diplomats with whom Kirk had dealt over the years was the fact that Sortino was also a retired Starfleet officer. She had reached the rank of commander, with advanced training as a sociologist and cultural specialist before accepting an assignment as the first officer of the *U.S.S. Lavinius*, a *Loknar*-class frigate assigned to patrol duty along the Federation-Klingon border.

"If you do not mind my asking, Ambassador," Spock said, "why did you choose to leave Starfleet for a career in diplomacy? Based on what I know of your service record, you were in line for promotion and your own command."

Sortino shrugged. "To be honest, I never really wanted my own ship. I never needed to be the one in charge; I'd rather be the one the person in charge turns to whenever they need something done. As for diplomacy, I'd had occasion to assist ambassadors and other diplomatic envoys from time to time, and I started taking an interest in the process. Of course, it didn't hurt that switching jobs also meant I got to stay home more often. My husband was quite happy with that new twist." Clearing her throat, she took another sip of her drink before turning her attention to Scott. "Anyway, I didn't come to tell my life story. Let's play some cards."

Smiling, the engineer nodded. "Aye, that sounds like a fine plan, indeed."

"I take it you're tired of reading mission briefings and status reports from the first-contact teams on Dolysia?" Kirk asked as Scott began to shuffle the deck of cards.

Sortino replied, "You have no idea. I think my eyes were starting to cross."

"You do not find the Dolysian people interesting?" Spock asked. "I must admit that I'm intrigued by what they've managed to accomplish, particularly given their current state of technological advancement."

"It's impressive," Sortino said, "there's no arguing that, Mister Spock. They're about on par with where Earth might have been in the mid to late twenty-first century, if your people hadn't seen fit to pay us a visit. A permanent presence on another world in their solar system, with regular traffic to and from it and an entire industry practically resting on the shoulders of that tenuous connection? It's fascinating as hell, if you ask me. I can't wait to see it for myself, and I can't believe this rift or energy field that surrounds the planetoid isn't something you're interested in studying, Commander."

The first officer nodded. "Indeed. So far as I am able to determine, the phenomenon is unlike anything ever before encountered."

"Any theories on what it might be, Spock?" Kirk asked. Though it was very subtle, Kirk was still able to note the almost minuscule change in his friend's normally inscrutable features as he pondered the question.

"I am reluctant to give voice to any hypothesis until

more information is available," replied the Vulcan. "However, the lack of any known precedent does tend to support the notion that it is not a product of nature, but rather artificial construction. It is worth noting that the sensor readings obtained and transmitted by the *Huang Zhong*'s science officer remain largely inconclusive."

McCoy leaned forward in his chair, and Kirk noted the look in the doctor's eyes as he asked, "You're not just saying that because of any feelings you might *have* for the *Huang Zhong*'s science officer, are you?"

Before Spock could answer, Scott tapped the shuffled deck on the table. "Five card draw, nothing wild," he announced as he began dealing cards to the other players, beginning with Spock to his left and proceeding clockwise around the table.

Seemingly content to leave Spock alone, at least for the moment, McCoy instead returned his attention to Sortino. "Ambassador, how are the Dolysians taking to the notion of having interstellar neighbors? First contact had to be something of a shock."

"At first," the ambassador conceded, "and that's not even considering the Prime Directive issues, which pretty much went out the window when the *Resolute* found the sleeper ship. Still, that was mitigated by returning the ship and the crew to Dolysia. There was some initial unrest and even panic in some quarters, but by all accounts most of the population seemed to accept the new paradigm without too much trouble. Still, there's been a small army of sociologists and other specialists working with government, scientific, and industry leaders for more than a year, helping to ease the burden of transition."

Spock said, "There would seem to be many issues to

address before Dolysia would be ready for Federation membership."

"Absolutely," Sortino replied as Scott finished dealing cards. Reaching for the five cards she had been given, she brought them up so that she could read them while straightening them with her free hand. "Still, they'll certainly receive protectorate status, and one of the reasons I'm here is to negotiate a long-term trade agreement. The ore they're mining out of the planetoid, erinadium, shows some serious potential to be useful in a number of areas. Don't ask me to tell you what those areas are; all I know is that some scientists back on Mars have been studying samples of the stuff for months, and they seem pretty excited over whatever it is they've found."

Guided by instinct, Kirk glanced at Spock, who was already lowering his cards and opening his mouth to deliver what the captain knew would be an in-depth recitation on the properties and possible uses of erinadium. "Your bet to open, Spock," he said, grinning as the Vulcan realized he had been thwarted.

"Very well," Spock replied, reaching for one of the stacks of chips representing his modest winnings from the previous hand. No sooner did he toss two blue chips into the center of the table than the familiar whistle of the ship's intercom sounded across the rec room.

"*Bridge to Captain Kirk,*" said the voice of Lieutenant M'Ress, the communications officer assigned to the bridge during the *Enterprise*'s beta shift.

"If you get up to answer that," McCoy said while looking over the tops of his cards, "you automatically fold."

Rising from his seat, Kirk grinned and tossed his cards facedown on the table. "I didn't have anything, anyway."

He crossed the room, offering greetings along the way to members of his crew as he made his way to a nearby wall-mounted intercom panel. After pressing the control to activate the panel, he said, "Kirk here. What is it, Lieutenant?"

"*I apologize for disturbing you, sir,*" the Caitian officer replied, her words soft and drawn out in a manner that could be soothing if not outright hypnotic. "*I've just picked up a distress call being broadcast on all Starfleet emergency frequencies. It's the* U.S.S. Huang Zhong, *Captain, calling from the Kondaii system. They've encountered some kind of trouble while investigating the spatial anomaly.*"

His brow furrowing in concern, Kirk asked, "Does the message give any idea as to the nature of the problem?"

"*No, sir,*" M'Ress replied. "*It's simply a distress call, and seems to cut out in mid-transmission before repeating on a continuous loop. A data packet containing their most recent sensor readings has also been attached to the message.*"

Not liking the sound of that, Kirk did not hesitate. "Send a message to Starfleet Command and Starbase 23, updating them on the situation. Instruct the helm to accelerate to maximum warp. Have navigation recalculate our arrival time and send that on to Starfleet, as well. And route the sensor data to the science station."

"*Aye, aye, sir,*" the communications officer acknowledged.

"Mister Spock and I are on our way up now. Kirk out." Severing the connection, the captain turned to his companions at their table, and noted that Scott was already reacting to the subtle shift in the pitch of the *Enterprise*'s massive warp engines as the ship began to increase its speed. The engineer was looking at him, his expression conveying the question he did not need to ask aloud.

Kirk nodded to him as he moved toward the table. "Break's over, gentlemen. Time to go to work. Scotty, I'll need you keeping an eye on the engines. Mister Spock, if you'll join me on the bridge?"

"What's going on, Captain?" Sortino asked, her own expression one of worry. "Something with the *Huang Zhong*?"

"It looks that way, Ambassador," Kirk replied, sighing as he wondered what they might find when they reached the Kondaii system.

THREE

Despite the best efforts of the bridge's environmental control system, the stench of acrid smoke from burned-out relays and scorched insulation still assailed Ronald Arens's nostrils. Normal illumination had been extinguished as a consequence of losing main power, replaced by emergency lighting that cast most of the bridge in shadows highlighted by the glow of workstations and status monitors. Though the alert sirens had been deactivated at least a full minute earlier, his ears still rang with their sharp warble. Because of that, it took Arens an extra moment to realize that the omnipresent reverberation of the *Huang Zhong*'s warp engines was notable by its absence.

"Position report!" he called out, pulling himself from his captain's chair and moving to stand behind Lieutenant T'Vrel at the helm. "Did we make it through the rift?"

The Vulcan nodded. "Affirmative, sir. We appear to have cleared the inner boundary and are now on a course toward the planetoid."

Arens directed his attention to the main viewscreen, which displayed the image of the small, seemingly orphaned Gralafi. Even from this distance, the captain was able to note the amalgam of grays and browns denoting the planetoid's surface, with only slight splashes of greens indicating sparse vegetation in various, isolated regions.

Considering there were no other destinations that seemed to present themselves, he ordered, "Take us to a standard orbit, T'Vrel. Let's park while we figure out what's what."

"Acknowledged," the helm officer replied, her fingers playing across her console as she entered the necessary commands.

So, what exactly is what? The thought rattled around in Arens's mind as he contemplated the past few minutes. Everything had seemed fine as T'Vrel maneuvered the *Huang Zhong* into the rift on a course toward Gralafi. The first indications that something might be wrong had come within seconds of entering the energy field, as Boma picked up distortions from inside the rift even as the ship made the transit through the barrier. The alarms from engineering seemed to start mere heartbeats after that, with the chief engineer, Master Chief Petty Officer Christine Rideout, contacting the bridge and advising Arens of fluctuations in the warp engines. Things had only proceeded to go downhill from there.

Looking about the bridge and seeing that the rest of his officers had already returned their attention to their respective stations and duties, Arens asked, "Commander Hebert, how are we? Is everybody okay?"

"We're good to go in that department, sir," April Hebert replied from where she stood at one of the workstations along the bridge's starboard bulkhead. "Everyone accounted for, and no injuries to speak of."

Arens nodded at the report. "Small favors, but I'll take them. Turning his attention to Rzaelir Zihl du Molidin, who had taken a seat at the unmanned console next to Hebert, he asked, "Advisor, are *you* all right?"

Zihl said, "Yes, Captain. Thank you. I am happy to hear your crew suffered no injuries."

"Just our lucky day, I guess," Arens said before looking again to Hebert. "Did you manage to get off the distress signal?"

"For the most part," the first officer answered. "There was some disruption as we passed through the rift, and the last part of the transmission was cut off, but most of it got through, along with the sensor packet. The *Enterprise* was already on its way here, so they'll likely still be the first ship to respond. They were four days away at last report. Assuming they accelerate to maximum warp, that'll put them here in just shy of twenty-five hours."

"If I know Jim Kirk," Arens countered, "he'll milk every last bit of speed from his ship's engines to get here as fast as he can. Until then, though, we're on our own."

T'Vrel called out from the helm station, "We have assumed a standard orbit above the planetoid, Captain."

Nodding at the report, Arens said, "Thanks, Lieutenant. All right, now that things have settled down for the moment, I'd like to know how we got to this point. Advisor Zihl, have your people ever encountered anything like what happened to us when we passed through the rift?"

Zihl rose from her seat, and the captain saw her expression contort into something approximating a frown. "No, Captain. At least, not so far as is publicly known. I have been through the Pass many times myself, and I have never experienced or witnessed anything like that."

"Okay," Arens said, not liking that answer but seeing little to be accomplished from beating the topic to death when other, more pressing matters demanded his attention. "We'll put a pin in that for now, but I'd like you to ask your government leaders about it when we get a chance."

Turning toward the center of the bridge, he added, "Mister Boma, did our sensors pick up anything?"

Sitting at his workstation, the science officer replied, "Judging by these readings we collected, I'd have to say that the rift reacted in some manner to our warp engines. If Rideout hadn't ejected the antimatter containment bottles when she did . . . well, I'd rather not dwell on that, if you don't mind."

"You're kidding, right?" Hebert asked, making no effort to hide her surprise. "Even with all the backup and safety systems?"

Boma leaned back in his chair. "When the disruption hit the engines, everything was out of whack for a period of about ten seconds. Backups were trying to kick in, but they were lagging, and that was with a fluctuation in the magnetic fields surrounding the containment bottles. Any delay in a system kicking in could be critical, even fatal. Rideout did the right thing by punting the antimatter."

As if on cue, the ship's intercom buzzed to life, followed by the voice of the *Huang Zhong*'s chief engineer, Christine Rideout. "*Engineering to bridge. Everybody okay up there?*"

Moving to his command chair, Arens tapped the control on the chair's right arm to open the intercom channel. "Everybody's fine, Chief. What's the story with the engines?"

"*It's a sad, sad tale of woe, sir,*" the engineer replied, "*and the ending stinks. Whatever we ran into, it torqued the warp drive pretty good. Even if I hadn't ejected the antimatter, I'd still have half a dozen burnouts in the warp coils. Hell, one of the things damn near melted, if you can believe that.*"

Though Arens already had a decent enough idea

regarding the answer to his next question, he asked it anyway. "Give me the short version, Chief. How much time to make repairs?"

"*Out here, by ourselves?*" Rideout asked. "*About a century, give or take a week or two. Even if we had replacement antimatter and a containment system to go with it, we'd still need a tow to a proper maintenance facility, sir. Other than the warp drive, we can probably take care of everything else in a couple of days or so. Less, if we get some help.*"

Behind him, Zihl said, "Though I do not know what we might do to help, we are certainly willing to offer any possible assistance, Captain."

"I appreciate that, Advisor," Arens replied, knowing there was little if anything the Dolysians could do to help with his ship's present situation. Still, there was no mistaking in Zihl's words and eyes the genuine desire to render whatever aid might be feasible. "I truly do." Returning his attention to the intercom panel and imagining the beleaguered expression on the face of his engineer, he said, "All right, Chief. Thanks for the update. Is there anything we can do to make your life easier?"

"*You could send me to Wrigley's Pleasure Planet for a month,*" the engineer replied. "*We're going to need to access some systems and components from the outside, sir. If you could set us down, that'd be a huge help.*"

"Consider it done," Arens replied, happy not for the first time that the *Huang Zhong*'s design allowed the vessel to make planetfall, rather than being forced to remain in orbit. "Keep me posted, and I'll see about getting you some more help."

Through the speaker, Rideout said, "*Much obliged, Skipper. I'll have plenty for folks to do. Rideout . . . riding out.*"

Despite the current situation, Arens could not help but smile at the chief's signature sign-off as the communication ended. With a quick wit and a sense of humor sharp enough to cut diamonds, Christine Rideout often shouldered the burden not only of keeping the *Huang Zhong* in top running order, but also of seeing to the morale of the ship's crew. As fast as her mind might be when coming up with a clever riposte whenever someone made the ill-fated decision to challenge her in a verbal sparring match, the chief's fingers also seemed to move at warp speed and as though possessed of their own will. Whatever repair obstacles she faced, Rideout would make short work of them, at least so long as she had access to the proper resources. Even with the damage to the ship, which was beyond her immediate means to address, Arens knew that under the chief engineer's watchful eye, they still were in decent shape.

"You just know she's back there, cursing loud and hard enough to strip paint off the bulkheads," Hebert said, offering a knowing grin as she moved from her station.

The captain nodded, chuckling at the image her statement evoked. "Oh, I know. Having to ask for a tow back to base is the engineer's equivalent of a captain being forced to evacuate and abandon his ship, at least so far as damage to the ego is concerned." He paused, looking around the bridge and taking stock of the situation by glancing at the array of workstation monitors and status indicators within his field of vision. "Advisor Zihl, may I have your permission to land on Gralafi in order to start our repairs?"

The Dolysian replied, "Of course, Captain. Our central colony settlement, Havreltipa, features several landing ports and a vessel maintenance facility."

At the helm console, T'Vrel said, "I have it on sensors, Captain. The facility has two unoccupied berths."

"Excellent," Arens said, liking the way the situation was beginning to show signs of improvement. "T'Vrel, make preparations for landing. Advisor Zihl, if you'll work with Commander Hebert, we'll put you in contact with the mining colony in order to secure their authorization." Looking to his first officer, he added, "Commander, set up a shift rotation and let's have all available hands sent down to engineering to give Rideout some help. We're not going to be able to do much else until the cavalry gets here." Given the size of *Archer*-class scouts and the small crews serving aboard them, assignment to such a vessel required that each crew member be cross-trained and proficient in at least two other starship occupational specialties. Such was the case aboard the *Huang Zhong*, with everyone including the captain possessing some form of engineering skill set that could be utilized during situations just like the one Arens and his crew faced.

Hebert replied, "Aye, aye, sir. We're on it."

From where he still worked at his science station, Boma said, "Captain, you need to see this."

Uh-oh, Arens thought. *Now what?* Stepping around his chair, he moved to stand behind Boma so that he could look down at the console over the other man's shoulder. "What's up?"

"Something odd on the sensors," the science officer replied, frowning. "Now that we're on this side of the rift, I'm able to get a better look at the energy field. Though I suspected something like this from the beginning, this is the first real indication that I might be right."

"Right about what?" Arens asked.

Boma gestured to one of his console's display monitors. "The rift. I'm sure it's being generated artificially, Captain."

"Really?" Arens asked, his eyes widening in surprise. "How?"

Shaking his head, Boma replied, "I don't know yet. It was almost an accident that I found it at all." He pointed again to his station. "Coming through the rift disrupted our sensors, and I had to reset and recalibrate the array. I was going through some diagnostics, checking different wavelengths and frequencies, and the scanners picked up an abnormality. When I took a closer look, I was able to detect a regular pattern within the energy field surrounding the rift. It was reacting to our passage, even without the disruption caused by our warp engines. The entire field was acting like some kind of passive sensor scan. It covered the entire ship in seconds. I have no idea what controlled it, or if any information was transmitted to or from it, but the pattern was unmistakable, Captain. Whatever that thing is, it's not a naturally occurring phenomenon. Someone or something put it there, deliberately."

"You're sure?" Arens asked.

"Absolutely." Reaching for his console, Boma tapped several of the multicolored buttons in sequence, in response to which one of the monitors began to display a pattern of lights, fluctuating in what Arens quickly surmised was a steady, measured rhythm. "The sensors picked up the repeating pattern," the science officer explained, "though it's much slower than what I'm showing here. I amplified the tempo so you wouldn't have to look at it for an hour."

Arens smiled. "Thanks for that. Okay, so the big question now is who or what is responsible, and where are they?" Even as he asked the question, he found himself looking up from the science station to regard the image of the planetoid, the upper third of which was now visible on the main viewscreen. "Anybody care to take a guess?"

"Gralafi makes the most sense," Boma said, "though I haven't yet picked up indications of any sort of broadcast or projection coming from it. We're conducting sweeps of the planet surface, but so far I'm not finding anything that can't be explained by the Dolysians' presence."

Turning at the sound of approaching footsteps, Arens saw Zihl moving toward him, her expression one of confusion. "Commander Boma, are you suggesting that someone other than my people may be living on Gralafi?"

Boma paused, glancing to Arens, who nodded for him to continue. "At this point, Advisor, I'm not prepared to make that determination, though it's certainly a possibility. So far, our sensor data remains inconclusive."

"You mentioned that you only caught the initial pattern when you were retuning the sensors," Hebert said as she crossed the bridge to stand opposite Arens on the other side of Boma's station. "Maybe whatever you're looking for is operating on another frequency altogether; something we can't easily pick up, either."

"Already on that, Commander," the science officer replied. "I'm running a program that will cycle through the sensor array with special emphasis on wavelengths we don't normally use." He sighed, shaking his head. "I swear it's like whatever we're looking for *knows* we're looking for it, or at least was designed to evade searches like this." No sooner did he speak the words than an alert tone sounded from his station, and Boma emitted what to Arens's ears sounded like a grunt of satisfaction. "Bingo." He tapped another string of commands to his console, and several monitors shifted their readouts to display what the captain recognized as sensor wavelength patterns.

"What are we looking at?" Arens asked.

"Power readings," Boma answered, "coming from somewhere on the planet."

His eyes now riveted to the planetoid on the screen, Arens pondered the mysterious potential it now harbored, if his science officer's report was any indication. "Can you locate its source?"

"Working on it," Boma said. "Hang on, I think—"

The rest of his report was drowned out as a new alarm klaxon began wailing across the bridge mere heartbeats before Arens felt the deck shift beneath his feet. He reached out to grip the back of Boma's chair, just managing to keep himself from being thrown off balance as the entire ship seemed to quaver around him.

"What the hell was that?" Hebert shouted over the siren and the groans of protest that seemed to be emanating from every bulkhead and deck plate. Like Arens, she had grabbed for anything that might keep her from being tossed to the deck, and now held on to one of the rails separating the bridge's command well from the perimeter workstations. A quick glance around the room told the captain that everyone else seemed to have avoided taking any nasty spills.

Holding on to her helm console, T'Vrel replied, "Something hit us, sir. Attempting to ascertain damage."

"Shields!" Arens barked.

T'Vrel shook her head. "Nonresponsive, Captain."

"It wasn't something that hit us," Boma called out. "It's latched on to us. Some kind of tractor beam!"

Tractor beam? What in the name of . . . ?

The thoughts tumbled about within Arens's mind as the ship lurched again, and this time the attack—if it was an attack—was accompanied by the voice of the *Huang Zhong*'s chief engineer exploding from the intercom.

"*Rideout to bridge! What the hell's going on up there?*"

Pushing himself away from the science station, Arens dropped into his seat and hit the intercom switch on the command chair's right arm. "Something's gotten hold of us, Chief! Where are the shields?"

"The shield generators are being disrupted by the beam," Boma said, cutting off the engineer. "Unless we can break free, they're useless."

Through the intercom, Rideout replied, "*I've tried everything to override, but it's not happening!*"

Before Arens could respond, everything around him shuddered once again, and a new alarm tone blared for attention. "Now what?"

"The beam's strength is increasing," Boma replied, his tone one of shocked disbelief. "We're being pulled out of orbit!"

"Reverse course!" Arens shouted. "Full impulse power!" For the first time, it occurred to him to look toward the main viewscreen, where he now saw the image of Gralafi beginning to move as the *Huang Zhong* shifted on its axis from its orbital course and began to head toward the planetoid itself. "Engineering, I need everything you've got transferred to propulsion! *Now!*"

Rideout's voice erupted from the intercom, "*I'm rerouting everything I can get my hands on, Skipper!*"

"It won't be enough," Hebert yelled from where she had retaken her station. "Not without warp drive!"

Slamming his fist down on the arm of his chair, Arens hit the switch to silence the alarms. The action did nothing to soften the growing whine of the ship's engines as T'Vrel fought to break free of whatever had ensnared the *Huang Zhong*.

"Captain," the Vulcan said, "even with full impulse, I am unable to maneuver against the beam."

Over the comm speaker, Rideout shouted, "*Impulse engines are starting to overheat! Either we break away or power down, or we lose everything!*"

His eyes glued to the planetoid, which now filled the viewscreen and was continuing to come closer, Arens gritted his teeth at the report. "T'Vrel! What's the story?"

"The beam is too powerful, sir," replied the helm officer while keeping her attention on her console.

"*Bridge!*" Rideout's voice was tight with strain. "*We're at critical!*"

Clenching his fists in mounting anger, Arens snapped, "Reduce power!" No sooner did he give the order than he could hear the whine of the impulse engines begin to subside as the *Huang Zhong* stopped its futile struggle against its unseen attacker. Was it his imagination, or did he feel the ship accelerating toward the planetoid? The image on the screen certainly seemed to be growing larger at an increasing rate.

"I think I've got something," Boma called over his shoulder, and before Arens could respond he added, "I'm tracking the beam to its origin point. Whatever it is seems to be masked from our sensors, but there's no mistaking the beam's coming from there."

"Is that where we're being taken?" Commander Hebert asked.

Boma shook his head. "I don't think so. As far as I can tell, the beam's main purpose seems to be just yanking us down from orbit."

"Our speed is increasing," T'Vrel reported. "At our present angle and rate of descent, we will crash on the planetoid's surface."

From where she still sat at a workstation adjacent to Hebert's, Advisor Zihl said, "It cannot be anything belonging to us. We possess no technology capable of such feats."

In truth, Arens did not believe the Dolysians to be capable of an assault of this nature on his ship. Every briefing he had read or received on the civilization and its level of technological advancement supported that contention. Not that such things mattered at the moment. Struggling to maintain his composure, he asked, "T'Vrel, time to impact?"

"Fifty-eight seconds," the Vulcan replied.

Enough of this! If they were going down, Arens decided they would go down swinging. "Engineering, stand by for maximum thrust to the impulse engines! Transfer all remaining power to structural integrity and inertial damping!"

"*Aye, sir!*" Rideout acknowledged.

T'Vrel said, "Forty seconds to impact."

"Helm," Arens continued, "target the beam's origin point with full phasers. On my mark, fire the full spread and then take us at full impulse on a lateral course away from the beam." Heartbeats seemed to stretch into eternity as he waited for the helm officer to complete her preparations, finally turning from her console long enough to meet his gaze.

"Standing by, Captain."

Hebert called out, "Twenty seconds!"

"Fire!" Arens ordered, leaning forward while gripping the arms of his chair. "T'Vrel, full power breakaway, now!" Subtle tremors vibrated from the deck plates into his boots as the phaser batteries released their first barrage. On the viewscreen, two glowing spheres of energy sailed out ahead of the ship, arcing down toward the surface of the planetoid, which was now much too close for the captain's comfort. Two more phaser salvos followed, and seconds later the strikes registered on the screen as brilliant plumes of orange-white heat. Arens had only an instant to see the results of the attack before the *Huang Zhong*'s trajectory shifted with such abruptness that he could feel everything shift as the inertial damping systems struggled to compensate.

"We're free!" Boma shouted. "The beam's gone!"

Arens ignored the report, his attention riveted on the movements of T'Vrel at the helm. Her fingers were a blur as she fought the console, and from his vantage point the captain saw several status indicators change from yellow to red just as new alarm sirens began to sound.

"T'Vrel, what is it?"

"The helm is slow to respond," the Vulcan replied. "I am having difficulty arresting our speed."

On the screen, Gralafi's surface was now highlighted by a reddish-purple sky occupying the image's upper third. The ground continued to rush past, and terrain features now were clearly visible, growing larger and more ominous with each passing second. A single thought echoed in Ronald Arens's mind.

We're not going to make it.

"Helm control is failing," T'Vrel reported, and this time

even her stoic demeanor seemed to be cracking around the edges. "Captain, I cannot prevent a crash landing."

Without hesitation, Arens once more hit the intercom switch with his fist. "All hands, this is the captain! Crash protocols! Brace for impact!" Then, looking to Hebert, he said, "Launch the buoy."

As the first officer moved to comply with the order, Arens could do nothing except watch as the last sliver of sky disappeared from the top of the viewscreen, leaving only the barren, uninviting surface of the planetoid to draw ever closer.

FOUR

Leonard McCoy hated waiting.

"All right, that's it," he said, reaching for the control to deactivate the computer terminal on his desk and swinging the tabletop unit so that its display screen faced away from him. "I'm now officially bored."

Entering the room from the doorway leading to the sickbay's adjacent laboratory area, a data slate tucked into the crook of her left arm, Nurse Christine Chapel regarded him with a look of amusement. "You've finished reviewing the *Huang Zhong* crew's medical records?"

"Three times," McCoy replied. "It's easy when they only have fourteen people." He had spent the better part of the past two days preparing for whatever might be found once the *Enterprise* was finally able to rendezvous with the *Huang Zhong*. "Where are we with the trauma team?"

Chapel consulted her data slate. "Everything you requisitioned has been staged in Cargo Bay Two," she replied.

Nodding in approval, McCoy recalled the hour he had spent earlier in the day, reviewing the details of the manifest he had prepared for the trauma team. It was one more endeavor that had kept the doctor's mind from envisioning ever more dire scenarios with respect to the *Huang Zhong* and its crew. By far, the worst thing that might happen upon the completion of the mission would be having to put every item he had requested back into ship's stores, unused because no one remained for him to help.

Always the optimist, aren't you?

Still consulting her data slate, Chapel looked up and said, "Oh, and I forgot to tell you earlier, but Doctor M'Benga has volunteered to lead the team."

Shaking his head, McCoy said. "I appreciate that, but tell him I'll be taking this one. I've got more field medical experience than he does, and this might end up being a tricky situation. According to her record, the first officer has a rare blood condition that might require an organic surrogate if she's lost a lot of blood or was exposed to some infection." Based on his review of the geological and climatological reports pertaining to the Gralafi planetoid, he did not expect to find anything like that when he finally had the chance to diagnose and treat the *Huang Zhong*'s first officer, but he felt better preparing for such eventualities.

On the other hand, any medical aid she might be receiving from Dolysian doctors, despite their best intentions and given their understandable lack of knowledge in the areas of space medicine and xenobiology, might end up worsening an already delicate situation. Broken bones could be set and lacerations could be sutured easily enough, McCoy knew, but from what he had read, physiology varied widely between the Dolysians and any one of the four distinctions of humanoid aboard the *Huang Zhong*. Ministrations of anesthetics or even simple pain relievers, let alone other medications deemed necessary by Dolysian physicians, would at best be pharmaceutical guesswork. Transfusions would be risky, assuming anyone else among the crew was a compatible donor, or if there were sufficient quantities of the right blood types in the ship's stores, and surgeries nearly impossible. Once there, he knew that he and his trauma team would act quickly and skillfully to aid those in need, but the thought that any one of *Huang Zhong*'s crew might be enduring pain or even dying without appropriate care unsettled him.

Of course, that's assuming there are survivors in the first place.

Irritated with himself over the errant thoughts intruding on his consciousness, McCoy eyed the empty cup sitting abandoned near the corner of his desk. Deciding that his mood might be improved in singular fashion with the introduction of fresh coffee into the mix, he retrieved the cup and moved from behind his desk. He was halfway to the food synthesizer on the other side of his office when the door leading to the corridor outside sickbay slid aside to reveal Ambassador Dana Sortino.

"Doctor McCoy," she said, smiling as she stepped into the room. "I hope I'm not interrupting." Her attire, a light-gray skirt and modest top paired with a mellow purple jacket, was formal without making her appear stiff or unapproachable. McCoy suspected it was a conscious choice on her part, her wardrobe seemingly selected to put at ease those with whom she might interact even in the most decorous setting.

Holding up the cup for her to see, McCoy replied, "You're hardly an interruption, Ambassador. I was just getting myself a cup of coffee. Care for some?"

Sortino shook her head. "No, thank you."

As he pressed the controls beneath the food slot and waited for the device to process his request, he said, "You've kept a pretty low profile since the poker game."

"I've been going over my briefings on the Dolysians,"

the ambassador said, sighing. "I think those files keep growing when I'm not looking."

The food slot's door slid up, revealing McCoy's coffee, and he retrieved it as he turned to regard Sortino. "I used to cram before a big test all the time, too. Not sure if it helped, but for some reason it always managed to put my mind at ease."

"Lucky you," Sortino countered. "All it does for me is put *my* mind to throbbing, and thus, the reason for my visit. I was hoping you might remedy that."

McCoy crossed back to his desk, setting the coffee down next to his computer terminal. "Congratulations. You've just been promoted to my most challenging case of the day." He gestured for her to follow him. "Follow me, Ambassador, and we'll have you fixed right up in no time." He led her into the laboratory area and toward the storage cabinets where he kept those curatives that were most often requested by his walk-in patients. Opening the cabinet containing mild analgesics and other low-dose medications, he selected a small vial and dispensed a single, small blue tablet into Sortino's open and extended palm.

"It'll dissolve as soon as it hits your tongue," he said. "Doesn't taste too bad, either, but I can get you some water if you like."

Sortino shook her head. "This'll be fine, thank you." Swallowing the pill, she closed her eyes and exhaled through her nose. After a moment, she said, "Is it supposed to work so fast?"

"Oh, yes," McCoy replied. "It's no mint julep, but it gets the job done." Replacing the vial in the cabinet and closing the unit, he asked, "So, what now? Back to reviewing briefing packets?"

"Nope," Sortino said. "Captain Kirk called down to my cabin a few minutes ago. Mister Spock has finished his analysis of the *Huang Zhong's* recorder buoy, and is ready to brief me on his findings. I'm on my way to the bridge."

Considering the ambassador's statement, he asked, "The bridge? That has to be more exciting than anything going on around here. Would you mind if I shared a turbolift with you?"

Sortino frowned. "You can just do that? Go up to the bridge?"

"I have clearance throughout the ship," McCoy replied. "One of the fringe benefits of being something of a counselor as well as the chief medical officer." He shrugged. "Not the job I trained for, but I guess it helps that I have a knack for reading people. So, I wander around the ship from time to time. It gives me an opportunity to observe the crew in their work spaces, rather than formalizing the process by bringing them in here and making them self-conscious about talking about whatever might be bothering them." Then he smiled. "Mostly, I just like snooping around."

Leaving sickbay, they navigated around other members of the *Enterprise* crew as they made their way through the curved corridor. A pair of crewmen dressed in maintenance coveralls, whom McCoy recognized as part of the engineering staff, were waiting at the turbolift doors as he and Sortino approached. Both men stepped aside, allowing him and the ambassador to enter the lift.

"Going up?" McCoy asked when the men remained standing in the corridor rather than stepping into the car.

One of the crewmen shook his head. "We'll get the next one, Doctor."

"Suit yourself." The doors closed, and McCoy reached

for one of the grips mounted inside the lift. "Bridge." He felt the gentle push beneath his feet as the car vibrated and whined to life before moving on a lateral track. As it continued to accelerate, he noted for some inexplicable reason that the light bands scrolling past the turbolift's motion indicator caused a strobe effect across Sortino's face. It was an odd, soothing sight, and it was not until Sortino turned to face him that he realized he was staring.

"Sorry," he said, feeling a wave of sudden embarrassment. "I was . . . lost in thought for a second."

If she saw through his weak fib, she had the grace and decency not to call him on it. Instead, she said, "Doctor, you mentioned your ability to read people. I'd like to think that I've acquired a similar gift."

McCoy nodded as he felt the lift slowing before the lights in the motion indicator switched to scrolling in a vertical pattern, signifying the car's ascent. "Given your chosen profession, I can imagine something like that coming in pretty handy."

"I'm not really sure what we're getting into out here with the Dolysians," Sortino said, "but I feel better knowing it's the *Enterprise* that's here with me. Your ship and crew have quite the reputation, you know."

Unable to resist a small chuckle, McCoy said, "You are most definitely nothing like any diplomat we've ever had aboard."

Sortino had time only to share a laugh at his comment before the turbolift slowed to a halt and the doors opened to reveal the bridge. The familiar sounds of activity filled the air as intercom voices relayed status reports from other areas of the ship, control panels beeped either to request their users' attention or in response to bridge officers' commands. As he and the ambassador stepped from the car, McCoy looked to the main viewscreen and the brilliant energy field displayed upon it.

"Wow," Sortino said, her attention also on the screen. "That's really something."

Nodding, McCoy replied, "You can say that again." He directed her away from the turbolift alcove. To their left, Montgomery Scott sat at the engineering station, and he nodded in greeting as he noted their arrival. Guiding Sortino to the right along the bridge's upper deck, McCoy glanced at Lieutenant Nyota Uhura as she looked up from her communications console. While Lieutenant Hikaru Sulu and Ensign Pavel Chekov manned the helm and navigation stations at the center of the room, the command chair behind them was empty. Its normal occupant, Jim Kirk, instead was leaning against the railing that separated the bridge's perimeter workstations from the command well. The captain's hands were clasped before him as he conversed quietly with his first officer, Mister Spock, who was seated at the science station. Looking up at their approach, Kirk straightened his posture and pulled down on his uniform tunic.

"Ambassador, thank you for joining us," he said, the casual manner he had displayed at the poker game two nights previously now replaced by a straightforward demeanor, or "command mode," as McCoy liked to call it. "As I told you earlier, Mister Spock has finished his review of the *Huang Zhong*'s distress buoy."

The buoy had been intercepted within moments of the *Enterprise*'s arrival in the Kondaii system less than three hours earlier. According to the preliminary information Kirk had shared with him, McCoy knew that the device had been found maintaining station outside the mysterious energy barrier surrounding the Gralafi planetoid, and was the only clue as to the current status of the *Archer*-class scout ship. Much to the doctor's relief, no debris or ship wreckage had been found.

"Does it offer any details about what happened?" Sortino asked.

His expression grim, Kirk nodded. "I'm afraid so. Spock?"

Folding his arms across his chest, the first officer said, "The data contained in the buoy's memory banks reports that the *Huang Zhong* sustained damage during its transit of the rift. Based on the sensor telemetry provided by the science officer, the energy field possesses properties similar to a passive sensor net, not unlike those used to protect sensitive ground-based installations. Further, the field reacted to the presence of the ship's warp engines, or perhaps the energy generated by the engines. The ship then encountered further difficulty after assuming orbit over the Gralafi planetoid. Information at this point in the record is somewhat incomplete, but there are indications of some sort of attack from the planet's surface."

"Attack?" McCoy repeated. "By whom? Surely not the Dolysians?"

Spock shook his head. "No, Doctor. The Dolysians do not possess the level of technology required to launch an assault on an orbiting space vessel. As to the identity of the responsible party, there is no data at present to support any preliminary conclusions."

"How about a guess, Spock?" the captain asked.

Though his face of course registered no outward emotional reaction, the Vulcan's voice seemed to lower an octave as he replied, "I would prefer to review the available information in greater detail before putting forth a hypothesis, Captain."

"Of course you would," Kirk replied, smiling. Then, he added, "But, even your initial analysis tells you it's probably not safe for us to enter the rift?"

It was Scott, having moved from his station and stepped down into the command well to stand next to Kirk, who replied, "I wouldn't think so, sir. Our warp engines would likely provoke the same kind of reaction. That'd be risky, even dangerous. I'd like to take a better look at the data for myself. I may be able to do something to reduce or eliminate the risk; alter plasma flow or modulate the warp field generators, perhaps. We could even deactivate the warp engines entirely, though that wouldn't be my first choice."

"Nor mine," Kirk said. "So, how close is too close?"

The engineer frowned. "Based on what I've been able to dig out of the sensor data so far, I'd say a hundred thousand kilometers is a nice buffer, just to be on the safe side."

"Mother hen, that's what you are." Sighing, Kirk nodded. "Okay, Scotty, look into that. See if you can find a way to let us pass through, but without doing anything to upset the field's natural stability."

"It's likely that 'natural' is an inappropriate descriptor in this case, Captain," Spock said. "The readings collected by the *Huang Zhong* sensors indicate a repeating modulation in its waveform, one precise enough that the odds of it occurring naturally are quite remote."

"Remote?" Kirk echoed.

McCoy asked, "Remote enough that the *Huang Zhong*'s science officer might've had it right all along?"

"Not now, Bones," Kirk snapped. "All right, so if it *is* artificial in origin, how is it the Dolysians haven't been able to figure that out for themselves?"

Spock replied, "The readings are such that very sensitive equipment would be required to detect the patterns, Captain. Current Dolysian technology precludes the existence of such equipment."

Before the conversation could proceed, an alert tone sounded on the bridge, and McCoy looked past Kirk to see the alarm indicator at the center of the helm-navigation console flashing bright red. Ensign Chekov turned in his seat, and McCoy saw the concern on the younger man's face.

"Captain, we're picking up the approach of a vessel. It looks to be a Dolysian transport, sir. It came out of the rift and is heading in our direction." Looking toward the main viewscreen, McCoy now was able to discern a small, dark shape highlighted by the intense illumination of the energy field. It was short and stout, resembling at least in some respects the sorts of low-warp long-haul freighters that were in common use from Earth during the previous century.

His attention also on the screen, Kirk hooked a thumb over his shoulder. "Uhura, broadcast a standard hail on all frequencies."

"Aye, Captain," answered the communications officer as she input the instructions to her console. After a moment, she reported, "We're receiving a reply to our hail. Audio and visual, sir."

"On-screen," Kirk ordered.

The image of the energy field on the main viewscreen faded, to be replaced by that of two figures—a Dolysian and a human male—standing in what to McCoy looked to be the transport craft's bridge. The Dolysian, also a male, wore what the doctor presumed was a sort of simple uniform, with a broad-shouldered dark green coat tailored to the alien's slender physique. His human companion was a dark-skinned man, sporting what McCoy noted was a nasty abrasion on one cheek and a large cut on his chin. Though he wore a simple gray tunic instead of a uniform, his hairstyle and sideburns identified him as a member of Starfleet.

As he was wont to do in such situations, Kirk spoke first. "I'm Captain James T. Kirk of the Federation *Starship Enterprise*. May we be of assistance?"

On the screen, the Dolysian replied, "*Greetings, Captain. I am Renchir Thay na Berrong of the Unified Police Force, and I bid you welcome. As it seems our names can be somewhat cumbersome for humans to pronounce, Thay will suffice. I have been sent to assist you. I have been ordered by the leadership council to escort you through the Pass and on to Gralafi, and to lend whatever support you may require due to the unpleasant circumstances which have brought you to us.*"

"Unpleasant and certainly unintentional," Kirk said. "On behalf of the United Federation of Planets, I welcome your assistance. We hope to remedy the situation as quickly as possible so as not to pose any further inconvenience."

McCoy sensed Sortino leaning toward him, and then she spoke just loud enough for him to hear, "He makes quite the first impression. Are you sure you even need me on this mission?"

"*We are eager to help in any way possible,*" Thay continued, before indicating his human companion. "*We have*

*brought with us one of your comrades, as we felt it appropri-
ate that you hear from him directly."*

Although he recognized the man's face from his review
of the *Huang Zhong* personnel files, it still took McCoy
an extra moment to recall the crew member's name. He
stepped forward so that Kirk could see him in his peripheral vision, then said in a low voice, "That's Ensign Suresh
Kari, Jim—one of the engineers."

Kirk nodded, acknowledging the doctor's report before
turning his attention back to the screen. "Ensign Kari, it's
good to see you. How are you feeling?"

"Bruised and a bit beat up, sir, but ready for duty," Kari
replied. *"I'm one of the lucky ones. Only three of us survived
the crash, and our injuries are fairly minor. The ship itself is
a total loss."*

McCoy forced himself not to offer any visible emotional
response to the report. Three survivors meant eleven casualties. Based on Kari's report, there would be no need for
his trauma team on Gralafi.

It was obvious that Kirk also was disheartened by the
report, but he drew a deep breath before asking Kari, "Captain Arens?"

The ensign shook his head. *"I'm sorry, sir. He died of his
injuries, along with Commander Hebert. Our science officer,
Lieutenant Boma, is the highest-ranking survivor."* McCoy
noted how Spock and Kirk exchanged knowing glances,
each recognizing the name.

Thay added, *"Those who survived the crash were transported to the medical facility at the Havreltipa colony on
Gralafi, Captain. None of their injuries are life-threatening,
but you likely will be better able to treat them."*

"We'll be doing that very shortly, sir," Kirk said. "Ensign

Kari, we're going to beam you aboard the *Enterprise* for a full debriefing. Thay, we have some final preparations to complete before we'll be ready for your escort through the rift. Please stand by."

The Dolysian nodded. "*Yes, of course. We shall maintain station here until you are ready.*" As the transmission ended, the image of Thay and Kari dissolved and the energy field once again was visible on the main viewscreen, serving as a wondrous backdrop for the transport ship.

Turning to face Spock once more, Kirk asked, "How much time do we have?"

Without any apparent need to consult his instruments, the first officer replied, "Three point six two standard days, Captain."

"Three days to get in and salvage as much of the ship itself as you can," Sortino said. "It'll be tight. You may end up having to destroy the wreckage, rather than leave behind anything you can't remove before our window closes."

Kirk nodded. "I know. We've already exposed the Dolysians to enough advanced technology just by being here. The last thing we need is them digging around through the *Huang Zhong* wreckage and finding something dangerous, or something they're just not ready to deal with yet." He cast a somber look in McCoy's direction. "It looks like there's not much work for you, Bones."

"At least we can help the survivors," the doctor said. "That's something, anyway."

Pausing as though to process that grim reality, Kirk closed his eyes and rubbed his temples for a moment before looking to Scott, who still stood near the railing in front of McCoy and Sortino. "Okay, Scotty; taking the *Enterprise* through the rift is off the table, and our safety cushion rules out transporters. What about our shuttlecraft? Can they be rigged to make the transit?"

The engineer replied, "Aye, we can deactivate their warp engines. From what I can tell, impulse drive doesn't seem to pose a problem with the energy field, but we can install extra shielding for added protection."

"How long?" Kirk asked.

Frowning, Scott said, "Five hours, I'd think."

The captain gestured toward the turbolift. "Make it less, if you can."

"Right away, sir." Offering nods to the captain as well as Sortino, Scott turned and made his way toward the alcove at the rear of the bridge.

Leaning against the red railing, Kirk said, "Bones, it looks like you and your team will be getting a taxi ride through the rift. Have Scotty allocate a shuttle exclusively for medical transport use. Treat your patients there only if you have to. Otherwise, bring them back to the *Enterprise*."

McCoy had already been thinking along those lines from the moment the notion was raised to make use of shuttlecraft. "You read my mind, Captain."

"Good," Kirk said. "Spock, take another shuttle and see what you can find out about the rift. If it *is* artificial, then maybe it and whatever brought down the *Huang Zhong* are related, somehow."

"Where are you going to be, Jim?" McCoy asked.

Indicating Sortino, the captain replied, "I'll be accompanying the ambassador to meet with the Dolysian leadership." He paused, tapping the railing. "We've got three days to do our jobs, people. Otherwise, whoever's on the other side of that rift when it closes will get to enjoy a rather extended vacation, courtesy of the Dolysians and who or whatever else might be on that planetoid. I want answers, and I'm sure the Dolysians do, too. "Any questions?"

"How soon do we get started?" McCoy asked, anxious to reach the *Huang Zhong* survivors and get on with helping them. His comment earned him a smile from the captain as he offered one final, curt nod.

"All right, then," Kirk said. "Let's go to work."

FIVE

Vathrael felt the sting of the *lirash* across the back of her right hand as she twisted her own weapon in a failed attempt to parry the strike. Her opponent grinned as he pulled his staff back, holding it with both hands across his body while sidestepping from left to right as he searched for another opening. Gritting her teeth to force back the pain from her hand, Vathrael turned and maneuvered to keep her adversary in front of her.

"Very nice," she said, returning the smile and nodding in approval. If the *lirash* had been the actual weapon with its bladed head and spiked base, rather than the wooden replicas used for training, she might well have lost her hand during that attack. As it was, Vathrael could see where the pale green skin across her knuckles was already beginning to darken.

"Thank you, Commander," replied Terius. Perspiration ran from the centurion's face and down the bare skin of his muscled chest, the only outward sign of exertion that the younger man displayed. Vathrael felt her own pulse racing and her breathing coming fast and shallow, the first signs of fatigue beginning to assert themselves. The sparring match had already gone on longer than she had anticipated, her poor estimate of the time needed to dispatch the centurion made worse by her gross underestimation of her weapons officer's prowess. Terius's skill with the *lirash* and his command of the *Ch'Vashrek* personal combat method was impressive, particularly for someone so young. While Vathrael was pleased to see such interest in the ancient fighting arts and old-style weapons, she had not expected to be challenged with such verve, especially not by someone under her own command.

Perhaps you grow complacent in your advancing age?

The teasing thought was not enough to distract Vathrael as Terius made his next move. Feinting right, the centurion changed direction, bringing up the lower end of his *lirash* and attempting to swing in underneath Vathrael's guard. The commander saw the move for what it was and adjusted her own stance, dropping her staff to parry the attack. The sound of polished wood smacking together echoed off the curved bulkheads of the *Nevathu's* exercise chamber, first once and then a second time as Vathrael swung her *lirash's* opposite end up and around. Terius's reaction was swift and precise, parrying the strike with his own weapon before launching a counterattack.

There it is.

Terius's enthusiasm was betraying him, and Vathrael now saw her adversary's weakness. Lunging forward, she released her right hand from her weapon's grip, using her other arm to push up and away. Terius raised his arms in defense to meet the upward swing, a maneuver which forced him to shift his stance. That one move, needed to block what was little more than a distraction, provided Vathrael the opening she needed. She struck with her right fist, landing a solid punch to Terius's unguarded left flank. The centurion grunted in surprise and pain, his *lirash* lowering as he attempted to adjust to the new attack. It was an unfortunate move that left his face exposed, and Vathrael took full advantage of the opportunity, jabbing with rigid fingers to the side of Terius's neck. Designed as a killing blow when delivered with full force, even something less than half-strength was enough to make the younger officer stagger backward before falling to one knee. The *lirash* in his hands dropped to the exercise mat, and Terius sat down, grimacing as he reached for his neck.

"Are you all right?" Vathrael asked, concerned that she may have injured her subordinate in the excitement of the moment.

The centurion nodded, coughing as he rubbed his neck. "Yes, Commander. I'm fine. You simply caught me by surprise."

Unable to resist a small chuckle, Vathrael stepped forward and extended her hand. "It was I who was surprised. You demonstrate exceptional skill, but you lost your focus. Had you not done that, you may well have bested me."

Terius took the commander's proffered hand and allowed himself to be pulled to his feet. "You honestly think so?"

"No," Vathrael replied, laughing before she turned and crossed the exercise floor to a bench where she had left a towel and a bottle containing a pale blue liquid. After first leaning her *lirash* against the bench, she retrieved the bottle and—with no small amount of reluctance—drank from it, doing her best not to grimace at the unpleasant taste while in the presence of Terius and other subordinates in the exercise area. She should not have bothered, as her effort proved futile.

"You do not like the *matnaral*?" Terius asked, offering a knowing smile.

Vathrael shrugged as she forced herself to take another long drink from the bottle. "It has its uses." *Matnaral* had been engineered to replace fluids and minerals that the body lost during prolonged exertion and perspiration. Designed as a dietary supplement for shipboard crews, it also served to reduce the demand for drinking water during protracted missions in deep space. Unlike water, it possessed a bitter tang that only grew stronger as a consequence of the ship's reclamation and recycling systems, which of course were impacted by the amount of time the *Nevathu* stayed out on patrol far from home. Vathrael knew that drinking the concoction served a purpose so far as contributing to the health of her crew while conserving the precious water supply, but one of the promises she had made to herself was that upon her retirement from the service, *matnaral* would never again touch her lips.

Reaching up to wipe her mouth, Vathrael asked, "You understand I was only joking about our sparring match? You honestly do possess formidable talent. I hope you will continue your studies."

Terius nodded. "I am honored and humbled by your words, Commander. Your reputation as a master of *Ch'Vashrek* is well known, after all."

"An artifact of my youth, Centurion," Vathrael said, retrieving her towel and using it to wipe perspiration from her face. Though hand-to-hand combat was taught at the military academies, their preferred style was an amalgam of different martial arts that had been blended and simplified for ease and efficiency of instruction on a large scale. Vathrael had acquired an interest in *Ch'Vashrek* while still a cadet, studying under the watchful eye of her maternal uncle—himself an acknowledged master of the ancient fighting art—during whatever fragments of otherwise unoccupied time she could bring to the endeavor. Upon graduating from the academy and receiving her commission as an officer, Vathrael had continued her studies, even going so far as to enter various competitions devoted to the discipline. Her uncle's ample, often grueling tutelage served her well, allowing her to win most of those contests. Though she had long ago given up such pursuits, her affection for *Ch'Vashrek* and the benefits it provided her mind and body continued unabated.

Reaching for her *lirash*, Vathrael began wiping the weapon's grips with her towel as she eyed Terius. "With your abilities, you should consider competing. I daresay you would thrive in such an environment."

"I have thought about it," the centurion replied, retrieving his own towel and proceeding to wipe his hands. "Perhaps if I had a tutor, someone with a passion for the sport and hard-won experience, to guide me, I might consider it."

Well, it certainly appears as though young Terius can add servility to his list of skills. Vathrael schooled her features so as not to reveal a betraying smile as the errant thought echoed in her mind. Despite the centurion's penchant for easy, transparent flattery—a talent seemingly developed by all officers with familial ties to influential people in the Romulan government—Vathrael was forced to admit that she found the idea of acting as a teacher to a student of *Ch'Vashrek* carried with it an appeal she could not easily dismiss. She had not even attended competitive matches since making the decision to refrain from participating, but she still retained her taste for the excitement to be found at such events. Given that she was approaching the end of her military career, the idea of dedicating time and energy to some other pursuit was something she had been considering for a while. Perhaps she could find some new fulfillment as a mentor, not only to Terius but to other young students seeking to master the revered fighting art. It was a notion, Vathrael decided, that would require further reflection.

Her attention was drawn to the sound of the exercise chamber's door sliding open, followed by a set of fast-moving footsteps echoing across the deck plating. Vathrael looked up to see Subcommander Sirad, her executive officer, enter the room while carrying a computer data tablet. As always, Sirad presented the epitome of a well-groomed Romulan officer. He did not walk so much as marched, his every movement a testament to military precision. His uniform was tailored to an exacting degree around his trim physique, to the point that Vathrael often wondered if the subcommander had himself sewn into the garments each day. His hair was cut in a short style that left the sides of his head exposed, trimmed to what Vathrael was certain was mathematical exactitude. The boots he wore were polished to a shine so bright that other officers joked about being able to see their reflections in them, though such observations were of course never made in Sirad's presence.

"Commander," he said, coming to a stop before Vathrael. His body was ramrod straight as he nodded in greeting. "I apologize for disturbing you, but we have received a priority message from Fleet Command." He paused, and Vathrael knew that his hesitation was due to the presence of Terius standing nearby, although the centurion had remained silent since Sirad's arrival. Whatever message her executive officer had brought her, the paranoid bureaucrats who populated the halls of power at Fleet Command likely considered it to be of a sensitive nature regardless of its actual content. It was Vathrael's experience that such administrative drones preferred to compartmentalize and classify any and all information as being worthy of secrecy, doubtless in a bid to maintain their illusion of relevance to those higher in the chain of command. Such thinking had been entrenched within Romulan government and military affairs since long before Vathrael had first donned a uniform, and she was certain it would continue long after she bid farewell to the service. She had come to realize that fighting such institutional inertia was a waste of time and energy better spent on other pursuits.

Regardless of her personal feelings, the regulations pertaining to such matters were explicit, and Vathrael knew that Sirad would observe them until the protocols were changed or the universe succumbed to entropy, whichever of those events should first come to pass.

"Centurion," Vathrael said, glancing to her subordinate, "if you will excuse us."

Terius offered a crisp nod. "Of course, Commander. Thank you again for the contest. Perhaps a rematch at some appropriate time?"

"Perhaps," the commander replied. After the weapons officer had taken his leave, Vathrael once again regarded her second-in-command. "All right, Sirad. What bidding do you bring us from our masters at Fleet Command?"

After first checking to verify they were not being overheard, Sirad said in a low voice, "We have been ordered to leave our patrol vector for a new assignment. The Federation has taken an interest in a star system which lies in an area outside their territory but in proximity to Romulan space. Fleet Command suspects that Starfleet may be considering establishing a presence there."

Frowning, Vathrael nodded. "And our superiors believe this represents a grave danger to the security of the empire?"

"That would seem to be a possibility, Commander," Sirad replied. "Would you not agree?"

"Things are not always as they might first appear," Vathrael said before drinking once more from her bottle of *matnaral*. "What would seem to be a foregone conclusion reached within a comfortable office on Romulus is often at odds with what faces the commander and crew of a vessel operating under orders dispatched from that office." Encounters with Starfleet vessels had been sporadic in the more than three *fvheisn* that had elapsed since Romulan ships had begun probing Federation territory for the first time since the war with Earth. Vathrael and the *Nevathu* had themselves been party to one such meeting, which had begun from misunderstanding and ended without violence. Such had not been the case during other incidents, and it was the opinion of many within the higher echelons of Romulan government and military power that another war with the humans and their allies might soon come to pass. For her part, Vathrael did not believe hostilities to be quite so imminent, regardless of whatever statements might be issued by Fleet Command. "What do we know of this system?"

"Very little, as it turns out," Sirad replied, holding up his data tablet so that he could read it. "Its entry in our stellar cartography database does not even give it a name, but according to what we have learned from Starfleet reports, it is listed in Federation computer files as the Kondaii system. It contains eight planets, only one of which supports any sort of intelligent life. The message from Fleet Command includes information on a spatial anomaly within the system—some form of interspatial rift that conceals a small planet. The rift is not believed to be a naturally occurring phenomenon."

Sighing, Vathrael could not help smiling as she shook her head. "Sirad, I know you were once a science officer before transferring to the command hierarchy, but kindly take pity on someone who has always been little more than a soldier, and translate that into some language she might comprehend? Am I correct in assuming what you meant to say was that this mysterious incongruity is artificially generated?"

"That is Fleet Command's contention," Sirad replied, "based on information obtained from the interception of subspace communications sent from the Starfleet vessel tasked with observing the anomaly."

This gave Vathrael pause. "A Starfleet vessel is already on station? Well, that will certainly make things more interesting. I assume that we also received instructions regarding stealth?"

Lowering his data tablet, Sirad nodded. "Yes, Commander. We are to avoid confrontation, and gather as much information as possible about the anomaly and whatever technology is responsible for creating and maintaining it."

Vathrael grunted in irritation as she moved to a laundry bin to deposit her perspiration-dampened towel. "There was a time when the mere mention of our empire's name and the presence of but one of its warships instilled fear within any would-be adversary. Now? We slink about like rodents foraging for food in the dark, hoping to latch onto some scrap left behind by those whom we should have beaten into submission in the first place." Noting the wary expression on her executive officer's face, she smiled. "What's wrong, Sirad? Surprised to hear me saying such things?"

"I will admit that it does seem somewhat out of character, Commander," Sirad replied. "Though your record of service is unmatched by all but a few senior officers, your views on the appropriate uses of military action are well-known. Some have even dared to label you a pacifist."

"So I've heard," Vathrael said. "Such people are ill-informed, at the very least, and you should know that even though you've only been aboard a few short *khaidoa*." While she had never shirked from her duties as an officer in the Romulan military, she did not share the enthusiasm expressed by many of her contemporaries when it came to armed confrontations with the empire's interstellar rivals. She had no reservations about defending against the actions of an enemy, and at a younger age she even was comfortable with playing the role of the aggressor if it served the empire's needs. Growing older had given her a clarity of thought she had lacked in her youth, and while she still believed in her solemn duty to protect the Romulan people, she had come to understand that the Federation was not a threat to the empire, nor had it ever been. Despite the propaganda being disseminated by her government, Vathrael knew that conquest was not the way of the Earthers and their allies. This, even though most of the planets that now comprised the Federation all had some past history of violent conflict, within their own civilizations as well as with other spacefaring races. Given the opportunity, the Federation would happily seek peace with the Romulans or any other rival. Though Vathrael was a creature of duty, born and bred for the uniform she now wore as well as all the responsibilities that came with it, she respected and even envied the prospect of a life and a culture that did not revolve around the tenets of war.

Perhaps one day, she mused, *though certainly not today*.

Sensing Sirad's gaze on her as he waited for instructions, Vathrael forced away her momentary reverie and returned her attention to the matters at hand. "Well, then, I think we've indulged ourselves long enough. Set a course for the Kondaii system and engage the cloaking device. Let us go and see for ourselves what has so intrigued our Federation friends."

She could only hope that they might do so without starting another war.

SIX

Standing at the edge of the tarmac that was but one of the eight landing fields servicing the Havreltipa mining colony on Gralafi, Samuel Boma could not help feeling small and even insignificant as he regarded the massive ore transport before him. It was one of three that had occupied the field at the start of the day. Two had since departed, bound for Dolysia with their cargo holds filled to capacity with tons of the valuable erinadium mineral. Other freighters would soon take their place as well as that of the ship now sitting before him, as part of the continuous cycle of transferring personnel, supplies, and ore to and from the Dolysian homeworld.

"Wow," he said. "Couldn't you find anything bigger?"

Standing next to him, Drinja Shin te Elsqa, the colony's administrator and his newfound friend, affected an expression that Boma recognized as one of confusion. "I am sorry, Samuel," she said, "but I am afraid I do not understand your comment."

Boma grunted as he adjusted the makeshift sling he wore over his left shoulder, feeling a short stab of pain in his right arm as it rested in the sling's cradle. "I was noting the size of your freighter. It's quite something, Shin." Like most of the structures comprising the main Havreltipa settlement, the freighter was a functional, aesthetically uninviting vessel, positioned so that it spanned the width of the landing pad. It was supported by eight struts, which elevated its enormous bulk several meters off the ground. Each of the supports terminated in a wide, multi-jointed foot, which Boma figured was designed to afford the ability to land atop different types of terrain.

"I see," Shin said. "Your statement was meant to be . . . ironic?" She shook her head. "I must apologize; even with the wonderful technology you command, the many nuances of your language are proving difficult."

"Don't worry about it," Boma said, reaching out with his undamaged arm and resting his hand on the Dolysian's shoulder. "I've been speaking it my entire life, and I still make my share of mistakes. Besides, you've been thrown into the deep end with all of this. It's not wrong to be a bit overwhelmed by it all."

Again, Shin frowned. "Into the deep end?"

Boma shook his head, releasing a small laugh. "Sorry, Shin. It's a human expression. Basically, it means that you've been confronted with a task or situation for which you've had no preparation, and yet you still have to find a way to be successful. Dealing with aliens from another planet? I'd call that the deep end, all right."

As though giving further consideration to the turn of phrase, Shin finally nodded. "Yes, I suppose that is an apt description."

Despite the physical and emotional toll the past two days had taken on him, her solemn delivery evoked a broad smile from Boma. "If it's any consolation, I feel the exact same way." As the senior of the three members of the *Huang Zhong*'s crew to survive the ship's crash landing on Gralafi, it had fallen to him to interface with the

Dolysian miners who had come to their rescue. Almost none of them had ever before encountered anyone from the Federation, owing to the isolation forced on them by the barrier surrounding the planetoid. Though the colonists had been getting a crash course in the latest current events during the weeks since the Pass had been open and convoy operations had been under way, that was no substitute for actual interaction with these visitors to their homeworld. In contrast, the people on Dolysia had been living and working with Federation representatives since the establishment of formal relations more than a year earlier. A scant few of them were among the new personnel transferring in to the mining colony during the period when the rift was open. Fewer still were among the group of colonists assigned to the rescue detail who had made their way to the wreckage of the *Huang Zhong* once word of the ship's troubles was communicated from the homeworld to Administrator Shin at the offices of the Jtelivran Mining Conglomerate here in Havreltipa.

Shin had wasted no time mobilizing colony resources in response to the emergency call, leading the team that had journeyed to the crash site. As the team leader, she had become the unofficial spokesperson for one of the more atypical first-contact scenarios on Federation record, with Boma himself holding up the other side of that meeting. Luck, fate, or perhaps something else, had seen to it that he, along with Ensign Suresh Kari and Master Chief Petty Officer Christine Rideout, lived through the *Huang Zhong*'s horrific crash. Some of the crew had died on impact or in the immediate aftermath, while others succumbed to their injuries during the ensuing hours. Though Commander Hebert and most of the bridge crew had perished in the crash, Captain Arens and the ship's Dolysian advisor, Rzaelir Zihl du Molidin, had survived, at least for a while. Zihl had passed away first, and Boma had held his captain's hand when he died, promising to tell his wife that he loved her even as the life faded from his longtime friend's eyes.

Good-bye, Ron.

With no way to know why he had been spared, sustaining injuries no more serious than a broken right arm, it had fallen to Boma to greet Shin and the contingent of Dolysian miners who formed their rescue party. Once the initial anxiety on everyone's part had passed, the medical personnel Shin had brought with her team wasted no time treating the three Starfleet officers. Though none of the injuries were life-threatening, there still was sufficient timidity on the Dolysian doctors' part, resulting in a very careful, moderate course of treatment. Tranketh Nole su Dronnu, the mining colony's senior physician and the one in charge of the rescue party's medical effort, had even taken the time to inquire about proper handling of the *Huang Zhong*'s dead. She had tasked her people with caring for the remains, sparing Boma the additional grief of having to place the bodies of his friends and shipmates into body bags. The eleven casualties had been ferried back to Havreltipa and stored in the medical facility until such time as they could be transported to the *Enterprise* for their final journey home.

As for Boma and his surviving companions, they too had been brought to the colony's small hospital, where physicians had continued to oversee the "alien" charges in their midst. Because Federation first-contact teams had been operating on Dolysia for more than a year, language had not presented a barrier during any of Boma's interactions with their hosts. Boma considered that nothing less than a blessing, considering that even if he had not been impaired by injury, the odds of finding a universal translator in the wreckage of the *Huang Zhong* were probably worse than finding a snowman on Vulcan.

"We have already learned so much from one another," Shin said, "and in such a short time. Perhaps there will be time for us to continue our dialogue once my replacement arrives and I return to Dolysia."

Boma replied, "Maybe, though I expect I'll be heading back to one of our starbases in pretty short order." As he spoke, something in the back of his brain clicked, and he realized that Shin's statement might have carried an additional meaning. Was she suggesting they meet in a more . . . social situation?

You're out of practice, Sam. You're missing the signals.

Shaking his head at the teasing thought, Boma looked up to regard the late morning sky, which carried something of a lavender tint, the coloring an effect of sunlight from the Kondaii star refracting through the energy field surrounding Gralafi. The light effect played off the clusters of two- and three-story structures—most of which were fabricated from unpainted metal plating and support struts—that characterized the rather sparse, utilitarian-looking Havreltipa town center. The effect seemed to reinforce the sensation Boma felt: that he was not standing on an actual planet, but rather an artificial habitat such as those found on larger starbases and ground-based stations constructed on moons or asteroids that did not possess atmospheres.

Before Boma could think of anything to say to Shin

that would—he hoped—not increase the sudden feeling of awkwardness now gripping him, the sound of approaching footsteps made him turn to see Tranketh Nole su Dronnu walking toward them. Behind him, keeping what Boma guessed to be what someone had decided was a discrete distance, were a group of Dolysians. From the looks of things, the small crowd—miners dressed in their protective clothing, as well as civilians, had followed Nole here. Looking past them, Boma saw perhaps two dozen more colonists on the narrow service road curving away from the landing tarmac and leading back toward town. If the doctor was aware of his entourage, he offered no response to it as he stepped closer to Boma.

"Samuel," Nole said, offering a smile. "We have just received word from our traffic control center. Your people will be arriving within moments. Your ordeal is nearing an end."

Nodding, Boma said, "I can't thank you enough for everything you and your people have done for us." The most difficult aspect of the past two days had been his dwelling on the loss of Captain Arens and so many other good people. Cramped conditions aboard the *Huang Zhong* and the enforced proximity they engendered had made the men and women serving aboard the ship as much a family as they had been a crew. The assignment had been unlike any other during his career, and Boma doubted it was an experience that would be duplicated. Losing them in such an abrupt, violent manner was something with which he knew he would have to come to terms, but for the moment he was coping well enough, and much of the credit for that was owed to Tranketh Nole su Dronnu, his team of assistants, and other members of the mining colony who had taken it upon themselves to make him, Kari, and Rideout welcome.

"We have been happy to do so," Nole replied. "From what we have been told, our two peoples have been working together in harmony for some time, even if meeting you and your companions was something of a shock to us." Glancing to Shin, he added, "I for one cannot wait to return to Dolysia and learn more about our new Federation friends."

Boma smiled at that. "I know I'm biased, but I think you're in for a treat." He saw the look of confusion on Nole's face, and realized he once more had fallen into the trap of using idioms, something with which universal translation software often had trouble. "What I meant was that I think you'll find a great deal to like about us. At least, I hope you do."

"I have no doubts that I will," Nole said. Then, she looked past him and up into the sky before pointing in that direction. Turning, he peered upward and noted the two small objects descending through the clouds toward them. Their slate-gray hulls appeared violet in the light of the Gralafi day, the sun's rays playing off the crafts' smooth lines as one followed the other toward the surface.

"A very simple, yet elegant design," Shin observed, watching with rapt fascination as the shuttlecraft slowed their rate of descent, banking as their pilots directed the vessels toward their assigned landing coordinates. "And such maneuverability."

Boma sighed. "They have their good and bad points," he said, his thoughts turning to another Starfleet shuttlecraft— one in which he had almost died. It was easy to recall the unpleasant memories of that day, particularly when considering the ship that had been dispatched to assist the *Huang Zhong*.

This should be fun.

The thought, tainted with no small amount of bitterness, occupied him as he watched the two shuttlecraft settle to the landing field, both ships having pivoted so that their main access hatches faced their audience. Boma read the familiar markings that indicated the craft belonged to the *Enterprise*, along with its own designation: *Columbus*. Its companion shuttle was emblazoned with the name *Einstein II*, and Boma could not help but wonder what fate might have befallen the previous shuttlecraft bearing the moniker, and whether this indicated a tradition aboard the *Enterprise*.

They must go through a lot of shuttles. There's probably a Galileo II *up there, too. I guess I should be glad they didn't send that one to fetch us.*

As the shuttles' engines powered down, he heard the familiar whine of escaping air heralding the release of pressurized seals as the access hatches opened on both craft. A Triexian officer stepped down from the *Einstein*'s hatch, dressed in a gold uniform shirt and what looked to be black shorts, tailored to fit his physique and accommodate his three arms and legs. However, it was the occupants of the *Columbus* that caught Boma's attention. Despite his best efforts and his own promise to himself not to overreact in this situation, he could not help the feeling of apprehension that came over him as he caught sight of the first figure emerging from the shuttlecraft: Spock.

"Here we go," he said, not realizing until he heard the words that he had spoken them aloud. Boma had not seen the Vulcan since before his own ignominious departure

from the *Enterprise* more than two years earlier, and seeing him now only served to bring forth all of the feelings
he had strived so hard to suppress. He drew a deep breath,
commanding himself to be at ease. Whatever past history
existed between him and Spock, Boma knew he had a duty
to carry out, here and now. The crew of the *Huang Zhong*
deserved nothing less.

As Spock stepped down to the tarmac, he was followed by a man wearing a red uniform tunic, whom
Boma quickly recognized as Ross Johnson, a friendly and
very capable officer. The third person to disembark from
the shuttle made Boma smile. He had always welcomed
and enjoyed the company of Leonard McCoy, something
that did not change in the aftermath of their ill-fated mission together to Taurus II, and he was pleased to see that
McCoy remained in place as the *Enterprise*'s chief medical
officer.

I wonder if he's still giving Spock grief at every turn.

Deciding that playing it by the book was the best
option at the present time, Boma stepped forward until
he stood before Spock, assuming a military stance as he
offered a formal nod. "Commander Spock: Lieutenant
Boma, acting commanding officer of the *Huang Zhong*.
Welcome to Gralafi. I only wish it were under different
circumstances."

To his surprise, Spock replied, "Greetings, Lieutenant.
While I appreciate the observance of protocol, it is not
necessary, given the circumstances." He paused as though
considering his next words, before adding, "I offer my con-
dolences on the loss of your captain and crewmates."

Unsure as to how to proceed, Boma nodded. "Thank
you, sir." Turning, he indicated Shin with the hand of his

uninjured arm. "I'd like to introduce you to Drinja Shin te Elsqa, administrator of the Havreltipa colony as well as the mining corporation's operations here on Gralafi, and Tranketh Nole su Dronnu, the colony's head physician." To the Dolysians, he said, "May I present Commander Spock, first officer and science officer of the *U.S.S. Enterprise*."

"It is an honor to meet you, Commander," Shin said, reaching as though to touch Spock before halting her motion, her expression turning to one of uncertainty. "Forgive me. Samuel briefed us on Vulcan greeting customs; I simply forgot in the excitement of the moment."

Spock shook his head. "You need not apologize, madam. No offense was intended, or taken. It is our privilege to meet you, as well. Captain James Kirk asked me to convey his own greetings, and that he anticipates meeting you himself at the earliest opportunity."

"We look forward to that, as well," Nole replied.

As though deciding to dispense with the formalities, and much to Boma's amusement, McCoy stepped forward, extending his left hand to Boma in deference to the lieutenant's injured right arm. "It's good to see you, Sam. How are you feeling?"

Boma took the doctor's proffered hand before reaching across to tap the sling supporting his right arm. "This busted wing is my biggest complaint. Nole here was able to set it, but it hasn't yet been determined what effects Dolysian pain medications might have on humans, and we haven't been able to salvage any medical equipment or drugs from the *Huang Zhong*. So, we opted not to chance it." He grimaced as he recalled the discomfort he had lived with these past two days.

McCoy wasted no time reaching for the medical kit on his hip. He extracted a hypospray and selected a small vial, which he attached to the injector mechanism. Moving to Boma, he placed the hypospray against his patient's left arm and activated it. The hiss of the device and the tingle of the application was a welcome feeling, but it was nothing compared to the immediate fading of the pain in his right arm. For the first time in more than fifty hours, Boma did not feel like hacking off his own limb.

"Thanks, Doctor. You have no idea how good that feels."

"I can guess," McCoy said as he returned the hypospray to his kit. "I can take care of the arm itself, too. I've got a bone-knitter aboard the shuttle. We'll have you fixed up in no time."

"That's the best news I've heard in two days," Boma said. "Chief Rideout has some torn ligaments and a couple of really bad cuts. Nole was able to treat those, too, but she'll probably be happy to see you."

"Doctor," McCoy said, looking to Nole, "I can't thank you enough for looking after our people. If you can show me to somewhere I can work, I'd appreciate it."

The Dolysian physician nodded. "Of course. If you will follow me, I will direct you to our infirmary. Perhaps I can observe as you treat your patients. I have heard that Federation medical knowledge and technology is far more advanced than ours."

After glancing to Spock, who nodded for him to proceed, McCoy looked to Johnson. "Lieutenant, would you mind helping me grab the bone-knitter and some other equipment from the shuttle?"

"Not a problem, sir," the security officer said, after

which McCoy invited Nole to join them as they began walking toward the *Columbus*. Boma watched the two physicians engage in conversation as they departed. Just having McCoy here seemed to make him feel better, he decided. The doctor's bedside manner and overall approach when it came to the patients in his care was but one of the many qualities Boma had always admired, and he was one of several people Boma had missed since leaving the *Enterprise*. In truth, he even missed Spock, he realized, as he turned back to face the Vulcan and the Triexian lieutenant, who introduced himself as Arex.

"Do you have a report of what happened, Mister Boma?" Spock asked, his voice as flat and devoid of emotion as his expression. Unable to read whatever thoughts might be lurking behind the impenetrable Vulcan façade, Boma felt the initial pangs of familiar resentment. It had been two years since the mission to explore the Murasaki 312 quasar, in which Spock had commanded a team of specialists from the *Enterprise*—including Boma—aboard the shuttlecraft *Galileo*. As he met Spock's steady, unwavering gaze, the memories of that mission came flooding back to the forefront of his consciousness.

Latimer and Gaetano, murdered by those creatures. The rest of us scared for our lives, and with every setback and every death, he just kept looking at me—at all of us—the exact same way. All we wanted was some reassurance, some compassion or understanding from our commanding officer, anything that might have told us we were going to be all right and make it out of that hell. But no, that wouldn't have been logical. *Instead, all we got was that same damned blank stare, you bastard.*

The thoughts came unbidden, and he pushed them

back. Now was not the time for rehashing the past. Cradling his sling and his wounded arm a bit closer to his chest, Boma cleared his throat, struggling to keep an edge from his voice. "I don't have a formal report, sir. Between caring for Kari and Rideout and being the Federation liaison for the colony, I haven't had the time to prepare one, let alone the equipment. I'm happy to tell you what I know for now."

"That will have to suffice," Spock said. "What can you report about the circumstances which led to the *Huang Zhong*'s crash?"

Frowning, Boma replied, "We were pretty beat up after passing through the rift. After we assumed orbit above Gralafi, we started a sensor scan of the planetoid, looking for something to support our theory that the energy field was artificially generated. I think we made somebody or something mad, because we were hit by some kind of tractor beam." He paused, recalling the *Huang Zhong*'s final moments. "It dragged us down from orbit. We managed to disable it with photon torpedoes, but by then it was too late."

Spock nodded at the report as Arex asked, "Do you have the coordinates for the source of the tractor beam, Lieutenant?"

"I don't," Boma answered, "but you can probably still scan for residual energy from the torpedoes. That should lead us right to it."

"Then that is where we shall begin," Spock said.

Still standing next to him, Shin asked, "Is there something we can do to be of assistance, Commander?"

"I do not believe that will be necessary," the Vulcan replied. "We will be able to use the sensors aboard the

Columbus. However, your continued help at the *Huang Zhong* crash site would be appreciated."

The Dolysian leader nodded. "We are at your service."

Boma said, "Be careful when you fire up your sensors, Mister Spock. There's no telling what kind of response you might get."

"A practical observation, Mister Boma." To Arex, he said, "Lieutenant, it seems we will have no further need for your shuttlecraft. Once Doctor McCoy has determined the extent of Master Chief Petty Officer Rideout's continued medical treatment, you will return with the *Einstein* to the *Enterprise* and notify Mister Scott that salvage operations for the *Huang Zhong* can commence immediately." Then, he turned back to Boma. "Lieutenant, are you available to accompany us?"

Caught off guard by the request, Boma almost tripped over his own mouth in his attempt to answer. He had assumed Spock would prefer to leave him behind for eventual transfer back to the *Enterprise*. Sensing an opportunity, he replied, "Absolutely, sir." He then held up his injured arm. "That is, if you think a one-armed science officer is any good to you."

His expression never once wavering, Spock said, "In the event Doctor McCoy is unable to treat your injury, I am certain that Mister Arex is prepared to compensate, at least until he departs for his return to the *Enterprise*." Saying nothing else, he nodded to Shin. "If you will excuse me, madam, there are some necessary preparations to accomplish prior to our departure."

Boma remained silent as the Vulcan and Arex left, still processing what he had just heard. "Was that supposed to be a joke? From Spock?"

"The nuances of your language continue to elude me, Samuel," Shin said. "Is the commander a frequent employer of humor?"

"Not usually, no," Boma said, sighing as he watched Spock's retreating figure. "Something tells me this is going to be one very odd couple of days."

SEVEN

"I'll say this for the Dolysians," remarked Ambassador Dana Sortino, her voice echoing across the vast chamber despite its lowered volume. "They've got style."

Kirk could only nod in agreement as he beheld the spacious, circular room that served as the rotunda for the headquarters of the Unified Leadership Council. The gallery, though simple in construction, harbored what to Kirk's eyes appeared to be a loving balance between form and function. The walls were constructed of stones cut in rectangular shapes of approximately two meters in length and height, their surfaces encrusted with all manner of minerals and other artifacts that played off the natural illumination provided by the chamber's transparent, domed ceiling. As for the stones themselves, they were fitted together in a staggered pattern, and so closely that the seams offered no apparent gaps of even the smallest width. The patterns and reflections from their individual faces resulted in a wondrous display of color in response to the cascade of late morning sunlight. The effect was broken only by the eight entryways spaced at regular intervals around the room, some leading to passageways while others accessed stairwells constructed from the same stones. To Kirk, the chamber resembled a cathedral, though there were no outward displays of anything that might denote a deity or other religious beliefs. Tapestries and other artwork adorned the walls, while sculptures of varying size and shape occupied niches carved into the walls or stood on pedestals around the room. As for the floor, it was created from a network of stones cut and fitted together in what looked to Kirk like a random placement, with each piece fitted into a light gray mortar that resembled an intricate spider's web stretching across the expansive floor.

"When I was a boy," Kirk said, regarding the floor's stonework with an appreciative eye, "my uncle and my brother and I built a walking path that looked something like this. It took us most of the summer to lay it out so that it connected his house to the barn. I can't imagine how long it took to put this together."

Sortino replied, "About the same amount of time, though they had more people pitching in than you and your uncle probably did."

Chuckling, Kirk nodded. "Definitely." He smiled as he recalled the effort they had expended on the project during one summer vacation he had spent at his aunt and uncle's farm in Idaho. Then there were the countless times he and his brother, Sam, had sprinted the length of that path, pretending it was the corridor of a mighty starship as they raced to head off the latest in an unending series of crises to spring from their fertile imaginations. Though Kirk could appreciate the craftsmanship required to create something so beautiful and durable, he lacked the necessary skill and passion to do something like it on his own. In contrast, his late brother had acquired their father's natural gift for working and building with his own hands, as evidenced by the homes he had built for his family, from the ground up, on two different worlds, Earth and Deneva.

You would've loved this, Sam. I miss you, big brother.

Someone walking toward him from his left made Kirk turn in that direction to see Lieutenant Uhura approaching, her expression one of frank admiration. "If you think the art they have in here is nice, you should see what's in the anteroom leading to their council chamber," she said as she drew closer, holding up her tricorder for emphasis. "It's some of the most beautiful work I've ever seen."

"The Dolysians have always held the arts in high esteem," Sortino said, "but even more so in the past few generations. According to the first-contact reports I read, they're enjoying something of a cultural renaissance that was already going strong, but seems to have gotten a boost in just the last year or so."

Kirk said, "I suppose they have us to thank for that."

"Yes, of course you're right, Captain," Sortino replied. "First contact with us definitely seems to have spurred on the Dolysians, and by all accounts that looks to be a positive development, despite the unusual nature by which the contact came about." She paused, releasing a small sigh. "I just hope we're not doing these people a disservice in the long run. Other cultures we've encountered that are on par with the Dolysians haven't always reacted well to being 'befriended' by an advanced civilization."

Kirk nodded, having seen in his extensive travels the sometimes disastrous results of good intentions when it came to contact with lesser-developed societies. "That's why the Federation sends people like you, Ambassador," he said, offering an encouraging smile. "To make sure that doesn't happen."

Anything Sortino might have said in reply was interrupted by the sound of footsteps echoing from one of the passageways leading into the chamber, and Kirk looked over to see a Dolysian male entering the rotunda. Like other males he had seen since their arrival, this one had no hair atop his smooth, pale-yellow skull, and his fair skin contrasted with the dark robes that concealed his body from neck to feet. The garment lacked ornamentation, with the single exception of a silver sash worn over his left shoulder, crossing his chest and falling to a point below his right hip. With his hands held together before him, he walked with a purposeful stride, covering the expanse of the chamber and reaching Kirk and his party in a handful of seconds.

"Ambassador Sortino," he said, and Kirk got the impression that the Dolysian had only just learned the name's proper pronunciation moments earlier, "my name is Phirol Jlen lu Brak, Chancellor Wiladra's assistant, though it likely will be easier for you to refer to me as Jlen. The chancellor has asked me to convey her apologies for keeping you waiting. The council's morning session took longer than expected to conclude."

Sortino offered a small bow of her head. "No apologies are needed, Jlen," she said, utilizing the custom—at least in the region of the planet from which the Dolysian hailed—of employing a shortened version of the formal given name. After introducing Kirk and Uhura, she added, "We are grateful that the chancellor is able to meet with us. I have no doubts that she and the rest of the council are very busy."

"The council only meets once each season," Jlen replied, "and it seems that the planners schedule every available waking moment. However, everyone is excited to meet with you." He gestured toward the door through which he had entered the rotunda. "If you will follow me,

I will take you to the chancellor's study. She has asked to meet with you in private before you are introduced to the rest of the council."

Kirk asked, "Does the chancellor have some concerns about our presence here?"

"I would not call them concerns," the Dolysian answered, then smiled. "Though she does have some questions, and she is simply exercising one of the few perquisites of her office."

Smiling, Kirk said, "Well, we can't blame a lady for that, now, can we?"

With Jlen leading the way, Kirk and Uhura followed Sortino from the chamber. The corridor leading out of the rotunda appeared to follow the same design aesthetic, though in this case natural light was provided by a series of narrow windows running along both sides of the passageway near the ceiling. For the first time, Kirk noted the presence of recessed light fixtures, though none of them were active at this hour.

"I'm amazed that so much light makes its way in here," Kirk said, recalling what he had seen of the council building's exterior while walking to it from the landing area where they had left their shuttlecraft. "I would think the angles of the building itself would mitigate it."

Slowing his pace, Jlen turned so that he could talk to Kirk as they walked. "A series of reflectors mounted at key points along the outside surfaces assist in redirecting the sunlight. It's a simple yet very efficient design, resulting in reduced energy usage throughout the council building." He indicated the light patterns reflecting off the faces of various stones they passed. "I must also confess that I love the effect."

"Absolutely," Uhura replied. "It's beautiful." When Kirk cast an amused look in her direction, she shrugged. "Well, it beats the light show where I normally work."

They approached a pair of large doors, each of them appearing to be cut from a single piece of wood that had been embellished with an intricate carving of what Kirk recognized from the shapes of land masses as an artistic rendering of Dolysia itself, centered inside a pair of intertwined ribbons. Like everything else he had seen since entering the mammoth council building, the doors looked to have been created and maintained with utmost care. When Jlen was within a few paces of the doors, they began to part, though Kirk detected no audible signs of an automated mechanism. Beyond the portal was a smaller passageway that lacked the luxurious appointments of the rotunda and the connecting corridor. Furnishings were tasteful without being lavish, and the captain got the impression that this was an outer office or visitor reception area. It was not, he decided, where impressions were made; it was where real work was accomplished.

"The chancellor's study is this way," Jlen said, crossing the anteroom toward another door, which did not open at his approach. Instead, the Dolysian stopped before the entrance, and Kirk looked up to see a sensor mounted above the door. A moment later there was an audible tone and the door slid aside to reveal another office. Jlen marched into the room and Ambassador Sortino followed him. Upon stepping through the doorway, Kirk gestured toward Uhura to stand with him near the entry, their vantage point offering them an unobstructed view of the office. A single, large span of curved glass or some other transparent material formed the room's rear wall, providing a spectacular view of a courtyard lawn and garden. Positioned before the window was a large desk consisting of a metal framework supporting a slab of dark, polished stone similar to granite or marble. Standing behind the desk was an older Dolysian female.

"Good morning, Chancellor," Jlen said by way of greeting. "You asked me to bring our guests as soon as possible." He indicated Sortino with a gesture. "Ambassador Dana Sortino of the United Federation of Planets, may I present Chancellor Wiladra Pejh en Kail, First Voice of the Unified Leadership Council."

Her hands at her sides, Sortino bowed slightly at the waist. "Chancellor Wiladra, it is an honor and a pleasure to meet with you on this day."

"The pleasure is mine, Ambassador," Wiladra replied as she moved from her seat. Her shoulders were stooped, and her face was a darker shade of yellow than Jlen's. When she placed her right hand on the edge of her desk to support herself as she moved, Kirk noted its minor trembling. Though obviously aged, she did not walk with the assistance of a cane or other support, and there was still a recognizable spark of intelligence and passion in her stark white eyes as she smiled in response to her visitors' arrival. "I have been looking forward to this for quite some time." After taking Sortino's left hand in both of her own and holding it for a moment, she turned her attention to Kirk and his party. "You are the leader of the space vessel?"

"Captain James Kirk, Chancellor," Kirk replied, "commanding the *Starship Enterprise*." He indicated Uhura. "My communications officer, Lieutenant Nyota Uhura. On behalf of Starfleet, I want to express our gratitude for the assistance you've provided to the survivors of the *Huang*

Zhong. Your people's timely intervention saved at least one life."

Wiladra straightened her posture a bit upon hearing his words. "That is very kind of you to say, Captain. Though my interactions with your Federation contact teams have been limited, they have given me a great deal of respect for your people. I am pleased we were able to help your ship and its crew. I myself have not yet had the chance to meet any of that vessel's crew. In fact, you are the first representatives from Starfleet I have met since your other ship returned our vessel to us." When she smiled, Kirk could not help but feel the enthusiasm she radiated. "On that occasion, the *Resolute*'s captain was kind enough to give me a tour of his ship. I hope that time and circumstances allow you to indulge me in a similar favor?"

"That would be *my* honor, Chancellor," Kirk replied.

Nodding in apparent satisfaction, Wiladra said, "Before I can indulge in such pleasant distractions, we must first address matters of much greater importance. I understand that we have much to discuss, and it is a conversation I have been anticipating. While situations like this are probably commonplace for you, I am sure you understand how very unusual it all still is for us."

"Think nothing of it, Chancellor," Sortino said. "To be honest, I myself have not participated in very many conversations like this one, but I can tell you that no two meetings have ever been the same. Each of the cultures we meet has its own unique curiosities and concerns, and answering those questions is always a very rewarding experience for me. I can only hope it will be the same with you and your people."

The chancellor nodded. "That is my fervent wish, as

well." Looking once more to Kirk, she asked, "And what of you, Captain? How many worlds have you visited? How many new societies have you encountered?"

Feeling somewhat self-conscious, Kirk cleared his throat. "I've seen my share, Chancellor. Unlike Ambassador Sortino, my primary mission is to travel to such worlds and meet with their representatives in order to learn about their cultures, and to bring that knowledge back to my people. I'd like to echo the ambassador's comments, in that each encounter is unique and has its own rewards." He could not resist adding, "And a few have brought their own distinctive challenges, as well."

Wiladra seemed to sense the underlying humor behind his remarks. "Perhaps there will be time for you to regale me with some of those tales."

"It would be my pleasure, Chancellor," Kirk replied.

Sighing, Wiladra shook her head. "Despite our best efforts to crowd our schedules with such frivolous pursuits, I imagine a great deal of our time will be spent on far more important matters. I have to say, Ambassador, that the citizenry has been quite vocal with respect to entering an alliance with beings from other worlds. As you doubtless know, the initial reactions upon learning that there really was intelligent life beyond our world were quite varied. Though many were and remain excited by the idea, some expressed fear." She smiled again. "I do not know why anyone would be so surprised by such a revelation; it seems logical that we would not be the only inhabited planet in the universe. And while many people seem genuinely interested and even enthusiastic about furthering relations with your Federation, there are those who believe you are here to exploit us in some manner."

"It's a natural reaction, Chancellor," Sortino said. "However, I hope you understand and will convey to your people that any alliance with the Federation is your choice to make, not ours. You've had our representatives living and working among your people for quite a while now—more than enough time for opinions to be formed. We can't deny that a relationship with your people will have tangible benefits for the Federation, but our hope is that the reverse is also true. If your ultimate decision is that you wish us to leave your world, then we shall do so, in peace, though with no small amount of regret."

Holding up one withered hand, Wiladra said, "I have spent enough time with your 'first contact' specialists by now to know that you speak the truth. After all, would any party wielding the obvious power you possess bother with the pretense of befriending us for such a long period, rather than conquer us outright? Perhaps it has occurred to you that my world would offer little in the way of defense against such an effort."

"That's true, Chancellor," Kirk said, stepping forward, "and now that you've opened a dialogue with us, you can be sure there are others out there who will take an interest in what happens here."

Wiladra nodded. "Yes, we have spoken of that, as well. The Romulans, as you call them."

"Yes, that's right," the captain replied. "Our being here in your system will be enough to get their attention." He knew that if a more permanent Starfleet presence was established here, Federation boundaries would extend in this direction, and the Romulans would surely respond in some fashion. Not direct hostilities, Kirk suspected, though he found it hard to imagine the empire not deploying some form of counterpart on their side of the redefined border.

As though pausing to consider and envision the scenario at which Kirk had hinted, the elder Dolysian leader turned from him and Sortino and made her way toward the picture window at the back of her office. "One wonders why they haven't made their own inroads into our system before now. Are we so primitive that we offer nothing of value?"

This time, it was Sortino who answered, "We fought a war with the Romulan Empire more than a century ago. It was a war our people only barely won. After a peace treaty was signed, the Romulans retreated far inside their borders, and there was little if any contact with them until just a few years ago. Since then, they've conducted infrequent probing actions into Federation space, though for the most part they seem content to keep to themselves. When they do venture outside their territory, with few exceptions they seem motivated by curiosity, mostly about what we're doing. I expect the same will be true here and now. They'll want to see what we find so interesting about you, your planet, and this star system. If the erinadium you extract from your mines proves useful to us, that might also hold true for the Romulans."

"There's also the matter of the energy field surrounding your mining planet," Uhura said, from where she stood just behind Kirk. "The Romulans will be curious about that, too."

"Well then," Wiladra replied, "the Romulans will join a very long procession of people who have been asking that question for as long as anyone can remember." Standing at the window, she gestured toward the sky. "It has always been there, appearing and fading as it does. Many of our most-accomplished scientists at least agree that something must be generating the field, but none among our people has ever been able to find evidence to support such a theory. The lack of such irrefutable substantiation has, of course, led some segments of our populace to embrace the belief that it is a creation of their deities. I myself am not spiritual, but even I have pondered that explanation more than once." She turned from the window and made her way back to her desk. "Our scientific community has certainly examined it using all the technology available to us, and even they are unable to reach a consensus. Then there are those who believe it to be the work of travelers from the stars. For generations, that particular theory was both applauded and derided." As she once more took her seat, she leaned forward, and Kirk thought he recognized a twinkle of mischief in her eyes as she asked, "What are *your* feelings on such theories?"

Kirk was unable to resist a small chuckle. "I know only that they have a tendency to evoke a variety of opinions, Chancellor."

"A very diplomatic answer, Captain," Wiladra observed, nodding in appreciation.

Stepping forward, Sortino said, "With your permission and assistance, Chancellor, we'd like the opportunity to find answers to those questions."

"We shall do what we can, Ambassador," replied the elder Dolysian. "Let us consider this the first of what I hope will be many acts of cooperation and mutual benefit."

"With all due respect, Chancellor"—Kirk turned toward Sortino to include her—"Ambassador, there are still some things we need to take care of."

Sortino replied, "Quite right, Captain. The *Huang Zhong*."

Dealing with the wreckage of the ship and caring for its survivors, as well as exploring the mystery of what had brought about the science vessel's untimely demise, were matters requiring his attention. If, as Kirk suspected, the explanation was somehow connected to the rift, and his people discovered that the energy field surrounding Gralafi was not some natural phenomenon, how would that affect the Dolysian people? Would it be the sort of paradigm-shifting revelation for this civilization that might do more harm than good? Though special circumstances had seen to it that the Prime Directive was not an issue so far as preventing Federation interference with the Dolysian people, there still existed the very real danger of detrimentally influencing this society. Kirk knew that he and his people would have to tread softly for the duration of this assignment.

It's certainly going to keep things interesting.

EIGHT

"It breaks my heart to see her like this."

Lieutenant John Kyle could not help but sympathize with Master Chief Christine Rideout as the engineer looked across the expanse of terrain before her, a good portion of which was covered with wreckage from her ship, the *U.S.S. Huang Zhong*. Debris from the *Archer*-class scout lay strewn across the plateau, covering an area perhaps two hundred meters in length. From where he stood next to Rideout, Kyle could make out the mangled remains of what had been the ship's warp nacelles, each having been torn from their mountings as the *Huang Zhong*'s helm officer, Lieutenant T'Vrel, fought to bring the vessel down in something approximating one piece. Despite that valiant effort, the ship had landed hard, carving a deep, ragged gouge into the planetoid's unforgiving surface without benefit of structural integrity fields or even the inertial damping field, which, according to Rideout herself, had failed just seconds before impact. It was a testament to T'Vrel's skills as a pilot that the scout ship fared as well as it had in the crash.

As for the rest of the *Huang Zhong*, the large lump of twisted, scarred metal lying at the head of the massive trough it had created was somewhat recognizable as the ship's primary hull. It had come to rest at what his tricorder told him was a thirty-two degree angle to starboard, thanks to a large boulder buried beneath the soil and onto which the ship had slid as it came to a halt. Kyle watched as engineers from the *Enterprise*, along with volunteers from the Havreltipa colony—many of them employees of the Jtelivran Mining Conglomerate who had offered to assist the salvage effort—moved about the wreckage. Even from this distance, he could hear the sounds of equipment at work, along with bits and pieces of different conversations, as his team and their Dolysian helpers got on with the business of cleaning up the crash site.

"At least everyone's accounted for," Rideout said after a moment, her gaze lingering on the main wreckage, as she fiddled with the closure on the front of her olive drab jumpsuit, which Kyle knew was the standard duty uniform worn by crews of smaller vessels like the *Huang Zhong* as they operated far away from the pomp, circumstance, and other protocol to be found on ships of the line. "So, there shouldn't be any surprises in that regard, anyway."

Kyle nodded, aware that a team of Dolysian volunteers, under the supervision of the colony's administrator and senior medical doctor, had undertaken the thankless task of collecting the remains of the eleven *Huang Zhong* crew members who had perished in the crash. While he was grateful he would be spared the sight of their bodies, he knew from Doctor McCoy's preliminary report that the deaths had been anything but pleasant, just as he knew that evidence of their passing would still be present in the ship wreckage.

Swallowing the nervous lump that had formed in his throat as he pushed aside those troubling thoughts, Kyle adjusted the strap of his engineer's satchel as he returned his gaze to the debris field. "It's a good thing you ejected the antimatter bottles when you did. Otherwise, the containment field likely would've failed, and we'd probably be looking at little more than a giant crater."

Releasing an audible sigh, Rideout replied, "That might've made things a lot easier, at least so far as cleanup goes."

"Perhaps," Kyle countered, his voice low, "but then you and I wouldn't be standing here." When she turned to regard him, he added, "I know what you're thinking, Chief, and what happened here wasn't your fault. You did everything you could to save your ship, but the cards were just stacked too high against you."

The chief engineer reached up to rub the corner of her right eye, and Kyle noted the tear before she would wipe it away. "I keep going over it in my head—every decision, every button I pushed. That's all I've done for two days, lying there in that damned bed." She eyed him. "Do you know the Dolysians have some of the most god-awful beds you'll ever sleep in? I've slept in holes in the ground that were more comfortable."

Chuckling at the unexpected observation, Kyle felt a momentary pang of guilt as he considered his surroundings. Laughter seemed so inappropriate here. Still, the brief diversion seemed to be somewhat therapeutic for Rideout, so he said nothing until she wiped her eyes a second time and cleared her throat.

"I wasn't in any shape to do any sort of checks after we crashed," she said after a moment, "but I knew about the radiation and other leakage. Administrator Shin told me that they found some isolated breaches, but it seems as though the safety systems worked, at least for the most part."

"That's right," Kyle said, "but it's all taken care of now."

He gestured with one hand back over his shoulder to where the *Ballard*, the shuttlecraft he had been given as part of his assignment to lead the salvage operation, sat parked several dozen meters from the site. "We ran a quick scan when we were on final approach, and didn't pick up any further contamination." His initial survey of the crash site had revealed varying levels of particle radiation emanating from containment systems breached in the crash. Though the indications were that the leaks were minor, Kyle had ordered the use of environmental suits for the first team to inspect the site. His past experience on similar operations, including an exploratory mission, just before his assignment to the *Enterprise,* at the crash site of a Klingon cargo vessel on Archanis IV, was enough for him to throw no caution to the wind. Once the sources of the *Huang Zhong*'s breaches were located, decontamination and neutralization of the hazardous materials was a straightforward process. This was a blessing, he knew, as it meant that, at least so far as the preliminary inspection was concerned, the *Huang Zhong*'s crash did not appear to have inflicted any serious environmental damage to the area. A more thorough scan would confirm that, of course, once the majority of the salvage effort itself was completed, ensuring that the incident, as tragic as it was, had brought no lasting harm to Gralafi or the people who called the planetoid home.

To achieve that objective, every piece of debris from the wrecked ship would have to be reclaimed or destroyed. While many of the vessel's critical or sensitive systems—computer core, sensors, weapons, and other key components—would be extracted and returned to the *Enterprise*, the bulk of the ship itself would likely be eradicated in place. In addition to securing equipment and preparing the remaining wreckage for demolition, Kyle had also been given another assignment by Captain Kirk to retrieve as much of the crew's personal effects as was possible in the allotted time. It was one more thing on a list of tasks that was already too long, but Kyle understood the reason for the captain's request. The recovery of such items would serve as a gesture to the families of those lost in the crash. He would do his best to carry out the commission with the same conviction he would bring to any other assigned task. It helped that the compact size of the *Huang Zhong*, designed as it was for short-duration missions, meant that the crew would not have had much space for personal belongings. Kyle hoped that most items of that nature would be confined to the habitation spaces, and it was his intention to retrieve anything that looked like a storage locker or duffel bag, or which otherwise did not appear to be Starfleet issue. With luck, he would be able to accomplish that along with everything else on his to-do list before they were forced to leave the planetoid.

Here's hoping.

"Your people aren't wasting any time, are they?" Rideout asked.

Kyle shook his head. "Not much time to waste." Less than eighty hours remained until the rift in the energy field surrounding Gralafi closed, not to open again for more than two years. Well aware of their rigid timetable, Kyle watched with approval as members of his team worked with the proper urgency. Near the rear of the wrecked ship, two engineers were using a pair of antigravs to maneuver an unwieldy piece of hull plating to a flatbed work vehicle supplied by the Dolysians. Closer to the vessel's midsection, another *Enterprise* crew member was employing a cutting torch to remove the remnants of an external sensor array.

"I guess I've done enough sightseeing for one day," Rideout said, a note of bitter somberness lacing her words as she reached up to rub her left shoulder.

"How's that feeling?" Kyle asked, pointing to her arm.

Rideout nodded. "Better. It's still a bit tender, but otherwise, I'm fine." Until just a few hours ago, most of the ligaments in it had been torn, but they had proven to be no match for Doctor McCoy's medical prowess. Giving her shoulder one final squeeze, she said, "Time to get back to work. I'm going inside. You coming?"

"Certainly," Kyle replied as Rideout set off across the plateau on her way toward what remained of the *Huang Zhong*'s primary hull. He jogged to catch up with her, using his right hand to hold his satchel against his hip. Though the chief engineer seemed to have refocused her attention on the matter at hand, he could not help studying the wreck as they moved closer. It was disquieting to see the vessel in such condition, knowing that it would never again take flight. The best he and his team—and Rideout, of course—could hope to accomplish was to collect the ship's most important and sensitive equipment. While some of those components, most notably the computer core, would be transported to a Starfleet research facility for study, some of the other pieces, if reparable, would be refurbished and installed in other vessels. Kyle could not shake the feeling that this unpleasant assignment was not at all unlike harvesting organs from a deceased person in the hope that transplanting them to someone else might benefit other lives. It was a laudable goal, made no less maudlin by the process required to accomplish it.

It's just a ship, he reminded himself, following the thought with a mental rebuke at what Montgomery Scott might say if he ever heard such a sentiment spoken aloud. Walking a few steps behind her, Kyle followed Rideout around to where a collapsible ladder had been installed to allow access to the ship via the docking hatch on the primary hull's port side. A small generator sat next to the ladder, lengths of cabling running from it toward other areas of the ship, including one string that extended upward alongside the ladder and through the open hatch. Rideout ascended the ladder with what Kyle figured was practiced ease, given the lack of turbolifts aboard the scout ship and the use of ladders and Jefferies tubes to navigate the vessel's interior.

"It's going to be tricky walking around in here," Rideout cautioned as she reached the top of the ladder and extended her arm to grip the side of the access hatch's threshold. "So, watch your step." She hoisted herself up and over the threshold, leveraging her way through the entryway, and Kyle heard her hiss in momentary pain as she pulled herself up with her recently repaired left arm. He followed, pushing himself through the hatch. He brushed dirt from his uniform trousers, letting his eyes adjust to the reduced illumination inside the ship. A string of emergency lights, powered by the generator at the foot of the ladder, helped to chase away the darkness, but they could do nothing to alter Kyle's sensation that he had entered a dead ship.

The listing of the ship to starboard caused the deck to slope downward ahead of him, and Kyle recalled the *Archer*-class scout interior schematics he had studied as part of preparing for this mission. The junction for the passageway at the center of this, the ship's main deck, was directly in front of them. Sickbay was to the right, and crew quarters would be to the left. The forward sections, including the bridge, were in that direction, as well. Engineering occupied the rear areas of this deck as well as the smaller deck above them, with cargo spaces one deck down.

Seeing the look of apprehension on Rideout's face, Kyle asked, "Are you okay?"

The engineer nodded, reaching up to wipe her eyes. "Yeah. Sorry. I was just . . . thinking for a second, that's all."

"I understand," Kyle said, sympathetic to the emotions she must be feeling, returning to where her friends and shipmates had perished. "I can do this, if you want to go outside and take a break."

Her expression softening, Rideout drew a deep breath, then forced a small, humorless smile. "I'll be okay, I promise. It's just . . . harder than I thought it would be." Clearing her throat, she asked in a stronger voice, "Where to first?"

Kyle replied, "The bridge. Since the consoles in the computer section are wrecked, that's the best place to access the main memory banks. We've managed to rig up auxiliary power, and initial reports from my team tell me we still have access to some systems. Maybe we can get some information out of the computer or the sensor logs that can help Mister Spock." Another of his tasks was to obtain and transmit to the *Enterprise*'s science officer any data that might prove useful in determining the cause of the crash, or offer any insight into whatever technology had been utilized to bring down the *Huang Zhong*.

"Sounds like a plan," Rideout said. "Follow me."

Negotiating the slanted deck was easier once they made the turn and began moving forward, walking with their left feet on the deck itself while they placed their right feet on the bulkhead where it met the floor. Debris littered the passageway, requiring them to step over sections of floor plating, access panels, and other detritus that had come loose during the crash. Kyle passed a dark stain along the bulkhead near his foot, the low lighting making it seem almost black against the wall's gray paint. Was that blood? He forced himself not to ponder the question.

They arrived at the door leading to the bridge. Like the rest of the ship's interior hatches, this one had been forced open by the first crew to inspect the wreck, allowing Kyle an unhindered look into the compact control center. The lighting here was better, owing to the hole that had been cut through the hull in order to allow cabling to be passed into the ship from outside.

Instead of following Kyle into the bridge, Rideout turned her attention to the open hatchway on the corridor's opposite side. "The computer core is in here," she said. "I'm going to check the power settings and make sure we don't get a surge or something that might hurt the core. I'll be right back."

"Sounds like a plan," Kyle said. As with the corridor they had just traversed, the bridge's loose contents—station chairs, data slates, and other small pieces of equipment, along with debris from shattered consoles and even sections of deck plating—had been thrown into a heap at its low end. The captain's chair as well as the helm console had been torn from their deck mountings and now rested against the perimeter stations along the starboard bulkhead. He noted a sharp odor, which he guessed to be some kind of disinfectant, and recalled what McCoy had told him about the recovery of the dead *Huang Zhong* crew members. The Dolysians who had taken on that unenviable duty had taken the extra step of cleaning up the worst evidence of the crew's untimely demise.

Thanks for that, mates.

Only one console, the science station, showed any signs of life, thanks to another emergency generator positioned outside the ship and supplying power not only to the bridge but also to the compromised computer system. With luck, Kyle would be able to access the memory banks from here, rather than being forced to wait until the computer core was extracted and connected to a diagnostic setup he had brought with him aboard the *Ballard*.

Don't jinx it, he mused as he navigated the slanted deck across the bridge to the console. The chair that normally would have been positioned here would be useless given the deck's angle, so Kyle braced his legs against the station's mounting as he eyed its instrument panel. Reaching into his satchel, he retrieved his tricorder and activated it, directing its sensor at the console. With the exception of a few burned-out connections, the data relays between the workstation and the main computer system were still intact and active, boosting Kyle's hopes that he would be able to access and retrieve the information he sought.

He swapped his tricorder for a trident scanner from his satchel, using it to track down the connections that required repair. That accomplished, he adjusted the flow of power being supplied by the emergency generator to the console, once again monitoring the status of the connection with his tricorder. Within just a few moments, he nodded in satisfaction.

"Now we're in business," he said to no one as he returned the tricorder to his satchel and set to work keying instructions to the console's rows of colored controls. As he worked, he heard footsteps behind him, entering the bridge from the main passageway.

"How goes it?" Rideout asked.

Kyle did not look up from the console as he replied, "So far, everything's checking out." He frowned as one of his diagnostic instructions returned a less than ideal status message. "Some sectors of the main memory banks are corrupted, but we had to expect some of that, right?" He had no idea if the damaged areas of the computer core could be repaired, or whether the data stored in those sections was beyond any hope of recovery. Making that determination would require more time than he was willing to spend on the endeavor at this point. "Did you find anything?"

Shaking her head, Rideout said, "The workstations in there are wrecked, but the core itself looks okay. I guess the protective force fields held during the crash, before we lost main power."

Small favors, Kyle mused as he continued to work. Entering the commands that would grant him access to the library computer and the sensor logs, he was pleased to see that the most recent information recorded in the memory banks appeared to be accessible.

"According to this," he said, "the last time stamp recorded is about twelve minutes after the log buoy was launched. I think we're in luck, here." Once more he reached into his satchel, this time extracting a standard data storage card, which he inserted into the console's reader slot. "I'm going to make a copy of the data before I try transmitting it to Spock, just in case this thing decides to give up the ghost while we're working."

As the computer processed his request, he set up another information stream, which allowed him to review data extracts from the sensor logs. He scrolled past the columns of numbers and figures representing velocity, trajectory, power readings, warning and alert messages from various subsystems at the time the *Huang Zhong* was making its harried descent to Gralafi's surface. Such information would be of interest to the engineers who soon would be tasked with determining the ultimate effects of the mysterious weapon that had crippled the scout ship beyond all hope of avoiding disaster. More important to him, however, was the information preceding and following the ship's encounter with the enigmatic tractor beam. Being able to read that data was key to determining the beam's source, which in turn might be the first step toward determining the as yet unknown masters of that technology.

Then, Kyle's stomach lurched as the deck beneath his feet and everything around him heaved upward.

"What the hell?" he exclaimed, lunging forward and grabbing onto the science station as the ship tilted to his left. The entire tortured structure of the ship seemed to groan in protest as it shifted, settling to port and reclaiming at least some of the list. In the corner of his eye he saw Rideout struggling to keep her balance and instead stumbling to her left and falling against the wall station on that side of the bridge. Kyle wondered if the bridge bulkheads or ceiling might just collapse inward from the additional stresses being placed upon them. He was trying to dig his nails into the workstation when the movement ceased, and the surrounding hull seemed to sigh in relief as it once more came to rest.

Leaning against the workstation that had prevented her from tumbling to the deck, Rideout looked across the bridge to Kyle. "You okay?"

"Yeah," he said, pushing himself off the science console, which he noticed, was still active. He felt a twinge in his back, perhaps from overextending himself while grabbing onto the console for support. Grimacing at the mild discomfort, he reached for his communicator, bringing up the device and flipping open its antenna grille. "Kyle to Hadley."

A moment later, the voice of Lieutenant William Hadley replied through the communicator's speaker, "*Hadley here. John, are you okay in there?*"

"We're fine, mate," Kyle answered. "Just a little shaken, is all. What happened?"

Hadley said, "*The soil beneath the surface all around the crash site looks to be fairly soft, and I figure the weight of the ship must've finally gotten that boulder beneath it to shift a bit. The good news is that you're mostly level now.*"

"Is there bad news?" Rideout asked.

"*Not yet, but the day's young. You two need anything in there?*"

Kyle shook his head. "Not right now, Bill, but we'll let you know. Kyle out." He sighed as he closed the communicator, holding it in his left hand as he used his right to tap a string of controls on the science station. After a moment, he said, "I think we're still okay, at least for now." His communicator beeped again, and he opened it with a flick of his wrist. "Kyle here."

"*This is Mister Spock,*" replied the voice of the *Enterprise*'s first officer. "*Do you have a status update, Lieutenant?*" There was some mild static, owing to the effects of the energy field surrounding the planetoid, but signal boosting equipment carried aboard each of the shuttlecraft assigned to travel through the rift was working to mitigate the worst of the interference.

"Yes, sir," Kyle said. "As you know, the ship's a total loss, but we're still able to access the computer banks well enough. I should have some data to transmit to you in a few minutes." As he made his report, he retrieved the data card—which now contained a copy of the *Huang Zhong*'s sensor telemetry—from the console's reader slot and returned it to his satchel. "Salvage operations are under way. We should be able to retrieve the most sensitive components, but we'll probably have to destroy the bulk of the wreck, sir."

Spock said, "*Understood, Mister Kyle. Carry on with that effort, and transmit the sensor data to me as soon as possible. Spock out.*"

"Real chatty, isn't he?" Rideout asked, offering a knowing grin.

Kyle chuckled as he returned his communicator to its place at the small of his back. "He has his moments." Drawing a deep breath, he resumed his work at the science console. "Well, back to it, I guess. Miles to go before we sleep, and all that." He resisted the urge to stifle a yawn, knowing that the next two days would provide ample opportunity for such things. "I just wish I'd thought to bring some coffee in here."

NINE

Spock aimed his tricorder at the smooth stone wall, adjusting the unit's scanning beam and watching its miniaturized viewscreen as he worked to bring into focus what was invisible to the unaided eye. The whine of the tricorder in operation, carried by the soft breeze blowing in this direction from the plateau where he and his landing party had set down with the shuttlecraft *Columbus*, echoed off the high walls of the narrow passage and was irritating to his sensitive hearing. He ignored that, concentrating instead on his data collection.

"Are you sure it's here, Spock?" asked Doctor McCoy from where he stood several meters behind the Vulcan.

Spock replied, "Our own scans as well as the data provided by the *Huang Zhong*'s sensors all indicate that at least one of the attacks occurred from this general vicinity, Doctor. My tricorder readings would appear to support that assertion. However, I am not, as you say, 'sure' that this is the precise location we seek, which is why I am continuing to conduct a sweep of the area." Keeping his attention on the tricorder's display, he noted the slight shift in energy readings as the scanning beam swept over a section of rock eight point five meters in front of him. He took a step in that direction, at the same time hearing what he recognized as a grunt of irritation from McCoy.

"A simple 'no' would've sufficed, Spock. There's no shame in saying you're not sure. In fact, it's quite understandable. After all, we have no idea what it is we're supposed to be looking for, right?"

Once again, the readings from his tricorder registered a fluctuation, and Spock's eyes narrowed as he looked up from the unit toward the expanse of rock directly in front of him. It looked very much like the surrounding hillside—dull gray with hints of vegetation at ground level, and minor sparkling as minerals in the rock reflected the violet-tinged sunlight. There seemed to be nothing to distinguish this section of the wall from any other portion of the hill.

That, logically, would be the point.

Behind him, Spock heard McCoy release a tired sigh. "Spock, this looks like a dead end. There are other passages leading into the hills from the plateau where we landed. Maybe we should split up and search those, too?"

When his tricorder beeped this time, Spock deactivated the unit and returned it to its resting place along his left hip, suspended there by the leather strap slung over his right shoulder. "That will not be necessary, Doctor," he said, before taking two steps toward the rock wall.

"Spock!"

An odd tingling sensation played across his exposed skin as he moved closer to the wall. Without hesitation, he took a third step in full stride, only partially expecting his foot to come into contact with the unyielding rock. Instead, his boot vanished, followed by his leg and then the rest of his body as he took yet another stride. The pale purple glow of Gralafi daytime did not vanish, though Spock did note that the breeze and the slight whistle accompanying it were now gone. Turning around to face the way he had come, he saw McCoy along with Lieutenant Boma and *Enterprise* security officers Johnson and Minecci running toward him, their faces each sporting an expression of shock and worry. When McCoy called out to him, Spock realized that the sound of the doctor's voice was muffled, as were the shouts of the other landing party members.

Interesting.

McCoy, ever the emotional one and with no apparent regard for his own safety, seemed poised to plunge headlong toward whatever had separated Spock from the rest of the group. He was held back by Boma and Lieutenant Johnson. The security officer had a firm grip on McCoy's left arm and was refusing in no uncertain terms to allow the doctor to advance.

"Doctor McCoy!" Spock called out.

That was enough to give the physician pause. "Spock? Are you all right?"

"I am, Doctor. Thank you. As you no doubt are surmising by now, the rock wall before you is a façade—a holographic projection. It is not real."

His features taking on what Spock long ago had come to associate with the doctor's ostensible default state of mild irritation, McCoy snapped, "The heart attack you almost gave me would've been real enough." He paused, drawing a breath before asking, "All right, now what? Do you want us to come through?"

"Remain there," Spock ordered, turning to once again face what he now saw was the actual wall of rock that formed this part of the hillside. An immense boulder sat before him, flanked at its base by smaller piles of stones. Something about the arrangement struck him as odd, even artificial. Was the boulder perhaps something more?

Looking at the dirt near the base of the massive rock, he noted slight imperfections in the soil beginning at the stone piles and curving out and away from the hillside. He knelt next to the grooves, tracing them with the tips of his fingers. How long had they been here, undisturbed by time or perhaps even the ravages of weather? He rose to his feet, eyeing the wall to the left of the boulder, and noted a portion of rock at chest level that seemed paler than the surrounding stone. The area was no larger than his hand, he surmised. With that in mind, he placed his hand on it.

The rocks began to move.

A faint reverberation emanated from somewhere behind the boulder, and Spock stepped back as it, along with the smaller rocks at its base, began to move as one conjoined unit, swinging to his right away from the hillside. Then the sounds stopped, along with the movement. The resulting opening, though still sufficient to allow passage, seemed too narrow to be of any practical use. Another glance at the grooves in the soil told him that this doorway, such as it was, should have opened even farther.

"Spock!"

Turning, he realized that he once again could hear the sounds of the breeze in the narrow canyon passageway, and it was obvious that McCoy and the rest of the landing party could once again see him. The holographic projection that had acted as camouflage for the true entrance had disappeared.

"Are you okay?" McCoy asked as he approached.

Spock nodded. "I am uninjured, Doctor, as I indicated the first time you posed that query."

"Would you look at this?" Boma said as he stepped forward, his attention on the now open portal. Reaching for his tricorder, he activated the unit and aimed it toward the entrance. "It looks to be some kind of passageway, Mister Spock, angling downward, into the hill and beneath ground level. I'm picking up faint power readings close by, with indications of a stronger source farther down." He stopped scanning, though he remained motionless for a few seconds with the tricorder still held before him. "If these readings are right, there's a massive complex down there." Allowing the tricorder to drop by its strap to hang from his shoulder, he reached for the phaser on his right hip. "The people responsible for bringing down the *Huang Zhong* could be here."

"Unlikely, Lieutenant," Spock said. "Aside from the Dolysians at the mining colony, we have detected no indications of life anywhere on this planetoid."

Boma regarded the phaser in his hand. "Whoever built the weapons used to destroy my ship made sure they stayed hidden. For all we know, they're still hiding somewhere our sensors can't reach. There's only one way to be sure, sir." As he spoke, Spock was able to discern the emotional battle the man was waging within himself. To this point, the lieutenant had seemed able to maintain his composure even in the face of the ordeal he had endured and survived. In addition to healing Boma's injured right arm, McCoy also had provided an initial psychological assessment, stating that the lieutenant showed no outward signs of post-traumatic stress disorder. The doctor seemed confident that Boma's emotional state was stable, though he conceded that could change at any time. For the moment, he seemed in control of his faculties, harboring none of the rampant emotionalism that had dominated his behavior during the disastrous mission on Taurus II.

Perhaps that itself is one of the outward signs Doctor McCoy seeks?

"Your hypothesis is plausible, Lieutenant," Spock said, "and investigation of this complex is warranted if we are to determine what really happened to the *Huang Zhong*. Therefore, we shall proceed."

Boma gestured toward the opening before casting a solemn grin at Spock. "Mind if I lead the way?"

Despite a notable absence of anything resembling evidence of inhabitants, there was no denying that the facility, whatever its origin, was aware of the landing party's presence.

"Okay," McCoy said from behind Spock as the group made its way farther down the tunnel leading from the entrance and deeper into the subterranean complex, "somebody was thoughtful enough to set up motion sensors or whatever for anyone stumbling around down here. Makes you wonder what else they set up."

Spock was forced to admit that the doctor raised a valid point. In response to their movement in the underground passageway, lighting fixtures already operating at a low level had grown brighter, revealing much in the way of detail. In addition to the illumination installed into the corridor's ceiling, other points of light had come on line at regular intervals along both walls.

"Mister Boma," Spock said as he studied his tricorder, "turn left at the next intersection." Ahead of him, the lieutenant nodded in acknowledgment as he approached the junction, followed by Lieutenant Johnson. Boma and the security officer paused before stepping into the widened section of tunnel where this passage and two others met. They studied the other paths, their phasers in their hands, though held low and near their sides. Then Johnson pointed to his left.

"There." Looking back toward Spock, he added, "It's a door or hatch of some kind, sir."

Spock nodded to Boma, and the lieutenant, as he had since the landing party's entrance into the complex, once again took the lead. He was the first to reach the hatch, its smooth, polished surface standing in stark contrast to the rough stone walls of the surrounding passageway. The door itself was hexagonal, elongated along its vertical axis.

A small square panel was set into the wall next to the door, featuring no buttons or other visible controls. Spock moved to it and scanned it with his tricorder.

"This appears to be the door's control mechanism," he said, "though if these readings are correct, the door itself is not locked." With no obvious option presenting itself, Spock chose the most logical action and reached out to touch the panel. For his efforts, a low mechanical whine echoed in the corridor as the hatch began to slide upward, disappearing into a slot in the wall above the door's threshold. Spock noted the door's thickness; locked or not, the hatch was intended to act as a protective barrier, but against what, he had no idea.

"It's the simplest approaches that always work the best," Boma said, nodding toward the door panel. Then, stepping forward so that he could see into the room, he paused at the entry. "Wow."

"Hardly a scientific observation, Mister Boma," Spock said as he got his first look at the chamber beyond the door. "However, it is understandable."

Rather than being a natural formation beneath the

surface of the planetoid, the room looked to have been carved from the rock. The walls and floor, constructed from a metallic compound, were smooth and possessed a polished gray finish not all that different from the interior bulkheads of a starship. Octagonal in shape, the room was, Spock estimated, perhaps twenty-five meters in diameter. Six of the room's eight walls contained mechanisms or consoles, while the remaining two featured doorways leading to what appeared to be anterooms. The rows of control banks and consoles were composed of dark, polished glass or some other transparent material, and while some of the stations were inert, others were active. Glyphs and text were visible on many of the console surfaces, displayed in a language Spock was surprised to realize he recognized.

"Fascinating."

Stepping into the room, he motioned for Johnson and Minecci to remain at the entrance. As the two security officers took up stations near the door, Spock looked up to see that panels that looked to be of similar material to that of the walls were set into the ceiling, which otherwise retained the only visible characteristics of carved rock. Some of the panels featured indirect lighting fixtures that cast a pale lavender tinge across the room. Others supported various apparatus whose functions Spock could not discern, but it was the object hanging from the ceiling at the center of the room that commanded his attention.

"Spock," McCoy said as the doctor moved to stand next to him, "is that what I think it is?"

A large cube, mounted in a manner that would allow it to preside over everything in the room, was lit from within, and emanated a low, monotonous hum accompanied by a continuous swirling pattern of multicolored lights. As he regarded the cube, Spock realized the light pattern bore more than a slight resemblance to the effect of the energy field surrounding Gralafi.

"If you believe it to be the same type of mechanism that you and Captain Kirk found on the Kalandan outpost planet, Doctor," Spock said, "then you would be correct."

Frowning, Boma asked, "You mean you've seen something like this before?"

"Seen it?" McCoy snapped. "More like almost killed by it."

Spock saw the confused expression on the *Huang Zhong* science officer's face, and added, "Several months ago, we encountered an artificial planet, thousands of years old and constructed by a race of beings who called themselves the Kalandans. The planet was an outpost, designed as a colony." He moved toward one of the banks of control consoles, scanning them with his tricorder. "Those who created it were long dead, having fallen victim to a disease they inadvertently created while building the planet."

"By the time we found it," McCoy added, "the colony they'd built had been standing there empty for thousands of years, with a defense system left on automatic; a kind of holographic projection that could literally kill you just by touching you." He shook his head as though recalling the events. "Before we even knew what was happening, we'd lost three people, including two on the ship."

Boma made no attempt to mask his disbelief. "Some kind of machine sent a hologram to the *Enterprise* to kill people?"

"It was not quite that simple, Mister Boma," Spock replied as he continued his tricorder scans, "though the Kalandan defenses were quite formidable. They were even responsible for transporting the *Enterprise* hundreds of light-years from the planet."

"What?" Boma asked, incredulous as he looked around the room. "And that same kind of technology might be *here*?"

Looking up from his tricorder, Spock said, "I cannot be certain, Lieutenant. However, this equipment appears to be much older than the technology we found on the Kalandan outpost. Nearly one thousand years older, according to my tricorder scans."

"So," McCoy said, "you're saying it's not as advanced?"

Spock nodded. "In some respects, Doctor, though it is still impressive, particularly if we are to believe that the Kalandans are somehow responsible for the energy field surrounding this planetoid." He paused, noting one of the status readings on his tricorder. "I believe I have found a means of interfacing with this equipment."

"I take it you were able to learn something about their language?" Boma asked.

"To a point, Lieutenant, thanks to our survey mission to the Kalandan outpost." Spock had spent some time working with the computer systems on that world, but it was Lieutenant Uhura who had conducted the most research into the ancient technology. Still, he had managed to acquire a working knowledge of the Kalandan computer systems and had some ability to interface with them. Monitoring the control console with his tricorder, he reached for the smooth, black panel and pressed several of its embedded controls. Each touch to the panel brought with it a mechanical tone that Spock likened to musical notes. As he pressed the last control in the sequence prescribed by his scans, he heard a high-pitched warbling sound coming from behind him.

"Spock!" McCoy exclaimed. "Look!"

Turning from the panel, Spock saw that the control cube hanging from the center of the room's ceiling had become more active, its interior illumination having accelerated. A beam of light shone forth from the cube's base to the floor, and within it was a female humanoid shape. She wore a jade-colored long-sleeved robe, which covered her entire body. Her silver hair was short, leaving her neck bare. Spock estimated her age to be comparable to that of a middle-aged human.

"Unbelievable," Boma said.

"I've got a bad feeling about this," McCoy added.

Having now coalesced into solid form, the projection of the woman seemed to smile at them, though her blue-green eyes seemed flat and unseeing. "*My fellow Kalandans, I offer you greetings. I am Meyeliri, caretaker of this facility. We have created what is now the preeminent repository of Kalandan knowledge ever assembled by our civilization. In the event our homeworld continues to deteriorate to the point where it can no longer sustain our civilization, this world will serve as the first step in reestablishing our society.*"

"This is incredible," Boma said, his voice barely a whisper.

Meyeliri continued, "*Despite its proximity to an inhabited planet, it is ideally suited for our people in terms of environment and natural resources. Therefore, we designed the energy field encompassing this world to protect this facility from the curious. The field will open for short durations at regular intervals in order to receive updated information from our homeworld. As residents of this repository, you have the means to make contact with the homeworld as necessary. Otherwise, you will live in solitude, overseeing the facility's operation until such time as replacement caretakers arrive. Again, welcome, and I wish you well."*

"I wonder if any Kalandans ever heard that message," McCoy said after Meyeliri's image faded.

Boma said, "It sounds like this whole planet is nothing but one giant contingency plan. They send people here to man it, make sure everything keeps running, but then what?"

"Perhaps they were afflicted by the same disease that eventually destroyed the rest of the Kalandan race," Spock replied. From what he and Lieutenant Uhura had learned on the other outpost, Kalandans dispatched to other planets throughout this part of the galaxy had been called back to their homeworld. That happened when the disease was beginning its deadly campaign, and before it was known that it would prove lethal to their civilization. "The answer may well be here, along with the rest of the information the Kalandans were able to amass."

Moving to look about the room, Boma said, "The complete history and knowledge of an entire civilization, right here at our fingertips? This is amazing. You could make a career out of studying something like this."

McCoy cleared his throat. "What I don't understand is, if this planetoid was supposed to be protected from the Dolysians, or anyone else for that matter, then why does the energy field open at all? If the Kalandans thought it needed to open from time to time, then why stay open so long? It doesn't make any sense."

"It may well be that the systems overseeing the rift are malfunctioning," Spock said. "After all, they have been in continuous operation for thousands of years. Even the most robust mechanisms require periodic maintenance.

It's logical to assume that some form of automated repair work takes place as required, but even those devices may be suffering the effects of age. It would be interesting to investigate that possibility."

"You have to wonder how the Dolysians are going to handle this," McCoy said. "I mean, they had to at least consider the possibility that the field around this planet was an artificial creation, but to have it confirmed? And then be faced with all of this?" He shook his head. "They're going to have their hands full, that's for sure."

"Indeed," Spock conceded. How would the Dolysians react to the knowledge that fate and circumstance had seen fit to appoint them custodians for the amassed knowledge of an extinct alien civilization? How would the information stored here affect their society, and what was the potential for disaster if access to that knowledge was left unchecked?

The situation, Spock decided, had just become a great deal more complicated.

TEN

Standing in the middle of the *Enterprise*'s hangar bay, Montgomery Scott watched as two of his junior engineering assistants maneuvered a container loaded with tools and other equipment into the cargo shuttlecraft *Caroline Herschel*. Each of the crewmen held an antigravity loader attached to one side of the container, simplifying the process of moving the heavy crate into the proper position to be put aboard the compact craft.

"Aye, that's it, lads," Scott said, nodding in approval as he held up the data slate he had been carrying with him all afternoon and used the device's stylus to mark the container on his inventory list as having been loaded. Double-checking the slate's information, he added, "Now, we just load the equipment we need aboard the *Copernicus*, and that'll do it."

One of the crewmen pushing the container through the shuttle's open hatch, a young, muscled fellow named Miles McLoughlin, shook his head. "I can't wait for the day when transporters are good enough to beam cargo from point to point around a ship."

Scott could not help smiling upon overhearing the remark. "What's the matter? You're not afraid of a little hard work, are you? Imagine having to do all of this without the antigravs. That'd make your day a wee bit pleasant, no?"

"Don't give him any ideas," said McLoughlin's companion, Crewman Scott Hertzog, offering the other man a playful smack on the arm. "We're almost done."

"That we are," Scott confirmed, using his data slate to point to the lone remaining container sitting on the hangar deck. "Let's get that loaded, and the first team will be ready to head out." With all of the necessary equipment now prepared for transport, he knew that the real work was only just beginning. "Grab a hearty meal while you can, lads, as you'll likely be getting your fill of field rations over the next few days."

"All the reconstituted beef stew you can eat," Hertzog said, offering a wide grin. "If that's not fancy living, I don't know what is."

McLoughlin's expression was one of mock derision. "How can you stand that stuff? It'll melt your stomach lining if you eat enough of it. Now, the chicken loaf? That's actually not too bad."

"I prefer that my meats be presented in non-loaf form, thank you very much," Hertzog replied. Turning his attention to Scott, the crewman asked, "So, all we have are three days, sir?"

Nodding, the chief engineer said, "Aye, that's it. We'll have to be working at warp speed to get it all done in time."

Under other circumstances, Scott would have been content to call it a day and have his people get a good night's rest before setting out in the morning to begin the salvage operation. However, time was a driving factor in his team's activities. The task given him by Captain Kirk to strip the wrecked *Huang Zhong* of all sensitive equipment and other components would, by the engineer's estimation, require almost continuous effort over the next seventy or so hours.

"Three days is an awfully tight window, sir," McLoughlin said. "Do you think we can get it all done?"

Scott shrugged. "We're certainly going to give it our best shot." While he would have preferred a longer period of time to carry out the assignment, the deadline was necessary in order to meet the goal of having all *Enterprise* personnel as well as the *Huang Zhong* survivors away from the Gralafi planetoid well ahead of the rift's projected time of closure. He had three days to remove and ferry away everything that could be salvaged from the crashed science vessel—weapons and defense systems, sensors, computer core, various components of the propulsion system, and whatever else could be crammed into the various *Enterprise* shuttlecraft that had been dedicated to the detail. Once that was accomplished, whatever remained of the ship at the end of the time allotted to Scott and his people would have to be destroyed.

"It's too bad," Hertzog said, sighing. "The *Huang Zhong*'s only been in service for a couple of years. If circumstances were different, we could tow it out of here and back to a shipyard for repairs."

"You want to babysit it for three years until the rift opens again?" McLoughlin asked, his grin wide as he regarded his friend.

Hertzog replied, "Okay, I guess Starfleet can build another one." Then, as though realizing the potential callousness of his remark, he added, "I just wish we could say the same about the people we lost."

"Aye," Scott said, considering the *Huang Zhong*'s captain and those members of its crew who lost their lives in the crash. He had not known any of them, but they were fellow Starfleet officers and enlisted personnel, so they were brothers and sisters. While he would rather be diverting his engineering expertise into learning what had contributed to the science vessel's demise, he knew that Commander Spock was heading up that effort. If anyone could learn the truth about what had happened here, it was the *Enterprise*'s formidable science officer.

We owe that much to Captain Arens and his people. Scott cleared his throat, thinking of the eleven caskets which had been placed with reverence in one of the *Enterprise*'s cargo bays. While it was not the ideal location in which to house the remains of the *Huang Zhong*'s crew, recovering the bodies and bringing them back to the *Enterprise*, so far as Scott was concerned, had been the first and most important of the tasks he had been given to complete.

"There's nothing we can do for those poor souls, lads," he said, forcing his attention back to the matters at hand. "What we *can* do is the job we've been given, and maybe help Mister Spock to find out what happened to them, and maybe prevent that from happening to anyone else." He certainly had no desire to see any more caskets come to rest in his cargo bay.

Seeing nods of approval and even determination from his subordinates, Scott nodded. "All right then. It looks like we're ready to go here. Go and grab something to eat, and be back here in an hour with your kit packed. The first team leaves at fifteen-thirty hours." According to the information he had been given, it was coming up on early morning in the region of the planetoid where the *Huang Zhong* had crashed. Fourteen hours of daylight would be available to his team on their first day of work, much more conducive to their efforts than if the rift surrounding Gralafi were closed. Scott had read in one of the briefings about the small, seemingly rogue world that, during the nearly three-year cycle when it was cut off from Dolysia, was shrouded in perpetual darkness. One of the rift's many odd properties was that it somehow blocked the sun from being visible from Gralafi's surface, even though it allowed light and heat from the star to reach the planetoid. The engineer tried to imagine what living and working as part of the mining community would be like under such conditions, never able to see the sun they knew was there, somewhere, hidden by whatever bizarre spectacle surrounded the odd little planetoid they called home. It was but one more mystery for which Spock would doubtless be trying to find an explanation even as he investigated what might have brought down the *Huang Zhong*.

Better him than me, Scott mused, realizing for the first time that he was alone on the hangar deck, the rest of his team having already vacated the premises to finalize whatever preparations might still need to be addressed before their scheduled departure for Gralafi. *I've got my own mysteries to solve, like how in the name of all that's holy am I supposed to get all of this done in three days?*

Despite the friendly nature of relations between the Dolysians and the Federation, miners living and working on the planetoid could not be allowed unrestricted access to the wreckage of the *Huang Zhong*. The measures about to be taken by Scott and his engineers—gutting and scuttling the ship—though extreme, were required by regulations when it came to the presence of Starfleet vessels in situations such as this, when operational security and the protection of classified material and information was at issue. With the pending closure of the rift, waiting for towing vessels to be dispatched by Starfleet was not an option, and neither was leaving behind a cadre of *Enterprise* personnel to safeguard the downed ship until the mysterious rift enveloping the Gralafi planetoid deigned to open once again. That left salvage and demolition up to Scott and his engineers, and accomplishing both tasks in the time allotted by Captain Kirk would prove challenging, to say the least.

Complicating the situation, if only slightly, was the fact that with both Kirk and Spock off the ship, command of the *Enterprise* had for the moment been left to Scott himself. This would prevent him from traveling to the planetoid, at least until the captain or the first officer returned. Therefore, Scott's senior engineering assistant, John Kyle, would be overseeing the salvage activities and was in fact already on the planetoid, taking care of various preliminary tasks in advance of the main work party. None of that diminished Scott's desire to be on Gralafi, watching over the delicate operation.

Such is life, he reminded himself. *I guess I'll just have to conjure this particular miracle for the captain via remote.*

His reverie was broken by the sound of an alert klaxon wailing across the hangar deck. Snapping his head toward an alarm indicator set into the bulkhead near the exit hatch, Scott noted that it was flashing a bright, blinking crimson. No sooner did that register than the intercom's whistle pierced the air over the sound of the siren, and was followed by the baritone voice of Lieutenant Hikaru Sulu.

"Red Alert! All hands to battle stations! This is not a drill. Mister Scott to the bridge!"

Sitting in the command chair at the center of the *Enterprise*'s bridge, Sulu kept his gaze fixed on the main viewscreen, doing his best to examine each of the stars highlighting the black curtain of space displayed before him. He stared, waiting for anything—the slightest flicker or blink—that might betray the presence of what he knew was lurking out there.

Come on, he thought. *Poke your head out here. Just once.*

"Shields are at full power," reported Lieutenant Manjula Rahda from where she sat at the helm console in front of Sulu. Normally assigned to gamma shift, she had been called to duty early in order to serve in Sulu's stead while he held the conn. "Fire control reports all weapons standing by."

Sulu nodded at the report. "Very well. Chekov, anything new on sensors?" As he spoke, he realized that he was gripping the arms of the command chair with such force that his fingers were beginning to tingle. He forced himself to release the tension in his arms, and even leaned back in his seat. The actions did little to lessen his heightened apprehension. *Relax, Lieutenant. How does the captain manage to make this look so easy?*

Standing at the science station and bent over the console's hooded scanner interface, his face bathed in a soft, blow glue, Ensign Pavel Chekov replied without looking up, "Negative, sir. There was a momentary surge of neutron radiation, but now there doesn't seem to be anything there."

"I think we all know better than that," Sulu replied, his eyes drawn if only for a moment to the Red Alert indicator, which still flashed before him from the center of the dual console that served both the helm officer's and navigator stations. Though he had ordered the audible alarms silenced, the illuminated signal was more than sufficient to communicate the seriousness of the situation. "They're out there, somewhere." The *Enterprise* sensors had taken only seconds to register the odd neutron radiation reading, which could not be attributed to the starship itself, the mysterious spatial rift, or any of the civilian ship traffic in or near the anomaly or the Dolysian planet. Instead, the scanners had within microseconds searched the memory banks of the *Enterprise*'s main computer and found a match to the collected readings. The computer then automatically routed that information to the vessel's defensive systems at the same time that it apprised the science station—and by extension, Sulu and the rest of the bridge—of what it believed it had found.

"A cloaked Romulan ship," Chekov said. Though the ensign remained composed, Sulu still heard the slight tension in the younger man's voice.

"And we're sure it's not a sensor reflection?" Sulu asked. "Or something else given off by the rift?"

Chekov shook his head. "I've double-checked the readings. The computer is certain we detected a Romulan ship, if only for a few seconds."

So, where is it? The unspoken question ringing in his ears, Sulu returned his attention to the viewscreen. There remained only empty space, punctuated by distant stars. Was he expecting the Romulan vessel to just reveal itself right before his eyes? Were that to happen, the helm officer knew that it likely would be a prelude to something far more disagreeable than the unease currently gripping him.

"I thought our sensors had been modified to identify cloaked ships," said M'Ress, the female Caitian lieutenant seated at the communications station. As always, her speech sounded low and even relaxed. Sulu often wondered if her voice was a reflection of how she truly felt, even during situations like this where anxiety would seem like a natural reaction, or if the felinoid officer was just very good at hiding her emotions in times of stress. He preferred to believe the former.

"The sensors were upgraded after Captain Kirk stole the cloaking device from that Romulan ship," Chekov said, "and Mister Scott was able to figure out, at least to a point, how it worked."

Sulu recalled Spock's briefing following the successful completion of Captain Kirk's top-secret mission to obtain by any means necessary a Romulan cloaking device, during which the captain had employed subterfuge and deception not only against the commander and crew of a Romulan warship but also the men and women under his own command. The *Enterprise*'s chief engineer had been able to study the pilfered technology for only a few days before the device was handed over to Starfleet's tactical division. Despite the limited opportunity afforded him, Scott was able to determine the cloaking generator's basic functionality, including the faint neutron energy signature it emitted while active and drawing power from the vessel in which it was installed. The signature it produced while fitted to the *Enterprise*'s propulsion system was different from those of Romulan vessels that had been scanned, but there was enough commonality between the various readings that Scott was able to program an algorithm for the computer subprocesses overseeing the ship's sensor array. It was this new set of instructions that allowed the scanners to identify the telltale clue of a cloaked vessel as it entered detection range. The question now troubling Sulu was whether the sensors were accurate, or if they had fallen prey to some heretofore unknown properties exhibited by the Dolysian rift.

Behind him, Sulu heard the pneumatic hiss of the doors to the turbolift opening, and when he swiveled his chair to look he saw Montgomery Scott stepping onto the bridge. The chief engineer's gaze was already focused on the viewscreen, and Sulu watched his features darken into a scowl as he attempted to process what he was seeing—or not seeing.

"What the devil's with the Red Alert?" Scott asked, stepping from the upper bridge deck into the command well as Sulu rose from the captain's chair.

Indicating Chekov at the science station, the helm officer replied, "Sensors tell us they picked up a cloaked vessel entering the system."

"Romulan?" Scott asked, his frown deepening.

"That's what it looked like, sir," said the ensign, "though our sensors registered the reading only for a moment."

Casting a brief glance back to the viewscreen, Scott folded his arms across his chest. "Status?"

"Our shields are up and weapons are on standby," Sulu reported. "We're continuing to conduct full sensor sweeps of the area, but except for the initial contact, we've found nothing, which doesn't make any sense if that new program you installed to detect cloaked ships is working."

Scott appeared to consider that before saying, "Unless the Romulans, or whoever we think might be out there, have found a better way of hiding themselves." Moving away from the captain's chair, the engineer made his way to the science station. "Mister Chekov, show me the sensor readings that triggered the alert."

It took the younger officer a moment to recall the data and display it on one of his console's monitors before stepping aside and allowing Scott to sit at the station.

"What are you thinking, Scotty?" Sulu asked, moving

to stand at the red, curved railing separating the command well from the upper deck. It required physical effort on his part to keep from repeatedly looking over his shoulder at the viewscreen. Part of him kept wondering when the Romulan ship—or whatever could be out there—might choose to reveal itself.

Grunting, Scott replied, "That either I or my cute little program isn't as clever as I thought we were." As he began to input instructions to the workstation, his fingers tapping various buttons and controls spread across the console, he glanced over his shoulder. "I tried to make the detection algorithm broad enough to account for variances in the energy surge created by the cloaking field generator when interacting with different power systems."

"It's not hard to think the Romulans found some way to either alter or conceal that energy signature for their ships," Chekov said, "particularly after we stole one of their cloaking devices."

Scott nodded. "Exactly. The trick now is to find a way to expand the program's search parameters and recognition protocols to better distinguish variations in the range of potential energy signatures, and do it in such a way that it doesn't trip a false alarm." He shrugged as he continued to work. "Of course, it's likely that whatever trick I come up with will only be a temporary solution."

"I'd be happy if it just worked once," Sulu said.

"Aye," replied the chief engineer. "I'll see to it, lad." His fingers paused in their work, and his hands hovered over the console, as though he was conducting a mental review of what he had just done. When he resumed tapping the controls in seemingly random sequences, he said, "There's only so much I can do without going in and reviewing the entire routine, but we don't have that kind of time." He punctuated his statement with a final stab at one of the controls, and in response the monitor on which his program code was displayed flashed a column of green indicators. Rising from the chair, he gestured toward the station's hooded scanner. "All right, Mister Chekov. Let's see what that does."

The ensign moved to the scanner and peered into its viewfinder, and without looking reached out with his right hand to adjust the unit's settings. It took only a handful of seconds before an alert tone sounded from the console. "Picking up a minor energy disturbance," he reported. "It's faint, but it's there, consistent and repeating." Looking up from the scanner, he looked to Sulu and Scotty. "It's definitely a ship. The profile's still obscured, but I'm fairly certain it's Romulan." He then nodded toward the viewscreen, and when Sulu glanced in that direction, he still saw nothing but open space.

"Can you track it?" Sulu asked.

Chekov replied, "The readings are still erratic, but I think it's on a direct course for the rift."

Exchanging glances with Scott, Sulu saw heightening concern on the engineer's face, and decided the expression had to be a match for his own.

"Lieutenant M'Ress," Scott said, his voice stern, "open a channel."

ELEVEN

Commander Vathrael noted the nervousness of the centurion standing before the sensor controls, despite the young officer's best efforts at maintaining his composure while keeping his attention on his instruments. Vathrael was sure that the subdued lighting of the *Nevathu*'s cramped bridge, along with the room's increased warmth as power for the ship's environmental control system was routed to more essential operations to serve the current tactical situation, only served to heighten the man's unease. There was no mistaking the rapid blinking of the eyes and the clenching of the jaw, but the single bead of perspiration running from beneath the centurion's helmet and down the side of his face was the obvious clue. Even with the seriousness of the current situation, Vathrael could not help but smile as she stepped close enough to the centurion so that she would be heard only by him.

"You are remembering to breathe, yes?" she asked, her voice little more than a whisper. "It is easy to forget such things during times like this."

Centurion Betria's body went rigid for the briefest of moments in response to his commander's proximity, but Vathrael was satisfied to see her words having the intended effect as the sensor officer snorted, just a bit, under his breath, before nodding. "Yes, Commander, I am." He paused, uncertainty evident in his eyes as he added, "I apologize for my conduct."

Vathrael shook her head. "Your apology is unnecessary, Centurion. Such reactions are to be expected from one so young and untried. Confidence comes with experience, which you will gain in time. For now, it is commendable that you are working to set aside any fear you might feel and concentrating on your duty."

"Thank you, Commander," Betria replied. Along with a handful of other personnel, he had joined the *Nevathu* as part of a normal crew rotation during the ship's last stopover at a resupply base. Fresh out of the military academy, the sensor officer was on his first true deep space assignment, his head doubtless swimming with unchecked thoughts of honorable service to the praetor and the people of the Romulan Empire. Though training scenarios at the academy endeavored to offer simulations that were as authentic as possible, nothing in that controlled environment could ever hope to recreate the uncertainty and unpredictability of actual ship operations in potentially hostile situations such as the one Betria now faced.

From the other side of the *Nevathu*'s cramped bridge, Subcommander Sirad called out, "Weapons officer, what is the status of the cloaking field?"

"Operating at full capacity, Subcommander," answered Centurion Terius from where he stood before the bridge's tactical station. "Weapons and defensive shield generators are on standby, ready to engage the moment we disengage the cloak."

His hands clasped behind his back as he walked a circuit around the narrow pathway situated between the bridge's perimeter stations and the control hub at the center of the room, Sirad nodded in apparent approval. "Very good."

Raising her voice so that it could be heard by the other bridge personnel, Vathrael said, "Centurion Betria, what do your sensors tell us about the Starfleet vessel?"

"It is maintaining position approximately forty thousand *mat'drih* from the edge of the anomaly, Commander," the young officer reported. "Its defenses are not active, though our readings indicate the ship is conducting an intensive sensor scan of the area." He raised his head from his workstation and turned to regard Vathrael, his expression one of concern. "Is it possible they know we are here?"

Vathrael crossed her arms, reaching up with her right hand to stroke her chin. "One thing I have learned, Centurion, is that when it comes to Starfleet, anything would appear to be possible." Using the knowledge of Starfleet technology she had gained from direct experience, the commander had ordered the *Nevathu*'s entry to the Kondaii system on a course that would use the inhabited fourth planet and the mysterious energy phenomenon to mask their approach.

"Maintain course for the anomaly," Vathrael ordered, stepping away from Betria and making a circuit of the bridge, her eyes missing nothing as she studied the different stations and the officers presiding over them. No doubt their thoughts mirrored her own and they too were wondering if the Federation ship might be wise to their presence in the system. Even traveling while cloaked, there could be no guarantees that the *Nevathu*'s approach would escape detection by the Starfleet vessel's sensors. Since the theft of a cloaking device by a Federation spy some *khaidoa* previously, an effort was under way to develop a new generation of cloaking field generator, as a means of mitigating the tactical ramifications that might come from whatever knowledge Starfleet gleaned from their study of the stolen technology. What might they have learned already? Without the benefit of information obtained by covert agents working within the Federation, the only practical means of ascertaining how far Starfleet might be exploiting whatever temporary advantage they possessed was to face off against one of their ships. Of course, that notion ran contrary to the orders Vathrael had been given to maintain stealth during this mission and to avoid contact with the enemy if at all possible. While she understood the directive, the commander's curiosity remained unsatisfied. Such was the way of duty, she reminded herself.

"Centurion Betria," Sirad said, "what do sensors tell us about the energy field?"

The young officer replied, "It is not like anything previously encountered, Subcommander. The energy it emits does not conform to any natural or artificially occurring patterns on record."

Directing her attention to the small viewing screen positioned on the bridge's forward bulkhead, Vathrael regarded the odd energy field it displayed. Though she had never seen with her own eyes any spatial phenomena such as wormholes or interspatial rifts, she knew such things existed, thanks to reports and computer simulations created from the sensor logs of vessels that had run across such bizarre manifestations. In keeping with what Betria had reported, the thing on the screen before her did not resemble anything listed in those logs.

"And our scans cannot penetrate it?" Vathrael asked, without turning from the viewing screen.

"No, Commander." Betria turned from his console. "All scanning beams disperse upon contacting the field. As a result, we are unable to ascertain what lies beyond the field's outer boundary."

Vathrael nodded at the report. "Perhaps that will change once we move past that boundary ourselves." If the anomaly was, as Fleet Command believed, the product of some kind of alien technology, then it made sense that effort would be extended to make the energy field appear as something other than an artificial construct, at least from the outside. It also made sense that the Dolysians, lacking the sort of advanced sensors carried aboard Romulan and even Federation ships, would not be able to make such a determination for themselves. What secrets might be revealed once the *Nevathu* made the transit to the other side of the rift? Had the Starfleet crew already made the discovery for themselves? If that was the case, then it would likely have at least some effect on the direction of political discourse between the Romulan Empire and the Federation. Currently, the Kondaii system was in nonaligned space, but that could change in short order if the Dolysians accepted the Federation's overtures for trade agreements, which would certainly lead to protectorate status and, eventually, possible admission to the interstellar "cooperative."

Those are problems for diplomats, Vathrael reminded herself, *not soldiers. Mind your duty, Commander.*

Before she could issue her next order, a telltale tone sounded from the bridge's communications station, and when the centurion manning that post, Odera, turned to face her, Vathrael saw confusion in the young officer's eyes.

"Commander, we are being hailed by the Starfleet ship."

It took an extra moment for Vathrael to process what

she had just heard, though she did not go so far as to ask the centurion to repeat his statement. Instead, she asked, "How is that possible?"

Odera shook his head. "I do not know, though it appears to be a repeating message."

Stepping closer to the communications station, Sirad said, "Perhaps they are not certain of our presence, and are simply sending out a standard hail?"

"If not to us," Vathrael countered, "then to whom?" She nodded to Odera. "Play the message, Centurion. Standard translation protocols."

The communications officer nodded before turning to carry out the order, and a moment later a male voice emanated from the bridge's intercom system.

"*Unidentified Romulan vessel, this is Lieutenant Commander Montgomery Scott of the Federation* Starship Enterprise. *Be advised that we are able to track your ship even with your cloaking device, and we know that you are on an approach course for the spatial rift. The rift has proven hazardous to vessels possessing warp drive. We have already lost one of our own ships after it attempted to enter the region. Do not enter the rift, as we cannot predict any effect it might have on your ship.*"

Sirad scowled. "It is a lie. They cannot possibly be tracking us."

Her eyes narrowing as she listened to the message play a second time, Vathrael shook her head. "If we are to assume they are not lying about their identity, then this is the vessel responsible for the theft of the cloaking generator from one of our ships. If anyone in their Starfleet were to possess knowledge on how to exploit or defeat our cloaks, it would be this ship and its captain." The vessel's commander, a human named Kirk, figured prominently in the report Vathrael had read detailing the device's theft. Unconfirmed accounts also named Kirk and the *Enterprise* as having engaged other imperial ships on several occasions over the past three *fvheisn*, including one incident when a warship's commander had been forced to engage his vessel's self-destruct protocols in order to avoid capture. If the information Vathrael had read told her anything about this human and his crew, it was that they were not to be underestimated.

And where was Kirk? No doubt he was busy ingratiating himself with the Dolysians, doing his level best to convince the primitive species that life under Federation rule was infinitely superior to the banal existence they currently enjoyed. So far as the Romulan Empire was concerned, the Kondaii system held little intrinsic value, with the possible exception of whatever technology might be responsible for the energy field the *Nevathu* now approached.

"Do we respond?" Sirad asked, prodding Vathrael from her brief reverie.

She reached up to wipe perspiration from her brow, noting that the power reduction to the environmental control systems was now quite noticeable. "No," she said. "Maintain communications silence and proceed on course for the rift." She did not need to look about the bridge to know that members of her crew, doubtless still thinking of the warning from the Starfleet ship, were now sharing expressions of concern. Was the message a ruse, intended to lure the *Nevathu* out of hiding? It was a calculated risk, Vathrael knew, but one she believed was worth taking. Still, despite her own confidence, her subordinates, doubtless imagining all manner of repercussions for daring to take the *Nevathu* into the anomaly, might not be feeling the same level of self-assurance.

She should have guessed that Sirad would not be so affected.

"Attend your stations," the subcommander snapped, eliciting a small smile from Vathrael. "The inhabitants of this system have been traversing the rift for more *fvheisn* than some of you have been alive," he continued, every word echoing off the bridge's angled bulkheads and low ceiling, "and doing so in spacecraft I would not trust to carry away our garbage. I should like to think that a vessel of the empire would fare somewhat better."

"Quite right," Vathrael said, nodding in approval. Sirad's words seemed to have the desired effect as everyone on the bridge seemed to turn to their duties with renewed energy and focus. Though she might not always agree with his views and methods, if there was one thing at which the subcommander excelled, it was ensuring that the *Nevathu* and its crew maintained efficiency and discipline.

From her left, the centurion manning the helm reported, "We approach the rift's outer boundary, Commander."

"Slow to one-quarter speed," Vathrael ordered. "Full power to the defensive screens, and I want a detailed sensor sweep as we pass through the boundary. Transfer power from any system except the cloaking field, if necessary."

At his station, Centurion Betria turned and called out, "Commander, the Starfleet vessel is now moving along what appears to be an intercept course with us. Their defensive screens are active, as are their weapons, though I am detecting no evidence of our being targeted."

"Well," Sirad said, "that would seem to remove any

doubts as to whether they can track us. Shall we engage our own defenses?"

"No," Vathrael replied. "They will not fire on us unless provoked. Will we reach the rift boundary before they intercept us?"

Standing at the helm console, Centurion Janotra answered, "Not at our present speed, Commander."

"Increase to three-quarter speed," Vathrael said, and she heard the omnipresent hum of the *Nevathu*'s engines shift in pitch as they responded to the increased power demands. Moving to a secondary systems station, she reached for the console and tapped a series of controls, in response to which a display monitor flared to life and offered her an image of the Starfleet ship. The vessel seemed to be moving with singular purpose, growing larger on the screen with every passing moment.

They will not fire.

"Crossing the outer boundary now," Janotra reported, an instant before the entire ship seemed to react to contact with the rift. The first clue that something might be amiss was the flickering of the bridge's overhead and recessed lighting, partnered with a noticeable warbling in the reverberations cast off by the *Nevathu*'s engines. Still leaning against the console, Vathrael was able to feel the first vibrations carrying through the bulkheads—vibrations that were already growing in intensity.

"Increase power to the shields," she ordered. "Reduce to one-half speed." In response to her command, the *Nevathu* shuddered around her with an even greater force, and Vathrael reached for the console to steady herself. "What's happening?" Could she have misjudged the human? Had he indeed ordered his weapons unleashed against her ship?

Betria replied, "The energy field seems to be reacting to our passage!" There was worry in the young officer's voice, and Vathrael saw the emotion reflected in the eyes of the centurion as well as the other officers, all of whom were gripping their consoles or anything else that might offer purchase.

Then something slammed into the ship and the deck pitched up and to the left, and Vathrael scrambled for a handhold as alarms began to sound within the cramped control room. "Emergency power to the shields!" she shouted. All around her, the *Nevathu* was beginning to make known its displeasure at the assault being inflicted upon it. The odd, labored rhythm of the engines had now been replaced with an irregular rumbling that to Vathrael's ears sounded as though the massive power plants might be doing their best to wrest themselves from their mountings.

"Commander!" shouted Centurion Terius. "The cloaking field is failing!"

Even as the tactical officer spoke the words, Vathrael could see the alert indicator flashing on the helm console, signifying a problem with the cloak generator, but that was the least of the problems she and her crew faced. If something could not be done to arrest the *Nevathu*'s shaking and trembling in the face of whatever the mysterious energy field was doing to the ship, there would be nothing to conceal except for an expanding cloud of debris. Besides, it was almost certain the *Enterprise*'s own sensors had now detected her ship's presence. Whatever advantage she might have held with respect to stealth likely had evaporated.

"Never mind the cloak!" Vathrael snapped, anchoring herself against the systems station by gripping the edge of the console with both hands. She could now feel the ship's incessant vibrations in her bones. "Transfer that power to the deflector shields, and increase speed to full. Betria! How much farther to the other side of the rift?"

The sensor officer replied, "We are less than halfway through, Commander!"

No sooner had he made his report than Centurion Janotra called out, "We are losing propulsion! The helm is not responding!"

Instinct told Vathrael that the energy field's effects would continue to worsen the farther the *Nevathu* traveled into the rift. What was it the *Enterprise* officer had said? The anomaly had somehow damaged another Starfleet ship? Why was that? Something about the energy field being harmful to vessels with warp drive?

"Deactivate the warp engine!" Vathrael ordered. "Do it now!"

The order seemed incredulous even to the normally stoic Sirad. From where he stood, holding a safety bar mounted to the bulkhead near the helm station, he asked, "Commander? If we do that, power for our defenses will be severely limited."

"I know that!" Vathrael snapped, feeling her own anxiety growing even as the *Nevathu*'s quivering around them continued to increase. "Do as I command!"

In response to the directive, Centurion Janotra fed the necessary instructions to his console, and a moment later Vathrael heard the distinctive drone of the *Nevathu*'s massive warp engine starting to fade. The loss of the ship's primary power source was evident as a litany of alert indicators and tones wailed for attention across the bridge, and the shaking grew worse, but only for a moment. As abrupt as the bizarre assault had begun, it stopped. The groans of protest from the surrounding bulkheads ceased, and all that was left was the chorus of alarms, which Sirad ordered silenced.

"Damage reports," the subcommander directed, moving to Centurion Odera, who had lost his hold on his console and tumbled to the deck.

Still tapping controls on the helm console, Janotra said, "The impulse engines are sluggish, Commander, though we are still able to maneuver. I am requesting a status report from the engineer."

"What of the cloaking field?" Sirad asked, moving toward the tactical station.

Terius replied, "It remains offline, Subcommander. No report yet on its repair."

Pushing away from the systems console, Vathrael gestured as though waving away the report. "It does not matter. The *Enterprise* knows we are here." From what she knew of Starfleet practices, the commander of the starship might even try to offer assistance if he discovered the *Nevathu's* condition. "Have they made another attempt to establish contact?"

Odera said, "Our communications array also suffered damage from the rift. Even the internal system is experiencing difficulty, but the engineer reports that repairs are already under way."

His gaze focused on one of the hub's status monitors, Sirad said, "He has posted his preliminary repair estimates. At present, it will be tomorrow at the earliest before full impulse power is restored."

"What about warp drive?" Vathrael asked.

"Fully functional," the subcommander answered. "Deactivating it was the correct course, Commander."

Vathrael nodded. "Of course, it will only prove useful if and when we pass back through the rift."

Moving away from the hub, Sirad reached up to wipe his brow, which was damp with perspiration. "The *Enterprise* will be looking for us."

"Almost certainly," Vathrael said, then paused, frowning. "However, there is no way to know if the energy field has any effect on its sensors which might benefit us." In truth, she did not believe that to be the case; she had said it in large part for the sake of her bridge crew, each member of whom was regarding her with a questioning expression. "For now, we will carry out our orders to the best of our ability, and obtain as much information as possible. Helm, move us toward the planetoid. I suspect the answers we seek are there."

Watching as her subordinates set to their various tasks, Vathrael allowed herself a small sigh. She did not like operating like this; her ship compromised, and likely now being hunted by an enemy vessel. Almost without thinking, she began to consider the likelihood of the *Nevathu* escaping the rift and Kondaii space, and she did not like the scenarios she was beginning to envision.

Enough of that unproductive nonsense, she mused, chastising herself. *Focus.*

She noted Sirad moving closer to her, and she regarded him as she continued to oversee her officers tending to their work. "Something else?"

The subcommander nodded, and when he spoke it was in a voice she could only hear with effort. "The human was being truthful." His words carried a note of surprise.

"It would seem so," Vathrael said.

In a rare display of emotion, the corners of Sirad's

mouth curved upward in the slightest suggestion of a smile. "Does this mean you trust him?"

"Do not be fooled by everything you have read or heard," Vathrael said, her tone one of caution. "Humans are not the treacherous thugs our leaders would have us believe them to be." Her own encounters with representatives of Earth had given her at least some insight in that regard.

"But do you trust him?" Sirad pressed.

After a moment, Vathrael shook her head. "No."

At least, not yet.

TWELVE

"Romulan vessel decloaking!"

Montgomery Scott glanced toward the science station in time to see Ensign Pavel Chekov push himself away from the console and point at the main viewscreen and the image of the energy field displayed upon it. Near the lower left corner of the screen, Scott could see something small and dark coalescing into existence.

Or trying to, anyway.

"Looks like your detection program worked, Mister Scott," Sulu said from where he had retaken his normal post at the helm console.

Scott nodded. "Aye, though you can be sure the Romulans will be working to make sure we can't get away with that for very long." He leaned forward in the command chair, scowling as he regarded the image of what looked to be the ghostlike image of a Romulan scout ship fading in and out of visibility. "Something's not right," he said, more to himself than anyone else. "Is the rift interfering with their cloaking device?"

"That'd be my guess, sir," Chekov replied, his attention divided between the sensor readouts at his station and the viewscreen. "It's completely inactive now. The rift is definitely reacting to the ship's presence, and the readings I'm collecting are similar though not exactly the same as those recorded by the *Huang Zhong* during its passage through the field." Leaning over to peer once more into his scanner, the ensign added, "I'm also picking up fluctuations in their warp and impulse engines, sir. Again, they're not identical to what we already have recorded, but very close."

"It might have something to do with their engine design," Scott said, perching his right elbow on the arm of the command chair and reaching up to stroke his chin. "Are you able to track them?"

Still hovering over his station, Chekov replied, "Partially, sir. The rift's still interfering with our attempts to scan past the rift's outer boundary, but I've got a lock on the Romulan ship now. Its shields look to be taking a beating."

"That doesn't seem to make any sense, now, does it?" Scott asked, trying to rationalize Chekov's reports from what he had already seen take place with the passage not only of Dolysian freight haulers in and out of the rift, but also that of *Enterprise* shuttlecraft. No disruptions or even fluctuations from the rift had been recorded. Though it now was obvious that the field was reacting in negative fashion to something unique to various forms of warp drive, the exact nature of the conduit's response remained cloaked in mystery. "What is it about warp engines that's making this thing throw such a fit?" Setting aside the question for the moment, Scott said to Sulu, "Get us as close as you can to the edge of the rift without getting it mad at us, but no closer than ten thousand kilometers."

"Aye, aye, sir," Sulu replied, his hands already moving across his console to carry out the order.

Looking over his shoulder to the communications

station, Scott asked, "Lieutenant M'Ress, have you picked up any transmissions from them?"

The Caitian shook her head. "No, sir. Nothing."

"Open a hailing frequency to them, then," Scott said. "Let them know we're standing by to render assistance if necessary."

The order earned Scott a cautionary glance from Sulu. "You don't really think they'll answer us, do you?"

Scott sighed. "I really have no idea, but I'd like to avoid a shoot-out if at all possible." Though the Dolysian system was in nonaligned space, it was close enough to Romulan territory that it was understandable for the empire to be curious about the presence of Federation starships in the area. Also, Scott figured that their longtime adversary would be interested in the enigmatic rift and whatever might be causing it. Despite this, he saw no reason for the situation to deteriorate to hostilities. If anyone was going to fire first, it would have to be the Romulans.

Assuming they manage to get out of that rift without their ship coming apart.

"Mister Scott," M'Ress said from behind him. "I'm not getting any response to our hails. I can't be sure they're even receiving our transmission."

"Maybe the rift's interfering with their communications," Sulu offered.

"Or they're just too busy to answer," Scott said. "Mister Chekov, anything new on the sensors?"

Turning from his station, the ensign replied, "The intensity of the field's reaction looks to be increasing. I'm seeing severe fluctuations in the field corresponding to the Romulan ship's position within the rift." He shook his head. "I don't know how they've managed to make it as far as they have."

"Romulan vessels are known for their robust construction," said Lieutenant Arex from where he sat at the navigator's console, having taken over for Chekov while the ensign manned the science station. Shifting in his seat, the Triexian turned his oversized, elongated head to face Scott. "My species learned that during our first encounters with the empire more than a century ago."

Scott nodded in agreement, recalling from his studies at the Academy that Triex's initial encounters with the Romulan Star Empire, which predated the Earth-Romulan War, were not dissimilar to the first confrontations experienced by ships of humanity's then-budding Starfleet. "Aye, they're tough beasties, all right."

An alert indicator from Chekov's station made the young officer look up in confusion. "Mister Scott, the field is beginning to stabilize."

Sitting up straighter in his chair, the engineer frowned at this latest news. "What do you mean?"

"I don't know, sir," Chekov replied as he once more directed his attention to his scanner. A moment later, he added, "I'm not detecting readings from the Romulan ship's warp drive. I think it's been taken offline."

"Did they sustain damage?" Scott asked.

Chekov shook his head. "The sensors didn't register anything. From what I can tell, the engines were deliberately deactivated."

Interesting, Scott mused, unable to suppress a small, wry grin. "So, they were listening to our initial hail, after all."

Looking up from his scanner, Chekov reported, "The field readings have returned to their original levels, and I'm no longer able to track the Romulan ship, sir. I think they may have made it to the other side of the rift."

"And we're still not able to scan to the other side," Scott said, frowning, "even this close to the field?"

"No, sir," Chekov said. "The beams scatter as they attempt to penetrate the farther they travel into the rift."

That did not sit at all well with the engineer. Swiveling the command chair so that he faced the communications station, he eyed M'Ress. "Lieutenant, we need to get word to the captain and the landing parties. Let them know what's happened and to be on the lookout for that Romulan ship. Make sure to repeat the message at least a few times. Hopefully that'll help punch everything through the static." With communications to and from the other side of the rift compromised by the energy field of the barrier itself, it was Lieutenant Uhura who had suggested using tight-beam transmissions broadcast through the *Enterprise*'s navigational deflector array, which would in turn be received by similar apparatus carried aboard the various shuttlecraft tasked with transiting the conduit. The resulting connections were still laden with static and other interference, but at least Captain Kirk and the other landing parties were not completely cut off from the ship while in or near the Gralafi planetoid.

M'Ress replied while turning back to her console and setting to the task of establishing the communications link. "Aye, aye, sir. Setting up the transmission now."

His attention on the main viewscreen and the image of the energy field displayed upon it, Chekov said, "I wonder if retuning the sensors to a tighter focus might help? Like we did with communications? We would probably lose some resolution, but we might at least be able to get a look past the barrier."

Scott nodded. "Aye, that might work. Notify engineering

of your plan, and have them get a team on it. In the meantime, Lieutenant M'Ress, send Lieutenant Kyle the updates I made to the search program, and have him detail the *Einstein*'s sensors to scanning for the Romulan ship." The sensor suite carried aboard the shuttlecraft did not carry the same power or range as the *Enterprise*'s systems, but it would have to serve, at least for the time being. "And inform all of our teams that the salvage operation is suspended until further notice." As much as he might not like it, the *Huang Zhong*, Scott decided, would have to wait, as he had no desire to expose more than necessary any more of the ship's shuttlecraft to potential danger.

There was, he realized, at least one more matter requiring attention, and one that was not at all minor. "M'Ress, prepare a message for transmission to the Dolysian governments and the heads of the mining operation. Alert them to the Romulans' presence, and that we advise them to suspend their freight transfer operations until the area is secured and the situation is under control."

"That won't go over very well," Arex said. "From everything we've been told, the shipping schedule to and from the mining colony doesn't have a lot of room for delays, and they've got only a few days to complete all their shipments before the rift closes."

"All true, Lieutenant," Scott replied, "but we have to warn them, at least." There would be nothing he could do if the Dolysians elected to continue their shipping flights, and in doing so they likely would complicate the situation so far as the Romulans were concerned. With their scout ship somewhere on the other side of the rift, possibly damaged, would its commander endeavor to avoid contact with Dolysian vessels? There was no way to know that for sure.

Despite Captain Kirk's wishes to keep the *Enterprise* outside the unexplained energy field, Scott now was giving serious thought to powering down the ship's warp engines in order to facilitate traversing the conduit.

"I can see what you're thinking," Sulu said, and Scott turned to see the helm officer regarding him with a knowing expression. "If we do that, we'd be compromising power to the weapons and the shields."

Releasing a tired sigh, Scott replied, "Aye, but you can figure on the Romulans being in the same predicament. We might even have an advantage, if we can get through the rift without sustaining damage like they did. Besides, I don't like the idea of the captain and our landing parties over there without the *Enterprise* to look after them." Glancing over his shoulder, he said, "Lieutenant M'Ress, let's get on sending that message to Captain Kirk."

After that, Scott knew, there was precious little he could do except wait.

THIRTEEN

Sitting in the co-pilot's seat of the *Galileo II*, Kirk rested his elbows on the arms of his chair, making a conscious choice to keep his hands at rest in his lap. Though he preferred to operate the controls himself on those rare occasions when he left the *Enterprise* aboard one of its shuttlecraft, he was doing his best to heed McCoy's advice—as the doctor had stated with no hint of eloquence—by "letting his people do their damned jobs." In this case, that meant allowing Lieutenant Uhura to guide the craft, rather than forcing her to sit idle as so many other junior officers and would-be pilots had been required to do during previous shuttle outings with their captain.

As though reading his mind, Uhura said, "I didn't have a chance to say it before, Captain, but thank you for bringing me along. I don't get to leave the ship very often, much less practice my shuttle piloting skills. I thought I might be a little rusty, but it all seems to be coming back to me."

"You are a qualified pilot, Lieutenant," said Ambassador Sortino from where she sat in the chair behind Kirk. "Are you not?"

Uhura nodded. "I am, Ambassador. I'm not as good as Mister Sulu, but I can hold my own."

"You needn't worry about your skills, Lieutenant," Kirk said, adopting a mentoring tone. "I dare say you could give

Sulu a run for his money." It was not meant as simple reas-
suring praise; Kirk was an accomplished pilot in his own
right, and recognized Uhura's natural affinity for controlling
the craft. Her deft touch had been evident from the moment
she had guided the *Galileo* out of the *Enterprise*'s shuttlebay,
and reinforced by one of the softest, precise manual land-
ings he had ever witnessed when the craft had arrived at
the grounds of the Unified Leadership Council on Dolysia.
Following the meeting with Chancellor Wiladra and Spock's
contact from Gralafi, the captain had let Uhura take the
craft's controls again as they, along with Sortino, set off for
the mysterious planetoid. The communications officer had
not balked at the notion of piloting the shuttle through the
energy field surrounding Gralafi, though Kirk himself had
experienced some measure of anxiety despite reports from
Spock and other *Enterprise* personnel that their respective
transits of the rift had been uneventful.

Lucky us, I suppose. The sobering thought seemed to
echo in Kirk's mind as he considered the ill-fated *Huang
Zhong* and its crew, and his mood darkened even further
as he contemplated the nature of the alien technology
responsible for the science vessel's crash. Even with the
preliminary reports offered by survivors as to what had
happened, it still had been more than a bit sobering to hear
Spock's confirmation of those initial suspicions. The greater
shock had come with the first officer's preliminary report
about the possible origins of what he and his team had
discovered.

"You look pensive, Captain," Sortino said as the *Galileo*'s engines powered down and Uhura keyed the control
to open the craft's main hatch. "What's on your mind? The
Kalandans?"

Kirk nodded, rising from his seat and moving to the now-open hatch. "We know so little about them, even after the time we spent exploring that planet they created. It's amazing that we might find another example of their technology."

Sortino asked, "How far away are we from that other planet you found?"

"I'm not sure," Kirk said as he exited the shuttlecraft, stepping down to the ground and taking his first look at the plateau that served as the *Galileo*'s landing site. "Two, maybe three weeks at maximum warp." He frowned, remembering what he could of the star charts of the region he had reviewed while the *Enterprise* was in transit to the Kondaii system. At the time, he recalled making note of the fact that they were in the same general vicinity as the Kalandan planet. It was the ship's first time back in this area of space since that original encounter with the artificial world, which ostensibly was built by the Kalandans as an outpost for reasons that remained shrouded in mystery.

"Given what we know of their technology," Uhura said as she joined Kirk outside the shuttlecraft, "that probably wasn't a huge distance to them. It doesn't sound all that crazy to think they might have more than one planet in the same neighborhood. And it wouldn't be the first time we've run into an alien species with that kind of ability."

"Lieutenant, has anyone ever told you that you can sound a lot like Spock when you want to?" Kirk asked, smiling.

The comment elicited a chuckle from Sortino as she exited the *Galileo*, then regarded Kirk as she stepped down next to him. "Remind me to read your report about that other planet when we get back to the *Enterprise*. I've never heard anything like that before."

Kirk replied, "I'll make the file available to you, Ambassador. I was planning to review it myself." The subsequent missions he and his crew had carried out were seeing to it that the less-interesting details of that particular incident were starting to blur. On the other hand, etched forever in his memory were the finer points of the time he had spent on that enigmatic world, stranded along with McCoy, Sulu, and Lieutenant Robert D'Amato—an *Enterprise* geologist who had lost his life to the planet's automated defense system.

Looking about the plateau, Kirk saw that it was bordered on three sides by hills and on the fourth by a yawning chasm that had looked imposing from the air as the shuttle made its descent. The shuttlecraft *Columbus*, to which Spock and his science team had been assigned, sat fifty meters behind the *Galileo*, closer to the edge of the massive ravine. Though the ground beneath his feet was little more than dirt and flat rock, lush vegetation covered the hillsides rising up around them. Unlike the areas near the mining colony, the air here was crisp and clean, and Kirk thought he detected the faintest hint of something sweet tickling his nostrils. As far as he could tell and with the exception of the two shuttlecraft, the region looked to be untouched by the intrusions of the Dolysians, or anyone else, for that matter.

"Absolutely beautiful," Sortino said. "This view is spectacular."

"No argument here," Kirk replied, before looking over his shoulder. "Lieutenant, how far are we from the Havreltipa colony?"

As she stepped away from the *Galileo*'s hatch, the communications officer replied, "About four thousand kilometers, sir; not quite halfway around the planetoid. According to the reports I've read, the Dolysians have explored most of the surface, though largely for the purposes of prospecting potential mining sites. This region apparently lacks any appreciable deposits of erinadium, so it's unlikely any real mining efforts will be established here."

"Coincidence?" Sortino asked, "Or just plain good luck for the Kalandans?"

"Excellent questions," Kirk said, conceding the ambassador's point. "As Mister Spock might say, it's logical to assume that if the Kalandans are responsible for what he found, then they were here thousands of years ago, well before the Dolysian people advanced to a technological level that allowed them to travel here from their homeworld. They would've known about the Dolysians, and perhaps even foresaw their interest in this planet. Maybe they even anticipated how the Dolysians would find erinadium useful."

Uhura said, "It wouldn't be the craziest thing we've ever run into, that's for sure."

"Precognition?" Sortino asked.

"Maybe," Kirk replied. "For all we know, the Kalandans may even have had plans for the Dolysians once they achieved a predetermined level of technological advancement." He glanced at Uhura. "It wouldn't be the first time we'd run into something like *that*, either."

Sortino smiled, shaking her head. "I need to review your mission reports, Captain. I've heard the stories, but somehow I think I'm missing all the really good stuff."

Looking around, Kirk asked, "Well, we're here, and the *Columbus* is here. Where's Spock? He said he'd meet us." Looking to Uhura, he prompted, "Lieutenant?"

"I'm not picking up any life readings, Captain," Uhura

replied over the quiet whine of the tricorder she held in her hands. "Wherever they are, they're not in the shuttle, or anywhere nearby."

Kirk reached for the communicator on his hip and flipped it open. "Kirk to Spock," he said as he held the device near his mouth. "Come in, Spock."

The first officer's voice replied from the communicator's speaker grille, "*Spock here, Captain. We noted your arrival, and I should be joining you in short order.*"

"Are you invisible, Mister Spock?" Kirk asked.

"*In a manner of speaking, sir.*"

A low rumbling sound rolled across the plateau from the direction of the hillside farthest from the chasm. Kirk turned in that direction, half expecting to see an avalanche despite the admitted absurdity of such a notion. Still, he was relieved to see no surge of tumbling rocks bearing down on them. Instead, there was only Spock, standing no more than twenty meters from them, before an opening in the hillside that Kirk was certain had not been there upon their arrival.

"Greetings, Captain," the Vulcan called out, his voice carrying across the open ground. His left hand gripped the strap of the tricorder he wore slung over his right shoulder, and Kirk noted the dirt stains on his uniform tunic and trousers.

"It looks like you've been busy, Spock," Kirk said as he and the others began walking toward him.

The first officer nodded, "Indeed we have. I think you will find what we've discovered below to be most interesting." As the landing party drew closer, he inclined his head toward Sortino. "Greetings to you, as well, Ambassador."

"And to you, Mister Spock." She gestured toward

the gap in the hill's rocky façade. "You make quite the entrance."

"No kidding," Kirk added. "That's some trick."

In response to the comments, Spock's right eyebrow arched as he turned to regard the opening from which he had emerged. "To borrow a human colloquialism, Captain, I believe that you have not yet seen anything."

In his travels, Kirk had seen his share of alien technology. While much of it was less advanced than that with which he normally interacted, there were those occasions where the sophistication of a computer or other mechanism far surpassed anything with which he was familiar. The Preservers, the Fabrini, and the Shedai, along with so many others, fell into that latter category. As he beheld the subterranean storehouse into which Spock had led him, he once again was reminded that the Kalandans also stood among such august company.

"It really is them, isn't it, Spock?" Kirk asked as he stepped through the archway leading from the underground passage into the chamber. Even as he asked the question, he already had his answer. Though some of the details were different, they were outnumbered by the similarities to the technology he recalled studying back on that unnamed world: the small, seemingly irrelevant planet guarded by the lone sentinel, Losira. "The Kalandans, again?"

"Even without the prerecorded message we found, the parallels in technology and instrumentation are unmistakable, Captain," his first officer replied as he stepped around Kirk on his way to a nearby bank of what could only be control consoles designed for unknown users. "There are some divergences, of course. First and foremost, this planetoid does not show any evidence of having been artificially created, as was the case with Kalandan Outpost 1." Kirk nodded at his friend's use of the planetary designator he had given to the peculiar, artificially created world, which the Kalandans had opted not to name—at least so far as Spock had been able to determine during his time spent studying the ancient technology they had found there.

Spock continued, "Just based on what we've been able to find to this point, the planetoid belongs to the Kondaii system, and was appropriated by the Kalandans for their use many thousands of years ago, well before the Dolysian society evolved on their world." He indicated his tricorder. "Our readings indicate that this chamber and the equipment in it is much older than what we encountered on the other outpost planet."

At one of the nearby consoles, where he had been working when Spock led Kirk and the others into the room, Lieutenant Boma turned and pointed to the cube hanging at the center of the room. "That's a computer control mechanism, sir. Our tricorder scans show that it has power and other connections running through the rock to and from other chambers in this complex. Some of those rooms have devices like this one, while others don't."

"A kind of network?" asked Uhura as she paced the room's perimeter, examining the different consoles and banks of controls.

Boma replied, "That seems to be the case. The whole facility actually looks to be laid out that way, with five clusters of rooms and other compartments all networked by a series of tunnels, with other, larger passages connecting the clusters. Each cluster looks to have its own power source, environmental control, and other self-contained systems, almost as though sections were designed to run independently of each other." Shaking his head, Boma blew out an audible breath. "We're still figuring a lot of it out, but Mister Spock's knowledge of Kalandan technology from your previous encounter is definitely coming in handy." Redirecting his attention to Kirk, he added, "Captain, we found what looks to be the Kalandan version of a medical bay in one room. Doctor McCoy's investigating it now."

Nodding at the report, Kirk held out his hand to Boma. "I'm sorry about the loss of your shipmates, Lieutenant."

Boma took the proffered hand and shook it, his expression turning solemn. "I appreciate that, sir."

"How are you holding up?"

As though uncertain as to the best response for the question, Boma paused, casting his gaze toward the floor before replying, "It's hard, thinking about it, but working helps. I was angry at first, but it's hard to be angry at people who've been dead for thousands of years." He sighed, shaking his head. "The *Huang Zhong* was a small ship, so we got to know each other pretty well, very quickly. They were good people, from Captain Arens on down."

"I'm sure they were," Kirk replied. The last time he had seen Boma was on the day the lieutenant had requested his transfer from the *Enterprise*, that act coming after Kirk had been forced to enter a notation into the younger officer's service record regarding his conduct during the events on Taurus II. His insubordination and near-mutinous conduct toward Spock on that occasion might have garnered him a court-martial from another starship captain, but Kirk had opted for nonjudicial punishment and a formal reprimand. It was obvious at the time that Boma regretted his actions, and even though Spock himself never again discussed the matter, Boma still felt that a new assignment to another ship or base was the best way to put the incident behind him. Kirk had tried to convince him otherwise, but to no avail.

Joining them after taking a circuit around the room and looking over some of the mechanisms for herself, Ambassador Sortino said, "The sophistication of the design looks astounding."

Spock turned from where he had taken up station at an adjacent console. "Indeed it is, Ambassador, though it also is worth noting that despite this equipment's relative complexity, it still lacks some of the more refined features we discovered on Kalandan Outpost 1."

"Well, it's a damned sight more advanced than anything I ever saw on border patrol," the ambassador countered.

Spock said, "Although our tricorders were not able to detect it, the system's own internal monitoring equipment revealed the presence of a massive energy plant, far beneath us and separated from the rest of the complex. Based on the amount of power being generated, it would appear that the plant is responsible for the energy field surrounding Gralafi."

"The source of the rift is here?" Kirk asked. "In this complex? If that's the case, we should be able to find evidence of broadcast arrays or some other means of focusing that power into space, right?"

Shaking his head, the Vulcan answered, "Only in a manner of speaking, sir. From what we've been able to determine, the planetoid itself, with its rich variety of particular mineral ores, acts as a form of antenna. Indeed, Gralafi and the energy barrier encompassing it would seem to be intrinsically linked. As Mister Boma earlier hypothesized and the projection of Meyeliri confirmed, the field has several uses, simple protection being its primary function. However, it does conduct the equivalent of covert sensor scans on any vessel passing through it, during which it assesses each ship's threat potential."

"That's incredible," Sortino said. "An entire planet, deliberately engineered to act as an energy field generator. Imagine what you could do with that kind of power, and the ability to broadcast it on such a scale. What's even more amazing is that these systems are still functioning even after all this time."

"Though not without issue," Spock replied. "Based on what we have learned about the generation of the energy field, the interval during which it remains open is much longer than originally intended. There would appear to be a fault in the control mechanisms overseeing the barrier—one from which the Dolysians have benefited for generations."

"How about that?" Kirk said, shaking his head. "One civilization's mistake or misfortune is another's gain, only in this case, it's an innocent reward, rather than something obtained via theft or conquest." He wondered how this revelation would affect Dolysian society once the truth became known. "So, this place just came on line once you found a way in?"

Spock replied, "We found evidence of very few systems in an active state, though other systems did later come on line. It appears some form of passive detection process is monitoring conditions within the complex, and reacts to the presence of living beings. For example, the air in these caves seemed rather stale and oxygen depleted, and it was cooler than it is now. An environmental control system has been activated in response to our being here."

Stepping closer, Boma gestured toward the stations. "And notice the lack of dust? Some kind of automated maintenance protocols are probably responsible for that."

"Precisely, Lieutenant," Spock said, nodding in approval. "There doubtless will be other systems which will cycle through periods of activity and dormancy, the longer we remain here."

Kirk cleared his throat and waved once more toward the suspended cube with its illuminated, rotating light color display. "Speaking of Kalandan technology reacting to our presence, you're sure there's no Losira lurking about, right? Or any of her brothers or sisters, for that matter?"

"Our initial scans have shown no mechanism comparable to the internal defense system we found on the Kalandan outpost," Spock said. "Nor have we found any indications of any device like the one which transported the *Enterprise* away from the outpost during our initial encounter with that planet. Based on our studies of that facility, I believe that the equipment powering and controlling its defense system is more advanced than anything we've so far discovered here. I suspect that any internal security systems will be as comparably primitive as the other mechanisms here."

Kirk asked, "And no mysterious portals that let you leap entire galaxies in a single bound?"

"We have found no indications of any such technology, Captain," Spock replied, his expression, as always, unreadable.

"I suppose that's a relief," Kirk said. Then, eyeing the cube again, he sighed. "All we need right now is this place doing its damnedest to kill us." No sooner did the words leave his mouth than he regretted the casual air of his statement. He glanced to Sortino, though the ambassador seemed not to have heard the comment. Despite Spock's assurances—such as they were—Kirk still was troubled by the possibility of having to face off against some ancient Kalandan security system, particularly given the current situation.

Commander Scott's report about the infiltration of a Romulan ship into the Kondaii system and its apparent traversing of the conduit had placed him on edge. He had already asked Sortino to alert the Kondaii government and mining colony leaders about the new development, and also had apprised all *Enterprise* personnel here on the planetoid, and concurred with Scott's recommendation that shuttle missions to and from the ship be suspended until further notice. If the Romulans decided to push a confrontation with him or his people here and now, there would be precious little Kirk could do about it unless and until he ordered the *Enterprise* into the rift. On the other hand, it had been nearly two hours since Scotty's report and the last verified sensor scans of the Romulan ship, which the chief engineer believed to have been damaged during its transit of the rift. For all anyone knew, the Romulan ship was disabled, drifting somewhere in space near Gralafi, and in no condition to present any sort of threat.

Wishful thinking, Kirk mused, rebuking himself.

Turning from the console she had been studying, Sortino asked, "Mister Spock, you're able to operate this equipment?"

The first officer replied, "Only to a point, Ambassador. Some of the Kalandan text is similar if not identical to script we found on the other outpost, whereas other samples are unfamiliar to me." To Kirk, he said, "Captain, I have scanned those marked surfaces we have encountered since entering the complex. I will require a link to the *Enterprise* main computer in order to proceed with my analysis, though due to interference from the energy field, such a connection is not reliable at the present time."

Kirk nodded at the report. "The next time we check in with Scotty, we'll ask him to figure out a way to link one of the shuttlecraft onboard computers to the *Enterprise*. In the meantime, keep doing what you can with what we have here."

From behind him, he heard Uhura say, "Maybe Kyle's team at the *Huang Zhong* site can find a portable computer we can use. We could at least bring that down here."

"An excellent suggestion, Lieutenant," Spock replied. He started to say something else, but his words were cut off by a new sound in the chamber rising above the omnipresent hum of the central cube. All around the room, control stations were coming to life, their flat black panels illuminating from within to display an array of blinking, shifting graphics and scrolling alien script.

"What's that about?" Sortino asked.

Without replying, Spock indicated for Boma to come with him toward one set of control banks, and Kirk watched as the two men began working in concert. Spock's fingers moved across the surface of one console as though the Vulcan had been operating the equipment for years, whereas Boma's efforts were more hesitant.

"Whatever it is," Boma said, pointing to one large, detailed graphic displayed on the wall panel between them, "it's activating systems throughout the network."

Spock nodded. "Agreed." As his right hand continued to work the controls, he used his left hand to activate his tricorder and raise the device so that he could observe its miniaturized display. "If I am correctly interpreting these readings, it appears to be the very defense system we have been seeking."

"An internal system, Spock?" Kirk asked, already feeling the first tinge of anxiety as he recalled the guardian Losira from the other Kalandan outpost. He felt his hand moving to the phaser at his waist and forced himself to arrest that motion before he could retrieve the weapon.

After a moment, Spock turned from the control console. "No, Captain. I believe the complex's central computer has enabled the planetary defense network responsible for attacking the *Huang Zhong*. It appears to have reactivated in response to a new threat it has detected in orbit above this planetoid."

"The Romulans," Uhura said. "It has to be."

Spock's eyebrow rose once more. "That, Lieutenant, would appear to be an accurate assessment."

FOURTEEN

Vathrael reclined on the small, narrow bed in her private quarters, leaning back against the headrest so that she could see the computer monitor sitting atop the desk at the room's far wall. The back of her head rested against the cool metal of the bulkhead, and she was able to feel the slight reverberation in the plating as generated by the *Nevathu*'s impulse drive. Experience told her that the sound and the feel of the engines were not quite correct; the pitch was lower than it should be. Mylas, the ship's engineer as well as one of her oldest friends, had made rapid progress repairing the damage inflicted upon the propulsion system by the odd energy field, but his work, so far as Vathrael was concerned, was not yet complete. Repairs to the cloaking generator were still under way, leaving the *Nevathu* visible, and vulnerable.

And Mylas will tend to it, Vathrael thought as the inclination to request an update from the engineer presented itself, even though she had received a status report at the beginning of this duty period. *He will finish with greater speed if he is allowed to work.*

Opting to leave the engineer to his duties without further interruptions, Vathrael instead returned her attention to the image of the planetoid now displayed on the computer monitor. It was small, yet it presented the appearance of a lush, fertile world. Continents and oceans were visible beneath a thin cloud cover, and for a moment her eyes were drawn to what looked to be a fierce storm over one of the oceans in the planet's southern hemisphere. The storm seemed to be moving toward one of the major land masses, but Vathrael knew from preliminary sensor reports that, with the exception of lower-order indigenous life-forms, the affected region of the planetoid was uninhabited.

Take caution in your thoughts, Commander, she chided herself. *Wylenn would have your head if he heard you being so dismissive of such things.* The thought of her husband berating her on this topic brought Vathrael no small amount of amusement. On Romulus, Wylenn was an outspoken proponent of environmental and wildlife conservation initiatives. He was always lending his time and energy to a number of efforts aimed at raising awareness of the plight of endangered plant and animal species, and the need for industrialized and expanding populations to be mindful and caring of the world that was their home. As he often argued when facing down government officials on this or related topics, the Romulan Empire might be comprised of many planets, but there was only one Romulus, and it needed to be nurtured, not pillaged until it was drained of every last natural resource.

This was not a cause Wylenn had adopted on his own, of course; such activism had been a hallmark of his family for generations. His paternal grandmother was one of the first advocates for preventing the dangerous process of dilithium refining from being moved to Romulus, and instead keeping it on the planet's sister world, Remus, from the center of which the ore was extracted in massive quantities. The refining process carried with it significant risks and resulted in the creation of hazardous by-products that were better kept away from the lush, fertile Romulan homeworld and contained upon the otherwise useless planet from which the mineral came in the first place.

As for Wylenn and his family, they had from time to time run afoul of aggrieved Romulan officials, though their particular brand of advocacy had always remained within the scope of legal protest. Still, Wylenn's efforts often rankled the sort of stuffy bureaucrats for whom Vathrael had little use, and it was but one of her husband's many qualities that had made her fall in love with him in the first place.

"Oh, do I miss you," she said to no one, her eyes moving from the computer monitor to the holographic image of Wylenn sitting next to it on the desk. The image showed him in repose, sitting on the low wall of the garden he had planted behind their home in Dartha, the capital city on Romulus. She had captured him in a moment of spontaneity while his attention was focused on his work, a wistful smile on his face as he tended to one of the garden's exotic plants. Vathrael had never been able to explain, to him or herself or anyone else, what it was she had found so alluring about him on that occasion, and she had long ago given up such futile efforts. It was enough that he had captivated her that day, just as he had from the moment they had first met.

A sharp, low-pitched tone sounded from her desk, signifying the activation of the *Nevathu*'s internal communications system. "*Commander Vathrael,*" a voice said, sounding tiny and distant and swathed in a blanket of static buzzing from the receiver, "*your presence is requested on the bridge.*" The disruption in the connection told Vathrael that the damage inflicted upon the communications systems during the ship's travel through the peculiar energy field had not yet been repaired.

Sighing in resignation, Vathrael moved to the edge of the bed and retrieved her boots before donning her uniform tunic and sash. "Duty calls, my husband," she said, her eyes lingering on Wylenn's image for an additional moment as she dressed herself. After verifying that everything was where it was supposed to be and that she once again presented the proper appearance of a Romulan ship commander, she exited her quarters and began the brief transit to the bridge. The first thing she noticed upon stepping into the corridor was the smell of something burning, accompanied by the unmistakable sound of a plasma torch in operation. As she came abreast of a junction, Vathrael saw a team of two centurions working before an open bulkhead paneling, behind which she knew were components of the ventilation and communications systems. It took her a moment to recall the chief engineer's report about various communications relays scattered throughout the ship requiring replacement.

She did not approach her subordinates to inquire about their status, knowing they would only stop their work in order to observe proper military protocol. Unlike some of her peers, who never seemed to grow weary of exploiting the positions they occupied and the power they commanded, Vathrael had no use for such ceremonial tripe even when formality was appropriate. There were times when it was necessary and even desirable, but the fewer and more infrequent they were, the happier it made her. Aboard ship, she preferred to dispense with it when the crew was engaged in carrying out their duties. As a consequence, those under her command demonstrated their loyalty as a natural outgrowth of their respect for her, rather than simply obeying orders.

Besides, she reminded herself, *I have Sirad to enforce all of that ritualistic nonsense.*

Stepping onto the bridge, the first thing to catch Vathrael's attention was the subcommander standing next to Centurion Betria, with the young officer focused on the controls, displays, and indicators of the sensor station at the room's control hub.

"Commander," Sirad said as he noted her arrival, and stepped away from the station in order to afford Vathrael an unencumbered view of the console's displays. "Betria has found something interesting."

Given his cue, the centurion turned to face Vathrael. "Commander, our sensors have detected faint power readings coming from beneath the surface of the planet."

The report caused Vathrael to turn toward the room's main viewing screen, upon which was displayed the image of the small, seemingly insignificant world that nevertheless was of great value to the system's indigenous population. "I assume you're about to tell me that these power readings are inconsistent with whatever technology the Dolysians have at their disposal?"

"It would seem so," Sirad said. "In fact, the sensors only detected a minor fluctuation during our scans of the surface, but attempts to localize and identify it were inconclusive." He nodded toward Betria. "It was only after the centurion retuned the sensors that the readings became clear enough to track with any degree of accuracy."

Vathrael said, "I'm afraid I don't understand. Are you saying the power reading was somehow masked from normal detection?"

"Yes, Commander," Betria replied. "If what we know of Dolysian technology is true, they would not possess anything capable of detecting the power readings in any form."

Crossing her arms, Vathrael frowned. "If that's the case, then it's likely the Starfleet ship and its people have detected these readings, as well. They're nothing if not resourceful."

"We've already located two of their transport craft on the surface near one location where the readings were detected," Sirad said.

What could they have found? The question teased Vathrael. Might it be some kind of ancient technology, from a long-dead civilization? Though her adult life had been spent in service to the military, Vathrael had as a child been interested in a number of topics that held no place in such an organization. Among those intellectual pursuits was archeology, which had begun as a simple exploration into the history of the Romulan people and how they had come to form their own society after long ago separating from their Vulcan brothers and sisters. That fascination soon extended to other cultures, starting with worlds that had been folded into the Romulan Empire and later those with which her people had interacted. She had even come to learn during her studies that Earthers in particular harbored an intriguing past, something she had discovered after forcing herself to look past the propaganda and even outright lies disseminated about them. From what she had read, the humans' own planet was home to ruins and artifacts from primordial civilizations about which almost nothing was known. Perhaps it was this lack of information, this inability to trace with absolute certainty the origins of their species, that pulled Earthers to the stars in search of knowledge and even answers as to their own heritage?

You're a romantic, Vathrael.

"Commander," Betria said, having returned to his station and resumed overseeing his instruments, "I'm detecting new power sources, from locations all across the planet." He paused, and Vathrael watched as he frowned, his fingers tapping a series of controls, which had the effect of altering the data being displayed. "Seventy-six different sites, all of them subterranean."

Stepping closer, Vathrael peered at the sensor displays. "This is the first time this has happened?"

Terius nodded. "So far as I'm aware, Commander. I've only just been able to conduct a full sensor sweep after the modifications which were required to better discern the power readings." He frowned, shaking his head. "It's almost as though something has reacted to our sensor probes."

Something about that troubled Vathrael. "Raise our alert status," she snapped, looking to Sirad. "Activate our defensive screens."

"Commander?" he said, his expression turning to one of concern. "What are you—?"

The question was cut off by a new alarm echoing throughout the bridge, accompanied by the momentary flickering of overhead illumination and the sound of the *Nevathu*'s engines increasing in pitch as new demands were placed upon them. Glancing to the weapons station, Vathrael saw that the defense systems had activated on their own, which only happened in response to a threat detected by the ship's sensors.

"We are being scanned," shouted Centurion Terius over the alarms. The weapons officer did not turn from his console as he reported, "It's a high-intensity beam, directed at us from the surface."

After signaling to another centurion to extinguish the alert sirens, Sirad said, "It could be a targeting scanner."

Nodding in agreement with the report as well as at the validation of her own instincts, Vathrael pointed to the centurion at the helm station. "Janotra, stand by for evasive maneuvers, and prepare to leave orbit." She was not yet ready to retreat, at least not until she could learn more about whatever might now be curious about her ship, but that did not mean she wanted to take any undue risks.

"What about our weapons, Commander?"

Vathrael studied the information streaming across the monitors at Betria's station. "From this distance, only the main plasma weapon has sufficient force to penetrate through the planet's surface to where these power readings appear to be originating." Using the weapon would tax the vessel's already strained power systems, particularly with the warp engines still inactive following the *Nevathu*'s passing through the energy field. Still, if they were being targeted, she did not wish to be caught unprepared to respond to any hazard posed by the planet's still-unknown technology. After a moment, she nodded. "Weapons officer, route power to the plasma cannon."

To her left, Centurion Odera turned from the communications station. "Commander, I am detecting an outgoing message from the planet. It appears to be someone from the Starfleet ship."

"Put it through, and activate the translation matrix," Vathrael ordered. A moment later the bridge's intercom system blared to life, with a male voice calling out from within a hiss of crackling static.

"*Romulan vessel, this is Captain James T. Kirk of the* Starship Enterprise. *Your ship is being targeted by a planetary defense system keyed to react to perceived threats. It can detect your engines, your deflector shields, and your weapons. The system is programmed to preemptively neutralize such threats. Your ship is in danger!"*

Sirad frowned. "Could he be lying? Trying to confuse us as he makes use of the alien technology?"

Though the same thought had occurred to Vathrael as she listened to the human's message, something behind the words convinced her that this was not a ruse. "I don't think so." Anxiety was beginning to gnaw at her. "Helm, increase our orbit to our maximum weapons range."

"Additional readings from the planet!" Terius called out, a new edge to the weapons officer's voice. "Massive energy buildup from multiple locations. I think they're weapons!"

"Helm!" Vathrael shouted. "Break orbit!" Even as she gave the order, she knew the ship's speed would still be compromised by the earlier damage. "Sirad, notify engineering that we need impulse power now!"

Moving around the central hub toward the helm station, the subcommander reached for a nearby communications panel and began relaying instructions. Vathrael did not listen or wait for whatever status update the chief engineer might provide. The matter was simple: if the impulse engines were not available, then there likely was little chance of the *Nevathu* being able to outrun anything directed at it from the surface. There would be no other option but to answer whatever attack might be coming. "Betria, have they locked on to us with any kind of targeting scan?"

"I don't know, Commander," the centurion replied, his nervousness now evident. "Wait. I'm picking up a new scan from one area of the planet. It's directing a beam at us."

That's it, Vathrael thought, now certain that the Starfleet captain and her own intuition had not been lying to her. "Route that information to helm and the tactical station. Terius, target those coordinates and stand by to fire."

Instead of acknowledging the order, the weapons officer suddenly shouted, "Incoming fire!"

"Evasive!" Vathrael ordered just before the proximity alert klaxon began wailing for attention. At the helm station, Janotra's hands were almost a blur as the centurion attempted to alter the *Nevathu*'s course of retreat from the planet. "Target the point of origin and return fire!"

"Brace for impact!" Sirad shouted, and Vathrael saw him lunge toward one of the central hub stations just before the deck seemed to fall from beneath his feet. Thrown to her right, Vathrael slammed into a nearby console, falling into the centurion doing his best to maintain his own balance. The entire ship lurched under the force of the brutal assault, with a chorus of new alarms sounding in the control room. Several of the displays and panels flickered, some of them remaining dark even after the ship began to stabilize.

At the weapons console, Terius reported, "We were struck by a focused ion beam. Our shields have dropped to less than half strength. The next strike will likely overpower them. We've returned fire, but our weapon seems to have had no effect!"

How was that possible? The plasma cannon was capable of inflicting unbelievable destructive power from distances far greater than that separating the *Nevathu* from its target on the planet's surface. How fortified was the enemy's weapons placements to withstand such an attack?

"Fire again!" Vathrael ordered, as the alarms once more

were silenced, "and route all available power to the shields, weapons, and propulsion." Shoving herself away from the console, she made her way to the helm station. "Move us out of here!" Without a functioning cloaking device, Vathrael knew that evasive action might prove futile.

Centurion Janotra shook his head. "I'm doing so, Commander, but our engines are still not operating at full capacity!"

Studying the helm display screens, Vathrael could see that retreat—already a questionable strategy given the circumstances—was no longer a realistic option. "Sirad, route power from propulsion to the shields."

The subcommander turned from where he now stood at the weapons station. "Commander?"

"Do it!" Vathrael barked. "We cannot escape, so we will have to stand and fight!" As she made the bold statement, she moved to the communications station and pressed the one control on the console reserved for use by only her and Sirad.

Watching her actions, Centurion Odera asked, "Commander? The distress message?"

Vathrael nodded, understanding the portion of the query the centurion had left unspoken. After all, the only reason to use the automated distress protocol was because the sender did not expect to be alive to receive a response. She had updated the information to be transmitted so that it automatically included relevant sensor telemetry and a brief status report regarding the rift's effects. Would it be enough to warn her superiors about this new threat? There was no way to be certain, she knew, and no time to worry about it.

"We are being scanned from several different points

on the planet's surface!" Betria reported, his voice rising in pitch and betraying his fear. "I'm picking up another energy buildup. . . . Wait! Incoming fire! Multiple attacks!"

Vathrael heard the order directing all remaining power from every other system to the shields bursting from her lips, but even as she spoke she knew it would be a futile gesture. Terius had already warned her about what to expect should the ship be hit a second time by the alien weapon. All around the bridge, the crew remained at their posts and carried out their tasks, readying for the next assault and hoping for the opportunity to respond in kind. To the last, they were remaining loyal to the empire, to the praetor, and to her. Though Vathrael's last words were in keeping with her duty, her final thoughts were elsewhere.

Good-bye, Wylenn.

FIFTEEN

"Did what I think happened just happen?"

Turning from the display screen at the center of the bank of control consoles along the subterranean chamber's forward wall, Kirk eyed Uhura, whose expression was a mix of concern and uncertainty.

The communications officer nodded. "Yes, sir. The Romulan vessel looks to have been destroyed."

Kirk redirected his attention back to the display. As with the other screens active in the control room, he was unable to read much of the Kalandan text scrolling across the screen. Still, and with Uhura's assistance, he was able to discern some of the graphical representations they depicted. At the center of one screen was a large white circle, which Uhura had told him represented the Gralafi planetoid. Within that graphic was scattered a collection of more than seventy pinpoints of green light, each indicating one node in the massive and heretofore hidden planetary defense network. Blue dots, more than a dozen of them, marked the location of underground complexes such as the one in which Kirk presently stood.

Then, there had been the red dot, outside the white circle, which had represented the orbiting Romulan vessel. That marker was now gone, disappearing as though it had never existed. Until a moment ago it had been there, accompanied by columns of alien text that had told him nothing, but which Spock reported indicated the status of the defense network as it took notice of the ship and initiated what it perceived to be a necessary protective action.

A small indicator flashed in the bottom left corner of the display, and Uhura pointed to it. "This is a communications monitoring process, and it detected the Romulan ship sending a final message before . . . before the end. If I'm reading this correctly, it was some kind of encrypted burst transmission, sir."

Nodding, Kirk said, "That'd make sense. Once somebody at their home base figures out they're overdue for return or check-in, they're probably going to send another ship to investigate. The ship's commander may have been sending a warning about the danger here." He released a small, exasperated grunt. "It's not like they had time to do much of anything else." The speed of the Kalandan defense system's decisions and actions had been uncanny as it reacted first to the presence of the Romulan ship in orbit above Gralafi and then as the vessel's sensors began their intense sweeps of the planetoid. Uhura and Spock had narrated the situation as it developed inside the space of a minute before the first officer reported the targeting of the Romulan vessel by the automated weapons stations.

"They never stood a chance, Captain," Uhura said, her voice low and quiet. For the first time, she allowed herself to lean against the control console, and Kirk could see how she was already beginning to shrug off the energy and stress of the past few moments. She had been afforded precious little time to prepare to help Spock and Lieutenant Boma understand and operate the Kalandan technology, but she had taken to the task as though she had been doing it for years. Kirk reminded himself that she had been in the party that had accompanied Spock into the depths of Kalandan Outpost 1, bringing to bear her remarkable xenolinguistic skills to assist in deciphering the extinct race's language.

"It was a damned slaughter," said McCoy, standing alongside Ambassador Sortino after having emerged from what Boma had described as the Kalandan equivalent of a medical bay. He and the ambassador remained several paces away from the consoles so as to give Spock, Boma, and Uhura room to work.

Unable to disagree, Kirk could only shake his head in disappointment. Might the tragic outcome have been avoided? Possibly, though Kirk could not fault the Romulan ship's commander for the logical, tactically sound steps he likely had taken to protect his vessel and crew, and which doubtless had brought about their destruction by a force against which they had stood no realistic chance of defending. There would have been no way for the Romulans to know that.

A waste, Kirk conceded.

Sortino added, "I don't understand. If this defense system—or whatever it is—activated automatically in response to the Romulan ship's presence and basically blew it out of orbit, why didn't it do the same thing to the *Huang Zhong*?"

Turning at the sound of approaching footsteps, Kirk saw Spock and Boma crossing the room toward them, coming from the consoles they had been monitoring during the engagement with the Romulan ship. "How about it, Spock?" asked the captain, already piecing together the likely hypothesis.

"I cannot be certain without further study, of course," the first officer replied, "but, based on what we know of the *Huang Zhong*'s crash, the vessel likely did not present itself as a threat in the same manner as the Romulan ship. It had already sustained heavier damage due to its passing through the energy field. Perhaps the defense system scanned the ship and determined its threat potential to be minimal."

Boma said, "Until we retuned our sensors and started poking around. As soon as we did that, everything went to hell. It must be programmed to react in different ways depending on the level of intrusion. Weapons likely bring about a more aggressive response, but even sensors capable of localizing power sources and other facilities are likely considered hostile, as well." He sighed and Kirk noted the haunted look in the lieutenant's face. "It's my fault. I'm the one who reconfigured the sensors so that we could get a better look."

Stepping toward the younger man, McCoy placed a hand on his shoulder. "You did what you were supposed to do, Lieutenant. You had no way to know what kind of reaction you'd get." He paused, letting his gaze wander about the room. "If there's one thing we know about the Kalandans, it's that they tended to overprepare, and their reactions to stimuli weren't always proportional to the provocation."

"There must be some kind of threshold observed by the system," Sortino said. "After all, it didn't destroy any of your shuttlecraft or, for that matter, the Dolysian freighters who've been coming and going from this planet for decades. It obviously doesn't see any of those vessels as threats."

"The system is obviously able to distinguish the capabilities of approaching vessels," Spock said. "Neither our shuttlecraft nor the Dolysian freighters or support craft pose an obvious threat, and the Dolysians possess no sensor technology capable of detecting the presence of these subterranean installations or the power generators required to operate them."

McCoy snorted. "Sure, but what would've happened in, say, fifty or a hundred years, when the Dolysians developed the kind of technology that would allow them to find this place? What might've happened then?"

"Depending on the scope of any hypothetical Dolysian probe or expedition," Spock said, "it is likely the Kalandan technology would have acted against any perceived threat in much the same manner it has already demonstrated."

"Yes, I know that, Spock," the doctor replied, rolling his eyes and waving as though to indicate the entire room. "We have to find a way to shut all of this off, before the Dolysians or some other innocent ship does something to make it mad."

Kirk looked to Spock. "What do you think?"

"Doctor McCoy is correct," the Vulcan said. "This equipment is too dangerous to leave operating on its own, particularly now that we have established formal relations with the Dolysians. The increased number of Starfleet and Federation civilian space vessels in this region only increases the threat represented by this technology." He paused, looking about the chamber, before adding, "However, the potential it holds should not be dismissed. This facility and the others like it are far more complex than the installation we found on Kalandan Outpost 1. The technology itself is less advanced, but based on what Mister Boma and I have already found, there would seem to be little doubt that this planetoid was intended for some greater purpose than the other outpost."

"What do you mean by that?" Kirk asked.

By way of reply, Boma made his way to the control console Uhura had been monitoring. He touched several of the console's flat black plates in sequence, each contact bringing with it a string of melodic tones accompanied by new lines of Kalandan text on the station's central display. "During our investigation, we discovered what looks to be a data storage facility located about two kilometers beneath us. The thing is massive. If I did the math correctly, we're talking about a data warehouse holding more information than Memory Alpha *and* Memory Prime *combined*."

"That's one hell of a lot of storage," McCoy said.

Kirk replied, "Bones, your talent for understatement knows no bounds." Memory Alpha, the central repository housing information pertaining to the historical, cultural, and scientific achievements for each of the Federation's member worlds, was among the largest such archives in existence and was available to anyone who wished to make use of its extensive collection.

"This is incredible," Sortino said, her amazement evident in both her voice and expression. "The library of an entire civilization, right here beneath our feet."

Boma nodded with no small amount of enthusiasm. "Exciting doesn't even begin to describe it, Ambassador."

"In addition to the data storage complex," Spock added, "there is evidence of a vast communications array, which we've been able to determine is activated soon after the energy field surrounding the planetoid opens and allows passage. It's quite possible that this system transmitted or received instructions during the intervals that the rift was open."

"Or updates?" Uhura asked. When Kirk and the others looked at her, she shrugged. "If it's supposed to be a library, it makes sense that the Kalandans would want to keep it updated."

"But they've been dead for thousands of years," McCoy said. "So, who the hell has this planet's computer system been talking to?"

Spock replied, "Most likely no one, Doctor."

"So," Kirk said, if this *is* an archive like Memory Alpha or some other kind of backup for their knowledge base, it makes sense for the Kalandans to have wanted to protect it."

Boma said, "It might not even be the only such repository they created. Redundant backup storage, that sort of thing. We certainly learned our own lesson on that front."

Recalling the incident that had resulted in the loss of a great deal of data from the Memory Alpha complex, Kirk could only nod in agreement. After sustaining damage during a freak attack by noncorporeal beings that actually had been targeting the facility's humanoid staff members, the ensuing loss of information had triggered the creation of Memory Prime and several other backup installations, as well as a network of smaller stations scattered throughout Federation space. It was hoped that the resulting division of information assets among the disparate data collection storehouses would reduce if not prevent further loss of such records.

"If what we learned at the other outpost we found is any indication," Kirk said, "the Kalandans were very interested in decentralizing their base of power. According to the records Spock was able to access, there may be dozens of planets like that one *and* this one, with examples of their technology and amassed knowledge storehouses. They obviously were planning ahead for some kind of major event so far as their civilization was concerned." Despite Spock's best efforts, however, the Kalandans' ultimate goal, if indeed there even was one, remained as much a mystery as the long-dead race itself.

"Imagine the information that might be down there," Sortino said, shaking her head in amazement, "It's obvious the Kalandans were more technologically advanced than we are, at least in some respects. Think of what we can learn from them."

Boma nodded as he looked to Kirk. "The information and equipment in this facility alone would take years of comprehensive study, sir."

"And Starfleet will send specialists here to do just that," Kirk countered, "but that might have to be postponed, unless we take steps to protect the Dolysians' interests here. We also need to be thinking ahead so far as the Romulans are concerned." There could be no forgetting the destroyed Romulan vessel and the signal it had dispatched just prior to its destruction. More ships would be coming, he knew, searching for answers and possibly even stumbling into the same trap. Then there was the possibility that someone from the *Enterprise* or even Dolysia might do something else to provoke the Kalandan defense system.

So, Kirk thought, *how do we prevent that from happening?* He held no real desire to see injury or death inflicted upon those who considered him their enemy, even when circumstances allowed no other option. So long as alternatives to taking life existed, he would seek them out and exploit them. "Spock," he said, "what can you tell me about getting control of the system and maybe even shutting it down? Or at least being able to redirect or countermand any actions it might take against perceived threats?"

"We have not yet gained access to those processes, Captain," the Vulcan replied. "The entire system is rigidly compartmentalized and therefore does not lend itself to easy access by unauthorized parties. If not for the knowledge we gained from the other Kalandan outpost, as well as the talents of Mister Boma and Lieutenant Uhura, we would not have made it this far."

From behind Kirk, Uhura said, "Captain, I think you need to see this." When the group turned to her, the captain saw that she had moved back to the console she had been monitoring during the attack on the Romulan vessel. She pointed to one of the monitors, which once again displayed row after row of what Kirk could describe with utmost generosity as gibberish.

Echoing his thoughts, McCoy said, "That looks worse than Scotty's technical journals."

Kirk ignored the comment as he stepped closer to the console. "What've you got, Lieutenant?"

"This monitor is displaying an extract from what Lieutenant Boma and I have determined to be—for lack of a better term—an activity log. There are entries here for all of the different tasks, actions, queries, and results processed by the computer network, including the defense system."

"So," Kirk said, "you're able to tell me everything this thing's been doing since it came on line?"

Boma replied, "If a complete archive of the system activity is recorded in that data storage beneath our feet, we should be able to tell you every action this computer has taken since it was first activated."

Setting aside the idea of what thousands of years of recorded computer data might look like, how long it might take to access it, or how much storage space such a massive amount of information might require, Kirk looked to Uhura. "I'm guessing you've got something to show us from the recent past, Lieutenant?"

The communications officer nodded as she gestured once more to the monitors. "Yes, sir. According to this, and if I'm translating the date and time computations correctly, the defense system recorded the actions it took when confronting the *Huang Zhong* and the Romulan ship. From what I'm seeing of the sensor data, the Romulan vessel was not destroyed."

"What?" Sortino asked, her eyes widening in surprise. "Are you sure?"

Uhura replied, "Not one hundred percent, but from the recorded data, the ship seemed to disappear just seconds before the final attack." She looked to Kirk. "Sir, I think they activated their cloaking device and managed to escape."

"Escape to where?" McCoy asked. "We'd have heard from the *Enterprise* if they had gone back through the rift, right?"

Spock said, "The sensor data recorded during the engagement noted the damage inflicted upon the Romulan vessel. If it did survive the attack, then it likely would require extensive repairs."

"If that's true," Kirk said, "we may have ourselves some party crashers, after all."

SIXTEEN

Standing at the foot of the ramp leading into her ship, Commander Vathrael looked toward the sky and noted the beginnings of the color shift signifying the onset of nightfall. Unlike the mauve tinge cast over everything during daylight hours, the effect of the energy field encompassing this world now was beginning to radiate a pale violet glow across the surrounding landscape, a hue Vathrael had come to find soothing. Though the barrier prevented the penetration to the planetoid's surface of direct sunlight as well as light reflected from the two moons orbiting the nearby inhabited planet, the light refracted from the barrier itself did a serviceable job of compensating for that loss. Vathrael wondered if those responsible for the energy field had intended such an effect, or if it was simply an odd consequence of the technology they had seen fit to place here.

An interesting question, she conceded. It was but one of many queries she had considered with respect to the planetoid as well as the technology it seemed to harbor and those who created it. The weapons certainly commanded her interest, given how it had disabled and—if not for the timely intervention of her engineer—nearly destroyed the *Nevathu*, and brought about its forced landing here. Despite any personal desire Vathrael might have to further investigate such mysteries, they would have to be set aside while she and her crew tended to the more immediate problems they faced.

Footsteps on the ramp behind made her turn to see her engineer, Subcommander Mylas, descending toward her from the ship. His face and hands, along with his uniform—a standard gray one-piece coverall designed for wear by crew personnel when performing labor-intensive tasks where the regular duty uniform was inappropriate— were smudged with grime. Thinning, stark white hair dampened with perspiration and bloodshot eyes rounded out his disheveled appearance, testifying to the extended period of time he had spent in the bowels of the *Nevathu*.

"You look tired, my friend," Vathrael said as she regarded him.

Mylas nodded as he came to a stop at the foot of the ramp. "I'll rest when the work is completed, Commander." Despite his words, he leaned against one of the ramp's support struts, a breach of protocol that Vathrael would never have tolerated from anyone but him.

Unable to resist a small smile, she said, "If you'd let Fleet Command give you the promotion you've already earned several times, by my count, you wouldn't have to crawl around in the belly of my ship trying to fix everything."

"I much prefer my present duties, Commander. I'm not a creature of politics, or even polished military bearing. My place is with the machines, and I am happy to continue serving in that capacity so long as the empire will have me."

Vathrael replied, "Fleet Command's loss is my good fortune." She first met Mylas when she was but a young centurion, recently graduated from the military academy on Romulus and having been posted to her first assignment to the warship *Bloodied Talon*. Mylas had been that vessel's engineer, and she recalled that even then he had projected the same attitude toward promotion or any other offer that might remove him from the position for which he was without question ideally suited. The two had become friends during that assignment, and continued to correspond even after duty and circumstance saw to it that they were separated and dispatched to different ships. Several *fvheisn* later, having been promoted several ranks herself and after receiving her orders to take command of the *Nevathu*, Vathrael learned that Mylas had not yet retired and asked him to transfer to her ship to serve as its engineer. It was a request he had obliged without hesitation, much to her delight, and in addition to his duties overseeing the scout ship and its systems, Mylas also resumed the other role he had taken on during her early career: that of her mentor, sympathetic listener, and even her conscience.

"How are the repairs progressing?" Vathrael asked.

Covering his mouth with one hand to stifle a yawn, Mylas nodded. "As well as can be expected, Commander. Life support is fully operational. The sensors are still off line, but we should be able to test the impulse engines by this time tomorrow." He paused as though considering his remarks, before adding, "Most of the actual repair work there is complete, but I wish to execute some tests and a computer simulation before we attempt to employ the engines."

"Have you no faith in your own skills?" Vathrael asked, suppressing the urge to smile once again.

Mylas shook his head. "I simply have an aversion to dying in an expanding ball of fire and gas, which is what will happen if our repairs to the impulse drive are incorrect, incomplete, or careless."

Trusting her friend's judgment, Vathrael replied, "Very well. It's not as though we will be in any hurry to depart." Then, realizing how her words could be interpreted, she added, "I'm sorry, Mylas. That was an inconsiderate remark."

Rather than appearing offended, the elder Romulan instead released a small, quiet chuckle. "Worry not, Commander. I understood your meaning. Of course, I do regret that there are limitations to what we can repair."

"You saved the ship," Vathrael countered. "Would you not agree that to be the primary concern?"

Mylas nodded. "In light of that, I bow to your wisdom, Commander." He punctuated the remark with another tired laugh.

The attack on the *Nevathu* from the mysterious defense system buried beneath the planetoid's surface had come within moments of being disastrous. From the pitched battle's beginning, Mylas had been taking steps from the depths of the engineering section. Though he was not fast enough to prevent the initial damage to the ship, it was his quick thinking and resourcefulness that had seen to the deactivation of all weapons systems as well as the haphazard deployment of the *Nevathu*'s cloaking device. The cloak's reactivation had come at the precise, necessary moment, rendering it invisible to the planetary defenses and allowing the ship to drop undetected from orbit.

Damage to the impulse engines, sensors, and life support systems had necessitated landing on the planetoid in order to effect repairs, anyway. Not for the first time, Vathrael was thankful she commanded a scout vessel capable of such action rather than one of the empire's larger and more prestigious warships. Otherwise, she and her crew might already be dead.

"You're certain there's nothing you can do about the warp drive?" she asked.

Mylas shook his head. "The ship will require dry-dock facilities and perhaps a complete system overhaul, which means that we will need assistance to return home."

"A not inconsequential obstacle, given our current predicament." Thanks to the *Nevathu*'s repaired cloaking device, the ship was able to maintain stealth. This allowed Vathrael some measure of relief while her crew continued the other repair efforts in a bid to return to space and, if they were fortunate, issue a call for aid. While that was a desirable goal, Vathrael knew that their paramount objective was to avoid revealing their presence to the *Enterprise*, which might still be outside the rift, monitoring the field and its effects. In addition to the potential danger it represented on its own, the Federation starship could also summon help, and there was a distinct possibility that any reinforcements it called would arrive here ahead of any Romulan vessels. Her standing order, identical to those given to every ship of the empire, was to destroy her ship in order to avoid capture once all other methods of evasion were exhausted. Vathrael would carry out that directive without hesitation, but also with a great deal of regret. Her obvious failure to the praetor would of course weigh on her conscience, but her last thoughts would be how she had betrayed the crew who had given her their trust and loyalty, and who would do so until the end.

We are not there just yet, she reminded herself.

"So long as the impulse engines are operational," she

said, "we can address the other considerations later, if necessary." She looked about the terrain, which stretched to the horizon in all directions. Taking a deep breath, she savored the gentle, enticing aromas cast off from nearby vegetation. Based on what her sensor officer had told her, this region of the planetoid had recently emerged from its short, mild winter, and the plant life here was currently in the stages of its seasonal bloom. "I think I speak for the entire crew when I say that regardless of how pleasant this little planet would appear to be, we do not want to spend the next few *fvheisn* here." How much time remained before the energy field surrounding this world became inaccessible again? Though Vathrael knew the situation would be temporary, if long-term, and as inviting as the surroundings might be, she had no desire to stay here, hiding from the indigenous population until rescue arrived or another opportunity for escape presented itself.

Mylas nodded. "I understand, Commander. I have no desire to spend what little life I might have left wandering about this place. I prefer to enjoy my retirement in the small house I recently purchased in the mountains north of Dartha—close enough to the city that I am not completely isolated from the best civilization has to offer, and yet far enough away that no one will bother me."

Laughing at the image that evoked, Vathrael shook her head. "Retirement? You? Considering how long I've known you, I would think you to be immortal."

"Only in spirit, Commander," the engineer replied, smiling.

Vathrael released a small sigh as she shook her head. "Mylas, you've been my closest friend since I was an untested centurion. You've more than earned my undying devotion and trust. You're allowed to address me by my name, at least when we're alone."

"I will take that under advisement, Commander," Mylas said, chuckling again.

Any protest Vathrael might have made was silenced by the sound of new footsteps on the ramp. She turned to see her executive officer, Subcommander Sirad, and her sensor officer, Centurion Betria, descending from the ship. Like Mylas, both officers looked tired and dirty from extended efforts as they contributed to the ongoing repair activities. The look on Sirad's face was enough to tell her that something was troubling him.

"Commander," Sirad said, offering a formal nod before extending a similar greeting to Mylas. "Our sensors have detected the presence two Starfleet transport craft."

Surprised at this, Vathrael eyed Betria. "The sensors are functioning?"

The centurion nodded. "Partially, Commander, but enough to show us what may be the source of the attack on our vessel. It's some distance from here, but still within the range of our transporter system."

"So, the humans are conducting their own investigation?" Vathrael asked.

Sirad nodded. "It's what they do, Commander. They investigate, discuss, document, and categorize anything and everything to the point of exhaustion." He paused, shrugging. "In that respect, they are quite formidable."

"That was difficult for you to admit, yes?" Mylas asked.

His expression remaining fixed, the subcommander replied, "It evokes a pain unequaled in my lifetime."

Laughing at that, Vathrael allowed the welcome feeling to linger for a moment before her smile faded and she returned to the matters at hand. "If the Starfleet group finds anything of value, they'll take samples or scan records of it back to their superiors." Based on the intelligence reports she had been given upon being given this reconnaissance assignment, she knew that Starfleet and the Federation already had made diplomatic inroads with the Dolysians. That relationship would only continue to grow and strengthen with time, and Starfleet ultimately would benefit from any advanced technology its officers might find while conducting their own survey missions here. During the attack on her ship, she thought the Dolysians themselves may have been responsible, but it was becoming obvious to her that the weapons employed against the *Nevathu* were far beyond the technology of the planetoid's current inhabitants. The more she considered that aspect of this evolving situation, the more she was coming to realize that another course of action was beginning to take precedence. Learning about this unknown technology and perhaps seizing it for the empire might well end up superseding the *Nevathu*'s need to depart the planetoid and escape the rift before it closed.

"Whatever is here," Sirad said, echoing Vathrael's unspoken thoughts, "we must find it first, and deny it to our enemies."

Mylas nodded. "That would seem to be the prudent course, even though doing so likely will threaten any stealth we might currently enjoy."

"Then that is the price we will pay for carrying out our duty," Sirad countered, his voice firm. Then, as though remembering his place, he directed his gaze to Vathrael. "Commander?"

After a moment spent in silence as she contemplated

her options even as her three officers regarded her, Vathrael drew a deep breath. "Yes, it is our duty." To Betria, she said, "Provide the relevant location information to the transport officer. I will lead a scouting party to the source of the readings, and see what there is to find." If whatever alien technology she might discover could not be collected and returned to the *Nevathu*, Vathrael knew it would have to be destroyed.

Whether that course of action might require her own death, or those of her crew, was a question that for now would remain unanswered.

That will be dictated by duty, as well.

SEVENTEEN

The reconstituted scrambled eggs looked real enough, Pavel Chekov conceded as he studied the clump of egglike mass perched atop his eating utensil. The color and texture, so far as he could tell, approximated the real thing. On the other hand, whatever the ship's food processors had decided this was supposed to be possessed nothing even close to the flavor he tended to associate with eggs.

Just eat, and get it over with.

"Ours is not to reason why," Chekov muttered before shoving the eggs into his mouth and doing his best to chew while not allowing the offensive pseudo-food to contact his taste buds. As he swallowed, he grimaced while making a mental note to report the possible food synthesizer malfunction to engineering at his earliest opportunity.

"Ensign, are you all right?"

Only when he heard the question did Chekov realize that his eyes were closed. Opening them, he looked up to see Lieutenant M'Ress standing on the other side of his table. The Caitian communications officer was holding a tray identical to his own, atop which was a plate stacked with some sort of green vegetables he did not recognize. A data slate was tucked under her left arm, and her coat of orange fur gave off a sheen thanks to the recessed lighting of the officer's mess, making Chekov wonder if she had recently finished grooming herself.

That's a stupid thing to think, now, isn't it?

As he started to stand, M'Ress held out a hand, smiling at him as she indicated for him to remain seated. "At ease, Mister Chekov. I noticed your expression as I was walking past. Are you ill?"

Eyeing his eggs, Chekov replied, "Not yet, but I'll let you know."

M'Ress laughed at the joke before gesturing to the empty chair opposite his. "May I join you?"

"By all means." Chekov gestured toward the chair with his free hand. "Be my guest, Lieutenant." Now self-conscious, he looked about the officer's mess, though no one seemed to care that M'Ress was taking a seat at his table, even though there were chairs available at other tables occupied by officers of rank commensurate to hers. Watching her fluid, graceful movements even as she performed the simple act of sitting seemed only to heighten his sudden bout of anxiety. For her part, the lieutenant seemed more preoccupied with her data slate than anything or anyone else. No sooner had she sat down than she pushed her tray to one side, giving herself more room for the tablet.

"I was under the impression that humans usually consumed eggs during their breakfast meal," M'Ress said, waving toward his plate. "You do not?"

Chekov smiled. "I do, but sometimes I also like eggs with a steak for dinner." It was a favorite meal of his, going back to his childhood. He, along with his stomach, was happy to know that while the *Enterprise* food processors might not always do well preparing eggs, they made up for it with their steak choices.

The explanation seemed to satisfy M'Ress, who nodded in understanding. Then, rather than picking up one of the utensils on her tray, she opted instead for her data slate's stylus. After a moment, she said, "I understand that you've been busy studying the energy barrier."

"Yes, that's right," Chekov replied, before reaching with his free hand for the chair to his left and holding up his own data slate, along with a trio of computer data cards. "I'm not supposed to go on duty for another hour, but I can't stop thinking about the field. How it's generated, why it opens and closes, what the Kalandans had in mind when they created it." He shook his head. "Even the way it reacts to the presence of other ships; there has to be a reason it does that. Is it defensive? Only the Kalandans can tell us, assuming they left the answer somewhere on that planet." He sighed. "It's amazing, and I wish I was with the landing party, having a look at that outpost for myself."

In truth he had worked a double shift on the bridge, examining the *Enterprise* sensor logs of the energy field as well as the data from the *Huang Zhong*'s distress buoy. The field itself was unlike anything on record, including the immense barrier at the edge of the galaxy, which the *Enterprise* had encountered three times. That it was an artificial creation made it all the more compelling a mystery. It was Chekov's hope that Mister Spock would see fit to request his assistance with the research currently being conducted on and beneath the surface of the Gralafi planetoid, so that he could see the technology responsible for the field's generation. Unless and until that opportunity presented itself, Chekov had enough to do just examining the energy field surrounding the planetoid and perhaps learning what might have happened to the *Huang Zhong* as well as the

Romulan vessel. To that end, he had immersed himself in his studies, becoming so preoccupied that Commander Scott had seen fit to order him from the bridge, not to return for duty until he had slept for at least four hours and eaten a decent meal.

"Don't overextend yourself, Ensign," M'Ress said, her tone quite soothing, Chekov decided. "We may be here a while, and if that's true, you'll likely get your chance to see the outpost. In the meantime, you would do well to conserve your energy. You never know when you'll need it." Her eyes lingered on him a moment before she returned her attention to her data slate.

Nodding, Chekov replied, "Your words to Mister Spock's ears. Until then, I have plenty to keep me busy." He scooped another bite of pseudo-eggs from his plate, and as he did so he noted M'Ress watching him, her eyes narrowing as though curious or perhaps confused.

"Is that a pew?" she asked.

Pausing as he was in the process of taking his next bite, Chekov glanced to his right hand, feeling a sudden rush of blood to his face as he realized for the first time what he was using to eat. Had he actually carried the thing from his quarters? Only then did he notice that the cutlery that he had taken from the dispenser near the food synthesizers remained untouched on his tray.

Talk about preoccupied.

Chekov hoped his forced chuckle covered the sound of his clearing his throat as he held up his "personal eating utensil," or "PEU," as it was known in Starfleet vernacular. Essentially a spoon with the end of its scoop molded to feature a trio of fork tines, the implement was a standard equipment item issued to cadets at Starfleet Academy.

Though generally used only during training missions on Earth or off-planet locations where even rudimentary dining facilities often were not provided, the "pew" was a vital component of a cadet's field gear. "I've had it since the Academy," he said, smiling at the memories the utensil evoked. "During a training mission on Andor, a fellow cadet broke three fingers on her right hand. We were in the middle of a ground combat exercise and no medical equipment was nearby, so I used this as a field-expedient splint."

Smiling in obvious appreciation—and perhaps a small bit of amusement—M'Ress nodded. "Its titanium construction would make it quite suitable for such a purpose. Very resourceful, Ensign."

"It was enough to immobilize her hand until help arrived," Chekov said, holding up the pew as he finished his story. "Once the exercise was over and we were on our way back to Earth, I decided it was a sort of good luck charm, and I've had it ever since."

M'Ress seemed to think about this for a moment before Chekov heard her emit a low purr. "I understand the concept of keepsakes and other talismans which their owners believe are imbued with special properties they hope will bring favorable fortune. I find it to be a quaint notion, though one to which I do not subscribe."

Once again feeling self-conscious as he considered the prized utensil in his hand, Chekov stammered before replying, "I don't really believe that. It's more a memento of that day." Then, remembering what his Academy instructor had told him upon learning of the incident, he added, "It's also a reminder that, sometimes, when you're faced with a complicated problem, the best solution is the one that's right in front of you." He shrugged, "Or, in this case, my field pack."

"Is that why you seem to carry it with you wherever you go?" M'Ress asked, and when she smiled, Chekov knew that the lieutenant was teasing him in good-natured fashion, and he laughed in response.

"No. I have it because for some reason, it was on top of my data slate when I left my quarters this morning." In truth, he had carried it with him on numerous occasions over the years, and even used it when eating in his cabin. It was not the first time he had brought it with him to the officer's mess; chances were good it would come with him again at some point. For now, however, he felt no pressing need to share that information with his dinner companion. Instead, he gestured with the utensil toward her data slate. "What are you working on?"

"I just finished decrypting the last message sent from the Romulan ship," M'Ress replied, punctuating her answer with a low growl from the back of her throat that was only just audible to Chekov's ears. "Even with the computer's help, I still struggled with it. When I first started looking at it, I could see that it was using a new encryption algorithm, different from anything we have on file. I had to write a new procedure for the computer to use for decoding the message, but it worked." Using her stylus, she tapped the data slate again. "Part of me wishes I had not been so successful."

Frowning, Chekov asked, "So, it was a call for help?"

M'Ress stared at the tablet before nodding. "It's as we expected. They included a distress call with their most recent sensor data. The records show that their ship was attacked by the Kalandan defense system, but the commander seemed to believe that they were being fired upon by the Dolysians. That was the final entry in the buoy's memory banks." She paused, her eyes widening in concern. "What if the Romulans think the Dolysians *are* responsible for the attack on their ship?"

"They won't be happy," Chekov replied, staring at his tray. "They'll send ships to investigate, or worse."

Tapping her data slate with the stylus in her hand, M'Ress said, "Commander Scott has already advised Captain Kirk of that." She paused, studying once more the information on her tablet. "The next day or two should prove to be anything but boring."

Such unpleasant news seemed to have become commonplace in the wake of Captain Kirk's report from Gralafi of the Romulan vessel appearing to have survived the attack on it by the Kalandan defense system. Though it was likely that the ship had sustained at least some damage, perhaps even on a scale comparable to what happened to the *Huang Zhong*, at present there was no way to confirm that theory. Were there Romulans on Gralafi, and if so, where were they and what were they doing? The landing party might be in danger, and though the captain's instructions remained explicit in that the *Enterprise* was not to enter the rift at the cost of deactivating its warp drive, Scott and his team of engineers were still searching for a means of shielding the starship's engines against the energy barrier's harmful effects. Chekov had volunteered to assist in that effort but was overruled by the chief engineer, citing his earlier order of food and sleep. Though he knew he was doing the correct thing by following orders, which in turn would aid in maintaining his alertness for his next duty shift or the next emergency, that knowledge did little to alleviate his guilt at sitting idle while others worked.

Relax, he reminded himself. *You've earned a little rest. Besides, Scotty will kill you if you disobey him.*

Finishing the remainder of his meal, he looked up to see that most of the other officers who had been making use of the dining facility had left, either heading for their stations or somewhere else to while away their precious few hours of off-duty time. He then noticed that M'Ress had yet to take even the first bite from her plate. "Are you not hungry, Lieutenant?" he asked.

"Please, call me M'Ress," she said as she glanced at her tray. "I thought I was, but in truth, I guess I'm still distracted with my work."

Chekov smiled, recalling Scott's final words to him before ordering him from the bridge. "You should eat, M'Ress. You wouldn't want to have your stomach growling while we're at Red Alert."

"So, you were listening to Mister Scott." M'Ress reached for the fork on her tray and began picking through the meal she had ordered. When she spoke again, her voice was lower and softer. "If you have nothing more interesting to do, you're welcome to stay. To be honest, I prefer not to eat alone."

Something about the way she said the words gave Chekov pause. Was she flirting with him? He had never been good at reading such signs. Further, he did not know M'Ress that well. When she had come aboard the *Enterprise* and had begun serving as a junior communications officer, he was immersed in a series of duty rotations orchestrated by Mister Spock as part of a mentoring program designed to provide him with educational and practical experience in a variety of disciplines. Under the Vulcan's watchful eye, Chekov had completed disparate assignments ranging from working with the ship's science teams to training with the security cadre. Such work had for several months limited the time he spent on the bridge as a navigator and even a backup science officer. While he had missed the excitement to be found while working in the starship's command center, he believed the time invested in such cross-training had not been wasted.

But, it didn't help you with this kind of thing, did it?

Praying with each word that he would not stammer, Chekov answered, "I have no better plans and I don't mind at all."

M'Ress seemed very pleased with that response. "Excellent, Pavel," she purred. "May I call you Pavel?" When she smiled this time, Chekov realized that he had no trouble reading that particular sign.

EIGHTEEN

"*Captain,*" said Chancellor Wiladra Pejh en Kail as she regarded Kirk from the small display screen on the *Galileo*'s cockpit console, "*please understand that I pose the following question with utmost respect, but have you lost all connection to reality or sanity?*"

On any other occasion, Kirk might have laughed at the query, and even now he could sympathize with the chancellor's concern. After all, it likely was not every day that someone told her she needed to interrupt one of her planet's vital industries based solely on the advice of an alien.

"You wouldn't be the first person to ask me that, Chancellor," Kirk said, hoping to ease the Dolysian leader's anxiety, if only the slightest bit. "Believe me when I tell you that I don't make such a request lightly. Based on the information currently available to us, the Romulan Empire knows about the Kalandan installation here, and they'll want to send other ships to investigate it."

Sitting next to him, Dana Sortino added, "At the very least, they'll almost certainly attempt to prevent us from examining the facility for ourselves, but it goes without saying that once they find out the potential this technology represents, they'll want to do everything to secure and exploit it for their own advantage."

"Exactly," Kirk said. The report Commander Scott had given to him after Lieutenant M'Ress's decryption of the encoded Romulan message only served to strengthen his suspicions and worry so far as the empire was concerned. For all he knew, another Romulan ship was on its way here even as he spoke to the chancellor. Unfortunately, the *Enterprise*, beyond launching additional shuttlecraft—which Kirk already had forbade—was not in a position to render assistance here on the planetoid. Sensors would not penetrate to this side of the rift, hampering any search for the lurking Romulan vessel. Scotty was working on a means of shielding the ship's warp engines from the effects of the barrier without having to deactivate them, but so far the chief engineer was having no success.

On the viewscreen, which made her seem small and distant, Wiladra's expression was one of helplessness. The effect seemed amplified by the quality of the connection, which was a result of interference from the rift. Most of the signal noise was being reduced by linking the *Galileo's* communications system with that of the *Enterprise*, which in turn was relaying the signal to Chancellor Wiladra's office on Dolysia.

"*I can only defer to your experience and judgment with respect to these Romulans, Captain,*" she said, "*but I must consider the needs and safety of my people. While we can and do continue to mine erinadium from our two moons, the simple fact is that those operations, even when their numbers are combined, do not match the output from Gralafi.*" She paused, leaning closer to the visual pickup of whatever communications device she was employing in her office back on Dolysia. "*As you are aware, we are coming to the end of the interval in which we will be able to transport the ore shipments through the Pass, and if we fail to meet our quotas, then the effects on our planetary infrastructure both here and on the moons as well as the Havreltipa colony will be severe."*

Kirk fought the urge to release an audible sigh, and it required physical effort to maintain his neutral expression. For the first time, he noticed that the air inside the shuttlecraft, even with its hatch open, was growing thick and uncomfortable in stark contrast to the slight breeze that had been blowing across the plateau as he and Sortino emerged from the hidden Kalandan complex. Glancing to where the ambassador sat in the shuttle's co-pilot seat, he noted her own impassive features as she leaned forward so that Wiladra would see her image transmitted over the communications frequency.

"Chancellor," she said, "we are very much aware of the situation. I have no doubts that if there were any other available option, Captain Kirk would be advocating it. The action he proposes would actually serve to protect the mining colony, as it would protect your people from undue harm, as well." Clearing her throat, she added, "The Romulans would have no reservations about forcing your people into servitude if they thought it might serve their needs here. I've seen firsthand the results of imperial conquest, and trust me when I tell you it is not a pleasant experience."

Though he nodded in agreement, Kirk said nothing. He had seen Romulan subjugation, himself, and while it did not approach the brutality of rule under the banner of the Klingon Empire, it was still a far less desirable alternative to simple freedom and self-determination.

Wiladra said, *"Ambassador, forgive this next question,*

but my duty to my people demands that I ask it: Though you say you are acting to prevent our possible exploitation by the Romulans, how do we know that you are not simply acting out of your own self-interests? You've said before that if we asked, you would leave us in peace. Does this still hold true?"

Pausing as she glanced to Kirk before answering, Sortino replied, "If that is your genuine wish, Chancellor, then we will leave, never to return until and unless you call upon us again. I would hope you wouldn't do that, though, as the threat to your people from the Romulans would still remain. While they are our adversaries at this time, we believe they will avoid direct confrontation with us if at all possible."

"But you cannot be certain of that," Wiladra said.

Kirk answered, "No, we can't be certain. However, I am certain that if we leave, the Romulans will step in." Leaning forward, he held out his hands in a gesture of supplication. "Chancellor, our people have been living and working within your society for more than a year now. You said it yourself: with our technology, we have no need to stage such an elaborate pretense in order to gain your trust. We're calling on that trust now, in order to help you. Let us do that."

For the first time since the communication had begun, Wiladra smiled. *"It is evident that you have our best interests in mind, Captain, and for that I am grateful. You say that closing the Pass is the only way to ensure the safety of the planetoid, whatever it is you have found beneath its surface, and our people at the colony. Once the danger has passed, how can you be certain that you will be able to reopen the passage again?"*

Looking to Sortino to see if she might want to field this question, Kirk almost snorted at the sight of the ambassador holding up her hands in mock surrender and shaking her head. Despite the momentary amusement her reaction evoked, the captain instead returned his gaze to the viewscreen. "My first officer, Commander Spock, and his team from my ship have been examining the Kalandan systems that oversee the energy barrier. While there's still much to learn, he's confident he can take control of those systems and direct the field to open and close at will. If he's right, then the barrier can most likely be programmed to remain open permanently, or even eliminated altogether. Think of what that will mean for your people, Chancellor."

"*But if your officer is wrong,*" Wiladra countered, "*what will that mean for us? Will the Federation stand by us after inflicting such lasting effects upon our society?*"

Kirk said, "Absolutely. You have my word on that." He knew even as he spoke that he possessed nothing to support his pronouncement save for whatever conviction he might muster. Was the force of his words sufficient to convince the Dolysian leader? Though he prided himself on his ability to read others, Wiladra was proving to be most difficult in that regard.

"Mine, as well, Chancellor," Sortino added. "Captain Kirk is one of the most honorable people I've ever met. His reputation for doing what is right, even when it means defying rules or regulations, is quite something."

In a lower voice, Kirk muttered, "I'm not so sure that's a good thing to add to the sales pitch."

Looking away from the video pickup for a moment, Wiladra turned in her chair, and Kirk recalled what he remembered about the layout of the chancellor's office.

He figured she likely was looking through the window at the rear of her private chambers and out onto the lush, manicured courtyard outside the building that housed the planet's Unified Leadership Council. It was easy to see that she was weighing what she had heard from him and Sortino, along with whatever opinions and feelings she had accumulated with respect to the Federation in the months that had passed since her people's introduction to the reality of having interstellar neighbors. What doubts had she gathered, as well? Would they be enough to negate whatever goodwill had been engendered by the Federation first-contact teams, which had been living in her people's midst all this time?

When she returned her attention to Kirk, she shook her head. "*I am sorry, but this is simply not a decision I can make without consulting the council as well as the mining colony leaders. There is just too much at stake to do otherwise. I hope you will understand and respect that.*"

"Of course, Chancellor," Sortino replied, even as Kirk gritted his teeth and forced himself to say nothing. "However, I urge you to have that meeting as quickly as possible. We will stand by and wait to hear from you at your earliest convenience."

"*Very well, Ambassador,*" Wiladra said, the corners of her mouth turning upward as she offered a small, worried smile. "*Thank you for bringing this matter to my attention. I will contact you soon.*" She reached forward to something off-screen, and a moment later the connection dissolved into static.

Now certain he would not be overheard by the chancellor, Kirk let loose with an unrestrained sigh of exasperation. "That went off wonderfully, don't you think?"

"For a man whose diplomatic skills are purported to be lacking," Sortino said, leaning back in her chair, "I thought you handled yourself with great poise."

Kirk chuckled. "Diplomacy is a skill I've acquired more out of a basic need for survival than from any real calling, Ambassador. It's most definitely not my strong suit." He reached up to rub the bridge of his nose, feeling the first signs of fatigue beginning to set in. How long had he been gone from the *Enterprise*? He had lost track of the hours that had passed, and looking at the chronometer on the cockpit's control console would only serve to enhance his growing weariness.

"All right, then," Sortino said after a moment. "What do we do now?"

Pushing himself to his feet, Kirk paused, stretching the muscles in his lower back before replying, "We told Chancellor Wiladra we'd wait for her decision, and I have no intention of going back on that. On the other hand, I don't like sitting around and waiting, particularly if there's still a Romulan ship lurking around somewhere. There's no reason we can't try to be ready when she does call back. With luck, Spock will have figured out the systems overseeing the rift by the time that happens." As he made his way to the shuttlecraft's open hatch, he saw from the corner of his eye Sortino rising from her seat to follow him.

"What are you thinking?" she asked. "Some kind of demonstration?"

"That's exactly what I'm thinking," Kirk replied, stepping from the *Galileo* down to the ground. "We need to convince the Dolysians that we—and they—can control or even eliminate the rift. It'll ease their worries, and show them that they no longer have to be subordinate to the whims of whatever the Kalandans had in mind when they created the thing."

Following him from the shuttlecraft, Sortino said, "The last year has been pretty dramatic for the Dolysians. I mean, even though they had to be expecting that they might one day encounter people from other worlds, the fact that it *happened* still sent some shock waves through their society. And now, we're here, living and working among them, and ohowing them all these possibilities for how their lives might improve. Making contact with these people was about as close to a Prime Directive violation as you can get and not actually cross the line." She shrugged. "Even though everything seems to be going well, you still have to wonder if and when another shoe's going to drop."

"I don't think you're giving the contact teams, and yourself, enough credit, Ambassador," Kirk said. "Compared to other cultures forced to accept the idea of life on other planets earlier than might have been appropriate, the Dolysians appear to be adapting to their new situation with very few problems." From his experience and after considering the various factors surrounding the Federation's engaging the Dolysians, Kirk believed this might be one of the smoother first-contact situations he had ever observed. "What we need to demonstrate now is that we're here for the long haul; that we'll stand by them during times of adversity even while allowing them to make the choices they believe are right for their people." That would be easier said than done, he knew.

Anything worth doing always is, Kirk mused, smiling to himself upon hearing the familiar nugget of wisdom as it had been spoken to him countless times by his father.

Light reflected off something in the corner of his right

eye. Looking in that direction, he was in time to see a figure ducking behind a large rock formation at the base of the hill on the plateau's far edge. He caught flashes of silver and blue, but it was the gold helmet that made his eyes widen in surprise. *Romulan.*

Muscles tensing in anticipation, Kirk reached for Sortino and grabbed her left arm, pulling her past him and sending her toward the *Galileo*'s open hatch. "Get inside!" he snapped as his right hand moved to the phaser on his hip, fingers curling around the weapon's grip as he pulled it free and raised it to take aim. Movement from the rocks was followed by a flash of light and a howl of energy, and something slammed into the dirt to his right. Ears ringing from the sudden attack, Kirk launched himself toward the front of the shuttlecraft. He tucked and rolled as his right shoulder struck the ground, momentum carrying him around the nose of the ship as a second disruptor blast struck the side of the *Galileo.* Regaining his feet, he maneuvered himself so that he could use the shuttle for cover as he scanned the hillside for threats.

"Ambassador!" he shouted. "Are you all right?" Instead of a reply from Sortino, Kirk's query evoked another barrage of disruptor fire from the hillside. At least one of the shots hit the shuttlecraft, and the captain felt the reverberation across the ship's hull as it absorbed the strike. Now somewhat protected, he was able to see the origin points of the attack. There were at least two shooters, he surmised, though there also could be more.

Always the optimist.

Ignoring the errant thought, Kirk aimed his phaser to where he had seen the weapons flashes and fired. The weapon spat a blue streak of energy that crossed the plateau and struck one of the larger rocks jutting from the hillside. He was not expecting to hit his target, at least not the first time, but he hoped his return fire might force the attackers to seek cover behind the rocks, perhaps even providing him with a window of opportunity to . . .

. . . *to do what, exactly?*

Another disruptor bolt chewed into the dirt near his right foot and Kirk jerked back, once more using the shuttlecraft's hull as a shield. "Not going to make it easy, are you?" he muttered, backpedaling to the *Galileo*'s rear and hoping a change of position might offer him a better vantage point. Kneeling aft of the craft's starboard nacelle, Kirk switched his phaser to his left hand and leaned forward, looking toward the hill in search of the Romulans. That was when he heard new weapons fire, and it took him an extra second to realize it was coming from a Starfleet phaser, and one not set to stun.

What the . . . ?

The report was followed by a second shot, along with what Kirk thought sounded like something exploding in the distance. He leaned around the rear of the shuttlecraft and saw two figures on the hillside, scrambling to get away from where repeated strikes of phaser fire were tearing into the rock formation that had been providing concealment. No sooner had the Romulans broken cover than another phaser beam, its pitch higher and sounding to Kirk's ears as though it carried only stunning force, rushed across the open ground and struck one of the enemy soldiers in the back. The Romulan stumbled and fell to the ground, and his companion turned and fired his disruptor back toward the *Galileo*. The energy bolt found the side of the shuttlecraft's hull as Kirk stepped into the open, raised his own phaser, and fired. His beam found its mark, catching the Romulan in the chest and sending him falling backward to collapse on the hill's gentle slope.

"Ambassador?" Kirk shouted as he maneuvered around the shuttlecraft, keeping his right arm extended and continuing to aim his phaser toward the hillside. Moving back to the craft's port side, he saw Sortino stepping down from the open hatch, wielding a phaser in each hand and aiming them across the plateau to where the two unconscious Romulans now lay. She glanced in Kirk's direction and, noting his quizzical expression, smiled as she indicated her weapons.

"Stun," she said, bending her right arm to indicate the phaser in her hand, then repeating the motion with the other weapon. "Not stun. Figured I could flush them out, then put them to sleep."

Nodding in appreciation, Kirk said, "That was some nice shooting."

"I still hold all the marksmanship records on the *Lavinius*," the ambassador replied, bobbing her eyebrows.

Kirk grunted in momentary amusement. "I'm convinced."

Seemingly satisfied that no further threats lurked nearby, Sortino lowered her phasers. "I guess there were only the two of them."

"They'll have friends," Kirk replied, nodding to the unconscious Romulans.

"I'm surprised they engaged us at all," Sortino said. "Romulans usually prefer stealth to direct confrontation."

His eyes on the stunned soldiers, Kirk shook his head. "That's probably my fault. They must have tracked us here, and were likely reconnoitering the area to see what all the fuss was about. If I hadn't seen them, they might've been content to sit and watch us." Would they have managed to find their way into the Kalandan base? That was still a possibility, Kirk knew, particularly if more Romulans came looking for their companions.

"What do we do now?" Sortino asked.

Gesturing toward the opposite end of the plateau, where the entrance to the subterranean complex was concealed, Kirk moved to the *Galileo* and tapped the controls on its exterior control pad to seal and lock its hatch. "Come on. We need to get back inside and warn the others. Something tells me we're going to have company." In addition to alerting his people to the new danger, there also was the matter of preventing the Romulans from getting inside the subterranean installation.

Even as he spoke the words, Kirk heard the high-pitched hum of a transporter beam, and turned to see five columns of energy coalescing into existence at the far end of the landing site, near the fallen Romulans.

"Okay," he said, reaching for Sortino to pull her with him. "Time's up."

The only thing left to do was run.

NINETEEN

Fools!

Vathrael's first shouts to cease fire were drowned out by the storm of disruptor energy as two of her centurions unleashed their weapons on the pair of running humans.

"Stop!" she barked, stepping forward and pushing the arm of the nearest centurion up and out of the way before he could fire again. When the subordinate looked at her with an expression of confusion and fear, she leaned so close that her face all but obscured his field of vision before hissing through gritted teeth, "They won't be able to answer our questions if you *kill* them." Capturing one or more of the human landing party and interrogating them was the entire reason for the covert reconnaissance, rather than simply disposing of them before she and her crew attempted to gain entry to the subterranean alien complex on their own. The centurions she had dispatched for that purpose obviously had acted carelessly, revealing their presence to the humans. Whatever element of surprise she might once have enjoyed had evaporated.

"My apologies, Commander," said the centurion, Sipal. "I saw them fleeing, and I reacted without thinking. My actions are inexcusable."

Standing next to him, his companion, Betria, swallowed

with obvious nervousness and added, "Mine, as well, Commander."

Ignoring their excuses, Vathrael returned her attention to the formation of large rocks at the base of the hill where the humans had disappeared. "Scan that area," she snapped, gesturing in that direction. "Find them."

Her order was answered by the low hum of a portable scanner one of the centurions had brought with him, and a moment later Betria said, "I am unable to detect their life readings, Commander."

"Are you certain?" she asked, then rebuked herself for even bothering to pose the question. The alien installation itself had escaped detection from the planet's indigenous population for generations. The *Nevathu*'s own sensors also had failed to find it, at least not until those systems were reconfigured. Vathrael suspected the party from the Federation ship would have been forced to make similar adjustments. Looking across the expanse of open terrain to where the pair of Starfleet shuttlecraft sat, she knew that the humans could not have been here very long before her arrival. Still, she did not discount any progress they might have made during that interval in their efforts to understand whatever they might have found beneath the surface.

Betria continued to study his scanner, making adjustments on the unit's control panel before saying, "Commander, I believe I have located an entrance to the underground facility." He pointed toward the hill. "It's where the humans were running."

"Of course it is," Vathrael said, resisting the urge to roll her eyes as she started walking in that direction. She paid no heed to the movements of her subordinates as they fell into step behind her, though she noted that they at least had the presence of mind to spread out into a formation that would offer some protection in the event of an ambush.

As she drew closer to the foot of the hillside, Vathrael saw a narrow opening, all but invisible from the plateau behind them, between two of the larger rock formations. Eyeing the ground at the base of the rocks, she detected signs of the massive stones having been moved to their present position. They seemed far too large to have been levered out of the way without some form of aid or mechanical assistance. As for the gap itself, there was almost nothing visible beyond the threshold save for the darkness beckoning to her.

"A concealed entrance," she said, more to herself than to the centurions behind her. "Some kind of automated mechanism to move the stones aside and admit entry, but why not close it to prevent us from entering?" Had the massive door somehow malfunctioned? Without any order from Vathrael, another of her soldiers, Centurion Drixus, stepped toward the opening, his weapon arm extended as he advanced.

Behind her, Betria said, "I am detecting no life-forms near the entrance, Commander." Now standing in front of the opening and using his body to shield hers, Drixus looked over his shoulder at her, waiting for instructions.

Vathrael nodded, her right hand coming to rest on the pommel of her own holstered disruptor. "Proceed, with caution." Following Drixus, she passed between the two large boulders and into the narrow gap. Once past that portal, she noted how the passage began to widen once they moved beyond the entrance. The darkness that seemed to shroud the opening was broken by a string of small, round light fixtures set into the tunnel's stone ceiling. The lights themselves varied in color, all soft hues and just enough illumination to proceed farther into the passageway. Vathrael noticed a soft, faint hum coming from the fixtures themselves, the noise amplified in the passage's narrow confines. It was cooler here as well, with a slight yet still perceptible breeze emanating from somewhere down the tunnel. Perhaps ventilation from a subterranean environmental control system? That was yet another question for which Vathrael hoped to find an answer.

A deep rumbling sound from behind her made Vathrael flinch, and she whirled to look in that direction, pulling her disruptor from its holster and extending her weapon arm toward the source of the sound. The three centurions who had been walking behind her were lunging forward, deeper into the tunnel, as the slice of light denoting the entrance from the surface began to narrow.

"Get away from there!" she yelled as the gap continued to close, and a moment later it vanished as though it had never existed. In response to the closure, the lighting within the tunnel increased, bringing the passageway's stone walls, floor, and ceiling into sharp relief. Turning to look down the sloping tunnel, she saw other shafts of light beginning to activate from within the walls. Power relays? Computer interface terminals? There was no way to know, at least not with the information she currently possessed.

"We're trapped," Betria said, holding up his scanner to emphasize his comment. "I am unable to read anything beyond the entrance."

Drawing a deep breath, Vathrael forced herself to maintain her composure. Despite the lighting's soothing effects, she still noted her odd twinge of apprehension as she regarded the enclosed space ahead of her. It was a fear that had stalked her since childhood, and even the *fvheisn* spent aboard the cramped confines of imperial warships had done little to help her surmount what she knew to be illogical angst.

Enough, she chided herself, ashamed that she had allowed the infantile sensation to impede her thinking even for a moment. "The door was closed," she said, "so it can be opened again, either by us or by those who closed it. All we have to do is find the mechanism to do that." Getting there likely would be difficult, of course, but the alternative was to stand here and do nothing, and Vathrael had never been one for such inaction. Her only concern was the loss of stealth; the Starfleet group had to know she and her people were here. Were they able to somehow monitor the complex's interior? "Betria, is your scanner able to detect any human life signs?"

After taking a moment to study the information being collected and displayed by the unit, the centurion shook his head. "Readings are indistinct, Commander, at least at a distance. I believe that some of the minerals in the surrounding rock have properties which interfere with my scans. However, I believe I'll be able to isolate their location the farther we move into the installation."

Vathrael nodded, only somewhat concerned with the report. Her years in command long ago had taught her to enter any potentially dangerous situation with the understanding that anything that might go wrong or present an obstacle was likely to make itself known. Such thinking tended to reduce surprises or the frustration that often came about as a result of being too reliant on a well-considered plan and not allowing for the realities of actual engagement with an enemy.

"Very well," she said before turning her attention to the fourth member of her party, Subcommander Atrelis. "It appears you'll get your chance to study whatever alien technology we find, if for no other reason than so that we might be able to report our discovery to our superiors."

The subcommander, a tall, thin soldier with dark hair, a thin, angular face, and thick, severely upswept eyebrows, nodded. "I accept that challenge, Commander," he said, his lips pressing into a small tight grin.

"Let's hope your confidence is not misplaced," Vathrael replied. Turning from the science officer, she made her way back down the tunnel until she came abreast of Drixus. The centurion, to his credit, stood where he had been since they had first entered the passageway, his weapon aiming down the long, narrow tunnel, on guard for any potential threat. Vathrael reached up to place a hand on his shoulder. "You are unwavering in your duty, Centurion, but whatever we are to face down here, I shall face it first."

Drixus nodded. "And I shall face it with you, Commander."

Comforted by the centurion's statement of loyalty, Vathrael stepped past him and began making her way down the tunnel, doing her best not to dwell on the feeling that the stone walls already were beginning to press in around her.

Reaching an intersection in the underground passage, Kirk, for perhaps the fourth time—he had lost count—brought his communicator to his mouth and called into it, "Kirk to Spock. Are you there?"

"*Spock here, Captain*," the Vulcan replied. Was it Kirk's

imagination, or was there more static clouding the connection now than there had been earlier in the day?

"Close the surface entrance to the complex. Romulan intruders are following us, and we can't let them get in here." He had tried and failed to close the entrance and reactivate its electronic shroud before he and Sortino were forced to flee deeper into the subterranean complex. The only hope now was that Spock could carry out that task from the control room. Kirk had no desire to try and fight the Romulans, outnumbered at least two and perhaps even three or four to one. A deep rumble echoed from somewhere back the way they had come, and Kirk sighed in momentary relief, realizing that Spock was acting on his instructions.

"Nothing says at least a few of them didn't get inside before it closed," Sortino said, a bit out of breath from the extended dash from the surface. "We need to keep moving, and get to the control room."

Kirk paused, catching his breath as he replayed the events on the surface. How long had it been since he and the ambassador had sprinted for the opening of the Kalandan complex, dodging disruptor fire as the Romulans transported to the plateau from an unknown origin point and gave chase? No more than three minutes, he decided, which likely meant only one thing.

"If they're already in here," he said. "They'll be trying to follow us." With his phaser, he gestured back the way they had come. "There are other tunnels and side passages. Most of them lead to chambers with no other exits, but we haven't had a chance to check them all. We have to go back and stop them from getting too far down here, before they find something they might be able to use against us."

Indeed, the more he pondered that line of thought, the angrier he grew with himself for not considering the possibility earlier, when he and Sortino could have taken more direct preventive action against their Romulan pursuers.

As though resigning herself to the situation, Sortino blew out her breath and tucked one of the phasers she had taken from the *Galileo* into her waistband. Holding up the second weapon, she appeared to check its power setting before returning her gaze to Kirk. "All right, then," she said. "Let's get this over with."

Despite the seriousness of the situation, Kirk grinned. "You're beginning to sound a lot like Doctor McCoy, Ambassador."

"If we're going to keep getting into firefights with Romulans," Sortino said, "you should probably start calling me Dana."

Shrugging, Kirk said, "Only if you call me Jim."

"Fair enough."

Leading the way back up the tunnel, Kirk wished he had thought to retrieve a tricorder from the *Galileo* before escaping back to the complex. That in turn made him wonder about the status of the two shuttlecraft outside, and whether the Romulans might take the time to ransack the vehicles in search of any valuable equipment or information they thought either ship might possess.

I doubt it, he decided. *All the fun is down here.*

Arriving at a T-junction in the passageway, Kirk paused, holding up his free hand and signaling for Sortino to remain silent. He inched his way forward, pressing his back against the stone wall and holding his phaser near his chest. Was it his imagination, or had a fleeting shadow played across the wall on the opposite side of the junction?

Something that sounded like cloth or leather against rock was just audible over the low drone of the overhead lighting. Kirk held his breath, straining to listen for other telltale signs of someone in the tunnel, but there was nothing. Still, instinct told him that he and Sortino were not alone here, and when he looked at her he saw that her features, obscured by shadow, were clouded with a suspicion he was sure matched his own.

Here goes nothing.

Kirk dropped to one knee as he leaned into the junction, bringing up his phaser and firing without even bothering to aim the weapon. The vivid blue streak of energy lit up the corridor, throwing into sharp relief the rock walls as well as the female Romulan officer standing no less than twenty meters away. She ducked to her right as the phaser beam struck the wall behind her, and Kirk noted four other shadow-laden figures lunging for cover in the passageway as he pulled himself back to safety. No sooner was he out of the way than a pair of disruptor bolts screamed past them, their shrill whines all but deafening in the tunnel as they drilled into the wall at the back of the junction. Kirk pushed Sortino in the direction of the passage leading deeper into the complex.

"Go!" he spat, back-stepping as he held his phaser out in front of him. Shadows undulated from the other tunnel, growing larger and more distinct. Kirk took aim at the lighting fixture illuminating the corridor junction and fired. The effect was immediate, destroying the lamp and evoking cries of shock from at least two of the Romulans.

Sortino yelled, "Come on!"

When he turned to run after her, he saw that the ambassador had taken up station at another bend in the passage, bracing herself against the wall as she aimed her phaser back the way they had come. "We've got to get to the others!"

Voices from beyond the intersection were growing louder with each passing moment as Kirk directed Sortino deeper into the tunnel. How far from the surface had they come? How much closer were they to the control room? Reaching for the small of his back, he grabbed his communicator and flipped it open as he continued his jog down the passageway.

"Kirk to Spock!"

This time, the Vulcan's response was immediate even though the quality of the signal was still lacking. "*Spock here, Captain. Are you all right?*"

"We're coming your way, Spock," Kirk replied, "and we're being chased by Romulans, so be ready for us."

"*Acknowledged, Captain,*" replied the first officer. "*You should also be aware that we are detecting the activation of several dormant systems within the Kalandan computer network.*" There was a pause before he added, "*We are not yet able to ascertain their exact purpose, but indications are that they are connected to the system's security protocols. Logic suggests there may be something taking place in response to the Romulan intruders, as well as weapons fire within the complex.*"

"*Blast your logic, Spock!*" shouted McCoy's voice from somewhere in the background. Then, as though the doctor had moved closer to Spock, he added, "*He's trying to say watch your back, Jim! You may have honked off something out there. Get the hell back here!*"

"We're working on it, Doctor," Kirk snapped, images and memories from the other Kalandan outpost rushing forth in response to Spock's new information. He pushed all of that aside. There would be time to deal with it later.

Maybe.

Three more turns in the corridor, and Kirk was just realizing that he now recognized where he was when a figure stepped into the tunnel ahead of them. Kirk's first instinct to raise his phaser and fire was quelled as he identified Spock. Lieutenant Ross Johnson and Ensign Nick Minecci, two security personnel who had accompanied the science officer from the *Enterprise*, emerged into the passage as Kirk and Sortino came abreast of them.

"They're right behin—" was all Kirk had time to say before a fresh volley of disruptor file exploded in the tunnel. Ducking into a crouch as something punched the rock wall behind him, Kirk gritted his teeth at the sting of stone shrapnel pelting his back. He put his hand between Sortino's shoulder blades and shoved the ambassador through the open portal leading to the control room at the same time that he felt a hand on his arm. In his peripheral vision he saw Spock standing to his left, the Vulcan's attention focused somewhere up the passageway.

"Get everybody in here and shut the door!" Kirk shouted, taking up a defensive position just inside the threshold and aiming his phaser up the corridor. He waited as a shadow played across the rock face at the rear of a turn in the tunnel, which was followed by a figure lurching around the corner. The Romulan soldier, his round gold helmet obscuring most of his features, halted his advance as he saw the reception waiting for him. It was all he could do before Kirk adjusted the aim on his phaser and fired. The weapon's blue beam caught the Romulan in the chest, and the centurion collapsed to the floor of the tunnel.

"Johnson! Minecci!" Kirk said, keeping his gaze directed ahead of him and waiting for the next intruder to show himself. "Get inside!" The security officers were moving past him and into the control room when the next Romulan appeared in the tunnel. Perhaps having learned from the mistakes of his companion, the soldier did not step into the line of fire, but instead hugged the corridor wall as he aimed his disruptor pistol toward Kirk. When the Romulan fired, Kirk ducked just long enough to avoid the attack before leaning once more into the passage and seeking a target with his phaser. Behind him, he heard the sound of something exploding, and he glanced back to see one of the consoles erupting in a shower of sparks and fire. The entire bank of monitors and interface panels went dark, after which a low, rumbling klaxon began wailing throughout the room and the corridor.

A sharp hum accompanied a vibration in the door frame he was gripping for support. Something made him look up, and it took him an extra instant to realize that the heavy, reinforced metal hatch was sliding down toward him.

Move!

He felt hands on him, pulling him to his feet and dragging him into the control room faster than he could have done on his own. Looking up, he saw Spock leaning over him, his stoic features betraying just the slightest hint of concern. The door finished closing, followed by the sound of metal locking into position with a loud, imposing snap. Though he had to strain to hear them, he still picked up the sounds of disruptor bolts striking the other side of the door.

Spock, talking loud enough to be heard over the alarm, said, "It would appear the Romulans are discovering for themselves the quality of Kalandan construction techniques."

"You okay, Jim?" McCoy shouted, moving forward and extending a hand to Kirk.

Nodding as he allowed the doctor to pull him to his feet, Kirk tried to ignore the klaxon as he eyed his first officer. "You could've warned me before you did that, Spock."

The Vulcan replied, "This was not our doing, Captain." Turning, he indicated where Uhura and Boma stood before the banks of Kalandan control consoles, several more of which were active and appeared to be operating at a more furious pace than when he was last in the room. As they watched, Boma ran his hand across one of the panels, and the annoying siren ceased.

"Thank you, Lieutenant," Kirk said, relieved to be free of the irritating sound as he turned back to Spock. "You were saying?"

"As I indicated," the Vulcan replied, "new systems have come on line. We are still working to ascertain their functions, but I believe at least some of them are dedicated to overseeing the complex's internal security protocols."

"And what might those be?" Sortino asked.

His expression never wavering, Spock said, "I cannot yet answer that question, Ambassador, but I would expect that the protection of key systems and other areas of the installation would be a high priority."

"Which would include intruder control?" Kirk asked.

Spock nodded. "That is a logical assumption."

"So," McCoy said, "what you're saying is, if the Romulans don't kill us, this place might do it all by itself?"

Turning to regard the doctor, Spock replied, "Colloquially expressed, yet essentially correct."

McCoy rolled his eyes. "I think I'm going to have that engraved on my tombstone."

Holding up his hand to put a stop to the banter, Kirk said, "Spock, can you do anything from here to override those systems, and maybe give us more control?"

Spock nodded before moving toward the nearest row of consoles. "We are endeavoring to do just that, Captain."

"Wait," Sortino said, and when Kirk looked at her he saw that she was frowning. "Does anybody hear anything?"

When Kirk realized what she meant, he said, "The Romulans. They've stopped firing."

"I doubt they're just giving up," McCoy said.

Now standing at one of the control consoles, Spock turned and called out. "They did not, Doctor. They were forced to retreat." He waited until Kirk and the others moved to stand next to him before he pointed to one of the console's display monitors. Kirk realized the image was that of the corridor outside the control room.

"A surveillance feed?" Sortino asked.

Spock replied, "Yes, Ambassador. It activated as part of the security subprocesses." He touched one of the circular clusters of colored lights on the flat black panel, and the image shifted to show the Romulans outside the room, firing at the door. "This is from a few moments ago." As they watched, new beams of energy rained down from a point beyond the image's borders, striking one of the Romulans. As he fell, his companions retreated out of the frame, somehow managing to avoid being struck by any of the beams.

"What the hell are those?" Sortino asked. "They weren't there before."

Spock answered. "No, Ambassador. They appear to be concealed weapons turrets—part of the complex's intruder control system, which is now quite active. From what I am able to determine, there are similar weapons deployed throughout the facility. We can only assume that the system will view us as a threat, as well."

"That can't be good," Kirk said, allowing a bit of sarcasm to lace his words as he watched the display's restored live feed. On the screen, two of the Romulans had returned, crouching as they pulled their fellow centurion out of sight around the bend in the corridor. "Is he dead, or just stunned?"

Boma replied, "Can't say for sure, Captain. According to this readout, the weapons can be set to incapacitate or kill, depending on the situation." He paused, clearing his throat before adding, "I'd rather not be the one to test the thing's limits."

Standing next to him, Uhura said, "There's something else, sir. It looks like the security system's not limited to just this planetoid."

It took Kirk an extra second to process the communications officer's statement before realization dawned. "The rift?"

Nodding, Uhura replied. "Yes, sir. It's closing."

"Spock," Kirk snapped, "can we stop it, or open it again?"

The Vulcan shook his head. "Not at present, Captain."

"Uhura, can you contact the *Enterprise*?" Kirk asked. "They need to know what's going on down here." The Dolysians doubtless would be alarmed at the rift's sudden closure and the effects it would have on their efforts to resupply the Havreltipa mining colony on Gralafi as well as transporting the erinadium ore from the planetoid to where it was needed on the homeworld.

"No, sir," the lieutenant said. "All frequencies are blocked, and our own communicators are being jammed, but I don't think it's coming from inside the complex."

"The Romulans?" Kirk asked, already knowing the answer.

Uhura nodded. "It looks that way, sir."

Damn it! Kirk thought. They were trapped down here, with no way to call for help even from the landing parties at the *Huang Zhong* wreck, much less anyone on the *Enterprise.* And if the Romulans were behind the jamming, then the team that had made it into the complex could call for help. "If the jamming were removed, could we use the Kalandan technology to contact the ship?"

Spock replied, "Possibly, Captain, but that would take time."

"Then we need a way to reach Kyle at the crash site," Kirk said. "I don't care how, just find something." Maybe his crewmen working the salvage operation might be able to help him.

Boma, still working at the adjacent console, turned and said, "I think we may have an even bigger problem."

"Of course we do," McCoy said, falling in behind Kirk as the captain and Spock moved to where the lieutenant pointed to one status display.

"What is that?" Kirk asked.

Before Boma could answer, Spock said, "A countdown, Captain. The security system has issued an emergency containment protocol, designed to go into effect when it believes it is under attack."

"The Romulans destroying that row of equipment over there?" Boma said, pointing to the ruined consoles along the wall near the door. "Those controlled access to the environmental control systems. An attack on that is like an attack on the entire complex."

Before Kirk could ask his next questions, a low whine cut him off, and he turned to see a beam of light cascading down from the control cube hanging at the room's center. Inside the beam, the indistinct form of Meyeleri took shape. She wore a dark blue robe and stood with her hands clasped before her as she seemed to fix her gaze on Kirk.

"*My fellow Kalandans, our defense system has detected a threat against this facility. In order to prevent the accumulated knowledge of our people from falling into the wrong hands, the system has initiated our final containment protocol.*"

"She's sure being nice about it," Sortino said.

Meyeleri continued, "*As caretakers of this repository, you undertook a pledge to protect it at any cost. Though it was hoped that such drastic steps would never be needed, no other choice remains. The sacrifice you are about to make on behalf of all the Kalandan people will always be remembered and honored. Thank you.*" She bowed her head as the projection faded before disappearing along with the cube's light beam.

McCoy asked, "Any more good news?"

"The explosion will consume this entire facility," the science officer replied. "The resulting shock waves could cause severe damage to the Dolysian mining settlement, and perhaps cause irreparable damage to the planetoid itself."

Releasing a snort of derision, McCoy said, "Does anybody besides me think that's more than a bit of an overreaction on the computer's part?"

"It might be that some key circuits related to decision support and response escalation were damaged by the

Romulans," Boma said. "We won't know until we start digging around."

Kirk felt his heart sink even as his mind raced to consider the safety of not just his people but also the Dolysians at the mining colony as well as the transport ships moving to and from the planetoid. "How much time do we have?"

"Two hours, twenty-six minutes, eleven seconds," Spock said, "converting from Kalandan time measurements, of course."

"What about the Dolysian miners?" Uhura asked. "Can they evacuate?"

Spock shook his head. "Even if we could warn them, there is insufficient time to effect an evacuation, Lieutenant. As it stands, the complex itself has been sealed, and each of the five clusters within the facility has also been locked down. We cannot get to the surface, though we can move to an adjacent cluster."

"We can't leave, even if we wanted to," Kirk snapped. "This planetoid is vital to the Dolysian people. Losing it or letting it suffer catastrophic damage would cause immeasurable harm to their society."

"Although not as important as protecting the Dolysians," Spock said, "there is also the Kalandan knowledge repository to consider. Given what we know of the Kalandan civilization's ultimate fate, it's very possible that the data stored here is irreplaceable. It should be preserved if at all possible."

McCoy said, "There's probably another planet like this one out there somewhere, Spock. Hell, there might be dozens of them, for all we know."

"If it comes down to the Kalandans or the Dolysians," Kirk said, "we're backing the Dolysians, not that it matters."

So far as he was concerned, there was only one course of action. "We have to stop the destruct sequence, no matter what."

"Or die trying," Sortino added. When Kirk turned to look at her, he saw the resolve in the ambassador's face, and nodded in agreement.

"Right," he said. "Or die trying."

TWENTY

Pavel Chekov frowned at the data being fed to him by the *Enterprise* sensors, not knowing what to make of the readings he was observing. "Mister Scott," he said, pulling his face away from the science station's hooded viewer, "I'm picking up a fluctuation from within the rift. Something's happening." Turning from his station, he looked to where Commander Scott sat in the captain's chair at the center of the bridge, an expression of concern clouding his features.

"Any idea what it might mean?" the engineer asked.

Chekov shook his head. "The readings aren't like anything we've observed since our arrival sir, and there's nothing comparable in any of the sensor data collected by the *Huang Zhong.*"

Gesturing toward the main viewscreen, which now depicted an image of the energy field as well as a Dolysian freighter on a course to enter the rift, Scott asked, "Could it be reacting to us, or even that ship?"

"I don't think so, sir," Chekov replied, returning his attention to the sensor viewer. Without looking, he reached to the rows of controls that allowed him to adjust the display of the data being routed to the viewer, switching between different displays that offered him all manner of information about the rift. Among the measurements and other statistical and tactical information was one figure that he now noticed was shifting. The number was decreasing, and beginning to do so at an accelerated rate.

"The rift's closing!" he shouted, turning from the science station to look back to the viewscreen, where it was now quite obvious that the energy barrier had started to contract. The gap in the field was growing smaller with each passing moment.

Rising from the command chair, Scotty asked, "Do we know what's causing it?"

"No, sir," Chekov replied. "At least, the sensors aren't telling us anything."

Sitting at the helm, Sulu pointed to the screen. "What about that freighter? Does the crew know the rift's closing?"

"M'Ress," Scott said, "hail that ship and warn them off."

"Opening a frequency now, sir," replied the Caitian lieutenant, turning to her station. After a moment, she added, "They seem to be aware of the situation, Mister Scott, and they are hailing us."

"On-screen, Lieutenant," Scott ordered.

The viewscreen display shifted from its depiction of the rift to that of a Dolysian female. She was dressed in a monotone green garment which to Chekov resembled a set of crewman's coveralls, and her hair was thick and unkempt. Standing at the center of what looked to be a cramped cockpit or bridge, her pale yellow skin looked almost white in the pale glow of the compartment's recessed lighting and the illumination cast off by the control consoles, which seemed crammed into every centimeter of available space.

"*Federation ship*," she said, her white eyes wide with

anxiety and confusion, "*I am Matrel Ketran ila Shul, master of the freighter* Yishayyk. *Can you tell us what is happening?*"

Stepping away from the captain's chair and around the helm console, Scott said, "Captain Ketran, I'm Commander Montgomery Scott, temporarily in command of the *U.S.S. Enterprise.* We registered the rift's closing at the same time you did. At this point, we have no explanation for what's happening. If I had more information, I'd happily share it with you. Do you know if there were other ships that might have been caught in the rift while coming from Gralafi?"

The Dolysian shook her head. "*I do not believe any of our ships were actually in the Pass at the time of the closing, but I do know that several freighters were scheduled to leave Gralafi in short order, each carrying full shipments of the erinadium ore produced by our mining facility.*" She paused, casting her gaze downward for a moment before adding, "*The situation would appear to have changed that, however. My ship contains replacement components for Havreltipa's environmental control and water filtration systems. If we are unable to deliver these supplies, it puts the miners and support personnel living there at risk.*"

Chekov nodded, understanding all too well that the rift's closure meant a disruption of the tight delivery window of crucial supplies and relief personnel to the Havreltipa colony. He had familiarized himself with the operation, marveling at the precision required to transport people and matériel on such a scale and within such a limited time frame. The process had been perfected over decades of practice, charging experienced hands like Captain Ketran with keeping the operation on its rigid schedule. Now, some unknown element had upset that delicate program, endangering not only one of Dolysia's primary industries but also the lives of hundreds of people living and working on Gralafi.

"Rest assured that we're investigating the problem with every resource at our disposal, Captain," Scott said to Ketran. "If there's anything we can do to assist you, please feel free to contact us directly."

On the screen, Ketran replied, "*Thank you, Commander.*"

As the communication was severed and the Dolysian's image was replaced once more by that of the rift, Scott turned to M'Ress. "Lieutenant, send a message to Chancellor Wiladra's office on Dolysia. Apprise her of the situation with the rift, and inform her that we're doing everything we can to figure out what's going on."

"Aye, sir," M'Ress said.

Turning from his station at the helm, Sulu looked first to Scott and then to Chekov before asking, "Do you think the rift closing might be connected to anything happening on Gralafi?"

"That was my first thought, Mister Sulu," Scott said, moving past the navigator's console on his way to the railing separating the command well from the upper bridge deck and the science station. "What do you think about that, Mister Chekov? Could the landing party have done something to trigger this? Can we rule out that the rift simply closed on its own the way it always does?"

Chekov resisted the urge to swallow the large lump that seemed to have taken up residence in his throat. "I'm not sure, sir, but I don't think the rift closed naturally. According to everything we know about it, the window for it remaining open is supposed to last at least for the next several days, and that's not even counting the safety margin the Dolysians factor into their schedule when planning the various transport runs. So long as they've been recording the rift's openings and closures, the window for passing through it has remained consistent."

"But none of those readings include anything that might have been caused by the passage of non-Dolysian ships," said Lieutenant Arex from where he sat behind Scott at the navigator's station.

Nodding, Chekov replied, "That's an excellent point, sir. Perhaps the Romulan ships or the *Huang Zhong* or even our own shuttlecraft have had some sort of unintended effect on the rift?" He had conducted all manner of scans against the energy field almost from the moment Mister Spock had assigned him to the task of filling in as the *Enterprise*'s science officer on the bridge while the Vulcan was away on Gralafi. No hints or clues to any sort of disruption that might have been caused by the passage of the shuttles had presented itself. Whatever had triggered the energy barrier's reaction to the ill-fated *Huang Zhong* and the Romulan scout ship seemed not to have had any lasting effects. Chekov had detected no obvious shift in the field's patterns prior to the closure, and now that the rift itself had disappeared, the barrier's readings appeared to have returned to normal. "Given that the Kalandan outpost on Gralafi controls the rift, I'm thinking that something there has caused this, either by accident or design."

"And what if it's because of something the Romulans did?" Arex asked. "The captain and the others could be in trouble, and we wouldn't even know it, much less be able to help them."

"Chances are the captain and the others know what's going on," Scott said, eyeing the image of the energy field on the main viewscreen. "I guess we should be thankful that whatever closed the rift didn't decide to boot us half-way across the quadrant."

Chekov nodded, recalling how the ship had been transported hundreds of light-years away from the other Kalandan outpost by the technology buried beneath the surface of that planet. It was not an experience he wanted to repeat, considering how the process had almost led to the ship's destruction.

"The captain might need our help," Sulu said, nodding toward the main viewscreen, "but with the rift closed, he can't reach us."

Scott sighed as he crossed his arms. "Aye, and vice versa. That field's not letting anything through, all right. So, we'll just have to figure out a way to get in touch with them, anyway." Eyeing Chekov once again, he asked, "Any thoughts on that, lad?"

"Not yet, sir," he replied, swallowing another nervous lump, "but I'll get on it right away." As Scott moved away from the railing on his way back to the command chair, Chekov turned to see Lieutenant M'Ress rising from her seat and walking toward him. She smiled, nodding to him as though offering encouragement.

"If you require any assistance," she said, "let me know." The offer and her tone were enough to cut through at least some of his anxiety, and for a moment he thought he might blush.

Swallowing the lump in his throat and trying not to look around the bridge to see if anyone was watching their exchange, he nodded and offered in what he hoped was a composed voice, "Thank you, Lieutenant. I'll be sure to do that."

M'Ress, either oblivious to his anxiety or else reveling in

it, smiled again before bringing her right hand from behind her back and extending it to him. When he looked down, he saw that she was holding his Academy-issued and never-returned personal eating utensil.

"For its good luck properties," she said, her eyes wide with amusement, though Chekov knew she was not mocking him. "I hope you don't mind, but I took it when I left this morning."

Now, he did blush. Taking the PEU from her, he again cleared his throat as M'Ress regarded him in silence for one final moment before turning and moving back to the communications station.

Chekov watched her go. Then, something made him glance toward Sulu, only to see the helmsman making an immense effort not to look in his direction. Was that a thin, knowing smile fighting to work its way onto his friend's face?

Wonderful.

Setting aside the distracting thoughts—and sights, welcome as they were—Chekov forced himself back to the matter at hand, and framed the issue in the simplest terms: until he solved the communications problem, the landing party was cut off from the ship and unable to request or receive aid, assuming they needed it. That was all the motivation Chekov required. While his skills and experience were no match for Spock's, he was comforted by the knowledge that the *Enterprise*'s science officer would not have placed him in this position of responsibility if he did not think him up to the task.

All I have to do now, Chekov mused as he tapped the PEU on the edge of the science station console, *is not let him down.*

TWENTY-ONE

Leaning into the tunnel so that her head and upper torso were exposed, Vathrael aimed her disruptor at the weapon turret mounted in the corner of the corridor intersection and fired. Heat from the pistol warmed her hand, and the energy discharge howled in the tunnel's narrow confines as the bolt slammed into the turret. A shower of sparks erupted from the weapon, and Vathrael saw part of it fall to the ground.

"So," she said, looking to where Subcommander Atrelis stood along with her centurions and nodded with approval, "they can be beaten."

Her science officer nodded as he reached up to brush a lock of damp, grayish-black hair from his face. "Based on the scan data I have collected, Commander, the defense system, while quite sophisticated, appears designed to operate within rigidly defined parameters. It seems to remain passive if not directly confronted, or if it fails to register threats against whatever it is programmed to protect."

"If not directly confronted," Vathrael repeated, stepping into the corridor and taking another look at the now-destroyed weapons mount. "Are you saying I didn't need to shoot that turret just now?"

Atrelis shrugged. "One can never be too careful, Commander. For all we know, there are additional weapons

which remain hidden, waiting to be triggered by some careless action on our part."

Sighing, Vathrael shook her head. Whatever was behind the activation of the automated weapons turrets
had also seen fit to disrupt communications, inhibiting
her ability to contact her ship and preventing her from
summoning reinforcements. This new complication only
served to heighten the anxiety she felt as she regarded the
tunnel walls and ceiling, which were far too close for her
taste.

Enough, Vathrael thought, irritated with herself for
allowing such distracting thoughts to gain any purchase
within her mind. There were far more urgent matters demanding her attention, not the least of which was finding
an exit from this underground maze. Finding and seizing
control of the alien technology at work here was still of
prime importance, but she already was beginning to wonder if that goal remained attainable. It was obvious that the
Starfleet team had acquired some measure of knowledge
and command of the mechanisms operating down here,
but how far did that influence extend? Vathrael recalled
the look of surprise on the human commander's face at the
moment the door to the control chamber closed. Had he
not been expecting that to happen? It was possible that the
ancient equipment was operating with complete autonomy,
and the humans were as powerless as she and her people to
affect anything.

An interesting notion, she decided.

Stepping closer to her, Atrelis held up his scanner.
"Commander, I believe I've located other areas within
this complex which might offer us access to the facility's
computer systems. If these readings are correct, then there

are other chambers containing equipment similar to that within the room the humans currently occupy."

Vathrael's eyes widened at this new information. "Are you certain?"

"Yes, Commander," replied the science officer. "There is considerable interference with my scans, but I was able to determine the location of one such chamber that is within a short walking distance. The others are at points farther away or deeper in the complex, and would require more time to reach. I was able to plot a path through the tunnels to take us to the chamber closest to us."

"Excellent," Vathrael said, already considering the potential of Atrelis's report. "If we can access this chamber, do you think you'll be able to interact with the technology we might find there?"

Atrelis glanced at his scanner before replying, "I believe so, Commander. I was able to collect some information during our skirmish with the humans. It is not much, but I think it is enough for me to begin deciphering the alien language, though I admit it likely will take some time."

"Not too much time, I hope," Vathrael said. Her next thought was interrupted by a string of chirps from the communications device on her belt. Retrieving the unit, she pressed its activation control and said, "This is Vathrael."

"*Commander?*" said the voice of Subcommander Sirad, much clearer and more free of static than was the case during her previous attempt to contact the *Nevathu*. "*Are you able to hear me?*"

"I am indeed," Vathrael replied. "It seems you've found a way to improve our communications."

The subcommander said, "*You can thank Mylas for that.*

A wizard, that one. He found a way of channeling power from the impulse engines to the communications array in order to strengthen our signal output and ability to receive. I do not pretend to understand a fraction of what he explained to me."

Buoyed by the knowledge that her first officer and the rest of her crew aboard the *Nevathu* were continuing to work at supporting her even while she was off the ship, Vathrael said, "Pass on my compliments to Mylas and his engineers."

"Our sensors are only just able to detect your life readings, Commander," Sirad said. *"We also register the presence of the humans. What are your orders?"*

"I want you to lead another team to our location," Vathrael replied. "If the humans are facing the same predicament that challenged us, they may be unable to contact their ship for assistance. For the moment, we may well have the advantage."

There was a pause, and when Sirad spoke again, there was a noticeable air of uncertainty in his voice. *"The advantage to do what, Commander?"*

Contemplating the enormity of the task she was about to undertake and realizing that her orders and her duty provided her with no alternative, Vathrael said, "To take this facility, or to prevent the humans from doing the same, by whatever means necessary."

TWENTY-TWO

Holding the pair of protective goggles to his face, John Kyle thought himself prepared for what was going to happen next, but he still flinched when the laser drill fired. The massive tool spat forth its beam of harsh, blue-white energy, carving with ease into the side of the *Huang Zhong*'s fractured hull. The accompanying whine of power emanating from the drill was enough to make Kyle wince in momentary discomfort and to scold himself for not remembering to don hearing protection before setting off the implement's firing sequence.

And you just know Doctor McCoy will be on you about that.

Standing behind the drill as it continued to fire, Kyle studied the unit's interface panel, noting the progress of the sequence he had programmed into its fire control system. It would take only seconds to cut through the targeted section of the *Huang Zhong*'s outer hull, and once it was out of the way the salvage party would be one step closer to having access to the ship's cargo space. He waited until the drill ceased operation, hearing the residual hum of the beam emitter before removing the goggles from his face. Looking up, Kyle saw Bill Hadley and Lieutenant Marshall Elliot moving into position with handheld antigrav supports, securing them to the section of hull plating he had just cut.

Working together, the two engineers were able to make short work of maneuvering the hull section out of the way, exposing the darkened interior of the wrecked ship.

"Wow," said Christine Rideout as she walked up behind him. "It's been a long time since I've seen one of those." The *Huang Zhong*'s chief engineer ran her hand along the laser's control panel, pausing as she studied the rest of the unit. "This one's not standard issue, though, is it? Looks to me like someone repurposed an old-style laser cannon."

Kyle smiled as he reached up to pat the rearmost of the drill's two spherical prefiring chambers. "Good eye, Master Chief." The chambers, mounted in sequence atop a movable and extendable support arm, were connected by a series of coils tasked with focusing the drill's beam and were linked to a short, wide barrel that was the tool's emitter. The entire apparatus sat atop a squat gray base into which was embedded the fire control panel and the unit's circular targeting scanner. The interface was but one of the many upgrades the drill had undergone since its conversion. "This thing was taking up space in one of the lower-level cargo holds. According to Scotty—sorry, Commander Scott—it hadn't even been used since before he came aboard as chief engineer. As the story goes, the *Enterprise* was surveying an uninhabited planet that was loaded with dilithium, and the geology team wanted to take some core samples. The laser drills they had weren't powerful enough to punch through the bedrock to get at the dilithium."

"And so your Commander Scott converted this behemoth into a supersized mining drill," Rideout said, nodding in appreciation as she reached up to wipe her forehead with the back of her hand. "Nice." The smudge of dirt or soot or whatever that had found its way to her face was now a streak, matching the one on her left cheek. Her dark green jumpsuit also was dirty, and there was a tear in the right leg just below her knee, which had occurred when the engineer was maneuvering through one of the *Huang Zhong*'s debris-littered corridors.

Shrugging, Kyle said, "He had to downgrade the power emitters and other systems, to make it more like a tool and less like a weapon capable of boring a hole straight to the center of a planet. It works well enough for various odd jobs."

"I guess so," Rideout replied. "Other than pictures in old technical manuals, I've never even seen one of these things outside of the Academy museum."

"They were always more trouble than they were worth," Kyle said. "When they're disassembled, you can't move the larger components without antigravs. Once they were set up, that's where they stayed, which isn't always the most practical idea, depending on the situation. Besides, if whatever you need to shoot at is too big for a phaser rifle, then you call up to your ship and let them have a go at it."

Rideout laughed at that. "And what if there's no ship in orbit?"

"Then you've got a whole new set of problems," Kyle replied. The thought made him look to where he had positioned *Enterprise* crew members on the perimeter of the crash site, each keeping vigil while the rest of the team continued the cleanup. The news from Mister Spock, that a Romulan scout ship might be somewhere in orbit or even on the planet, had caused a blanket of unease to settle over the entire team. Though he had posted the guards, along with people overseeing the sensors aboard both shuttlecraft, Kyle knew there was precious little he could do to prepare for any kind of Romulan attack. He could only hope that the Romulans were too busy elsewhere to bother with a simple salvage effort.

Looking away from the *Huang Zhong*, he saw that Hadley and Elliot had finished moving the separated section of hull plating to one of several collection points set up around the wreck. Most of the material placed at these locations had been deemed scrap and would be destroyed before the salvage team departed the planet. As for the unsalvageable items and other detritus, these were being hauled to these locations by *Enterprise* crewmen as well as volunteers from the Havreltipa mining colony.

"I have to say," he mused after a moment, "the Dolysians are no strangers to hard work, are they?" He had observed the volunteers as opportunity presented itself, and noted how they had labored tirelessly in support of Kyle and his team.

Rideout replied, "Just watching them makes me want to go and take a nap." She even punctuated her statement with what to Kyle's ears sounded very much like an authentic yawn. "I've been getting a lot of questions about some of the stuff we're stacking up to scuttle. More than a few miners have expressed their regret that so much material's being destroyed, rather than recycled in some form." She shrugged. "I can't say I blame them."

"If we were on Dolysia," Kyle said, "where our Federation liaison teams could work with them, that'd probably be okay, but once the rift's closed, the people here are on their own. Even melting some of this stuff down, if it's not done right, could produce toxic vapors or who knows what." Shaking his head, he added, "No, the best option is to remove it or destroy it." The sensitive equipment and other components earmarked for transport to the *Enterprise* were being staged in or near the *Ballard* and *Heyer*, the pair of shuttlecraft assigned to him in support of the salvage effort. Other shuttles had been committed to the task, but none of them had been able to leave the ship before Commander Scott placed a temporary hold on additional runs to and from Gralafi. Kyle gave silent thanks that the laser drill had been loaded aboard the *Heyer* and not the *Copernicus*, which still sat in the *Enterprise*'s shuttlebay, stuffed with additional equipment for him and his team. The salvage crew would have to make do for the time being, but the drill at least was able to assist with the necessary task of extracting the sensitive computer equipment, weapons, and other matériel from the *Huang Zhong*.

"Speaking of potential problems," Rideout said, "even with the pace we're keeping, there's no way we're going to be finished before we have to leave." Blowing out her breath, she added, "I guess we should be thankful we didn't crash something bigger."

Kyle nodded. "I suppose that's one way of looking at it." Scarcely sixty hours remained before he and his team would be forced to change from salvaging equipment components to destroying them, after which they would flee the planet and the energy field surrounding it. "Still, you're right; we'll never get to it all before we have to shut down the operation, and I don't particularly want to stay here for the next three years."

When he turned to look at her, he saw that Rideout had cast her gaze toward the ground, and her expression was one of sadness. "I wouldn't mind it," she said, her voice little more than a whisper. "I'd be okay with it, if Captain Arens and the others were stuck here with me."

As he had on the previous occasions during the past day they had spent working together and the engineer had allowed some of her grief to show through the façade she had erected around herself, Kyle remained silent, not wanting to say or do anything to upset her further. She had already demonstrated that she was more than capable of handling the understandable onslaught of emotions without assistance, though she did so by forcing back those feelings before they could overwhelm her. That carried its own cost, Kyle knew, and these brief moments were her way of releasing some of that pressure.

Aware that he was watching her, Rideout looked up at him and offered a small smile. "Sorry. I got distracted there for a second."

"No apologies necessary," Kyle offered. "You haven't had a chance to catch your breath, much less take the time to rest or recover from what happened." He made a mental note to ask Doctor McCoy to talk with her when the opportunity presented itself. Though he was not a licensed psychiatrist or mental health professional, being the chief medical officer of a starship crewed by more than four hundred people tended to hone one skills in those arenas. Further, Leonard McCoy's natural affinity for helping people identify and seek solutions to their problems and difficulties made him the ideal shoulder on which to lean.

After another moment, Rideout smiled again, and this time Kyle saw that it did not seem to be a forced response. "Okay, that's enough break time to hold me for a while. Time to get back at it."

Kyle heard footsteps approaching and turned to see Liadenpor Ceeda hu Novi, the group leader for the Dolysian miners helping the *Enterprise* team, walking toward them.

Like everyone else involved in the salvage work, Ceeda's clothing and exposed skin were disheveled, and though Dolysian facial expressions did not always correspond to human responses, Kyle was still able to tell that the miner was tired.

"Lieutenant," Ceeda said, then bowed his head in greeting to Rideout. "I wanted to inform you that we have completed our sweep of the crash site and have collected all loose debris. Most of it appears to be unsalvageable, but we did find a few components which we think your team should examine before a final determination is made."

Smiling in appreciation, Kyle replied, "Excellent, Ceeda. Thank you, and thank you for everything you and your people have done to assist us. We could not have made this much progress without you."

Ceeda seemed pleased with the compliment, if not a bit self-conscious. "You are very kind, Lieutenant." He paused as though considering his next words. "I must admit that when we on Gralafi heard our home planet had been visited by beings from another world, there was a variety of emotional reactions. Excitement, fear, curiosity, confusion, doubt; everywhere you turned, someone had a different opinion, and a different prediction. Not a few of us wondered if you had come to conquer us." The corners of his mouth turned upward in the Dolysian equivalent of a smile. "I am happy to say that my initial belief was proven wrong."

Laughing at that with an intensity that nearly brought her to a coughing fit, Rideout took a moment to regain her composure. "Nicely played." After covering her mouth for one last cough, the engineer asked, "Are you one of the colonists who will be staying here after the rift closes?"

"No," the Dolysian answered. "My assignment with the colony is at an end. I will be leaving on the last transport once we are finished here. My family has already departed and is back at our home on Dolysia."

"You were able to bring your family with you," Kyle said. "That must've made things a lot more bearable."

Ceeda nodded. "I have spent more time with my children during this assignment than when I was sent to our lunar mining colony. That facility does not possess the same amenities as Havreltipa, owing to its easy accessibility. Rotations there are shorter, as well, but it can still be lonely without family." Looking first to Kyle and then Rideout, he asked, "Do you have families?"

"Not me," Rideout replied. "Maybe after I decide to leave Starfleet and settle somewhere, but I don't see that happening any time soon."

Kyle added, "Same for me. This life doesn't really lend itself to raising a family, but maybe one day."

"John!"

Startled by the shouting of his name, Kyle turned to see Lieutenant Donovan Washburn running toward him. A tall, lanky man, Washburn's blue uniform tunic seemed almost a size too small as he jogged over the expanse of open ground separating what remained of the *Huang Zhong* from the *Ballard* and the *Heyer* as well as the Dolysian cargo transport, which was perhaps twice the size of the *Enterprise* shuttlecraft. He ran with his right arm extended, and Kyle saw that he was holding a communicator.

"It's Captain Kirk!" Washburn called out between breaths as he ran up to Kyle. "Something's happened!"

Kyle took the communicator, hearing the static

emanating from the unit as he adjusted its antenna grid. "Lieutenant Kyle here, sir."

"*Kyle, we've got some serious problems here,*" Kirk said. "*Romulans have infiltrated the facility, and the defense system has reacted by sealing off the complex and closing the hole in the energy field. It's also initiated a self-destruct sequence. We're trapped here, so we're doing everything we can to stop it.*"

"What?" Rideout exclaimed, her eyes wide.

"It's true, Chief," Washburn replied. "I just tried to contact the *Enterprise*, and I'm getting nothing but static. We're trapped here."

Ceeda also was troubled by this news. "The Pass has already closed?"

Ignoring the side commentary as he listened to the static engulfing the channel, Kyle said, "We're getting a lot of interference, Captain."

"*We think the Romulan ship may be jamming our frequencies,*" Kirk replied. "*Mister Spock and Lieutenant Uhura were able to punch through that, but I don't know how long it'll last.*"

"What can we do, sir? Do you need us to come and help get you out of there?" As he asked the questions, Kyle was looking to Washburn and motioning for him to start alerting the others about the change in the current situation.

"*No,*" the captain snapped. "*Stay away from here. Whatever happens when this place goes up, it'll be powerful enough to take out the entire complex, and it might damage the colony, too. Your help might be needed there if we can't stop it. For now, though, I need you to find that Romulan ship.*"

Now confused, Kyle frowned in confusion. "I don't understand, sir."

"*I need you to find that ship, and stop whatever they're using to jam us,*" Kirk said. "*If we can do that, we may be able to use the Kalandan equipment to reopen the rift and contact the* Enterprise."

"Find a Romulan ship, sir?" Kyle was not sure he could believe what he was hearing. How could he, with two shuttlecraft and less than twenty people, do anything of use against a Romulan vessel?

"*Lieutenant Kyle,*" a new voice said, "*this is Mister Spock. The ship you are seeking is a scout-class vessel, lightly armed and with a small crew. Based on the strength of the jamming signal, I believe the ship is somewhere on the planet's surface. You should be able to use sensors to track the signal to its source.*"

That part seemed easy enough, Kyle conceded, but that still left one very large and very unexplained part of Captain Kirk's plan. "And if we find the ship, sir?"

Kirk's voice, punctuated by bursts of static, now held a new edge. "*Do whatever you have to do, Mister Kyle, but stop that signal.*"

After wishing him good luck, the captain terminated the communication, leaving Kyle to stare with mounting anxiety at Rideout, Washburn, and Ceeda.

"Just when you think it can't get any weirder," Rideout said.

Washburn nodded. "Amen to that, Chief."

Stepping forward, Ceeda held out his hands toward Kyle. "We stand ready to assist you, Lieutenant."

Appreciating the unsolicited offer, Kyle shook his head. "I can't ask you to do that, Ceeda. If this goes according to the captain's plan, then it's liable to be dangerous."

"I understand," Ceeda replied, his tone firm, "but these

Romulans threaten my people, too. That cannot stand, and neither can we stand and allow you and your people to accept risk on our behalf. Let us help you."

Uncertain as to how he might proceed with the aid of the Dolysian miner and his companions, Kyle surveyed the crash scene. *Enterprise* crew members and Dolysians alike were gathering, waiting for their next instructions. What was he going to tell them?

Tell them that the race is on, in more ways than one.

TWENTY-THREE

Scott shifted in the captain's chair on the *Enterprise* bridge, as always feeling self-conscious about occupying the most powerful position on the ship. In truth, he had never been comfortable assuming command, no matter how short the duration. He did not like sitting and watching while others performed their assigned duties, waiting for those same fellow crewmates to report to him as circumstances required. Instead, he preferred to preside over the vessel's inner workings from the welcoming environs of the engineering decks or, if circumstances warranted, the network of crawlways and Jefferies tubes that gave him unfettered access to the ship's most sensitive systems. There, he could put his hands directly on the source of a problem and solve it through the measured application of knowledge, experience, and—in some rare instances—even blunt force if the situation called for such action. It was there that Scott was in his element.

Here and now, however? He never failed to feel as though he were casting about, searching for the proper solutions to problems better addressed by those more competent than he. Whereas training and experience had taught him how to lead the engineers and technical specialists he oversaw as part of his primary duties, such skill was not a natural aspect of his character. Other officers, James

Kirk in particular, harbored within them an innate ability to seize command of a situation and guide with unwavering confidence any who would follow them. Scott, on the other hand, had always found such demands a struggle. Indeed, he recalled with some amusement the first time Captain Kirk uttered to him the most frightening words the engineer had ever heard on the bridge of a starship: "Mister Scott, you have the conn." Once he had pushed past his own anxiety, Scott realized on that first occasion that Kirk would never leave him in command of his ship so long as he possessed any doubts about his chief engineer's ability to carry on in his absence.

So, carry on, then.

Drumming the fingers of his right hand on the arm of the command chair, Scott leaned back into the seat as he studied the main viewscreen and its image of the roiling sphere that was the energy field encircling the Gralafi planetoid. At this moment, the field was indeed a barrier in every possible sense, not only separating the *Enterprise* from Captain Kirk and the rest of the landing party, but also preventing Scott from contacting them, as well.

Then there was the much larger issue of the impact the closing of the rift was having on Dolysian shipping traffic. Reports from the Jtelivran Mining Conglomerate as well as the Unified Leadership Council were coming at regular intervals, each one more anxious than the last. Given the limited window of opportunity to transit the Pass, every shipment was critical, and the schedule to move ships through the rift in both directions was coordinated to an exacting degree. Any delay carried with it the potential to disrupt the schedule for hours or days at a time, increasing the risk of needed personnel and matériel not making it to

Gralafi. If the rift could not be reopened, the planetoid's mining colony would be denied equipment and other supplies it needed in order to sustain itself for the nearly three years it would be cut off from the Dolysian homeworld. Further, what if whatever had closed the rift in the first place had done so in such a manner that it could not be reopened? What would that do to the Dolysians?

That just won't happen. Captain Kirk won't allow it. Not while there's breath in his body.

"Are we ready to launch the buoys?" Scott asked.

"I believe so, sir," replied Ensign Chekov as he rose from his seat at the science station. "Lieutenant M'Ress has completed her modifications and is on her way back to the bridge."

Scott nodded, satisfied with the report. While he had been the one to suggest the use of a subspace relay buoy to enhance the strength of any signal broadcast via the ship's communications system, it was M'Ress who had figured out the necessary modulation requirements for the device's transceiver array. The Caitian officer also had been the one to figure out that using two such buoys, each programmed to broadcast via different yet complementary oscillating frequencies, might provide the variations in signal strength and clarity necessary to punch through the energy field. M'Ress had likened the idea to harmonizing different musical instruments, about which Scott at first had expressed skepticism. The lieutenant's computer models had convinced him of her idea's merits, and she set to work making the necessary modifications to the pair of buoys Scott had ordered pulled from cargo storage. It was a lot of effort, he knew, but without any other means of contacting the captain or the other members of the *Enterprise* crew on Gralafi, he saw no other alternative.

We might as well try every crazy idea anyone can come up with, Scott mused, *because I'm not leaving here without the landing party.*

He heard the doors to the turbolift opening behind him, and he swiveled his chair to see M'Ress emerging from the car.

"All modifications are complete, Mister Scott," the lieutenant reported by way of greeting. "We can proceed whenever you're ready."

"Excellent work, Lieutenant. Thank you," Scott replied, letting his chair return to its normal forward-facing position. "Seems like now is as good a time as any. Let's see if all our jury-rigging has bought us anything. Mister Arex, transfer navigational data to the buoys and stand by to launch." While M'Ress saw to the tasks of making the physical modifications and software configuration changes for the subspace relays, it had been up to the navigator, with Chekov's assistance, to plot the best placement of the relays in proximity to the energy field.

As he tapped a series of controls on his console, Arex nodded without looking up from his station. "Aye, sir. Co-ordinates have been fed to the buoys. Standing by."

"Lieutenant M'Ress?" Scott prompted, looking over his shoulder to the communications station. "Ready?"

The Caitian turned in her seat. "Yes, Mister Scott. All monitoring systems are on line, and I've established the link to both buoys' frequencies."

"Send them on their way, Mister Sulu," Scott ordered. As he watched the helmsman carry out the order, he imagined the pair of compact devices leaving the *Enterprise* from their launch tube on the underside of the secondary hull, careening away from the ship as they followed their prescribed courses toward their designated positions near the energy field's outer boundary.

Arex said, "Both buoys on course. Estimate reaching final positions in twelve seconds." The Triexian pressed another control, and the image on the main viewscreen changed to a computer-animated representation of the energy field and the pair of buoys as they described independent arcs toward their prescribed coordinates.

"Is the field reacting to their approach?" Scotty asked, frowning as he eyed the viewscreen.

Hunched over the hooded scanner at the science station, Chekov replied, "I'm not picking up any new fluctuations, sir."

"It could be that they're too small to attract any attention," Sulu offered.

"That could be," Scott replied. He had not thought to consult any of the reports regarding Dolysia's space exploration efforts as submitted by the Federation first-contact team. Perhaps there was something in there detailing the Dolysians' initial studies of the energy barrier with unmanned probes and the field's reactions to those attempts.

It's a little late for that now, isn't it?

An indicator tone sounded on Arex's console, and the lieutenant said, "The probes have reached their designated positions and are now station-keeping."

"M'Ress, open a channel to Captain Kirk," Scott ordered.

"Aye, sir," the lieutenant replied, entering the necessary commands to her console. With her left hand, she reached for her Feinberg receiver and inserted it into her ear. "Frequency open. Sending the hail now."

Instead of a response from the captain, there was only

the sound of a wailing alarm. Scott flinched as it bellowed from recessed speakers around the bridge, loud enough to make him grit his teeth.

"Turn that thing off!" he snapped, rising from the captain's chair and looking to Chekov. "What's happening?"

The ensign was dividing his attention between the scanner and the science station's other status displays. He dropped into his seat, both hands moving across the rows of controls as he worked. "Some kind of fluctuation in the buoys' communications relay, sir. It's like the signal's being reflected back, but at an increased strength." Then, Scott saw the younger man's entire body tense before he shouted, "M'Ress, cut the signal!"

Though she moved with startling speed, the Caitian's response still was not quick enough. Just as she was reaching for her own console to sever the communication, status indicators at her station changed from green to red, and a litany of alert tones clamored for attention. M'Ress ignored them as she tapped several controls, and a moment later the annoying warning signals fell silent. As he moved around the captain's chair and stepped toward her station, Scott was still able to see several of the status displays flashing in alternating shades of harsh crimson.

"What went wrong?" he prompted, leaning past her and punching several controls as he called up a series of diagnostic protocols.

M'Ress said, "Some form of feedback loop, sir." She pointed to one of the status monitors. "The signal was refracted when it came into contact with the barrier. It generated a feedback pulse that almost overloaded our entire communications array. I was able to sever the connection, but it still managed to damage some of our systems."

Able to see that much just from his scrutiny of the console's status monitors, Scott replied, "It doesn't look too bad. Mostly circuit burnouts, but I guess we shouldn't try broadcasting through the barrier again." He shook his head. Though the damage from the signal surge was for all intents and purposes minor, it still would impede the ship's communications abilities. His eyes lingered on the status message notifying him that long-range transmissions via subspace were compromised, preventing him from dispatching status updates—or requests for help—to Starfleet. "Notify engineering to assign a team to the repairs, Lieutenant. You take charge, and keep me informed."

"Aye, sir," M'Ress acknowledged. She turned back to her console, and Scott heard her contacting Lieutenant Palmer, one of the *Enterprise*'s junior communications officers, to report to the bridge as her relief.

Moving back to the command chair, Scott rested his left hand on its armrest, pondering whether he should retake the seat. With repairs—even minor ones—about to get under way, he knew he did not want to sit idle. His instinct was to put Sulu in charge so that he could oversee and perhaps accelerate the mending of the beleaguered communications system, but he dismissed the notion. He could justify leaving the bridge for an emergency, but his duty at the moment was here, and he would have to trust in M'Ress and his own staff to carry on without him looking over their shoulders.

Easier said than done.

The alert indicator at the center of the helm-navigation console flared red, accompanied by its dull beeping tone, at the same time that both Sulu and Arex looked over their shoulders in his direction.

"Deflector screens just went up," Sulu reported.

Scott looked to Chekov, who was already manning the sensor viewer at his station. "Long-range sensors are detecting vessels approaching," he said. When he twisted his body to look away from the viewer, Scott saw the apprehension on the ensign's face. "Three ships, sir. Romulan."

"Birds of Prey?" Scott wondered aloud. "Or Klingon D-7s?"

Chekov took an extra moment to study the sensor readings before answering, "Definitely not Klingon design, sir. Most likely Birds of Prey."

That was something of a relief, Scott decided. Though the *Enterprise* had already encountered Romulans crewing Klingon battle cruisers as the result of a technological exchange pact between the two powers, the most recent intelligence reports indicated that only a small number of the larger, more powerful vessels had been included in that trade. Given a choice, Scott would rather face the Romulans' own warships.

Well, maybe not three of them.

"They're not cloaked?" Arex asked.

"No, sir," Chekov replied, "and they're definitely heading in this direction. I estimate their arrival within the hour."

Sulu added, "Probably looking for their missing ship." He shook his head. "They're not going to be very happy when they get here."

"Aye," Scott said, "you can be sure of that. Lieutenant M'Ress, signal our liaisons for the Dolysian leadership council and the civilian mining company. Alert them to the current situation, and advise them that they should restrict all space traffic until further notice."

M'Ress said, "Acknowledged, but even such a short-distance communication will have some loss of signal clarity."

"Just make it clear enough to be understood," Scott replied. "We'll worry about the formalities and proper explanations later."

"They're not going to like that," Chekov noted.

Nodding, the engineer said, "I know, but the last thing we need is to offer up any easy targets." Dolysian spacecraft would be susceptible to damage from Romulan weapons fired at even a minimal setting. He did not want to think about the results should one of the approaching warships elect to fire on an unshielded civilian freighter with the full might of its offensive weapons.

He frowned as he once more regarded the energy field on the viewscreen. Somewhere beyond that barrier, Captain Kirk and the rest of the landing party waited, perhaps needing help from the *Enterprise*, and there was nothing Scott or anyone else could do at the moment to help them. Likewise, Scott himself was without the guidance he might have sought from the captain. Even if he could call for assistance from Starfleet, there was no way such aid would arrive in time to be of any practical use. Whatever happened in the next twelve minutes, it would fall to him to lead the way, and Captain Kirk would be counting on him to carry out that duty to the best of his ability.

Releasing a small sigh of resignation, Scott moved to the command chair and sat.

He had the conn.

TWENTY-FOUR

His lungs beginning to burn from extended exertion, Kirk sprinted down yet another stretch of underground tunnel, searching for threats. Despite the cool air permeating the complex, he still felt sweat beneath his clothes and running down the sides of his face. Slowing as he approached the next turn in the passageway, he pressed himself against the rock wall and peered around the corner. Perhaps ten meters away and mounted just beneath the ceiling at the corner of a three-way junction was another of the automated weapons placements. Unlike the last turret he had dispatched moments earlier, Kirk saw that this one was operational. The faint glow of its multidirectional motion sensor cast a faint crimson glow across the rock of the nearby walls. As for the weapon itself, it swiveled in a ninety-degree arc from left to right and back again, scanning the three segments of passageway before it.

He held up his left hand, making a fist and indicating for Sortino and Ensign Minecci to maintain their positions. "We're here," he said, keeping his voice low and confirming to the others that they had reached their destination. "There's a turret. Active." He gestured toward the tricorder Minecci held in his hand. "Anything?"

The security officer shook his head. "Muddled readings,

sir. Whatever's interfering with the scans, I think it's getting worse."

Kirk grunted in irritation, even though Minecci's report was something he had anticipated as they drew closer to the operations chamber, which was their goal. From the moment the Kalandan outpost's internal security systems had come on line, they had caused problems for him and the landing party. Communicating with the *Enterprise* was for all intents and purposes out of the question, given Spock's report that the rift within the energy barrier surrounding Gralafi had closed. Even with the extra boost provided by routing signals through the communications systems of the two shuttlecraft on the surface, the barrier itself prevented any connection. It was a reality the Dolysians had faced for decades since the establishment of their mining colony here, but one for which Kirk had little patience at the moment. Tricorder scans, already compromised to a degree thanks to the scattering and other damping fields working to conceal the outpost's presence, were further hampered by the security measures now in play. Spock, Uhura, and Boma were at this moment attempting to fashion some sort of workaround to that issue, but they had their hands full just trying to find some way to override the complex's impending self-destruct protocol.

It's always something.

Even without the benefit of a tricorder, Kirk's gut told him one thing: if the turret at the end of the passage was active, it had detected something it considered a threat. Did that mean the Romulans were close by? Given that the operations chamber the weapon guarded was the closest such facility within easy walking distance, it did not make sense for the Romulans to be anywhere else if they were looking for a fast way to gain access to the outpost's technology. They doubtless were suffering the same sorts of setbacks thanks to the security system, and were without question looking for their own tactical edge in what was fast becoming a game of subterranean cat and mouse.

"What are you doing?" Sortino asked, watching as Kirk adjusted the power setting on his phaser.

"I don't feel like waiting for the Romulans to pin us down," the captain said. Peering around the corner again, he noted that the turret was swiveling away from him. He figured he had perhaps five seconds before the weapon began to swing back in his direction. That would be enough, he decided as he stepped into the tunnel and took aim at the turret. He sighted along the top of his phaser, focusing on the base of the weapon just as the unit's motion sensor glowed brighter and its inner mechanism hummed louder. Its speed accelerated as it swept back toward him, and he knew that the thing had detected his presence. The turret locked on him just as he pressed his phaser's firing stud and a blue beam spat forth, the whine of the weapon's discharge all but deafening in the narrow tunnel. There was a brief flash of light as the beam struck the turret, a shower of sparks erupting from its base. Kirk kept his phaser trained on the unit until he saw the motion sensor fade to black, and the hum of its internal motor died.

"That thing could've cut you in half, you know," Sortino said.

Kirk sighed as he reset his phaser to stun force. "I try not to think about it like that." Now free from the scrutiny of the defense system, at least in this section of the complex, he moved forward into the tunnel. With his phaser held out before him, his eyes focused on the metal door set into the stone on the left side of the corridor near the junction. "According to Spock, this door leads to the second control chamber."

Behind him, Minecci said, "That tracks with the readings I'm getting, sir. Whatever's behind that door, it's pulling a lot of power."

"Let's just hope whatever instrumentation we find in there is compatible with the other room's," Kirk replied. "Otherwise, this little field trip will have been for nothing." Based on what Spock had told him, each of the five operations chambers located at different points within the underground complex seemed to have been designed to operate independent of the others. Despite this, and as far as the science officer had been able to determine, each of the rooms was subject to override by any of its counterparts. In theory, if the Romulans were able to seize control of just one of the remaining operations centers, they might well lock out Spock and his team, and perhaps even turn the outpost's defenses against the *Enterprise* party.

So, Kirk mused with no small amount of apprehension, *let's try to avoid that, shall we?* As things currently stood, the Romulans could cause enough trouble, and that was without considering the ticking clock that was the outpost's containment protocol. In order to protect whatever chance Spock and the others might have of aborting the outpost's destruct sequence, Kirk saw no alternative but to do everything possible to deny the Romulans access to any of the Kalandan technology.

"Come on," he said, motioning for Sortino and Minecci to follow him. As he moved closer to the door, he was able to see the openings leading to the other two passages meeting at this junction. The door was positioned between the corridors, and each of the tunnels curved away in different directions. Kirk recalled what Spock had told him about this area of the complex, remembering that the closer of the two corridors charted a path deeper into the bowels of the underground facility and the massive generators supplying power. The other passage cut a lateral swath through this part of the installation, intersecting with other tunnels and rooms, including what looked to be an environmental control plant as well as yet another of the operations chambers.

Separating him from that area of the facility, Kirk knew, were yet more of the weapons deployed as part of the internal security system. So far as Spock had been able to determine, the mounted turrets were the extent of such weapons, but even the ever-reliable first officer had expressed doubts when considering the incomplete information available to him. Despite the lack of concrete knowledge regarding the full extent of the outpost's defenses, Kirk had no choice but to risk venturing deeper into the complex in a bid to stop their Romulan adversaries from gaining access to any of the ancient yet still quite dangerous Kalandan technology.

Kirk paused before crossing the threshold of the other tunnel and looked over his shoulder at Minecci. "Readings?" he asked, his question little more than a whisper.

The security guard frowned as he studied his tricorder. "The interference is getting stronger the closer we get to the ops room, sir." Returning his phaser to his hip, he reached up to manipulate the tricorder's control panel. "I don't understand it, Captain. Whatever this is, it wasn't there before."

"Something new from our Kalandan friends?" Sortino asked, leaning closer to look over Minecci's shoulder at his tricorder.

"I don't know," Kirk replied, "but whatever it is, we have to find a way around it. Until we can reopen the rift and warn the *Enterprise* about the Romulans down here, we're on our own." Poking his head around the threshold leading to the other tunnel, he saw nothing but more rock walls, floor, and ceiling. Except for one darkened area perhaps three-quarters of the way down the tunnel, overhead lighting fixtures were spaced at regular intervals down the length of the passage until it came to a bend, perhaps fifty meters from where he stood, that curved to the right.

Wait.

No sooner had he pulled back from the junction than Kirk realized something about the corridor was . . . *wrong*. What had vied for his attention, if only for a fleeting moment?

"Jim?" Sortino asked. "What's the matter?"

Shaking his head, Kirk replied, "I don't know. I just—" He stopped as his eyes fell on the tricorder in Minecci's hand. The device had proven all but useless during their move from the operations chamber, a difficulty explained by interference created as one part of the facility's security protocols, but what was it Minecci had said? Something new had taken to disrupting his tricorder?

Son of a—

Without warning, Kirk stepped back into the intersection, aiming his phaser at the patch of darkness created by the pair of extinguished lighting fixtures near the far end of the corridor. He fired, the beam striking a point along the rock wall, and the reaction was immediate as shadows broke away from the sides of the tunnel and lunged into the illumination cast by other lights farther down the hallway. Kirk caught sight of silver and red and even a reflection of something gold and rounded—a Romulan centurion's helmet.

"Kirk!" Sortino snapped. "What the hell are—?"

A hailstorm of disruptor fire exploded from the mouth of the tunnel as Kirk jumped across the threshold, seeking cover on the other side of the passageway. Energy bolts slammed into the wall behind him, sending a cloud of stone shrapnel into the tunnel. Kirk stepped farther from the tunnel mouth, his back to the doorway leading—he believed—to the operations chamber. The assault from the corridor faded, and Kirk was sure he heard the sounds of footsteps running toward him. At least two assailants, he figured, possibly more. He would not have time to try his hand at opening the door the way Spock had instructed him, and he and his team might find themselves outnumbered in short order. What to do?

Dana Sortino provided the answer.

"Ambassador!" was all Kirk could shout at Sortino, who was once more brandishing a phaser pistol in each hand as she stepped into the tunnel and fired both weapons. Twin streams of blue energy lanced down the passageway as Ensign Minecci took a position next to her, dropping to one knee and firing his own phaser. Kirk leapt forward, unwilling to let his charges take on that kind of risk without him, and added his own weapon to the fray. The darkness at the halfway point of the tunnel was illuminated by the flashes of phaser fire, and Kirk saw at least two figures lying unmoving on the tunnel floor. Another figure had already retreated to the far end of the corridor, taking refuge around the passage's bend.

"Come on!" Kirk shouted, gesturing with his free hand for Sortino and Minecci to head for the operations chamber's doorway. Pausing before the panel set into the wall that controlled access to the room beyond the door, he already could hear more sounds of running in the corridor, but he was certain they were coming from more than one direction. Within seconds, by his estimate, he and his team would be outflanked, so long as they remained in this corridor. The only options were running for safety or getting through the doorway, and overriding the door's control panel even with Spock's detailed instructions would take far too much time.

Kirk aimed his phaser at the door panel and fired.

Dashing up the corridor, Vathrael paused to kneel beside Betria and Sipal, her two fallen centurions. In the near darkness, she had to feel her way to each soldier's neck in order to check his pulse, and was relieved to discover that neither of her subordinates was dead. Whatever she might think of humans, she knew that it was not their normal habit to kill unless they felt no other option was available. The human who had first fired on her and her subordinates, the one with the gold uniform tunic and the insignia of a Starfleet captain, obviously felt that the current situation had not yet deteriorated to the point where killing was necessary. Though Vathrael could admire that restraint, her next thought—born of training, experience, and instinct— turned to how she might fashion this insight into some form of tactical advantage.

"Come," she said to Subcommander Atrelis and Centurion Drixus, both of whom had managed to avoid falling victim to the humans' abrupt attack. "We have to keep moving." She had no desire to be pinned down here in the tunnels and at the mercy of her human counterparts, even if they were refraining from the use of lethal force. The hurried plan she had put into action in order to attempt to ambush the Starfleet group had almost ended in utter failure. Despite Atrelis's success at effecting a low-level disruption of the humans' portable scanning devices, the Starfleet captain had somehow figured out the ploy. Vathrael cursed herself for the decision to extinguish some of the lights in the tunnel as a hasty means of providing momentary concealment. She had been counting on the humans being so involved with accessing the sealed compartment—the same chamber to which she sought entry—that they might fail to notice the irregularity. Once again, the human captain had seen through the ruse, which Vathrael conceded had been poorly considered.

Another enemy might well have made you pay for your ineptitude with your life. Think, fool.

Vathrael reached the mouth of the tunnel just as another, single burst of Starfleet phaser fire erupted somewhere ahead of her. It was followed by the sound of something exploding, but no sooner had that noise echoed down the corridor than she heard a new, low hum.

"Captain!" shouted a male voice. An instant later there was another burst of energy, followed by shouts of warning.

Lunging into the passageway, her disruptor held before her, Vathrael was in time to see the Starfleet captain running up the corridor and lunging for cover. His companions, one female in civilian clothing and a male in black trousers and a red Starfleet tunic, also were running away from her. As the captain caught sight of her crouching at an intersection at the far end of the corridor, his eyes grew wide with alarm even as she raised her disruptor and took aim at him.

Another burst of energy howled in the corridor, and instinct screamed for Vathrael to drop to the ground just before something hot and bright passed over her. Then she felt something grip her shoulder and looked up to see Centurion Drixus pulling her along with him.

"Wait!" she shouted, but there was no time for anything else as the human woman and the other Starfleet officer were turning toward her, weapons raised.

"Take cover!" the human captain shouted, just as more energy whined in the tunnel, and for the first time Vathrael saw a new weapon turret, this one mounted above the still-sealed doorway leading to the alien control chamber. It swiveled in its mount and spat forth twin beams of yellow energy that struck the tunnel walls near where the humans had been standing. Additional blasts tore into the tunnel's rock floor, sending stone shrapnel hurtling in all directions.

"Fall back!" Vathrael heard the human captain shout even as Atrelis and Drixus were pulling her out of harm's way and back toward the other tunnel. She saw the automated turret continuing to fire, loosing salvos in the direction of both parties, until she was ushered out of its line of sight by Drixus. Now under cover, she listened to the weapon's ongoing assault for an additional moment before it ceased firing. Her ears still ringing from the maelstrom that had just been unleashed, she finally held up a hand and signaled for Drixus to halt their retreat.

"Are you all right, Commander?" The centurion's concern, Vathrael saw, was genuine, yet another demonstration of his unwavering loyalty to her.

Reaching up to pat him on the shoulder, Vathrael nodded. "I'm uninjured. Thank you, Drixus." She paused, wiping perspiration from her brow, before looking to Atrelis. "What was that?"

"The intruder control system," the science officer replied. "It seems designed, at least as a first measure, to disable weapons it perceives as a threat. I did not comprehend that feature during our initial encounters with the automated turrets, Commander."

Vathrael frowned. "Are you saying that so long as we don't use our weapons, the turrets won't harm us?"

"I would not proceed from that assumption," Atrelis said. "As I said, it may only be a preliminary countermeasure. I cannot help but think that the system will employ more robust methods if we attempt to infiltrate an area it deems worthy of protection."

Drixus asked, "So, what are we to do?" He held up his disruptor for emphasis.

"The humans face the same dilemma we do," the science officer replied, from where he now knelt next to the still unconscious form of Centurion Sipal. "We would seem to be on equal footing, at least in that regard." Rising to his feet, he gestured to the fallen soldier. "They should be reviving soon, Commander."

Nodding as she absorbed the report, she asked, "This security system. Is it something you could countermand, assuming you're able to gain access to the control room and decipher the components?"

Atrelis replied, "Perhaps, but the humans destroyed the panel controlling the door, Commander. I may be able to bypass the damage they inflicted, but it likely will take considerable time and effort."

That was unacceptable, Vathrael decided. There still were other comparable chambers scattered throughout the complex, not counting the one to which the humans had already gained access, but they were much too far away to be of any immediate use. She harbored no doubts that the Starfleet captain and his group meant to deny her entry to any of the other chambers, using whatever means were at their disposal and even as they too dealt with this new complication presented by this installation's security protocols. The only true advantage she possessed, thanks to overhearing the Starfleet captain moments earlier, was the knowledge that he and his people were alone here, without the support of their ship, which hovered somewhere beyond the energy field, which for some unknown reason had become impassible.

If that ship cannot come in, then you cannot leave. It was a simple statement, but one carrying a great deal of weight. Unless and until a way could be found to traverse the energy barrier, there would be no way to alert Fleet Command of her findings here. There was nothing to be done about that at the moment, Vathrael reasoned. For now, she faced more immediate problems.

"Where are the humans now?" she asked.

Scrutinizing his scanner, Atrelis nodded back toward the mouth of the tunnel. "They appear to be retreating down the other passage. It may be an attempt to circle back to the other members of their party."

"Then that is where we must go, as well," Vathrael said.

TWENTY-FIVE

"Mister Spock, I think we've got something."

As he crossed the Kalandan control room in response to Boma's summons, Spock saw the lieutenant and Uhura eyeing him with obvious anticipation. He also noted that several of the alien workstation's previously darkened displays now were active and offering lists of scrolling text in one of the ancient Kalandan written languages. Though he suspected that the information was moving much too fast for either Boma or Uhura to read, he still was able to discern enough of the moving data to gain a rapid understanding of what his two companions were doing. "What is it, Lieutenant?"

Boma gestured to one of the displays. "The security system, sir. I think we've found a way in." He paused before indicating Uhura. "I mean, I think Lieutenant Uhura's the one who found a way in."

"We did it together," countered the communications officer before turning to Spock. "I've been able to decipher some of this computer code, sir. If I'm reading it correctly, we may be able to counteract or work around at least some of the protocols that are currently active."

Spock stepped closer to the workstation, tapping several of the illuminated keys on the console's polished black panel. In response to his instructions the scrolling text on one display slowed to a halt, allowing him to read and translate it. "An inhibitor field?"

"That's right," Boma said. "It's been active since the system came on line. We think it's what's jamming our communications and interfering with tricorder scans. Basically, it's designed to sweep for active frequencies and overload them to the point that they're useless."

"And you believe you can deactivate that process?" Spock asked. "What of the destruct sequence?"

"We're still working on that, sir," Uhura replied. "These areas of the system overseeing it look to be shielded by several layers of protection algorithms. We haven't isolated the programming behind that, but I think we can code a workaround. If it works, we should be able to filter out certain frequencies that'll let us use our tricorders and communicators again, and maybe send a warning to the Dolysians."

Nodding in approval, Spock said, "Interesting." Uhura and Boma had shown great alacrity in their efforts to understand the alien technology, working with the information Spock had provided from his research of the original Kalandan outpost planet. While he had expected the usual difficulties that came with attempting to decipher and interact with any new language or methodology, both officers had comported themselves with distinction. "However, defeating the security protocols should be our primary concern, as we now have one hour and forty-eight minutes until the destruct program is carried out. Do you require assistance with the new programming scheme?"

"We know how much time we have," Boma snapped. Then, realizing his lapse of bearing, he sighed. "I'm sorry, Mister Spock." He indicated Uhura again. "Between the two of us, I think we've got a handle on it."

"Whatever you're going to do, you'd better hurry," said a voice from behind them, and Spock turned to see McCoy at another workstation, pointing toward one of the displays. "Because I think we've got a bigger problem here."

Spock made his way to where the doctor was standing and scrutinized the monitor, which depicted a visual feed of the area outside the control room's door, as well as the pair of Romulans lurking outside it.

"I do not recognize either of them from our earlier encounter," Spock said. Was it possible that other Romulans had somehow found their way into the complex, despite his efforts to keep the surface entrances sealed?

Grunting in what the Vulcan took to be an expression of exasperation, McCoy again pointed to the screen. "Spock, that doesn't really matter right now. Look! See what they're doing?"

It was not until the pair of Romulans ran out of the camera frame and he saw the small, dark object affixed to the door that Spock realized the implications of the doctor's concerns. "Mister Johnson!" he said, not quite shouting. "Stand clear of the door!"

He turned to see the security officer backing away from the reinforced metal hatch before a section of the door exploded inward. Spock had time to recognize the effect of the shaped charge as he grabbed McCoy by the arm and yanked the doctor toward the nearby wall. The blast sent a spherical section of the metal plating shooting across the room, where it fell to the floor and skidded across its smooth surface before impacting against the far wall. Though smoke obscured the new, ragged hole in the door, Spock still saw figures moving in the corridor beyond. He reached for his phaser just as the first Romulan appeared in the door's new opening, disruptor pointed ahead of him and firing without any apparent target in mind. Bolts of energy screamed into the room, impacting against walls as well as various control consoles. Spock, mindful of the possible damage being inflicted to the room's valuable equipment, fired his phaser, its beam striking the centurion in the chest and causing him to collapse across the threshold of the newly created entrance.

"Spock!" Boma shouted. "Watch out!"

The lieutenant's words were still echoing across the room when Spock heard the hum of some mechanism above and behind him. He dropped to the floor just as a brilliant yellow blast tore into the nearby wall. The pungent smell of scorched metal and other compounds hung in the air, and when he looked up he saw the ragged hole caused by the turret.

"Come on, Spock!" McCoy snapped, gripping the Vulcan's arm and pulling him farther into the room. Looking to where he thought the energy beam had originated, Spock saw a weapon turret that until this moment had not been present on the wall. He reasoned that it must have resided within a hidden compartment, activating now in response to the use of weapons fire in the room.

Another phaser firing caught his attention, and Spock looked to where Lieutenant Johnson was crouching against the far wall, closer to the door. He was firing at the Romulans, and before Spock could warn him the security officer glanced toward the turret ceiling before lunging to his left. Just managing to avoid the automated drone as it fired at him, Johnson threw himself to the floor and slid into another of the control consoles. Scrambling to his feet, the lieutenant brought up his phaser and again aimed it at the door, firing even as he dodged to his right and doing his best to avoid the new threat within the room. The Romulan now in the doorway fired his disruptor at Johnson, and for his effort was rewarded by a blast from the automated turret. The salvo struck the centurion and he cried out, pushing himself back through the doorway to relative safety.

"Our weapons!" Spock heard Boma shout. "The system's designed to react to weapons fire!"

Johnson, reacting to the warning, turned and pointed his phaser at the turret and fired. The blue beam struck the weapon, but the stun setting did nothing to affect the drone before it fired again. Though Johnson dodged to avoid the attack the turret was faster, its beam catching the security officer in the back and sending him crashing to the floor. The whine of another phaser, this one much more powerful, wailed in the room, and Spock turned to see Boma firing at the weapon mount. Erupting in a shower of sparks and debris, the turret came apart and pieces of it crashed to the floor.

Standing next to Boma, Uhura had brandished her own phaser and now was firing multiple strikes toward the door. The shots drove back the Romulan centurion trying to make his way through the entry before one beam struck his shoulder and he fell forward, crumpling to the floor inside the room. Another figure appeared behind him, and Boma dispatched him with speed and accuracy. The centurion's body fell backward and out of sight.

"Mister Boma, secure the entrance," Spock said, following McCoy as the doctor crossed the room to where Johnson had fallen.

Boma shouted, "Aye, sir!" Moving forward, he took an

extra moment to collect two disruptor pistols dropped by their Romulan owners before taking up a kneeling stance near the compromised door. "Mister Spock," he said, and when the first officer looked in his direction, Boma was holding two small, dark objects in his left hand. "Charges, like the one they used on the door. This isn't the sort of thing Romulan soldiers typically carry, is it?"

"No," Spock replied. "It's not." Were these Romulan reinforcements? How had they gotten into the complex? "Mister Boma, use your tricorder to scan for additional Romulan life signs."

The lieutenant's tricorder emitted its characteristic high-pitched whine as Boma conducted a sweep, after which he nodded. "Readings are still fluctuating, Mister Spock, but I'm definitely picking up more Romulans than we had before. Looks to be a half dozen or so."

"Are you able to ascertain whether the surface entrance has been breached?" Spock asked, returning his attention to watching McCoy work on Johnson.

Boma said, "Not from here, sir. Scans are being scattered beyond three hundred meters or so, but they had to come from somewhere."

Moving to take up a position on the opposite side of the entryway, Uhura held her phaser ready as she glanced to where McCoy was kneeling next to Johnson. "Is he all right, Doctor?"

McCoy replied, "I don't know yet," even as he held his medical tricorder in his left hand while extracting one of his diagnostic scanners from the unit's accessory compartment. For his part, Johnson, lying on his side, was conscious, though Spock could see that the man was suffering some degree of pain.

"Feels like my back's on fire, Doc," he said, gritting his teeth and clenching his eyes shut.

Waving the scanner over the injured security officer's back, McCoy said, "There's some cellular disruption." He glanced at Spock, "Not all that different from that trick of Losira's on the other Kalandan planet."

"Perhaps a precursor to that weapon?" Spock asked.

"I don't know," the doctor snapped, "and right now, I don't really care, but at least now I know how to treat it." He deactivated the scanner before reaching for the medical kit on his left hip and extracting a hypospray. Fitting the device with a capsule of medication from the kit, McCoy leaned forward and pressed it to Johnson's right arm. Spock heard the hypospray's pneumatic hiss as the medicine was administered, and seconds later Johnson's body relaxed as the drug took effect, the look of discomfort already fading from his features.

"Thanks, Doc," Johnson said, his words soft and slurred, doubtless from the effects of whatever medicine McCoy had given him. "For a minute, I was starting to worry that my luck might finally be running out."

Though he had often found himself uncertain as to what he might offer to an injured subordinate if circumstances like this presented themselves, Spock said, "If I'm not mistaken, Lieutenant, you have managed to endure numerous dangerous situations while serving as a member of the *Enterprise* crew. I expect that even while suffering Doctor McCoy's ministrations, your record will remain unblemished once this mission is concluded."

McCoy, in the midst of reaching for Johnson—presumably to inspect the injured man's back—stopped in midmotion before turning to regard Spock with an expression the Vulcan recognized as surprise. "Who are you, and what've you done with Spock? Aren't you forgetting something, like this whole place getting ready to blow up and us with it?"

"I have forgotten nothing, Doctor." Rising to his feet, Spock moved to where Boma still guarded the door. "A most timely intervention on your part, Lieutenant."

Offering a small smile, Boma said, "Seemed like the logical thing to do, sir. I thought you of all people would appreciate that."

"Indeed," Spock replied.

Across from Boma, Uhura said, "I was able to read part of the programming code, sir. The security system's designed to escalate its responses based on the threats it identifies. First it targets other weapons, based on usage. If Mister Boma hadn't taken out that turret when he did, it eventually would've neutralized all of our phasers at once, and probably us with them."

"The same would've been true with the Romulans," Boma added, "but I figured it was better not to chance waiting to see what the computer would do." Frowning, he added, "What I don't understand is why it targets the weapons rather than the people carrying them."

"It could be that the system was designed to remove threats to sensitive equipment and other inhabitants without causing undue harm to persons," Spock said.

"Maybe," Boma replied. "Still seems kind of odd, though."

Still hovering over Johnson, McCoy said, "The alternative could be Losira or one of her sisters and her little love touches, you know."

Spock cast glances toward the scorched remnants of

several consoles at different points around the room. "Mister Boma, did the Romulans cause sufficient damage as to render the equipment in this room unusable?"

Shrugging, the lieutenant answered, "I'm not sure, but they did hit several stations we were using. We need to take a closer look."

At Spock's request Uhura moved to one of the consoles that was still functioning, though several of its control panels and displays were inactive. After a moment, she shook her head. "I don't know if I can work with the equipment in this condition, Mister Spock."

Not surprised at that report, Spock reached for his communicator and activated it. "Spock to Captain Kirk." In response to his summons, he received nothing but static.

"Where are they?" McCoy asked as he helped Johnson to a sitting position.

"Based on his last status report," Spock said, "I presume the captain is still attempting to access the third operations chamber, or at least deny the Romulans from doing the same." So affected had communications been at that point that the captain had barely been able to report his encounter with Romulans near the second control room. Spock knew that the quality of signal would only grow worse the deeper Kirk and his team ventured into the Kalandan complex. The larger problem, he knew, was that it would take precious time for the captain and his party to reach that area of the facility, and that was without the added impediment of any Romulans who might be in pursuit.

"Gather your essential equipment," he said. "We are moving to the next operations room."

Still kneeling next to Johnson, McCoy asked, "What are you doing, Spock?"

"If we are to secure control of this facility," Spock said as he slung his tricorder over his shoulder, "we must regain access to the internal network. As this room is no longer serviceable, our only option is to relocate. That is also very likely our best option for regaining contact with Captain Kirk."

McCoy gestured to Johnson. "He's in no condition to travel."

"I'm okay, sir," the security officer said, though Spock noted how weak he sounded. "Just give me something to get me back on my feet."

"Why did I know you were going to say that?" the doctor asked, muttering something else even Spock could not hear as he once more pulled the hypospray from his medical kit. Looking up as he readied the injection, he asked, "Jim said he sealed that control room—destroyed its control panel or some such damned thing. How are you planning to get in there?"

Spock turned back to Boma as the lieutenant was placing the pair of shaped charges into his utility satchel. "If I'm unable to bypass the door's access controls, then I believe the Romulans will provide us with everything we'll need."

The only complication, Spock knew, was getting to that room ahead of the Romulans.

TWENTY-SIX

"Commander?"

Vathrael almost fired her disruptor at the figure who stepped into view at the far end of the corridor, but raised the weapon at the last instant upon recognizing the new arrival as her first officer.

"Sirad," she said, allowing more than a hint of relief to creep into her voice. After the brief, trouble-laden communications she had shared with him upon his forced entry into the complex and the difficulties he had reported facing after his first encounter with the Starfleet group, it was good to see that he had weathered that incident well enough.

"I lost two centurions during our skirmish," the subcommander reported. "So far as I'm able to determine, they've been incapacitated, though not killed. Despite this, it's reasonable to assume that the humans know our numbers are now greater than theirs."

Standing behind Vathrael along with Drixus and the other centurions in her party, Subcommander Atrelis said, "I don't know that simply outnumbering our opponents is an advantage, given their obvious greater knowledge of this complex's technology."

Sirad replied, "Agreed, which is why I decided to confront the humans directly. I thought that a prisoner might prove useful to our understanding of the equipment."

Based on what Vathrael had observed as well as what Sirad had reported, it seemed that the humans' command of the alien mechanisms within this complex was even greater than could be justified by the brief period of time they had been here. Was it possible that Starfleet had encountered other examples of the technology contained within this underground installation? If that was the case, then information pertaining to such a discovery likely was sealed away under stringent security, as was Starfleet's habit when it came to such important findings. While covert Romulan agents had proven efficient at stealing even the most protected secrets from within the halls of Federation and Starfleet power, it stood to reason that some things escaped even their calculated scrutiny. Of course, it also was possible that the very information she might find useful here and now was in fact known to her superiors, who in turn may have chosen to withhold that knowledge for their own enigmatic reasons.

Your paranoia will serve you well, should you ever decide to seek election to government office, Vathrael mused.

"While I agree with your initiative," she said as she regarded her first officer, "we must proceed with some caution." She had already seen the consequences of haste, and of not giving careful consideration to all the facets of the current situation. Further mistakes could not be tolerated if they were to have any success at seizing control of this facility. "I have even given some consideration to abandoning this effort and returning to the ship. Fleet Command must be made aware of what is here, even if we are unable to secure it for the praetor."

Sirad greeted her comments with a fleeting scowl, though his effort to conceal his momentary lapse in bearing was commendable. "Commander, I don't understand; the praetor must be made aware of the full potential this technology carries. We cannot ascertain that if we leave it in the hands of the humans. If what you've told me is true and a Starfleet captain is here, unable to contact his ship, would taking him prisoner not provide us with an advantage?"

"I suspect that the Starfleet captain's ship is not simply waiting to hear from him," Vathrael countered. "They will be looking for any means to contact him. We have a very narrow window of opportunity here; it must not be wasted. Where are the humans now?"

Consulting his scanner, Atrelis answered, "The readings continue to be imprecise, but I believe they are still separated into two groups. One is moving in the direction of the control chamber we investigated earlier. The other is moving through the complex on an adjacent level."

"They have to know our location, as well," Sirad offered. "If we divide our resources, we may be able to overpower them before they're able to consolidate their numbers."

Nodding at the suggestion, Vathrael said, "Agreed, though I cannot believe the human captain won't be anticipating our strategy. We must move quickly."

If she was going to gamble on capturing one or more of the Starfleet contingent in a bid to exploit their knowledge of this facility and the secrets it contained, she needed to do so now. How much time remained before the presence of her ship and crew on this world was revealed? Vathrael had no way to know. For now, and until circumstances changed, her most viable course of action would seem to be carrying out her original mission and obtaining as much information about this installation as possible before making a stealthy escape. Whether she might be able to transmit her findings to her superiors in the empire was an issue to be resolved later, assuming she and her crew survived to address it.

As always, she reminded herself, *the best course is that of duty*.

Kirk and the Romulan saw each other at the same time.

Despite the look of surprise on the centurion's face, he wasted no time bringing his disruptor to bear. Kirk was faster, his phaser up and firing even as the Romulan was taking aim. The beam caught the enemy soldier in the upper chest and he fell backward, collapsing against the corridor's stone wall.

"Captain!" yelled Ensign Minecci as the security officer lunged forward, raising his own phaser and aiming it toward a second Romulan who was lurking beyond the intersection at the passage's far end. The soldier ducked out of sight to avoid the strike, and the phaser beam instead hit the wall behind where he had been standing.

"I guess your trick worked," said Dana Sortino from where she crouched along the wall on the tunnel's opposite side. She was holding only one phaser, having tucked her second weapon into her waistband at the small of her back.

Kirk nodded. "Looks that way." He had instructed Minecci to duplicate the tactic the Romulans had employed against them earlier, by setting his tricorder to emit an active broad-based scanning beam at the device's maximum output. The Kalandan outpost was still doing its best to disrupt internal scans, but Kirk hoped that the tricorder, upon getting closer to the Romulans, would interfere with whatever scanning devices they were carrying. At best, Kirk figured they might get a slight edge on being able to determine the Romulans' location once they were close enough, but he would be happy with neither side being able to track the other.

Keeping his attention focused on the intersection, Kirk said, "Minecci, any idea how many there are?"

The security officer looked down to study his tricorder, then grimaced. "No luck, sir. They're still jamming us, too."

A stray thought as to whether the Romulans might have retreated was answered when a shadowy figured darted from right to left across the junction, too fast for Minecci to follow with his phaser.

What the hell are they doing?

The centurion disappeared from view, avoiding Minecci's shots. Another Romulan appeared on the right side of the intersection, and Kirk fired at him. His shot also missed, and only then did Kirk think to look for some sign of a turret hub or any other facet of the complex's internal defense system.

Sortino was thinking along similar lines. "I don't see any of those weapon ports."

"I didn't see any of them before, either," Kirk countered, tightening his grip on his phaser as he fired at the spot where the Romulan had crossed. "I think they're going to try to catch us in a crossfire. We can't stay here."

Her eyes focused on the junction, Sortino said, "What have you got in mind?"

Adjusting the power setting on his phaser, Kirk took aim at the lighting fixture illuminating the intersection. "This," he said, before pressing the phaser's firing stud and releasing a short burst. The weapon's beam drilled into the roof of the corridor, sending large chunks of rock plummeting to the floor. A cloud of dust began to fill the corridor as Kirk ran forward.

"What the hell are you doing?" he heard Sortino shout, but ignored her as he plunged ahead, searching for movement. Rewarded with a dark figure emerging from the dust, he fired at it, his phaser whining as its beam found the target and sent the Romulan tumbling to the ground.

To your right!

Kirk turned as something moved in his peripheral vision, cringing at the sound of another weapon's discharge. A phaser beam crossed from behind him toward another Romulan emerging from around the tunnel's corner, and he gasped in shock as the strike knocked the centurion back against the wall. Kirk glanced over his shoulder to see Sortino advancing, her phaser clasped in both hands as she moved toward the junction and fired again. A burst of disruptor energy tore through the dissipating dust and screamed past Kirk before he heard a muffled groan behind him. It could only be Minecci, but there was no time to check as Kirk loosed several shots from the direction of the disruptor. Sortino followed suit, both of them saturating the tunnel with phaser fire. His ears ringing from the various salvos, Kirk moved forward to see three more bodies splayed on the ground. One of the Romulans had tried to seek cover around a bend in the passage before a phaser beam caught him in the back. The fallen centurion's disruptor lay next to his hand where he had dropped it, and Kirk moved to kick it out of reach.

As he came abreast of the turn in the corridor, he sensed movement behind him and to his left, but when he turned to aim his phaser in that direction something large and fast was moving. Sortino shouted a warning before

Kirk saw the Romulan slam into her, driving her against the nearby rock wall. Rather than the cold helmet of a centurion he instead saw black hair laced with gray, and a blue sash over one shoulder as the Romulan grabbed Sortino's weapon hand at the wrist and twisted it up over her head, forcing her to drop her phaser.

"Dana!"

The Romulan was holding Sortino so that she blocked any shot Kirk might take. As he started to move closer, the ambassador jerked her body to the left and lashed out with her free hand, punching the side of the Romulan's head. While not sufficient to free her from her attacker's grip, it was still enough to give her some maneuvering room and she struck again, this time aiming for the centurion's face. The edge of her hand found his nose, evoking an angered, pain-racked cry. This time the Romulan hit back, but Sortino blocked the blow before driving her knee into the soldier's groin. The hold on her wrist loosened and she wrenched her arm free, using it to push back from the Romulan before throwing one more punch to her opponent's jaw. When the centurion dropped to one knee, Kirk moved in, taking aim with his phaser.

"Don't!" he barked, holding up his hand as he saw Sortino pick up the closest weapon in reach, the Romulan's own disruptor, and aim its muzzle at the centurion's head. "I want one of them conscious. Oh, and just in case I forget to say this later, you're crazy. Do you know that?"

Moving to retrieve the phaser she had dropped, the ambassador said, "Me? All I did was defend myself. You're the one who charged into the fray. *That's* crazy."

"I prefer to think of it as unorthodox," Kirk said, leveling his gaze on the Romulan before him. Studying the soldier's uniform insignia and accessories, he realized this was not a rank-and-file centurion, but instead a subcommander—a member of a ship's officer corps. "You're a first or second officer, aren't you?" To his total lack of surprise, the Romulan remained silent, leaving Kirk with nothing except the chalky taste of dust in his mouth.

Handing the disruptor to him, Sortino said, "Minecci's dead, Jim."

Anger and grief pushed at Kirk's consciousness. The ensign, so far as he knew, was the first casualty of this mission. Would there be more? How many had preceded him just during the time Kirk had commanded the *Enterprise*? Too many, he knew. One was too many, regardless of what admirals or instructors and simulations at Starfleet Academy told him about death being a harsh reality of duty. He had never subscribed to that mind-set; every life was precious, and none more so than those he commanded. There would never be a time when he viewed the death of any member of his crew as an acceptable loss.

For the briefest of moments, Kirk glanced at the power level on the disruptor Sortino had given him. Though he was unfamiliar with the precise characteristics of Romulan sidearms, the weapon was set to what he believed to be a nonlethal force. It would take little effort to increase the power setting before shooting his prisoner.

What was that you just told yourself about every life being precious? The rebuke was enough to make him relax his grip on the disruptor, and he stepped back from the subcommander, taking a moment to draw a breath and regain his bearing.

"Your soldier's death was an accident," the Romulan said. "My centurions were given orders to subdue, not kill."

Confused, Kirk frowned. "You were trying to capture us? Why?"

Sortino moved to stand next to him. "Hostages? That's usually not in the Romulan playbook."

"It is if whoever you want to capture has information you need," Kirk said, "like how to access the systems in this place." Gesturing with his phaser to the Romulan, he asked, "Isn't that right?"

The Romulan continued to scowl at him. "Find your own answers, human." Despite his bravado, his eyes betrayed him, and Kirk nodded in grim satisfaction.

"Yes, that's it." With mounting irritation beginning to gnaw at him, he glared at the Romulan. "Do you know this entire complex is set to self-destruct in less than two hours? Everything in here will be gone, and maybe a good chunk of the planet itself along with it. You've got a ship somewhere, on the surface or in orbit. They might be in danger, to say nothing of the Dolysians at the mining colony."

When the Romulan refused to answer him this time, Kirk shook his head in annoyance. "Fine. Have it your way." He fired his phaser. The Romulan's face went slack as the beam enveloped him, and he fell unconscious to the ground.

"Now what?" Sortino asked.

Indicating the other Romulans, he said, "Grab their weapons. We need to go, and we're running out of time." His eyes lingered on the lifeless body of Nick Minecci, his thoughts turning to the message he knew he would soon have to compose and send to the fallen man's family.

Later, he chastised himself. There would be an appropriate time and place to honor the ensign for his sacrifice, but for now, Kirk knew there still was a job to do. He considered the disruptor he held. It had been some time since he had last held such a weapon and it felt odd in his hand, being heavier and somewhat more unwieldy than a phaser. Still, he decided that it might have its uses.

Sortino collected the remaining disruptors from where they lay scattered on the tunnel floor, "You think they're going after Spock and the others?"

Kirk nodded. "It's what I'd do."

TWENTY-SEVEN

Why is it so damned hot in here?

Sulu stood in front of the captain's chair and just behind the helm console on the *Enterprise* bridge, holding his hands at his sides and resisting the overwhelming urge to wipe them on his trouser legs. The collar of his uniform tunic felt like a rope around his neck, and dampness encroached beneath his arms and between his shoulder blades. Was it his imagination, or could he feel rivulets of sweat threatening to drip from his fingers to the deck?

Ignoring the unspoken question, he forced himself to stand without moving the slightest muscle, displaying his best poker face as he eyed the Romulan officer on the main viewscreen. The image, rather than offering the normal high-resolution clarity to which Sulu was accustomed, instead was being inundated with static and the occasional loss of focus, evidence of the damage the communications system had sustained during the failed attempt to contact Captain Kirk. "I'm Lieutenant Hikaru Sulu, temporarily in command of the *U.S.S. Enterprise*. It's my duty to advise you that your vessels have violated the Neutral Zone separating Romulan and Federation space, and that you are currently in violation of the peace treaty between our two governments. Do you require assistance?"

The Romulan, his image shifting and even blurring for

a moment before snapping into something approaching normal focus, said nothing at first, opting instead to tap the fingers of his right hand atop the desk or table at which he sat. Behind him was nothing but a flat gray wall, making Sulu wonder if the commander was addressing him from his private quarters or a broom closet, or perhaps just from a station on his ship's bridge that was oriented so as not to provide clear sight lines to any sensitive equipment. He looked older than many of the Romulans Sulu had encountered, with deep lines creasing his face and a shock of pure white hair. Despite his age he appeared to be in prime physical condition, with his uniform—the familiar ensemble of a ranking officer—stretching across a broad, muscled chest.

"*I am Commander Grathus,*" the Romulan said. "*You seem to be experiencing some form of technical difficulty, Lieutenant.*" As the last words left his mouth, the viewscreen's image chose that moment to coalesce into perfect resolution. The annoying static and other bothersome interference were gone, leaving only Grathus to stare at him with an unreadable expression.

Sulu shrugged. "I'm not sure I understand what you're talking about. Everything's fine on our end." The comment was enough to make the Romulan's eyes narrow, and he pressed his lips together as though biting back a retort.

Instead, Grathus said, "*It is my understanding that this system occupies nonaligned space, not that I am interested in discussing this matter with you. Where is your captain?*"

Forcing himself not to take the obvious bait, Sulu replied, "The indigenous population of this solar system has entered into an alliance with the Federation. In the interests of maintaining civil discourse, I recommend we chalk this up to a simple misunderstanding, Commander."

His attempt at polite concession did not seem to impress the Romulan. "*I am not in the habit of speaking with Starfleet underlings, Lieutenant. I consider it an insult that your captain chooses not to confer with me himself. Where is he?*"

"Captain Kirk is unavailable at the moment," Sulu replied, "but I've been authorized to speak on his behalf." He decided that this Romulan did not need to know the current location of the captain or Mister Spock, or even that Mister Scott, next in line so far as taking command while Kirk and the first officer were off the ship, was at this moment down in engineering. Though he had been reluctant to leave the bridge, the Romulans' imminent arrival and the difficulties encountered by M'Ress in repairing the ship's compromised communications system had forced him to lend his hands and experience in the hope of fashioning a quick remedy. Sulu suspected the chief engineer also was communing with whatever deity would provide him with a miracle to improve the odds should the *Enterprise* be required to withstand a simultaneous assault from the three Romulan warships.

Grathus leaned forward, his face filling the image on the viewscreen. There was no mistaking the menace in his voice as he glared at Sulu. "*Then speak to me, Lieutenant, about the Romulan vessel which has gone missing in this star system.*"

From his right, Sulu heard Chekov say in a low voice, "Mister Sulu, all three Romulan ships are maintaining a formation as they approach. Computer estimates twenty-four minutes, eleven seconds until they're within weapons range. Sensors show they're carrying disruptors and plasma torpedoes, though they do not appear to be armed at this time."

Sulu did not acknowledge the report, keeping his attention focused on Grathus. Affecting what he hoped was a casual air, he looked behind him before retaking his seat in the captain's chair, using the opportunity to glance at the status indicators on the helm and navigation consoles. It was enough to tell him that the *Enterprise*'s deflector shield generators were at full power, and that the starship's weapons were in a standby mode. No targeting information had yet been supplied, of course, as the enemy vessels remained well out of range. Based on his knowledge of Romulan weapons as well as past experience facing off against them in combat, Sulu was confident that the *Enterprise* might be able to hold its own against one, possibly two of the enemy warships, but three?

Let's not try that, okay?

"Our sensors did detect another Romulan ship in this area," he said. "We tried to communicate with its commander, but our hails were ignored. Likewise, our warnings about the energy field in this system also went unheeded. The ship encountered difficulty when it tried to cross the barrier in order to reach the planetoid on the other side, after which we lost all sensor contact with it." Sulu paused, knowing that the next part of his recounting of the events was not something the Romulan commander was going to want to hear. Did he at least not suspect what had happened to the other ship? Would he not have been given information from the encrypted message that had been transmitted from the ill-fated vessel before its demise, and which Lieutenant M'Ress had decoded?

He knows, Sulu concluded. *He's just testing me.*

As though sensing the hesitation, Grathus regarded Sulu with undisguised contempt. "*And then?*"

Deciding that he had had enough of whatever game the Romulan commander might be playing to gauge his reactions, Sulu leaned back in the captain's chair and forced himself to relax into the seat. "And then you know what happened. Your ship was attacked and presumed destroyed, by an automated defense system installed on the planetoid by an unknown party."

"*This mysterious, enigmatic enemy,*" Grathus said, "*crippled a vessel of the Romulan Empire? I find that hard to believe.*"

"We saw the sensor telemetry data the ship transmitted," Sulu fired back. "It bears out what I'm telling you. What reason would I have to lie?"

The Romulan glowered at him. "*I imagine you would say anything if you believed it might spare your ship from the wrath of my weapons.*"

Sulu heard the turbolift doors open and glanced over his left shoulder, offering silent thanks to whoever or whatever had seen fit to send Montgomery Scott to the bridge. His gaze was locked on the viewscreen as he moved to stand before the railing behind the captain's chair.

"*You are not the captain, either,*" Grathus said, noting the engineer's arrival. "*Another subordinate, I assume?*"

Resting his hands on his hips, Scott replied, "Lieutenant Commander Montgomery Scott, chief engineering officer."

Grathus nodded in apparent recognition. "*Yes, your name is familiar to me. You were the one who successfully installed a stolen cloaking device into your ship's power systems. Please accept my compliments on your obvious technical prowess.*"

Appearing less than impressed with the disingenuous praise, Scott said, "Commander, I have no doubts that

Lieutenant Sulu inquired as to the reasons for your crossing of the Neutral Zone. What are your intentions?"

"As your captain would seem to be too cowardly to address me himself," Grathus replied with mounting irritation, *"I suppose I shall have to make my intentions known to you. I am here to ascertain the status of our missing ship,"* the Romulan replied, *"and to seek appropriate retribution against those responsible."* He paused for what Scott presumed was some sort of dramatic effect before adding, *"Now, is your captain the one I should be suspecting, or is this situation due to an action you ordered?"*

Scott's eyes narrowed. "We took no action against your fellow ship. It was attacked by some form of automated planetary defense system."

"Then it would seem that my quarrel is with the inhabitants of this star system," Grathus said. *"As you know, attacking a ship of the empire without provocation is not something we tolerate."*

"As it happens, it's not something we fancy much ourselves, Commander," Scott replied, and Sulu heard the edge behind the engineer's words. "The defense system on that planetoid has been there for thousands of years, long before it was colonized by anyone from the neighboring planet. The indigenous population is not to blame for what happened. All evidence would seem to point to this being a very tragic accident."

It was obvious that Grathus was tiring of this conversation. *"That is for me to determine, human. My advice to you is not to become an obstacle as I attempt to do that."*

"We're not looking for a confrontation, Commander," Scott said, "and I don't think you'd risk interstellar war by launching an attack on a Federation vessel well outside your borders. Wouldn't you rather find out what really happened here? We're certainly willing to help in that regard."

On the screen, the Romulan frowned, but Sulu could tell that Scott's words had registered with him. Could the chief engineer be right? Might Grathus not want a fight? It was possible, of course, but the current state of political affairs between the Federation and the Romulan Empire, military maneuvering and bluster and a genuine need to know what happened to their ship, to say nothing of simple pride were all but certain to be coloring the commander's perspective. If Grathus was not prepared to take action against the *Enterprise*, then he at least was doing a first-rate job selling his ruse.

You can do that when you outnumber your opponent three to one.

"Mister Scott," Chekov called out, and both Sulu and the engineer looked to where the ensign was standing over the sensor viewer, his expression one of worry. It was obvious he had something to report, but when he glanced to the viewscreen Sulu realized his friend was unwilling to talk while Grathus could hear.

"Mute transmission," Scott said to Lieutenant Palmer at the communications station, and Sulu saw the expression darken on the Romulan's features in response to no longer being the focus of attention. "What is it, Chekov?"

The young officer pointed to the viewer. "Sensors are picking up a pair of Dolysian freighters, sir. They're still in orbit above the planet, but they're coming around from the far side. Their trajectories indicate they're on a course for one of the Dolysian moons."

Chekov did not have to say anything further for Sulu

to understand the chief cause of his concern. "They'll be sitting ducks by the time the Romulans get here. Can't we warn them off?" Sulu asked.

Shaking his head, Chekov replied, "There's not enough time to get them out of danger."

"Then we'll have to think of something else," Scott hissed, turning back to the viewscreen and motioning for Palmer to reestablish the communications channel's audio. "I apologize for that interruption, Commander, but it was a sensitive matter."

"*Would it have anything to do with the pair of civilian transport vessels currently departing the system's fourth planet?*" Grathus asked. There was no mistaking the confidence in the Romulan's voice.

Scott said, "We are aware of the ships. They are unarmed and pose no threat to you, Commander. I respectfully request that you leave them in peace."

"*As they represent this system's native population,*" Grathus replied, "*then they may be in a position to provide us answers about this mysterious ancient defense system you claim destroyed our ship.*"

Stepping forward, Scott's tone hardened. "Commander, we've been over this. The Dolysians do not know anything."

"*We shall soon see,*" the Romulan said.

"You'll force me to take action to protect them," Scott snapped.

Leaning back in his chair, Grathus sat in silence for a moment, and Sulu was certain he detected just the very hint of a smile tugging at the corners of the Romulan officer's lips.

"*That should prove interesting.*" He made a gesture with his left hand that Sulu did not recognize, but then the meaning became clear when Grathus disappeared from the screen, replaced by an image of space and the now quite familiar energy field.

At the science station, Chekov reported, "Their speed is increasing, sir! Sensors are also detecting their weapons are arming and that they've activated their shields!" He paused, leaning even closer to the viewer, to the point that Sulu thought his friend might try to drive his forehead through the device. "They're also breaking off from the formation they were keeping. At their present speed, they'll be here in a little over eighteen minutes."

"They may be moving into positions to try and surround us," Sulu warned. His knowledge of Romulan space battle tactics was a bit sketchy, but three ships at his disposal would give Grathus all the latitude he required to assume a variety of attack postures and formations designed to exploit his numerical advantage over the *Enterprise*.

Scott muttered something that was only just audible, and Sulu was sure he comprehended at least a few of the more colorful if now seldom used words from the Scotsman's ancestral home on Earth. "Sound Red Alert," he said as he moved to the captain's seat and thumbed the intraship communications switch on the chair's right arm. "This is Commander Scott," he said, his voice echoing through the bridge's intercom speaker. "All decks to alert status. All hands to battle stations. This is not a drill. Repeat: this is not a drill. All decks acknowledge."

As he resumed his position at the helm, Sulu noted that the battle stations indicators for each deck as displayed on his console were changing from red to green, indicating that designated officers were reporting their deck as ready for battle. "What are we going to do, Scotty?" he asked as he maintained watch on the indicators. "Those Dolysian freighters don't stand a chance against the Romulans."

"We're the only chance they have, lad," Scott said, his voice muted and carrying with it an air of reluctant acceptance. "Energize main phasers, Mister Arex. Bring all weapons to full power and place them on standby. Route power from all nonessential systems to the shields." Then, his voice somewhat muted, he added, "If they're really going to do this, at least we'll be ready."

On his console, Sulu saw the last of the indicators flash green.

The *Enterprise* was ready for battle.

TWENTY-EIGHT

Lying on the floor in the *Nevathu*'s engineering section, Mylas pulled himself away from the hole created by removing one of the deck plates, which in turn had given him access to the section of power routing conduit he had been repairing. He looked up at his junior engineer, Daprel, as he handed the younger man the laser seal he had just finished using to service the conduit.

"That should do it, I think," Mylas said as he pulled himself to a sitting position. "We can replace this deck plate and move to the next junction." He reached for the towel he had placed atop his tool kit and began using it to wipe his hands.

Daprel nodded. "Yes, Mylas."

With a grunt, Mylas pulled himself to his feet, wondering if the snaps and pops emanating from certain joints were his body's way of informing him that he might finally be growing too old to be crawling through the bellies of space ships. Perhaps it was time he traded places with younger, eager-to-please junior engineers like Daprel?

I think not. At least, not yet.

Wiping his forehead with his towel, he noted the look of disdain on Daprel's face. When he glanced down at himself, Mylas realized that very few areas of his jumpsuit were free of grime or dirt. "What troubles you, Centurion?" he asked, smiling. "Dirt on one's hands never sullied an officer's career, particularly that of an engineer. You don't think I'm going to keep doing this forever, do you?"

Rather than feeling disheartened about his appearance and the prospect of the time needed to clean himself once his work was done, Mylas instead relished the evidence of his hard work. Though he had tried to instill this attitude into the impressionable minds of the apprentices Fleet Command and Commander Vathrael saw fit to assign to his mentorship, he had come to realize as he grew older that such effort, more often than not, was a waste of time for all involved.

Is it the young officers who are so inflexible, or perhaps someone else? Not for the first time, Mylas considered that notion, and came away thinking that it had to possess at least an element of truth. He knew that his days serving as the engineer even of a small ship such as the *Nevathu* were coming to a close. Fleet Command could not afford the luxury of allowing senior officers with little or no prospects of advancement to linger within the ranks, not when so many promising young candidates were entering the service. His superiors had been tolerant of Vathrael's insistence that he serve under her command, but he suspected that their patience would be at an end once Vathrael made her report about the failure of the mission here. Vathrael herself would almost without question be sanctioned in some manner, and Mylas knew that Fleet Command would use this incident as an excuse to send him to retirement. If he was fortunate, he might be granted an instructor's position at the military academy's engineering school. Barring that, there were numerous learning institutions on Romulus that would welcome his skills and experience.

You concern yourself with matters which have no immediate importance, he reminded himself. *Better to concentrate on the problems at hand.*

Moving out of the way so as to allow Daprel to restore the section of deck plating to its proper place, Mylas had set to the task of returning various tools to his kit when he heard heavy footfalls coming in his direction from the engineering section's forward area. There were, at present, only four people aboard the *Nevathu*, and he did not have to look up to know that the heavy, measured footfalls belonged to Centurion Terius. It was not until Mylas had placed his laser seal in the kit's proper storage slot that he looked up to see the weapons officer standing at the corridor junction. Mylas could not help noting that Terius was wearing a disruptor pistol on his hip.

"What is it?" Mylas asked as he closed his tool kit and retrieved his hand towel.

The centurion said, "Our sensors are detecting the approach of an unidentified craft. It does not appear to be moving on a direct course toward us, but that does not alleviate my concerns."

Daprel, his eyes wide, asked, "One of the Starfleet transports?"

"No," Terius replied, shaking his head. "It's too large, and its construction too primitive. Most likely, it's a craft belonging to the indigenous population."

"That seems unusual," Mylas said, continuing to clean his hands. "From what Commander Vathrael told us earlier, their primary settlement is some distance from here. Is the vessel armed?"

"I don't believe so," the weapons officer answered. "Even if it is, nothing these people might bring to bear has any chance against our shields or even our hull plating."

Mylas eyed the centurion. "You do realize that the defensive shields and the cloaking field are off line at the moment, yes?" He had been forced to deactivate both systems in order to effect repairs to the power conduits running beneath the engineering deck. "Without them, we might still be vulnerable to some form of projectile weapon or explosive." That the efforts he and his Daprel had expended and the systems they had labored to repair might be at risk of further damage from some primitive attack by the natives of this tiny planet was not a comforting thought, to say the least.

"Why would they even be in this area?" Daprel asked. "We were told the inhabitants were conducting mining operations on the other side of the planet."

Terius said, "The obvious conclusion is that they are searching for us." Looking to Mylas, he asked, "Is it possible they were able to detect our descent from orbit, even while we were under cloak?"

"Possible?" Mylas considered the question. "Given our condition at the time, the ship may have been emitting some energy reading our cloaking field was unable to conceal. I won't know unless I conduct another review of our systems."

Waving away the suggestion, Terius replied, "There's no time for that. The ship is here, now. That is our primary concern."

"So, what are you suggesting?" Mylas asked. "The commander's orders are that we maintain stealth. We're not certain these primitives can even locate us."

Daprel added, "And even if they can, we still outmatch them so far as weaponry is concerned."

"The ship's weapons only matter if we're in flight," Terius snapped, glowering at the junior engineer with disdain. "Sitting here on the ground like a wounded animal? They're useless. We need to get the cloaking field back into operation."

Their conversation was interrupted by a series of three tones sounding from the intercom system. Terius looked up as the pings were followed by a click and a short burst of static before the voice of Ciluri, the lone centurion on duty on the Nevathu's bridge, called out, "*Terius, the Dolysian ship is changing course! It is now heading directly toward us!*"

Muttering what Mylas recognized as a very old and even anachronistic Reman profanity, Terius smacked the nearby bulkhead with the flat of his hand. "It seems the 'primitives' can track us, after all." He pointed to Mylas and Daprel. "Arm yourselves, and move to the landing ramp."

"You're suggesting we attempt to repel them with hand weapons?" Mylas asked.

"I'm not *suggesting* anything," Terius answered. "We will defend this ship, no matter the cost."

With the weapons officer shouting like one of his old military academy instructors to move ever faster, Mylas and Daprel each retrieved their personal weapons from a locker near the engineering deck's forward compartment. As they neared the still-open hatch leading to the landing ramp, Mylas saw that Terius and Ciluri were already there, both of them brandishing disruptor rifles, which of course were much more powerful than the standard-issue sidearms they all carried. They, along with Mylas and Daprel, comprised the entire crew left aboard the *Nevathu*, with Commander

Vathrael and Subcommander Sirad off the ship and both having taken sizable scouting parties with them.

"I don't understand," Mylas said as he followed Terius down the ramp. "Our cloaking field has only been deactivated for a short while. They could not possibly have tracked our location—not this quickly."

Terius did not look back at him as he replied, "Maybe they're benefiting from outside aid."

"The humans?" Mylas shook his head. "That is not their nature."

"We can argue this later," the centurion barked, reaching for his disruptor as he approached the edge of the ramp.

Stepping down onto the ground, Mylas offered a nod of encouragement to Daprel and Ciluri, both of whom were allowing their fear and inexperience to affect their composure.

"Look," Ciluri said, pointing toward the horizon. "There."

A small black shape had come over the mountains in the distance, and was now growing larger with each passing moment. To Mylas's practiced eye the craft was an ungainly creation, with straight lines and bulky components attached seemingly at random to the transport's wide, boxlike primary hull.

"Scan them again," Terius said.

In response to his order, Ciluri activated the portable scanner he had carried slung over one shoulder and aimed it in the direction of the approaching ship. "I'm detecting two life signs which aren't familiar to me. They must be Dolysian."

"What is that?" Mylas asked, pointing to one of the scanner's indicators. "A power reading?"

"Yes," the centurion replied. "Their engines are putting

out far more energy than should be needed for propulsion." Shaking his head, he added, "I am at a loss to explain it, sir."

Looking away from the scanner, Mylas watched as the Dolysian transport slowed its approach, shedding altitude as it began to pivot on its axis.

"Come with me, Ciluri," Terius said, bringing his disruptor rifle up and stepping away from the *Nevathu*'s landing ramp. Ahead of them, the Dolysian craft had completed its turn. Doors on its underside parted and a quartet of landing gear lowered into position. At the same time, a hatch on its aft end started lowering. A cloud of dust and dirt was thrown into the air as the ship made its final descent. When it made contact with the ground, its landing gear flexed as the craft's weight settled and the aft hatch continued lowering.

Mylas was the first to see the barrel of the massive weapon. "Wait!" he shouted, but by then it was too late.

A brilliant blue beam of energy erupted from the cannon or whatever it was, accompanied by a piercing shriek as it chewed into the ground in front of Terius and Ciluri. No sooner had the first barrage concluded than a second followed, ripping another gouge into the soil. Mylas felt Daprel's hand gripping his arm before the junior engineer, his disruptor drawn, began backpedaling and pulling Mylas with him toward the ramp.

"Return fire!" Terius shouted, dropping to one knee and taking aim at the craft. A third salvo spat forth from the weapon inside the ship, sending the centurion diving to the ground for cover. Ciluri mimicked his movements, throwing himself toward a slight depression and whatever meager protection it might offer.

How is this possible? The question screamed in Mylas's

mind as Daprel continued dragging him up the ramp. Where had the Dolysians obtained such weaponry? Though it was not as advanced as Starfleet phasers, the technology had to be related, of that Mylas was certain.

His suspicions were confirmed when he saw multiple figures, each wearing black trousers and either gold, red, or blue tunics that could only be Starfleet uniforms.

"Now!"

The instant the rear loading hatch cleared the laser drill's muzzle, Kyle gave the order, Christine Rideout hit the firing control, and the weapon responded by belching forth its powerful beam. Thanks to the chief engineer's inspired tinkering, the drill had been converted from a simple tool back to something resembling its original purpose. Though not as powerful as it once had been, it was still enough, judging by the way the laser beam shredded the ground in front of the Romulan ship and sent two armed centurions lunging for cover.

"Let's go!" Kyle shouted, jumping with phaser in hand from the open hatch to the ground. No sooner had his boots touched the soil than he was running forward, weapon arm extended and sighting down on the two Romulans who were scrambling to bring their own disruptors to bear. To either side of him, Bill Hadley and Donovan Washburn fanned out so as to approach the Romulans from different angles. Other members of the salvage team were following him, also spreading out and forming a skirmish line as the team advanced on the enemy scout ship.

Light reflected off something near the vessel's landing ramp and Kyle saw the two Romulans, one much older than the other, making their way back into the ship. The younger

of the two soldiers was holding a weapon, and Kyle wasted
no time aiming his phaser and firing at the potential threat.
The single beam lanced across the open space separating
him from the Romulans, striking the centurion in the chest
and causing him to collapse onto the ramp. Beside him, the
older Romulan moved to help his companion rather than
brandish his own weapon, leaving Kyle to see to the more
viable threats.

One of the centurions on the ground was fast—damned
fast. He was on his feet and pulling his large, ugly disruptor
rifle to his shoulder when Hadley, cradling his phaser in
both hands, fired. The beam hit the soldier in the shoulder
and he sagged, the stun effect already washing over him as
he fell backward to the ground.

"Stop right there!"

Washburn was yelling at the remaining Romulan, who
also had recovered his rifle and was bringing it to bear, but
the lieutenant fired his phaser first. The centurion dropped
to his knees, his rifle falling from his hands before he
pitched face-first to the dirt.

"That should be all of them," Hadley barked as he
moved to verify that the two fallen Romulans were unconscious. At the same time, Washburn retrieved their weapons as Kyle, flanked by other members of his landing party,
ran toward the landing ramp leading up into the Romulan
scout ship. The older Romulan was still there, kneeling next
to his companion. When he saw Kyle approaching him, he
held out his hands to show they were empty before pointing to the other fallen centurion.

"He's injured," the Romulan said. "His head struck the
railing when he fell."

Wary of deception, Kyle kept his phaser trained on the

Romulan as he stepped closer for a better look. Seeing the thin line of green blood streaming from the open gash on the side of the fallen soldier's head, he asked, "Do you have some kind of emergency medical kit nearby?"

The Romulan nodded. "At the top of the ramp."

Motioning toward Hadley, Kyle said, "This officer will accompany you to retrieve it." As they moved up the ramp, he turned and saw that Washburn, Rideout, and the others had completed the process of securing the other two Romulans. A tricorder in her hand, Rideout was using it to scan in the direction of the scout ship.

"I think I've found whatever they're using to jam communications," Rideout said. "It shouldn't take much to disable it."

Kyle held up his free hand. "Not so fast." Indicating the older Romulan who was being escorted by Hadley back down the ramp, he asked, "We're sure that's all of them?"

"Four life signs total," Rideout said. "That's still checking out."

"We'll sweep the ship, anyway, just to be sure," Kyle said. "Washburn, get a boarding party organized for that." As the lieutenant and Rideout set about preparing to enter the scout ship, he turned his attention to the Romulan as he set to work treating his unconscious companion. "Will he be all right?"

"I believe so," the Romulan said. "His injury does not look severe." Pausing, he turned from his work to regard Kyle. "Thank you."

"Your other men are only stunned," Kyle replied. "They'll be fine in a little while."

Nodding in apparent approval, the Romulan resumed hovering over his friend, extracting items from the medical kit. "How were you able to deceive us? We did not detect your human life signs aboard the ship."

"Just an old trick I learned," Kyle said. By having the transport's pilot, Liadenpor Ceeda hu Novi, increase the output of the craft's engines to their full capacity—something required to provide power to the laser drill, anyway—one of the resultant effects was masking the life signs of anyone standing in proximity to the ship's generators. As for using the drill, it had been Rideout's idea to mount the implement inside the ship's rear cargo area, giving Kyle and his team an extra advantage against the Romulan disruptors.

The Romulan seemed to process Kyle's remark before nodding. "I see. Well, where would we be without our little secrets?" He glanced to his friend before adding, "I suppose that we are your prisoners, now."

"That's for my captain to decide," Kyle replied. He could only guess as to the political ramifications of the Romulans sending ships here, endangering the local inhabitants and taking aggressive action against Starfleet personnel. Whatever discussions were to be had or decisions to be made, they would take place far from here, and likely involve no small amount of teeth gnashing from anyone unfortunate enough to be involved. For now, he had plenty to keep him busy.

He looked up to see Rideout descending the ramp, holding her tricorder against her left hip. Eyeing the Romulan, she said, "I've disabled their jamming hardware. You should be able to contact your captain now."

"Fantastic, Christine," Kyle said as he reached for his communicator and flipped it open. "Kyle to Captain Kirk."

There was a short burst of static before the captain's

voice replied, "*Kirk here. Since we're talking, I guess that means you were successful. Excellent work, Lieutenant. Any casualties?*"

"None, sir," Kyle replied. "One Romulan sustained a treatable injury, and we have them all in custody. What do you want me to do with them?"

Whatever answer the captain might have provided disappeared in a hiss of static loud enough to make Kyle wince. Pulling the communicator away from his face, he regarded the device with confusion. "What the hell is this about?" He looked to Rideout. "You're sure you disabled the jamming?"

The chief engineer nodded. "Absolutely. No question." She held up her phaser for emphasis. "I used my favorite tool to turn it off."

Scowling at the seemingly useless communicator in his hand, he grunted in irritation. "Maybe the Romulans in the complex are giving the captain and the others trouble."

"That is a sensible hypothesis," the Romulan said, and he seemed unfazed by Kyle's withering stare. "My commander is quite resourceful in that regard."

Kyle nodded. "Well, then I feel sorry for your commander, because no one makes trouble the way Captain Kirk does."

TWENTY-NINE

Uhura's eyes burned with the sting and grit of fatigue, and not for the first time did she reach up to rub them. The array of information being fed to the control console's seven display screens was starting to become one large, unending blur, she decided. Bracing her hands against the console, she arched her back, reveling in the sensation as she stretched and worked the kinks from her tired muscles. That accomplished, she drew a deep breath before returning her attention to the swirl of data before her. Was she really that tired, or had the ancient Kalandan text become even more difficult to read than just five minutes earlier? She reached up to stifle a yawn, aware once more of the mounting strain beneath her temples and at the base of her skull.

In less than an hour, none of that will really matter, right?

"You okay?"

It took her a moment to register the question, and when she did she turned to see Boma regarding her from a nearby console, concern evident in his eyes. She cleared her throat before replying, "Why do you ask?"

Boma pointed to her hand. "Because you look like you're about to punch something, or someone."

Glancing down, Uhura realized that her right hand was clenched and shaking as it rested atop the flat, polished console. Releasing the fist, she flexed her hand and felt the tingle and rush of warmth as blood flow returned to her fingers. "Sorry," she said, offering a sheepish expression. "It's been a long day."

"I know how you feel," Boma replied, closing his eyes as he reached up to rub the bridge of his nose.

"How are you feeling?" Uhura asked.

Leaning against the console, Boma crossed his arms and released a tired sigh. "All things considered, I guess I'm doing okay." He dropped his gaze to the floor. "Sometimes it's hard not to think about Captain Arens and the others. I try to keep busy, but that doesn't always work." He paused, wincing as he rubbed his right bicep.

Uhura pointed to his arm. "Still hurts?"

"A little," Boma replied. "It's more irritating than anything else. Doctor McCoy told me it'd be like that for a couple of days. Beats wearing a sling, though." He indicated their console with a nod of his head. "This is tough enough with *two* hands."

"Amen to that," Uhura said. The struggle to access and understand the Kalandan computer system, as well as their run-in with the Romulans and now the stress of trying to abort the underground complex's self-destruct protocols, was beginning to wear her down. Her latest discovery, that the Kalandan computer system had initiated a new protocol blocking all communications to and from the complex, was but the latest in a long string of obstacles thrown in their path. What other tricks might the ancient technology still have waiting in reserve?

After abandoning the original operations chamber, they had made their way to this counterpart control room, after which Spock—without using the explosive charges they had confiscated from the Romulans—had managed to work past the damage inflicted by Captain Kirk on the room's door access panel in order to open the portal. The downside to his achievement was that he was uncertain as to how he might reseal the door or, if necessary, open it yet again. This left no other choice than to station Lieutenant Johnson at the open hatch in order to guard against Romulan intruders. So far, and for whatever reasons, the Romulans had seen fit not to attack them while all of this was going on, leaving Spock and the rest of the landing party to once again work at regaining control of the ancient Kalandan technology in the hopes of aborting the destruct protocol. Despite the obvious need for urgency, Uhura found she was having trouble settling back to the tasks at hand.

"I guess I'm just not used to this sort of excitement," she said. "It's a long way from my station on the bridge."

"You wouldn't know it to watch you work," Boma said. He nodded to where Spock was working at a console on the other side of the room. "I mean, Spock understands this stuff because his brain's wired to. I'm running as fast as I can just to keep up, but you? You're a natural." Pointing to the console and the screens of streaming data, he shook his head. "Everything we've been able to figure out so far is because of something you saw in there, or even thought you saw."

Frowning, Uhura countered, "That's not true. We've been working together all day. You've been right here with me the whole time."

"I may have seen one or two things here and there," Boma said, "or helped you finish a thought, but that was only in response to something you said, or started to say.

The fact is, we're where we are right now because you're here." He paused, then released a small chuckle. "That didn't come out quite the way I intended."

Uhura smiled. Despite the current situation, she found herself buoyed by the unexpected compliment. "That's all right. I was able to translate the meaning, and I appreciate it." Drawing a deep breath, she forced herself to relax and to will away the aches in her back and neck. This mission had provided her with a rare opportunity to work beyond the technical demands of her primary duties and employ some of the skills and natural aptitude that had guided her to joining Starfleet in the first place. Thanks to the wonders of modern, computer-driven universal translation protocols, her innate talent for recognizing and adapting to alien languages—spoken and written—was tested only on rare occasions in her capacity as the *Enterprise*'s chief communications officer. Though the universal translator had proven useful here, as well, what it often failed to discern was the context and intent behind the words being interpreted. Insight into the mind of the speaker or writer also was necessary, and was part of the mystery and challenge of decoding an alien language. It was just such a test that Uhura relished.

So, get on with it.

Turning back to her console, she said, "Here, look at this." She waited until Boma moved to stand next to her before pointing to one of the station's displays. "I managed to get back into the security system. What do you see?"

Leaning closer to get a better look, Boma tapped his fingernails on the console as he studied the scrolling data. "That's code from the master control processes, right?"

"Yes. It oversees and instructs everything else, based

on information sent to it by the other hubs in the security system network." Uhura reached for the console and tapped several illuminated controls on the flat panel, and one of the displays shifted its image to show a series of nine status indicators. Each was labeled with its name in Kalandan script and a blue icon except for the next to last marker, which was yellow. Pointing to that icon, she said, "See this? It's the environmental control system."

Boma shook his head. "I don't understand. The system's inactive?"

"The system itself is fine," Uhura said. "But the computer process overseeing it isn't. Remember the firefight in the other control room?"

"Of course," Boma replied. "The control banks for the environmental system were damaged, but why would that affect the software? Those processes were active in the central network, right?"

"It would appear something was interrupted by the loss of the system console," said a new voice, Spock's, as the Vulcan and Doctor McCoy emerged from an adjoining room and walked up behind them. "Either as a consequence of the physical damage or perhaps a design feature or flaw in the system itself, that process has been compromised."

"Not just compromised," Uhura said, again pointing to the display, "but it's waiting for a diagnostic to be executed against it. That's what this indicator means. Until a corrective action is taken, it's operating in a standby mode."

"I know the feeling," McCoy said. "Where the hell's Jim when you need him? If anybody can convince a computer to do something it doesn't want to do, he can." Uhura stifled a smile, amused by the doctor's observation, which even garnered a raised eyebrow from Spock.

"Despite the captain's unusual proclivity in that regard," replied the first officer, "this computer system lacks the sort of interactive voice response technology to which we are accustomed. Indeed, interfacing with this system requires—"

"Mister Spock!"

Everyone turned at the sound of Lieutenant Johnson's shout, and Uhura saw the security officer moving back from the open doorway where he had been standing guard. He was pointing his phaser in that direction when something small and dark flew through the opening and bounced toward the center of the room.

"Take cover!" Spock called out, and Uhura felt Boma dragging her toward the floor before the entire room vanished in a brilliant white light. No sooner had she thrown up an arm to shield her eyes than a piercing shriek assaulted her senses. The whine seemed to stab directly into her brain, and she pulled her hands to cover her ears as she curled into a fetal ball on the floor.

Some . . . kind of . . . sonic . . . pulse . . . ?

Though the effect lasted only seconds, the ringing sound continued even as the light faded and Uhura rolled onto her side to see that the room itself seemed to have been affected by the blast. The overhead lighting was flickering in mad fashion, while displays and control panels on various consoles around the room were blinking on and off. Even the cube hanging from the center of the ceiling seemed to be reacting to the attack, its multihued swirl of incandescent illumination now a flashing and stuttering frenzy.

Looking toward the door, she saw dark figures charging

into the room. She heard a dull, droning hum and looked up to see one of the Romulans firing his disruptor at the turret high on the wall, his targeted strikes successfully neutralizing the automated weapon. White spots continued to dance in her vision as she reached for the phaser on her hip, but the motion was arrested by a hand on her wrist. She looked up to see the face of a Romulan centurion scowling down at her from beneath a heavy gold helmet.

As she was hauled to her feet, she saw Boma struggling with another Romulan. He was no match for the soldier's greater strength, as the centurion twisted the lieutenant's arm up and behind his back before slamming him face-first into a wall console. Boma grunted in pain as his knees buckled and he fell to the floor.

Fighting against her own captor's hold, Uhura jerked her head around to see McCoy already under guard. Johnson was faring better as he engaged a centurion in hand-to-hand combat. He blocked the enemy soldier's punch before grabbing the Romulan's arm and lashing out with his foot, kicking his opponent just below the right knee. Even with her compromised hearing the soldier's cry of pain was still audible to Uhura, and she saw him stagger away from Johnson as another centurion moved in behind the security officer.

"Watch out!" was all Uhura was able to say before the Romulan struck the back of Johnson's head with the butt of his disruptor. The lieutenant collapsed, falling against a nearby console before dropping to the deck.

On the other side of the room, Spock fought with another Romulan. The soldier was fast but Spock was faster, ducking under his opponent's attack and reaching for the centurion's exposed neck and shoulder. As the Romulan's body went slack and Spock allowed him to sag to the floor, Uhura saw another figure approaching him from the doorway, weapon drawn and aiming it at him.

"Spock!"

As he turned toward the new threat, the Romulan, a female with short black hair, pointed her disruptor pistol at the first officer's face, and he halted in place.

"The automated systems within this complex may still react if I shoot you," she said. "Please don't force me to test their effectiveness." She gestured to Spock with the muzzle of her disruptor. "You are the leader of this group, yes?"

Holding his hands out and away from his body to demonstrate his surrender as one of the centurions relieved him of his phaser, Spock nodded. "I am. Commander Spock, first officer of the *U.S.S. Enterprise.*"

Her features softening as she smiled, the Romulan said, "Yes, of course. I should have recognized you, given how prominently you, your captain, and your vessel factor into so many of the reports I receive from my superiors. As it happens, I also failed to recognize your captain when I encountered him in the tunnels. Kirk, is it not?"

"That is correct," Spock said. "Is he injured?"

Vathrael shrugged. "I do not know, nor do I care." Raising her voice, she added, "I am Commander Vathrael, and I claim this facility in the name of the Praetor of the Romulan Empire. You and your party are my prisoners. Conduct yourselves like the proper Starfleet officers you are supposed to be, and you will be treated well." She looked around the room at the centurions who had accompanied her, and her eyes locked on Uhura's for a moment before she said, "Collect them and put them in that other room."

The Romulan guarding Uhura pulled her phaser from her

belt and prodded her toward the adjacent chamber's doorway, where she looked down to see Boma still unconscious on the floor. For the first time since the attack, it occurred to Uhura to look around the room until she saw the weapon turret, which had not been there before, having emerged from behind a wall panel above the bank of control consoles on the far side of the room. The cube hanging from the center of the ceiling was glowing brighter now, its swirling light patterns having grown more agitated. On the far wall, the torched remnants of the weapon turret sat, smoking.

Why had the weapon not responded to the Romulans' assault on the room? It took Uhura only a moment to realize that the enemy soldiers had refrained from using their disruptors at the outset of the surprise attack, relying instead on the flash grenade they had tossed into the room. That act had been enough to trigger the chamber's security system and bring the turret out of hiding, but why had it not evoked a more aggressive response?

"They tricked it," she said, keeping her voice low. The sonic grenade, she decided, somehow must have impaired the turret's sensors, preventing it from taking action once it was deployed. She wondered if the Romulans could have anticipated that effect, and might instead have benefited from a minor yet still decisive stroke of luck.

Why can't we get that kind of break?

"I'm a doctor! Let me check Johnson and Boma!"

Uhura turned to see McCoy eyeing the soldier guarding him with a menacing stare. He was looking past the centurion to his commander before indicating the centurion Johnson had wounded. "I can treat your man, too, if you'll let me."

"See to my centurion first," Vathrael replied.

McCoy shook his head. "His leg is injured, but I doubt

it's life-threatening. Our people have head wounds. I need to determine their condition."

"Tell your physician to treat the centurion," the Romulan commander said to Spock, "or I will order your officers killed."

Spock shook his head. "That won't be necessary, Commander." Glancing over his shoulder, he said, "Doctor McCoy, please see to the centurion's injuries."

Mumbling something under his breath that Uhura could not hear, McCoy moved past the Romulan guarding him to where the wounded centurion was sitting on the floor near one of the control consoles. The soldier eyed him with suspicion as the doctor knelt beside him.

"Don't worry, son," McCoy said, his voice low. "I promise I'm not here to hurt you." He held up his tricorder for Vathrael to see before opening its storage compartment and retrieving the small diagnostic scanner housed there. Activating the unit, he began waving it over the centurion's leg. As he worked, other centurions collected Johnson and Boma and dragged them to the room, leaving them at Uhura's feet. There was no door to close, but one of the Romulans took up station outside the room, positioned so that he could watch his charges while still keeping an eye on Spock and Vathrael. Kneeling beside Johnson, she reached for his neck to check for his pulse, and breathed a sigh of relief when she felt the gentle throbbing beneath her fingers. The same was true for Boma, though there was a thin line of blood oozing from the back of his head.

"Commander," Spock said, "you need to be aware that a self-destruct protocol has been initiated. This entire facility is scheduled to be destroyed in fifty minutes and nineteen seconds."

Her eyes narrowing in doubt, Vathrael replied, "You will abort that protocol."

"I cannot," the Vulcan said. "At least, not at present. We were in the process of determining how to do that before your arrival."

"Then you will continue that effort," ordered the Romulan.

Uhura saw Spock's right eyebrow rise, his expression's only concession to the commander's directive. "And what, precisely, will you do if and when we succeed in canceling the destruct protocol?"

Stepping closer so that the tip of her disruptor was mere centimeters from the science officer's face, Vathrael answered, "Whatever my praetor orders me to do."

"The Federation will not stand by while you attempt to annex the Dolysian people into your empire," Spock said.

"What the hell are you babbling about, Spock?" McCoy barked from where he continued to examine the injured Romulan. "If this place goes up, it could kill who knows how many Dolysians at the colony!"

Without shifting his gaze from Vathrael, Spock replied, "I am aware of that, Doctor. Please keep your focus on your patients." Then, he gestured to where Uhura knelt next to Johnson before saying to the Romulan commander, "Despite my own misgivings regarding your motivations, I cannot refuse to act when so many lives are at risk. Nor can I allow the loss of the irreplaceable information and technology contained within this facility." Uhura saw the first officer pause, knowing he was weighing the lives of everyone in danger against the potential of losing the Kalandan outpost to the Romulans. If this were a Starfleet facility, the choice would be easy, made so by the fact that anyone wearing a uniform would know and have accepted the risks associated with their choice of career. The Dolysians, on the other hand, had made no such decision, but instead were at the mercy of a situation in which they had played no role. Beyond the potential for loss of life here on Gralafi, there was no way to predict the impact on the Dolysian homeworld. While there were tactical considerations so far as allowing the Romulans a chance to obtain and study the Kalandan technology, Uhura knew Spock, and was therefore certain how he would decide.

"I will require Lieutenant Uhura's assistance," the Vulcan said.

Uhura saw the skepticism in the commander's eyes as she considered Spock's request. Was she wondering what sort of trickery he might be attempting? That made no sense; surely the Romulan knew that Spock, like most Vulcans, would not employ deceit. On the other hand, Uhura had seen the first officer carry out what might be charitably described as misdirection. Might he be doing something like that now? She doubted it. There were just too many lives at stake, and Spock knew the best course of action, at least for the short term, was to continue the effort to override the destruct protocol and take that threat out of the equation. As for whatever strategy or other bold move might come next? To that, Uhura had no clue, and hoped Spock, at least, was thinking that far ahead.

And that was when the situation, already complicated and uncertain, looked as though it might be ready to begin careening toward total chaos as Captain Kirk and Ambassador Sortino stepped into the room.

THIRTY

Standing just inside the control room's entrance, the Starfleet captain and his female companion held their hands out from their sides, their empty palms demonstrating that they held no weapons. They made no attempt to reach for the phasers on their hips, though as he met her gaze Vathrael saw the determination in the captain's eyes. The human's audacity was, in a word, astonishing.

"Commander," he began, "my name is—"

"Captain James Kirk," Vathrael said, cutting him off even as Centurion Drixus moved toward him. "Fabled commander of the *Enterprise.*"

Kirk said nothing as Drixus relieved first him and then the female of their phasers, though Vathrael noted how the captain watched the centurion's movements as though gauging vulnerabilities or other openings to exploit. This one was dangerous, Vathrael decided. Prudence demanded she place both humans in custody, or even kill them. On the other hand, the information Kirk possessed on any number of subjects would be of certain interest to Fleet Command and even the Praetor himself. Delivering him as but one trophy of a successful mission could not help but elevate her standing in the eyes of her superiors.

An interesting notion, she mused, *assuming you survive the day.*

"Your reputation does indeed precede you, Captain," she said. "Fleet Command's file on you is rather extensive and illuminating, not to mention quite entertaining."

"I'm flattered," Kirk replied as Drixus stepped away from him, still covering the captain and his companion with his disruptor. Vathrael watched his eyes scan the room, lingering at a point behind her, where she knew his subordinates were being held. Glancing in that direction, she saw that the other human female, one of Kirk's crew, was kneeling beside the fair-skinned male in the red shirt, while the second male, darker-skinned and dressed in a blue uniform tunic, was pulling himself to a sitting position and holding one hand to the back of his head. Outside the room, the human doctor continued to hover over Centurion Sipal, and when he looked up from his work Vathrael saw him exchange glances with Kirk. The silent communication was evident even to her. No doubt the doctor and his captain were troubled over the welfare of their subordinates, and her theory was confirmed when Kirk spoke again, this time to his own first officer.

"Spock," he said, worry obvious in his tone and his features, "how are Johnson and Boma?"

"Unknown, Captain," replied the Vulcan.

Returning his attention to Vathrael, Kirk said, "Commander, your injured soldier seems to be okay, thanks to my doctor. May he now treat my officers?"

Vathrael considered the request, and saw no need to deny it. So long as his focus was solely on the safety of his people, Kirk would be resistant to any demands she placed upon him. Better to alleviate at least some of his concerns, and perhaps earn a small degree of trust. With that in mind, she looked to Centurion Betria and nodded. The doctor's expression turned to one of gratitude as he eyed her.

"Thank you," he said, before Betria directed him to the room with his injured companions. That left Atrelis to guard Spock while Vathrael stepped closer to Kirk. Stopping several paces from him, she holstered her disruptor.

"My name is Commander Vathrael, Captain. In all honesty, and though I say this with full knowledge that such comments might well be viewed as treasonous by at least some of my superiors, I have wanted to meet you for some time. Your Fleet Command file describes you as being quite intelligent and resourceful, if not impulsive and even a bit arrogant." Of course, such adjectives routinely were employed when describing the commanders of Starfleet's most powerful vessels, though Kirk's name seemed to be the one most often associated with such behavior. "Even knowing that, I still wouldn't have expected you to simply walk in here. You are either very brave or very stupid." Pausing, she smiled. "I suspect it is actually some mixture of the two."

Kirk shrugged. "You're not the first person to tell me that. Come to think of it, you're not even the first person to tell me that today."

The comment raised an important question, and Vathrael forced herself not to curse as she realized it was something about which she should already have inquired. Her suspicion mounting, she said, "You weren't skulking about the tunnels all alone. Where is the rest of your party?"

"My security officer was killed during a firefight with some of your people," the captain replied, and Vathrael observed how his jaw clenched and his eyes hardened as he spoke. "I think I may have injured your first officer. He'll be okay, but his head's probably going to be hurting for a day or so."

Her eyes narrowing in skepticism, she studied Kirk's face and came to the conclusion that he was not lying. Despite any concern she felt for Sirad and the other members of her crew, Vathrael had no intention of giving the human any satisfaction from an emotional display. Still, the death of Kirk's subordinate was not something in which she took pleasure.

"I apologize for what happened to your officer, Captain. Though duty sometimes requires us to take life, it is not something I pursue with any enthusiasm."

Kirk appeared unconvinced by her apology. "Look, Commander," he said, his voice turning hard and demanding, "we're here because, by now, I'm sure Mister Spock's informed you that this entire facility is about to be destroyed."

"He has," Vathrael replied, more than a bit taken aback by the captain's sudden shift in demeanor, "and I've directed him to continue his efforts." Looking to where Spock still stood, covered by Drixus, she said, "You may proceed."

"Spock, don't," Kirk snapped, and when Vathrael turned back to face him she saw the raw determination, even defiance, in the man's eyes.

Unable to resist a small smile, she asked, "Captain, surely you're concerned for the safety of your crew, to say nothing of the people living on this planet?"

"Of course, I am," Kirk replied, "but living under Romulan rule isn't exactly paradise, is it? Maybe I'm doing them a favor by not stopping this detonation."

He was being aggressive for a purpose, Vathrael

concluded, perhaps to distract her from some other gambit he was attempting, but what could that be? "Drixus," she called out, not taking her eyes off Kirk as she drew her disruptor and aimed it at Spock, thereby freeing her centurion for a new task. "Since the captain appears to be uncooperative, kill one of his subordinates."

"You do that," Kirk said, "and you might as well kill us all, because I'll stand here until the clock ticks down to zero or you shoot me, whichever comes first. Surrender now, and we'll do what we can to abort the self-destruct. Refuse, and we all die."

Considering his brash demand, Vathrael shook her head. "Captain, please don't confuse any admiration I have expressed with stupidity. Humans are notoriously weak-willed when it comes to such sacrifice."

"Don't believe your propaganda," Kirk snapped. "For the right reasons, we humans are more than capable of sacrificing ourselves, but we'd rather live. But if the difference between possibly living and certainly dying means doing something bold or even crazy, then so be it."

His expression changed, and he even shook his head as he regarded her with what Vathrael thought might be a small, grim smile of resignation. Only then did she comprehend the full meaning behind his words, and by that point Kirk's hand was moving as though to reach for something.

Pulling the disruptor from where he had tucked it at his back and beneath his shirt, Kirk felt its weight as he raised his arm. The weapon was still awkward in his hand, but he ignored that as he concentrated on simply aiming the damned thing. In front of him, Vathrael recoiled from his sudden movement, turning to bring up her own disruptor to aim at him as Kirk leveled his weapon at his intended target.

"Kirk!" the Romulan shouted as he fired.

He felt the vibration coursing through his hand as the disruptor whined and spat forth its bolt of controlled energy, which screamed across the space separating him from the control cube hanging from the center of the room. The bolt struck the cube, followed by a second and third salvo as Kirk fired again. This entire gambit, shaky as it was, had relied upon the Romulans focusing on confiscating his and Sortino's phasers and not considering the possibility that they might be harboring other weapons.

The greater risk, Kirk figured, was firing directly on the sensitive control mechanism even with the disruptor set to a lower power setting. He had no idea how it or the rest of the security system might react, considering the Romulans had already disabled the room's automated defense weapon. Was there another turret lurking somewhere else in the chamber, or was there some other, possibly lethal countermeasure waiting to be deployed? What other tricks might the long-dead Losira and her creators have hidden up their respective sleeves? Whatever was going to happen, Kirk was certain it would happen in the next handful of seconds.

It took rather less time for fate—or whatever it was that had looked after Kirk on so many occasions over the years as it tolerated even his more aggressive and often outlandish tactics—to choose once more to smile upon him.

The cube's internal light show accelerated and the patterns it emitted turned from fluid to chaotic as displays and lights began flaring and blinking on various panels around the room. The overhead illumination faded, dropping the room into near darkness broken only by the light cast by the surrounding control consoles. Maybe his shots had only disoriented the cube and this was its way of resetting itself, but there was no way to know for sure. Behind him, Kirk heard the drone of hidden motors as the reinforced hatch began to slide downward.

"Commander!" a male voice shouted. "The door!"

As the door continued to close, Kirk saw Dana Sortino lunge to her right, away from him, as she pulled her own captured disruptor from behind her back. Rather than seek cover, the ambassador was moving forward, searching for a target and firing with seemingly reckless abandon in the general direction of two centurions, prompting the Romulans to drop in search of cover.

That woman is certifiable.

The thought echoed in Kirk's mind as the door sealed itself, locking everyone within the room. Visibility was compromised due to the diminished lighting, but he was able to see Spock dispatching one of the centurions with a nerve pinch. He was fast, turning to face Vathrael at the same instant the Romulan commander perceived his movements. Rather than shoot him, she blocked his arm before he could reach her neck, then lashed out with her other fist, punching him in the midsection. Spock stumbled in the face of the sudden attack, though he did not fall or even back away. His right hand struck hers, freeing her grip on her disruptor and sending the weapon across the room, where it bounced off a control console.

"Spock!"

Despite his training and experience, the Vulcan seemed

to be no match for Vathrael, who Kirk could see possessed formidable unarmed combat skills. Raising his disruptor, he raced forward, taking aim at her back as she kicked Spock with sufficient force to slam him into the nearby wall.

"Commander!" he snapped. "Stop right there!"

Moving with startling speed, Vathrael pivoted on her left foot and ducked just as he pressed the weapon's firing stud, dropping beneath the energy bolt that tore through the space she had occupied heartbeats earlier. Kirk adjusted his aim, trying to track her, but she was too fast. Her right foot caught the end of the disruptor, and Kirk felt it rip from his hand. He had no time to think about recovering the weapon before Vathrael was closing on him, and then he felt the first strike to his rib cage. Pain exploded in his side and he gasped from the intensity of the punch even as instinct pushed him away from the attack. He felt a hand on his right arm as Vathrael latched on to him, gripping part of his shirt as she tried to move closer. Kirk jerked away from her, twisting his arm until he heard the material of his shirt sleeve begin to tear. The material stretched and Vathrael tried to wrap her hand around it in a bid to keep Kirk from escaping. He saw the next hit coming from his left, and lowered his arm to block the strike. As Vathrael began to pull back her arm he grabbed it, twisting his hand around her bicep. The Romulan responded by swinging at his head with her right fist, which Kirk also deflected. Their movements brought them face-to-face, centimeters from each other just as the room's lighting stabilized and returned to normal levels, and he now saw the fury in the commander's eyes.

"Kirk!" she hissed through gritted teeth, followed by

something he did not understand, spoken in her native language. There was no way to decipher the invective.

He smashed her face with his forehead.

Stars danced in his vision, but he ignored them along with the sharp ache above his brow, feeling Vathrael sag as she recoiled from the attack. It was enough for him to free his right arm, and he used it to strike a second time. The edge of his hand caught the side of her head, but she held her ground, bringing up her arm in an attempt to retaliate. Kirk, having shaken off most of the pain from Vathrael's initial assault, pressed forward, landing two fast jabs to her sides and forcing her backward. Wincing in obvious pain, the commander tucked her left arm close to her ribs as though protecting them even as she recovered her footing, and Kirk knew she was readying for another attack. He moved to his right, trying to come at her from her weakened left flank. His eyes locked with hers, and he saw the mounting hatred in the Romulan's eyes.

So focused was he on trying to anticipate her next move that he was almost caught by surprise when her expression flattened and her body went limp. Only then did Kirk see Spock's hand on her shoulder. Vathrael collapsed into the Vulcan's arms, and he lowered her with care to the floor.

"If it's the last thing I ever do," Kirk said, catching his breath as he regarded the torn material of his uniform shirt, which had separated at the shoulder, "I'm going to learn how to do that."

"I remain optimistic, Captain," Spock replied, rising to his feet. "I hope that you did not take offense at her suggestion regarding improper physical relations with your ancestors."

Straightening what remained of his tunic, Kirk eyed the unconscious Romulan. "Is that what that was?" He and Spock turned to see that Ambassador Sortino had done an admirable job subduing the other Romulans. The two who remained conscious were now under the watchful eye of Uhura and Boma, both of whom now wielded the disruptors Sortino had given them.

"Very nicely done, Ambassador," Kirk said.

Sortino smiled as she recovered the phasers confiscated from the landing party and held one out to him. "Are you kidding? I haven't had this much excitement in years. And didn't I tell you to call me Dana?"

The comment evoked a chuckle from Kirk as he made his way over to Boma. "Lieutenant, are you all right?"

Boma nodded. "I'll be fine sir. Just a bump on the head."

Emerging from the smaller room, McCoy stepped around Boma and looked to Kirk. "Johnson will be okay, too. A couple of days' bed rest and he'll be ready for duty, assuming we get out of this, that is."

"Spock?" Kirk prompted.

The first officer was already moving toward one of the consoles. "Understood, Captain. Lieutenant Uhura, I shall require your assistance once again."

McCoy made his way to where Vathrael still lay on the floor. Glancing at Kirk as he knelt beside her, he muttered, "Fine way to treat a lady. This isn't going to do your reputation any favors, you know."

"Next time, I'll let her punch you," Kirk replied, rubbing his side where Vathrael had hit him and wondering about the size and color of the resulting bruise he knew would be there in a few hours. Making an attempt to tuck in the edge of his torn sleeve, Kirk sighed in resignation.

"You were overdue for that to happen, weren't you?" McCoy asked.

Though he smiled at his friend's playful jab, Kirk chose not to respond and instead nodded toward Vathrael. "Is she all right?"

Waving his diagnostic scanner over the unconscious Romulan, McCoy's business-like manner returned. "She'll be right enough once I'm finished."

"Can you wake her up?" Kirk asked.

The doctor deactivated the scanner before returning it to his tricorder's storage compartment. "Are you sure you want that? She was a handful before."

Kirk nodded. "It'll be fine."

McCoy administered a hypospray and a moment later Vathrael stirred. She grimaced, perhaps from some lingering pain from her injuries during the fight. Reaching up to rub her forehead where Kirk had struck her, she cleared her throat.

"So," she said, "I am your prisoner."

"For the time being, anyway," McCoy replied, returning his hypospray to the medical kit on his hip.

Kirk turned as Boma moved to stand beside him, aiming his phaser at Vathrael. "We're a bit shorthanded, so far as guards are concerned," he said, and Kirk could see that the man was still enduring some residual discomfort from his own skirmish with the Romulans.

"Thank you, Lieutenant," Kirk said before moving to where Spock and Uhura were working at the control console. "Spock? How much time?"

"Thirty-five minutes, eleven seconds," the Vulcan replied, not turning from the console.

Kirk gestured toward the console. "Can you at least

break through whatever's jamming communications?" He had been cut off from Lieutenant Kyle without warning, and now worried that the young officer, having secured the Romulan ship, might be considering making his way here in order to assist his captain. "We've got to tell the rest of our people to stay away, and warn the Dolysians what's coming."

His attention still on his workstation, Spock replied, "I do not believe we will be able to do that and disable the destruct protocol in the time remaining to us, Captain."

Time and options were running out, Kirk knew. Looking to Vathrael, he said, "You still have time to evacuate, Commander."

"What?" Boma asked, frowning.

"Are you kidding, Jim?" McCoy asked, his expression one of disbelief.

Shaking his head, Kirk kept his gaze on Vathrael. "She was only following whatever orders she was given." To the commander, he said, "If you leave now, there should still be time for you to warn your people on the surface." As he spoke the words, he imagined there would be people in the upper echelons of Starfleet Command who would disagree with his thinking, but none of them were here at the moment.

So, to hell with them.

His thought was interrupted by the sound of a new alert tone emanating from the console where Spock and Uhura stood. Turning to look, Kirk saw the expression of worry on Uhura's face even as Spock's hands seemed to move with greater speed across the panel.

"What's going on?" Kirk asked.

Spock replied, "We appear to have triggered some other

form of anti-intrusion device, Captain. The result is an acceleration of the countdown."

Feeling the knot of anxiety already forming in his gut, Kirk asked, "Tell me you can stop it?"

"Unknown at this time," Spock said.

"Well, how much time's left?" McCoy asked.

His hands moving across the panel's surface, Spock's index finger paused on one illuminated red control before replying, "Twelve minutes, forty-two seconds, but the countdown is continuing to accelerate."

"Wait!" Uhura shouted. "I think I can . . ." The rest of her sentence faded as the lieutenant leaned closer to the console, reaching toward one of the displays she had paused. Kirk saw her eyes narrow as she studied the depiction of Kalandan text, her fingers tracing over a grouping of characters and other symbols he did not recognize.

Movement from his left caught his attention and he turned to see the two remaining conscious Romulans looking to take advantage of the current chaotic situation. Sortino, as though anticipating the maneuver, was ready for them. The ambassador did not hesitate, firing her phaser and catching both centurions before they could even take their first steps. Both Romulans collapsed back into the adjacent room, and Kirk looked to where Vathrael was still under guard by Boma, her features clouding with irritation.

"They're just stunned, Commander," Kirk said. "You're free to join them, if you like."

Scowling at his flippant comment, Vathrael said nothing.

Kirk returned his attention to where Uhura was still

working. "Lieutenant?" he asked, but she ignored him, her long fingers moving across the interface panel and its rows of illuminated controls as though possessed of their own will. One display on the wall above her showed a grouping of characters that was refreshing at an alarming rate, which Kirk interpreted as the countdown timer.

"Somebody say something!" McCoy barked.

Uhura tapped a long, seemingly unending series of keys on the smooth panel, before reaching out with her right hand and slapping her palm against a triangular blue control. There was an audible tone, and the indicator that was the focus of Kirk's attention froze. Other displays on the workstation halted in place, as well, their representation of text and graphics now static.

"What just happened?" Kirk asked.

Vathrael said, "I presume you were successful."

"You presume correctly, Commander," Spock replied, stepping back from the console. "The destruct protocol has been halted."

"So has my heart," McCoy added. "While I try to restart it, will somebody tell us what all that was about?"

It was Boma who answered, "It was the diagnostic, wasn't it?"

Uhura turned from the console, smiling as she nodded. "I was able to forge the necessary credentials to give us access to the environmental control system. Once I was inside, it was easy to cross over to the master control protocols and halt any process currently being executed." She shrugged. "So, I just canceled the program with the code to tell it that everything was fine and the crisis was over."

"Absolutely wonderful," Sortino said, crossing the room to join the group.

Even Vathrael, Kirk noticed, seemed appropriately impressed. "A simple, yet elegant solution."

"And that's it?" McCoy asked, not bothering to hide his skepticism.

"Sometimes that's all you need, Bones," Kirk replied, grinning. "Computers will listen to any instruction they're given; you just have to know how to talk to them. Isn't that right, Lieutenant?"

"Yes, sir," Uhura replied.

Placing a hand on her shoulder, Kirk said, "Very nicely done, Nyota."

As though self-conscious at the praise, Uhura cast her gaze to the floor before replying, "Thank you, Captain."

A now-familiar whine began from behind them, and everyone shifted their gaze to the cube at the center of the room, the illuminated interior of which once more was oscillating in a regular pattern. From its base was emitted the shaft of light aimed at the floor, which coalesced into the shifting, translucent image of Meyeliri. As in the previous transmissions offered by the control cube, the doctor once again was wearing a long-sleeved robe—mauve, this time—that concealed her body from neck to feet. The beam's intense light highlighted her short-styled silver hair and her piercing blue-green eyes.

"*Greetings, fellow Kalandans,*" she said. "*Our systems indicate that the threat to our outpost has been eliminated, the containment protocol is no longer required, and the storehouse of knowledge we have strived for generations to collect is no longer in danger. Unless and until such time as this repository is called upon to fulfill its primary function, the responsibility for its care and protection falls to you. If we are fortunate, our society will continue to thrive and endure, and we will never have need for such contingencies. Let us all hope that is always the case. Regardless of what the future may hold, I wish you well."*

"The Kalandans never did seem to catch a break, did they?" McCoy asked.

Kirk shook his head, considering the sobering message he had just heard. "They anticipated the fall of their civilization, and prepared for it, but they were so worried about external enemies, they never had a chance against the threat from within."

"I'm sure there's a lesson or three in there, somewhere," Sortino offered.

"For another time, Ambassador," Kirk replied before turning to Vathrael. "Commander, we seem to be at a crossroads here."

The Romulan nodded. "I know you may not believe what I said to you earlier, Captain, but I do regret the loss of your security officer. As for everything else that has transpired here today, you were correct when you observed that we were merely following our orders, but that does not lessen the effect of a needless death."

"I appreciate that, Commander," Kirk said, his instincts telling him that her remarks were genuine, rather than a ruse. Before he could say anything else, he was interrupted by a new beeping from the console behind Spock and Uhura. Frowning, and more than a bit worried about what other surprises or booby traps might still be waiting to be triggered, Kirk asked, "What's that?"

Uhura replied, "Sensors, sir. We've accessed what looks to be the entire network. This equipment's able to scan beyond the barrier."

"Is it still closed?" McCoy asked. "Can we contact the ship?"

Once again working next to Uhura, Spock replied, "I am able to detect the presence of the *Enterprise*, but we are still endeavoring to access the communications subsystem." He paused, his fingers moving across the console before he added, "Captain, the *Enterprise* is not alone."

THIRTY-ONE

Dividing his attention between the main viewscreen and the chronometer set into the astrogator panel situated between Sulu and Arex, Scott watched time slipping away as the image of the Dolysian freighter grew larger with every passing second.

"We're within transporter range," said Sulu from the helm.

Scott felt the ache in his back and shoulders, a consequence of his hunched posture while sitting in the captain's chair. "Extend our shields, Mister Sulu. Lieutenant M'Ress, notify the transporter room to stand by." He looked to Chekov at the science station. "You've verified the life signs?"

"Five, sir," the ensign replied. "Just like the first freighter."

Wishing he had remembered to read whichever briefing report might have informed him of the standard crew complement of Dolysian cargo freighters, Scott instead elected to thank whoever was responsible for seeing to it that he could beam everyone to the *Enterprise* at one time.

"Shields extended," Sulu said, and Scott saw him glance at the chronometer. "The Romulans should be in weapons range in under a minute."

Despite the escalating tension he could feel permeating the bridge, Scott still found a moment to shake his head in mild amusement. "Mister Sulu, what have I told you about your irritating habit of keeping time?"

Sulu, picking up on the joke, looked over his shoulder. "I believe you called it an annoying fascination for time-pieces, sir."

"Aye, so I did," Scott replied before looking to M'Ress. "Tell the transporter room to beam those Dolysians aboard."

The Caitian communications officer acknowledged the order, and Scott heard her talking to the crewman on duty in the transporter room, though his attention once more was focused on the chronometer before him. The seconds were continuing to evaporate before his very eyes, but were they now dwindling even faster?

"Transporter room reports all five Dolysians are safely aboard," M'Ress said.

Sulu added, "Their ship's navigation system is continuing on automatic for its destination at the second moon. It's programmed to meet up with its companion freighter and assume a standard orbit once it gets there."

"That'll do," Scott said, rubbing his chin as he leaned back in the captain's chair. Once this situation was resolved—and assuming it was concluded in something resembling a peaceful manner—the crews of both freighters would be returned to their ships so that they might carry on with their tasks.

The Red Alert indicator flashed on the helm console, and Sulu called out, "Romulan vessels are now within weapons range. They're still maneuvering into attack positions."

"Reset shields to normal configuration," Scott ordered, "and move us away from the freighter. I want some breathing room. Is that escape course plotted?"

Nodding, Arex replied, "Course plotted and laid in, sir. Ready to execute at your command."

Though he did not want to leave the system so long as other options presented themselves, Scott knew that if the situation devolved into a shooting fight, the *Enterprise* would be vulnerable. With that in mind, he had ordered a contingency plan to take the ship away from immediate danger should circumstances warrant such action. He vowed it would be an option of last resort, as he had no intention of abandoning Captain Kirk and the landing party.

"Tactical plot on main viewer," Scott said.

Sulu pressed the appropriate controls on his console, and a moment later the image on the viewscreen shifted from the Dolysian freighter to the computer's cold, lifeless rendering of the *Enterprise*'s current situation. At the center of a white grid was a blue icon representing the starship, with three green avatars depicting the Romulan vessels. A smaller red marker indicated the Dolysian freighter, near the screen's lower left corner and moving beyond the image's boundary. The schematic shifted, morphing the grid into a three-dimensional cube with the *Enterprise* at its heart, and the three enemy warships moving toward it from different directions and angles, forming a multi-axis attack formation.

Chekov said, "They're moving to surround us. We still have some maneuvering room, but not for long."

"Mister Sulu, maneuver us closer to the energy field," Scott ordered.

Surprised by the command, Sulu looked over his shoulder. "Sir?"

"Use the field as partial cover as we maneuver," the engineer replied, understanding the lieutenant's confusion.

"They have to know what the rift did to their other ship. Maybe they'll be hesitant to get too close. If nothing else, it might be able to keep them from flanking us." Scott knew it was a long shot, but at this point such gambles seemed appropriate.

"Mister Scott," M'Ress called out. "We're being hailed. It's Commander Grathus."

"Of course it is," the engineer muttered under his breath, unable to suppress a small smile. "Put him on-screen."

The image on the viewer changed to that of the Romulan commander, once again seated at whatever alcove or hole in the bulkhead that served as his communications station.

"*So*," Grathus said without any introduction, "*you have deemed it necessary to take the civilians under your protection.*"

Rising from the captain's chair, Scott replied, "As I told you earlier, Commander, the Dolysians have entered into a cooperative partnership with the Federation. As such, we are duty-bound to protect them from external threats. I'm also required to remind you that your presence here is in violation of the treaty between our governments. I suspect that my superiors will be contacting yours in due course."

Grathus leaned across his desk, to the point that his face all but filled the viewscreen. "*We do not recognize the validity of your 'partnership' with these people, and even if it does exist, it does not absolve them of guilt for the destruction of a vessel of the Romulan Empire. If you choose to stand as their advocate, then it is you who will be held accountable for their actions.*"

"Commander, we've been over this," Scott snapped. "The Dolysian people had no knowledge of the technology buried beneath the surface of the planetoid. It's been there since well before they even achieved space flight. Why are you continuing to perpetrate an obvious falsehood?"

"*It is not a falsehood, human,*" Grathus replied. "*Romulans simply do not believe in the notion of ignorance as an excuse from responsibility. The Dolysians claimed that planet and all the riches it affords their society. Therefore, they are culpable for any offenses it commits.*"

Sensing the futility of arguing with the Romulan, Scott could only shake his head. Had he misread Grathus? During their earlier conversation, the commander had seemed pragmatic, if determined, with respect to finding an explanation for the loss of the other scout ship. Though he had not responded to Scott's earlier assertions that he wanted to avoid triggering an interstellar incident, his mannerisms had suggested as much. Was it possible that the Romulan was just that effective at presenting a demeanor that caused others to underestimate or misjudge his motives? Could it be a simple matter of bruised ego, and the perceived need to assert dominance? Grathus commanded a small armada; did he need to demonstrate his strength, perhaps to subordinates who might see an opportunity for advancement if an ineffective leader were removed from their path?

"I'm certain my government will see things differently, Commander," Scott said, making one last attempt at fostering civil discourse. "And I can't believe yours won't feel the same way, so what is it you're hoping to accomplish here, other than possibly starting a war?"

The scowl that had been clouding Grathus's expression softened, and he almost smiled. "*You claim some insight into the minds and attitudes of my people, human. After all*

this time with us as your enemy, you have learned nothing."
His face vanished, replaced by the tactical schematic.

Sulu released an annoyed grunt. "Well, that was enlightening."

"Mister Scott!" Chekov called out, his voice nearly a shout. "The Romulan ships are accelerating to full impulse power, maneuvering to envelop us."

"Evasive course," Scott ordered. "Increase our speed to maximum and stand by weapons."

"Aye, sir," Sulu responded, his hands almost a blur as they moved over his helm console. "Executing evasive maneuvers."

"Sensors are detecting minor fluctuations in the energy barrier," Chekov called out. "It's almost like it's reacting to our presence."

Scott frowned as he processed the report. "Are we in any danger?"

"From the field?" Chekov asked as he returned his attention to the science station's sensor viewer. "No, sir. The Romulans seem to have that covered." A moment later he blurted, "Incoming fire!"

There was no time to issue any warnings to brace for impact before the first salvo struck. Scott felt the deck shudder beneath his feet as the *Enterprise*'s deflector shields absorbed the brunt of the attack. An alarm klaxon wailed for attention, but he waved to Chekov to silence it.

"Hit on port side, aft," Chekov said, and Scott heard the anxiety in the ensign's voice. "Shields holding."

Sulu asked, "Should we return fire?"

"Target their engines," Scott answered. "Wait for my order." He did not want this fight, but he did not see anything else in the way of options. Grathus was going to force this confrontation, perhaps destroying the *Enterprise* in the process. He would then be free to tell his superiors whatever version of fact or fiction suited his needs, perhaps even justifying further action against the Dolysians, who at least for the short term would be defenseless against Grathus and his small fleet. None of it made any sense to Scott, with the possible exception of simple pride, and the need for the Romulan commander to demonstrate that he—and, by extension, his people—would not be intimidated by their interstellar neighbors regardless of whatever territorial borders might exist between them.

Another strike impacted against the deflector shields, and everything around Scott trembled in protest. The quivering was channeled through the command chair and into his arms. Like the first round, he knew that this also was a solid hit.

They've got us dialed in, all right.

Chekov looked up from his viewer. "Another hit aft. Shields are still holding. For now, anyway."

"Are they playing with us?" Sulu asked as he alternated his attention between his console and the main viewscreen, which continued to update the tactical schematic as the skirmish evolved. "Or are they worried about the barrier?"

"You just keep hugging it, Mister Sulu," Scott said. Maneuvering the *Enterprise* closer to the energy field seemed to be producing the desired results, based on the information being relayed by the tactical plot. The Romulans, at first eager to give chase, now appeared to be giving the barrier a wide berth, even though they remained well within the operational range of their warships' weapons. Glancing over his left shoulder, he asked, "Lieutenant Masters, any effects from the field?"

Seated behind him at the bridge's engineering station, Lieutenant Charlene Masters, a young, dark-skinned officer, replied, "There's some minor flux in the warp engines, but otherwise everything's in the green, sir. I don't know what might happen if we get any closer."

The bridge was jolted by yet another salvo of disruptor fire, one after another in rapid succession. This time the effects were more pronounced, with consoles blinking and the overhead lighting dimming for a moment as power was automatically routed to the ship's deflector shield generators.

"Now it's getting interesting," Scott mumbled to himself, before prompting in a louder voice, "Damage?"

Chekov replied, "Aft shields down to eighty-seven percent, sir. Rerouting power to compensate."

"Masters," Scott said, "direct the computer to alternate power to the shields based on which side is facing the energy field. Draw power from that side to shore up the weakened areas." He knew it was a tall order given Sulu's maneuvering, which entailed whatever turns, banks, and dives he might execute as part of the evasive course he had plotted along with any improvisation he might employ based on the Romulan ships' movements. Such rapid calculations and action were beyond the limits of regular flesh and blood engineers, but Scott reasoned it would be easy enough for the *Enterprise*'s main computer.

Blowing out his breath, he said, "All right, Mister Arex, let's try giving them something to think about. Fire at your discretion."

Before the Triexian could respond, there was a notable disruption in systems across the bridge. Once more consoles and their display monitors wavered and the lights flickered, and Scott thought he even felt the briefest of tremors in the deck plating. Instead of resetting themselves as they had before, the interruptions continued, showing no signs of abating.

"We weren't hit," he said. "What's causing that?"

At the helm, Sulu's hands moved across his console, with the lieutenant stabbing button after button in a flurry of chaotic motions. "It's the energy field. I think I got us too close."

"The field's definitely reacting to us," said Chekov, once more bent over the viewer. "The Romulan ships are backing off. They must be seeing what's happening." Then, he looked up from his station. "If I'm reading this correctly, there's a distortion at the field's boundary corresponding to our relative position."

Scott moved from his seat just before another disruptor barrage struck the shields. The effects of the impact were more pronounced this time, triggering new alarms at different stations around the bridge.

"Firing phasers," Arex called out, and Scott heard the deep resonating hum of energy being channeled to the starship's weapons banks. "Direct hit on the lead vessel's forward shields. They're still maintaining their distance."

"Our aft shields are down to sixty-three percent," Chekov said.

Acknowledging the report, Scott pointed to the science station. "Show me the distortion."

Chekov nodded, pressing a series of controls on his console. One of the two large monitors above his station changed to a computer-realized interpretation of the energy barrier as recorded by the sensors. Pointing to the field's outer boundary, the ensign said. "See this area right here at the edge? It actually retreated on itself as we passed, then resumed its normal configuration after we moved away. The pattern repeats as we traverse the field."

"Our warp engines," Scott said, more to himself than to anyone else. "The barrier reacts to the presence of an active warp drive. Every time a ship passed through the rift, the field responded with distortion, but those ships were moving at sublight speeds." He studied the monitor, seeing for the first time what had been right before him—before them all—from the beginning. "What if a ship were to penetrate the barrier at warp speed?"

"What?" Chekov asked, his eyes wide with disbelief. "Enter the barrier? Sir, the rift's not open. The Dolysians told us that every ship and probe they've sent into it has been destroyed."

The ship trembled around them once more, the ship's reaction to the attack even greater this time. How many more hits could the shields take before the generators were overloaded?

"None of those ships had warp drive," Scott said, holding on to the railing to keep his balance. "Arex, plot a course for the other side of the barrier, using the *Huang Zhong's* navigational data."

"What are you thinking, Scotty?" Sulu asked.

Scott returned to the captain's chair. "Warp jump, Mister Sulu. Precision piloting. You up for that?"

"It beats staying out here," the helmsman replied. "But what if you're wrong?"

"Then Captain Kirk's liable to be pretty angry with me. Standard view on the screen, please." Though Scott could not be certain his idea would work, the sensor data seemed to support what his gut was telling him was possible.

Instinct emboldened by experience had always helped to see him through one enormous challenge after another during his career—none greater than some of the trials he had faced during his tenure aboard this ship—but would that be enough now? There was only one way to know, and any lingering doubts he might have vanished as another double disruptor strike slammed into the *Enterprise*'s shields.

"Aft shields failing!" Chekov shouted above the new wave of alarms.

Clinging to the arms of the captain's chair, Scott snapped, "Mister Arex!"

"Course plotted!" replied the navigator. The Triexian was gripping the edge of his console with two hands and using his third to manipulate his console's controls.

Scott gritted his teeth, glaring at the roiling mass of energy at the center of the main viewscreen. "Now, Sulu!"

The helm officer did not reply, but instead stabbed one button on his own control panel. Scott had the briefest of moments to note distant stars on the viewscreen begin to stretch as the energy barrier seemed to lunge toward him. Yet another alarm whined, and everything seemed to shake and rattle as though preparing to come apart.

"Energy distortion!" Chekov yelled over the klaxon.

Then, the field was gone, replaced by the small green-brown sphere that was the Gralafi planetoid. The tremors subsided, leaving only the alert warbling and drowning out all other sounds on the bridge. Before Scott could order it silenced, Sulu pressed a control and terminated the annoying siren.

"That's it?" Chekov asked, making no effort to hide his skepticism.

"We're secure from warp speed," Sulu said.

Scott cleared his throat. "Status? How are the warp engines?"

Behind him, Lieutenant Masters replied, "Everything looks nominal, sir. All decks are reporting no damage."

His eyes still on the planetoid, Scott asked, "What about the energy field? Any change in its readings?"

Peering into the sensor viewer, Chekov answered, "Readings appear normal, Mister Scott. No apparent disruptions based on our passage."

"The subspace field," Sulu said, turning from his console. "That's what did it, right?"

"Aye," Scott replied. "At least, I think so. If I'm right, the field generated by our warp engines actually acted as a sort of agent against the energy within the barrier. A ship moving at sublight speeds was slow enough that the barrier was able to . . . retaliate, if you will. But, by moving at warp speed, we didn't give it that chance." He would have to examine the sensor records as well as diagnostic and sensor information recorded by the ship's computer with respect to the warp drive's performance, but for now, he was satisfied with the explanation.

His theory was strengthened by the appearance of a Romulan warship on the viewscreen, flying into view as though from nowhere as it completed the transition from subspace. It loomed before him, crowding the screen's edges on all sides, and Scott imagined he could see the vessel's weapons bristling as though ready to fire.

"Distance sixty-one thousand kilometers!" Sulu shouted, peering into the targeting scanner which had risen out of the left side of his console.

"Full power to forward shields!" Scott yelled, with just enough time to comprehend how the enemy vessel had duplicated their escape maneuver before he saw a sphere of undulating orange energy spew forth from the Romulan ship's disruptor bank. At this range the effect was immediate, and the *Enterprise* rocked from the full force of the strike. Streaks of diffused energy played across the viewscreen image, and Scott felt his seat drop from beneath him before he was slammed back into the chair. "Return fire!"

Arex pressed the firing controls, and twin beams of blue-white energy streaked across the space separating the *Enterprise* from the Romulan ship. Its shields flared in response to the attack, absorbing the strike even as the navigator fired again. Next to him, Sulu manipulated the helm controls, trying to give the starship some maneuvering room. On the screen, the Romulan warship unleashed another barrage, once more bathing the *Enterprise*'s shields with unharnessed energy as the entire ship groaned in protest.

"Forward shields down to thirty-eight percent!" Chekov yelled.

Scott said nothing, his attention drawn instead to the second and third Romulan ships, which had just appeared on the screen. No sooner had they dropped from subspace than they began moving off in different directions, each banking in such a manner that Scott was able to make out the elaborate markings—ominous predatory birds—on the underside of each vessel's hull for only a moment before the ships moved out of view.

At the science station, Chekov called out, "They're moving to surround us!"

"Evasive, Mister Sulu!" Scott ordered, but his next command died in his throat as, on the viewscreen, the remaining Romulan ship was rocked by an enormous writhing globe of green energy slamming into its hull. It took Scott an extra second to realize that the attack had penetrated the warship's shields as though they were nonexistent, continuing through until it ripped into the vessel's port nacelle and destroying it with a single salvo. The Romulan ship lurched in response to the attack as it was sent careening away from the *Enterprise*.

"It's from Gralafi!" Chekov called out. "I'm picking up massive energy readings from multiple locations around the planetoid. The other two Romulan ships have also been targeted and have already been disabled. I'm detecting massive power loss in all three vessels."

"What about us?" Scott asked. "Are we being targeted?"

Chekov shook his head. "Not that I can see, sir. Only the Romulans."

"Let's have a look at all three ships, Mister Chekov," Scott ordered. The image on the viewscreen was now split into three parts, each displaying one of the three Romulan warships. In addition to the vessel Scott and the bridge crew had seen attacked, its two companions also were adrift. One ship, a massive wound in its underside, spiraled as warp plasma vented from both nacelles. The third vessel had taken a strike along the top of its primary hull, and all of its external lighting had gone dark.

"Life signs?" Scott prompted.

Nodding, Chekov replied, "I'm picking up readings on all three ships, sir. One ship has lost main power, but its life support systems look to be running on emergency batteries. The other two ships still have power, but all three ships appear to have had their weapons and primary propulsion systems disabled by the attack."

"All weapons on standby," Scott said. "And lower our

shields. Lieutenant M'Ress, open a channel to all three ships. Notify them that they are free to transport whatever crew or supplies they need between their vessels. We will not fire on them, and we stand ready to offer any needed assistance."

"Aye, sir," M'Ress acknowledged. Then she said, "Mister Scott, I'm receiving an incoming message. It's from Captain Kirk! Audio and visual!"

I should've known, Scott thought, allowing a broad smile onto his face. "Put him through, Lieutenant."

The image of the three injured Romulan ships disappeared from the main viewer, replaced by the somewhat disheveled, very exhausted yet still oddly satisfied countenance of James Kirk. His uniform tunic was torn and dirty, and what looked to be a bruise was visible on his forehead. Despite his obvious fatigue, the captain was able to muster a small, tired smile.

"*Scotty! Are you all right?*" It was not until Kirk spoke that Scott realized the signal connection was free of static or other interference, despite the *Enterprise*'s proximity to the energy barrier.

Rising from the command chair, the engineer offered an enthusiastic nod. "Aye, sir. A few minor things to fix, but nothing we can't handle. Was that you responsible for the attack on the Romulans?"

Kirk nodded. "*You can thank Mister Spock, Lieutenant Uhura, and Lieutenant Boma for that. They were able to access the Kalandan defense systems.*"

"And in the nick of bloody time, too," Scott replied. "A fine trick, if you ask me."

The smile on Kirk's face grew into a broad grin. "*If you liked that, you're going to love this.*" He then nodded to someone off-screen. A moment later, another alert tone sounded, this time from the science station. Chekov, frowning at the new advisory, moved to the sensor viewer and once more peered into it.

"I don't believe it!" the ensign exclaimed before looking away from his station and locking eyes with Scott. "Sir, the energy barrier! It's gone!"

THIRTY-TWO

Sunlight, actual sunlight and not cursory illumination, refracted through a maelstrom of colliding energy thousands of miles away in space, shone down upon the metal exteriors of the Havreltipa mining colony. The violet tint that had lain over everything was gone. All around the outpost's clusters of buildings and support structures, people stood in the narrow streets and other thoroughfares, looking up at the wonder that was the Kondaii star as it hung in the sky at midday.

Standing on the roof of the building that served as the headquarters for the colony administrator and her staff, Kirk turned from his view of the open-air plaza that was the settlement's town square, lifting his face toward that sun and closing his eyes. As he allowed the warmth to soothe his skin, he drew a deep breath, marveling at how the very air seemed fresher and perhaps even charged with some new excitement as it filled his lungs. While he knew that could not be true, of course, it still pleased him to consider such thoughts, particularly on this day, which in some ways had brought with it a sense of change, if not outright renewal.

"You know," a voice said from behind him, "a blue sky really suits this place."

Opening his eyes, he turned and smiled at the sight of

Spock and McCoy walking toward him. "I was thinking along those same lines, myself." He gestured toward the southern horizon, where perhaps two-thirds of Dolysia itself was visible through the sky's blue haze. "How about that view, Bones?"

McCoy nodded. "Nothing short of breathtaking, if you ask me. I can certainly imagine the miners thinking of home as not seeming quite so far away now."

"The dissolution of the energy barrier has done nothing to alter the distance between Gralafi and Dolysia, Doctor," Spock said, standing next to the physician with his hands clasped behind his back.

Turning his eyes skyward, McCoy released a heavy sigh. "No, Spock, but now that it's out of the way, maybe somebody up there will finally answer my prayers for mercy."

Unable to suppress a chuckle, Kirk asked, "Are the Romulans on their way?"

Spock nodded. "Affirmative. The ship which was forced to land here achieved orbit eighty-four minutes ago, after which it rendezvoused with its companions. All four vessels are at the extreme range of *Enterprise* sensors, continuing on course toward the Romulan border."

"Excellent," Kirk said. Each of the Romulan vessels had required some form of mending in order to restore warp speed capability for their return home. Kirk had authorized repairs sufficient to allow the ships to leave the Kondaii system under their own power, after first ensuring that each vessel's weapons systems remained disabled. With the work carried out under the supervision of Commander Vathrael as well as the watchful eye of sensors, both from the *Enterprise* and from the Kalandan defenses, the repairs were concluded without incident and the ships allowed to depart in peace. As for the larger ramifications of what had taken place here, Kirk had no doubt that the next weeks and months would be filled with diplomats from both governments arguing and downplaying the incident. Despite whatever propaganda the Romulans might disseminate to their people, Kirk did not believe the empire truly wanted war.

I guess we'll see.

"That Romulan commander doesn't like you very much, you know," McCoy said.

Kirk replied, "Well, at least she's in good company." Clearing his throat, he asked, "Any word from Starfleet Command?"

Spock replied, "Lieutenant Uhura reports that the *U.S.S. Potemkin* will be in orbit within thirty-six hours to assess the situation here. With the approval of Chancellor Wiladra and the Unified Leadership Council, a long-term plan will be submitted for protecting the Kalandan outpost, as well as the Dolysians, due to the Romulans' obvious interest." Kirk knew that the proximity of the Kondaii system to the Romulan border would doubtless play a considerable factor in the decision making process.

"Something tells me the Kalandan outpost can take care of itself," McCoy said, "and the Dolysians, too, for that matter."

As though ignoring the doctor's comment, Spock continued, "Starfleet also has dispatched a detachment from the Corps of Engineers to take over the salvage of the *Huang Zhong*. Now that the barrier is no longer a concern, the decision to destroy the ship has been rescinded, and the recovery operation will continue. Lieutenant Boma and the other survivors have requested that a proper memorial service be conducted prior to their departure."

New footsteps on the roof made the trio turn to see Ambassador Sortino and Lieutenant Boma escorting the mining colony's administrator, Drinja Shin te Elsqa, and—to Kirk's surprise—Chancellor Wiladra Pejh en Kail. Whereas Shin was dressed in the now-familiar gray one-piece garment favored by most of the miners, Wiladra wore radiant emerald green robes that accented her pale skin while catching the light from the sun. Her expression was, in Kirk's opinion, one of unrestrained delight.

"Chancellor," he said as the elder Dolysian and her entourage drew closer, "it's a pleasure to see you again."

Stepping up to Kirk and taking his hand in both of hers in a mimicking of the greeting she had offered during their first meeting, Wiladra said, "Captain, the pleasure is mine, and on a wondrous day such as this." Releasing her hold on his hand, she extended her arms away from her sides as though indicating the world around her. "I've always thought Gralafi to be a beautiful world, but I never imagined that such allure was hidden from our very eyes for so long."

Her enthusiasm was infectious, as evidenced by the grins warming the faces of everyone save for Spock, of course. Even Kirk could not resist the effect her zeal was having on him as he introduced her to his first officer and McCoy.

"It is an honor to meet you both," Wiladra said. "Commander Spock, I cannot thank you enough for the service you have provided us. It is a debt we can never repay, but I hope you will accept my sincere thanks on behalf of all Dolysia."

Offering a formal nod, Spock replied, "The effort was not mine alone, Chancellor. I am pleased that the results will prove beneficial to your people."

"In ways I cannot even begin to appreciate," Wiladra replied. Moving toward the parapet encircling the administration building's rooftop, she waved one hand toward the town square. "Without the Pass as an influence, discussions are already under way as to how this will affect our operations here on Gralafi. There is talk of additional mining and increasing the frequency of the export shipments, of course, and the planet's new accessibility is also attracting those wishing to be assigned to the colony, or to travel here for scientific research, tourism, and even permanent relocation." She cast a glance in Sortino's direction. "As your ambassador told me, it is not an understatement to say that an entire new world has been opened to us. I have also been having some rather illuminating conversations with her regarding alternative energy production methods. We may even one day be able to eliminate our need to mine erinadium from Gralafi and our moons, to say nothing of Dolysia itself." She paused, shaking her head as though overwhelmed by the possibilities. "The very idea of such change is exciting, if not a bit frightening."

"But we'll be with you," Ambassador Sortino said, "every step of the way. If you'll let us, that is."

Once again, Wiladra smiled. "Oh, yes, of course. As I said, we owe you so much, and we stand to learn so much more."

"As do we," Sortino replied, "from you and the Kalandans."

McCoy chuckled. "An understatement if I've ever heard one."

"Agreed," Kirk said. "Meyeliri and her people left a lot of information for us, after all. It'd be a tragedy for it to remain buried down there."

Sortino said, "The chancellor and I have already spoken at length about the Federation and Starfleet science teams that will be conducting extended investigations of the Kalandan complex. Now, I'm not a science type, and never was, but I have to admit that sounds exciting even to me. Even though I expect to be tied up with the chancellor and the leadership council as we negotiate the terms of this new cooperative venture between Dolysia and the Federation, I hope to sneak back here from time to time, just to see how things are going."

"I wouldn't mind doing that, myself," Kirk replied. Once the crisis had passed and the Romulan ships were sent on their way back to their territory, he had considered destroying the underground complex. At first, he thought that might be the best option so far as the Dolysians were concerned. Upon further reflection, he had come to the conclusion that the Kalandans—whatever their initial motives for scattering from their homeworld to the stars even though that action ultimately doomed them—deserved far better than to have such a lasting monument to their civilization discarded, even if such action served some short-term goal of increasing security or decreasing volatile tensions between interstellar neighbors. With that in mind, he had recommended to his superiors at headquarters that Starfleet establish a permanent presence in the Kondaii system, subject to the approval of Wiladra and the leadership council. The Dolysians would still retain custodial responsibility for the Kalandan repository, but Wiladra already had accepted the offer of Federation assistance, due to the sheer immensity of the task.

The chancellor nodded in apparent agreement. "It seems that our newfound friendship is off to a solid start."

Then, her smile faded. "I would also like to volunteer our continued assistance with the salvage efforts for your other ship, Captain. We owe a debt to those lost aboard that vessel, as well. The leadership council has also put forth the measure of erecting a permanent monument here on Gralafi, in memory of the ship and those lost aboard it. The entire Havreltipa colony is ready to assist."

Standing next to her, Administrator Shin said to Boma, "Lieutenant, I understand that you are planning to hold a form of ceremony to honor your fallen comrades. The chancellor and I wish to attend, if you'll allow it."

Boma, as though self-conscious in the face of the Dolysian leader's attention, cleared his throat. "By all means, ma'am. That's most kind of you both. I know how busy you must be, especially now."

"It would be our great privilege, Lieutenant," the administrator replied.

"I'll see to it that you have everything you need, Mister Boma," Kirk said. "And, once we're on our way back to Starbase 23, I'd be happy to help with notifying the families of those lost in the crash." He figured it was the least he could do, considering that the sacrifices made by Captain Ronald Arens and his crew had directly contributed to the improvement of Dolysian society on a global scale.

The lieutenant said, "I appreciate the offer, Captain, but I've already prepared individual messages for each of the families. If you'd make sure they're transmitted in a timely manner when you reach Starbase 23, I'd be very grateful, sir."

Frowning, Kirk asked, "You're not coming with us?"

"No, sir," Boma replied. "I've asked Starfleet to let me stay on here, as a member of the scientific cadre assigned to study the Kalandan outpost. Thanks to Meyeliri and her people, there's a lot to learn in there, and it'll take a long time to go through it all. Though I don't have Lieutenant Uhura's knack for understanding the Kalandan language, I'd like to think I can still help in some way."

Shin added, "We are already in the process of converting some of our unused billeting and administrative spaces for use by Mister Boma and the other researchers upon their arrival here, Captain." Glancing at the lieutenant, she added, "As our brothers and sisters on Dolysia have so amply demonstrated, there is much to learn from your people, as well, and I for one look forward to working together to explore the secrets of our world."

"That makes two of us," Boma replied, smiling as he regarded the administrator.

Though he said nothing, and he made certain to keep his facial expressions in check, Kirk was sure he noted something between Boma and Shin. Could it be that interplanetary romance was in the air? Given what the man had been through, Kirk figured he was entitled to a bit of happiness.

Turning to Spock, Boma said, "Commander, I enjoyed working with you again. I only wish it could've happened under more pleasant circumstances." He paused, clearing his throat. "I still owe you the apology you should've gotten from me before I left the *Enterprise*. I hope you'll accept it now."

Spock shook his head as he regarded the younger man. "No apologies are required, Lieutenant. You comported yourself with distinction during this mission, and I have already forwarded to Starfleet a notation to that effect for your service record."

"That's . . . unexpected, sir," Boma said, his expression conveying his confusion. "Thank you."

"I was merely informing Starfleet Command about the accomplishments of a skilled officer, Lieutenant," Spock replied, "whose actions and conduct during his most recent assignment should be given their due consideration when examining opportunities for the next stages of his career."

Leaning closer, his voice low but not so faint that Kirk could not hear, McCoy asked, "Spock, you're not going soft on us, are you?"

The Vulcan's only reply was the slight arching of his right eyebrow.

"I am going to miss you once you've left us, Captain," Wiladra said, punctuating her words with a hearty laugh. "It is a pity you cannot stay longer. You and your crew are most welcome."

Sortino said, "He may be back sooner than you think, Chancellor. If you and your leadership council approve Starfleet's request to establish a base here, then several starships will use it as one of their support stations in this region. That might well include the *Enterprise*."

"That's right," Kirk confirmed. For now, the Dolysians, and the Kalandans, for that matter, would have to get along without him and his crew. He was eager to turn over his current responsibilities to the captain of the *U.S.S. Potemkin*, because he already had orders for a new assignment, one that would return the *Enterprise* to its primary objective of exploration. He greeted that new task with growing anticipation, wondering where it might take him and what he might see along the way. Despite that eagerness, Kirk often lamented the reality of not always being able to return to a civilization encountered during a previous mission.

Such was the case with many of the worlds he had visited in his travels. It would be regrettable if the Dolysians were added to that list, and he wondered when Starfleet orders and fate might conspire to bring him back here.

One day soon. Well, one can hope, anyway.

Moving so that she was able once again to grasp Kirk's hand, Wiladra said, "I understand all too well the demands of duty, Captain. With luck, your superiors will see fit to bring you back here, if for no other reason than to behold whatever secrets the Kalandans might reveal."

"I look forward to that day, Chancellor," Kirk said. It would take months, if not years, to pry the secrets of the ancient race from its subterranean storehouse. Given what the Kalandans had revealed so far, what other wonders were there, waiting to be found and brought out from beneath the protective cloak of the past? It was a question for others to answer.

Meanwhile, James Kirk knew that his proper place, as always, was aboard his ship and with his crew, on a course for the future.

ACKNOWLEDGMENTS

Thanks of the first order go out to my editors at Pocket Books, for their invaluable assistance throughout the writing of this book. As always, their guidance was and remains greatly appreciated.

Special thanks go out to my friend and frequent writing partner, Kevin Dilmore, with whom the story for this novel was developed. Due to circumstances beyond his control and the pressing need to see to more important matters, he wasn't able to stay on as co-writer for this outing, and while I know he regrets not being able to participate, I have no doubts that he made the right call. We'll get 'em next time, bro.

A nod of appreciation is extended to Michael Richards, the writer who supplied the original story for "That Which Survives" to the producers of the *Star Trek* television series, and to John Meredith Lucas, who wrote the teleplay on which Mister Richards' story is based. I'd also like to tip my hat to Lee Meriwether, who portrayed Losira in the episode. While a conscious choice was made not to reuse Losira in this story, there is still something of a tribute in the form of Meyeliri, the holographic character who is described as appearing much like Ms. Meriwether does as of this writing.

Finally, I'd also like to thank James Estes, Ross A. Isaacs, Evan Jamison, Steve Kenson, Steve Long, Richard Meyer, Christian Moore, Peter Schweighofer: authors of *The Way of D'Era, Book 1: The Romulans,* a sourcebook for Last Unicorn's *Star Trek: The Next Generation* Roleplaying Game, for terminology and other small bits of lore and trivia I used to pepper certain scenes throughout the book.

ABOUT THE AUTHOR

DAYTON WARD. Author. Trekkie. Writing his goofy little stories and searching for a way to tap into the hidden nerdity that all humans have. Then, an accidental overdose of Mountain Dew altered his body chemistry. Now, when Dayton Ward grows excited or just downright geeky, a startling metamorphosis occurs.

Driven by outlandish ideas and a pronounced lack of sleep, he is pursued by fans and editors as well as funny men in bright uniforms wielding Tasers, straitjackets, and medication. In addition to the numerous credits he shares with friend and co-writer Kevin Dilmore, Dayton is the author of the *Star Trek* novels *In the Name of Honor, Open Secrets,* and *Paths of Disharmony,* the science fiction novels *The Last World War, Counterstrike,* and *The Genesis Protocol,* as well as short stories in a number of anthologies. For Flying Pen Press, he was the editor of the science fiction anthology *Full-Throttle Space Tales #3: Space Grunts.* He also provides regular content for *Star Trek Magazine,* Tor.com, and StarTrek.com.

Dayton is believed to be working on his next novel, and he must let the world think that he is working on it, until he can find a way to earn back the advance check he blew on strippers and booze. Though he currently lives in Kansas City with his wife and daughters, Dayton is a Florida native and maintains a torrid long-distance romance with his beloved Tampa Bay Buccaneers. Visit him on the web at daytonward.com.